CARTOON NETWORK

OVER THE GARDEN WALL.

CIRCUS FRIENDS

OVER THE GARDEN WALL: CIRCUS FRIENDS, October 2019. Published by KaBOOM!, a division of Boom Entertainment, Inc. OVER THE GARDEN WALL, CARTOON NETWORK, the logos, and all related characters and elements are trademarks of and ® Cartoon Network. A WarnerMedia Company. All rights reserved. (S19) KaBOOM!™ and the KaBOOM! Logo are trademarks of Boom Entertainment, Inc., registered in various countries and categories. All characters, events, and/or institutions depicted herein are fictional. Any similarity between any of the names, characters, persons, events, and/or institutions in this publication to actual names, characters, and persons, whether living or dead, events and/or institutions is unintended and purely coincidental. KaBOOM! does not read or accept unsolicited submissions of ideas, stories, or artwork.

For information regarding the CPSIA on the printed material, call: (203) 595-3636 and provide reference #RICH - 862815.

BOOM! Studios, 5670 Wilshire Boulevard, Suite 400, Los Angeles, CA 90036-5679. Printed in USA. First Printing.

ISBN: 978-1-68415-455-5, eISBN: 978-1-64144-572-6

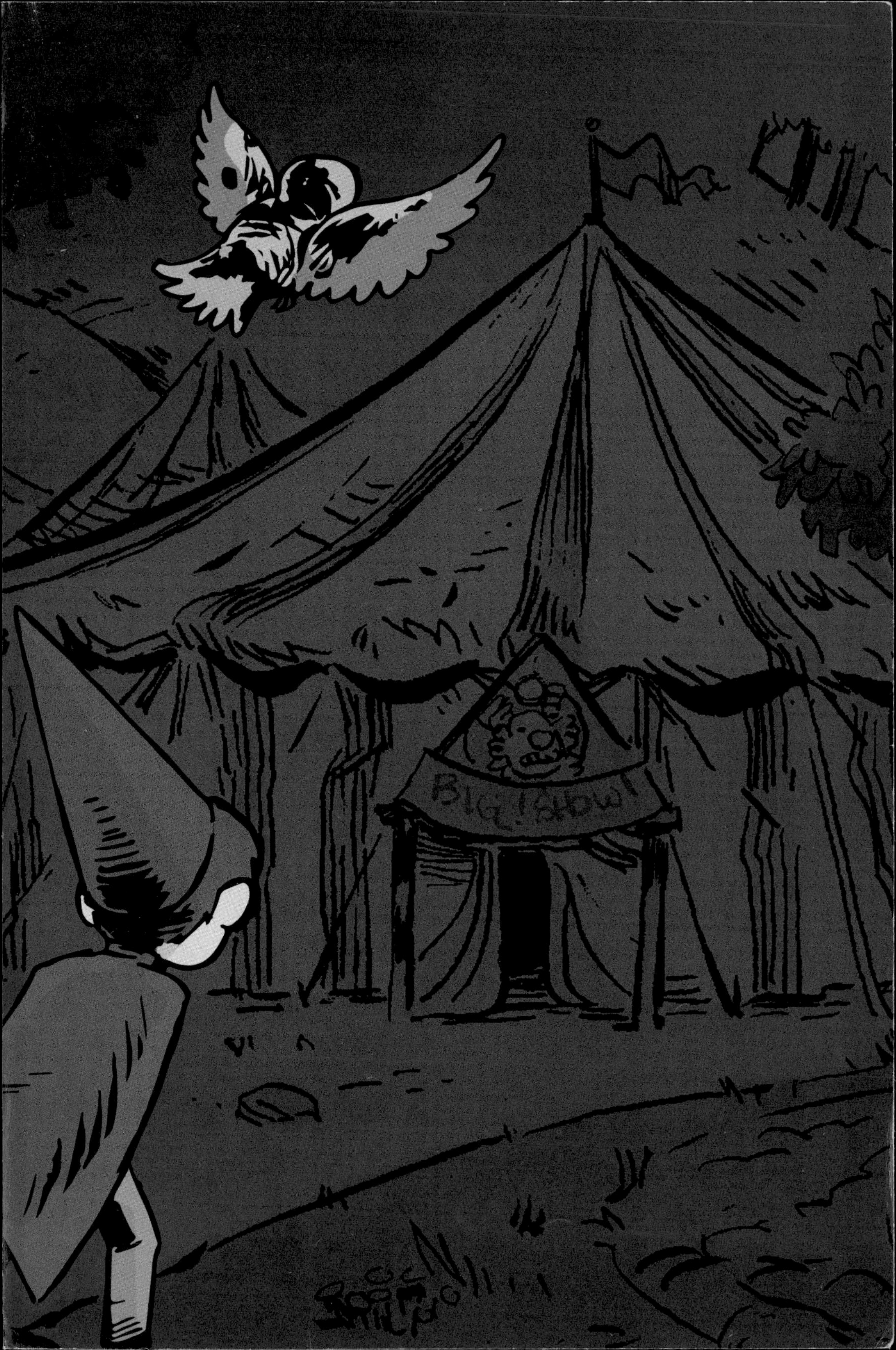
BIG!SHOW!

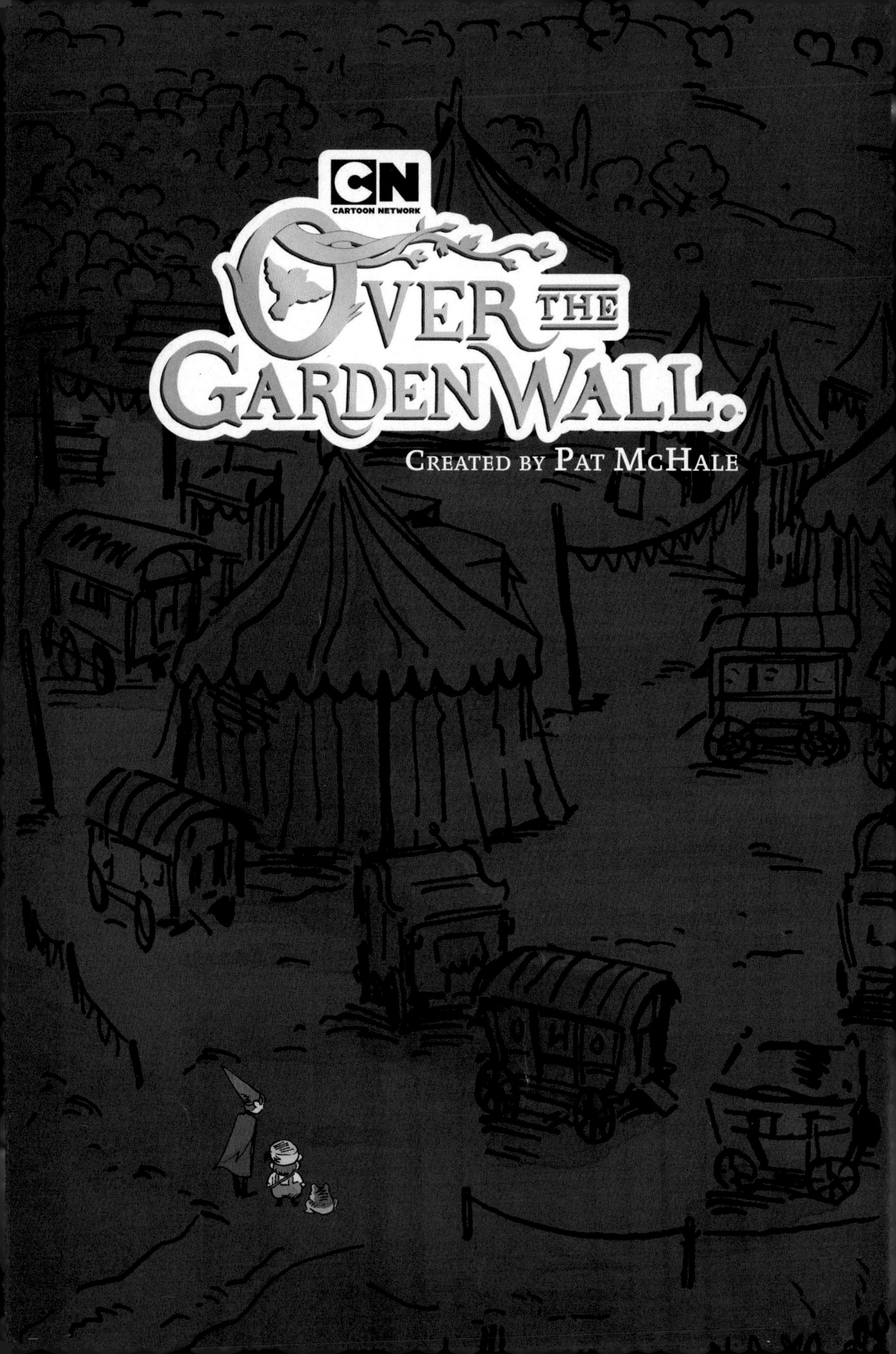

Over the Garden Wall

Created by Pat McHale

"Circus Friends"

WRITTEN BY
Jonathan Case

ILLUSTRATED BY
John Golden

COLORS BY
SJ Miller

LETTERS BY
Mike Fiorentino

COVER BY JIM CAMPBELL

DESIGNER JILLIAN CRAB
ASSISTANT EDITOR MICHAEL MOCCIO
EDITOR MATTHEW LEVINE

WITH SPECIAL THANKS TO JIM CAMPBELL AND
VERY SPECIAL THANKS TO MARISA MARIONAKIS,
JANET NO, AUSTIN PAGE, PERNELLE HAYES
AND THE WONDERFUL FOLKS AT CARTOON NETWORK.

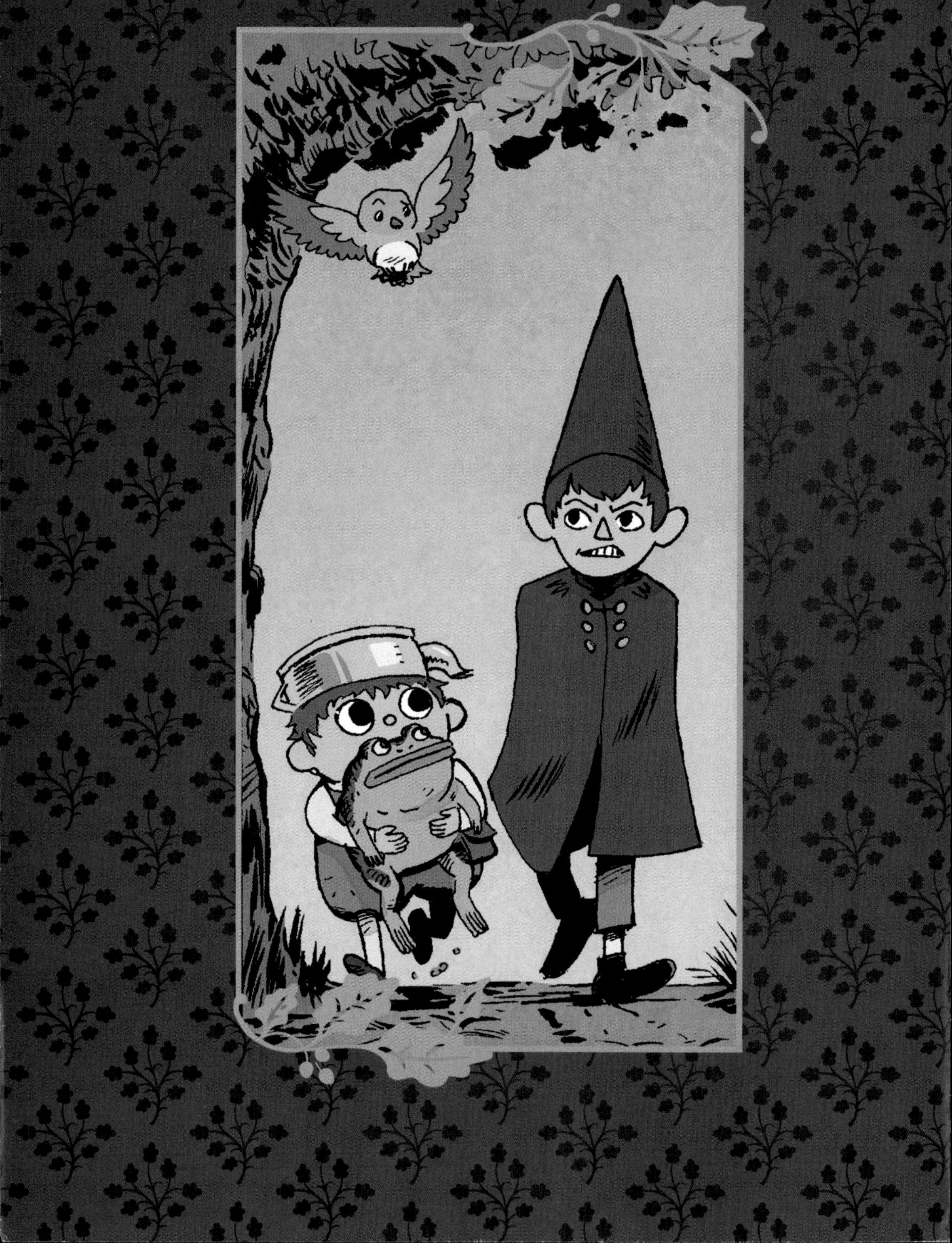

ACT ONE

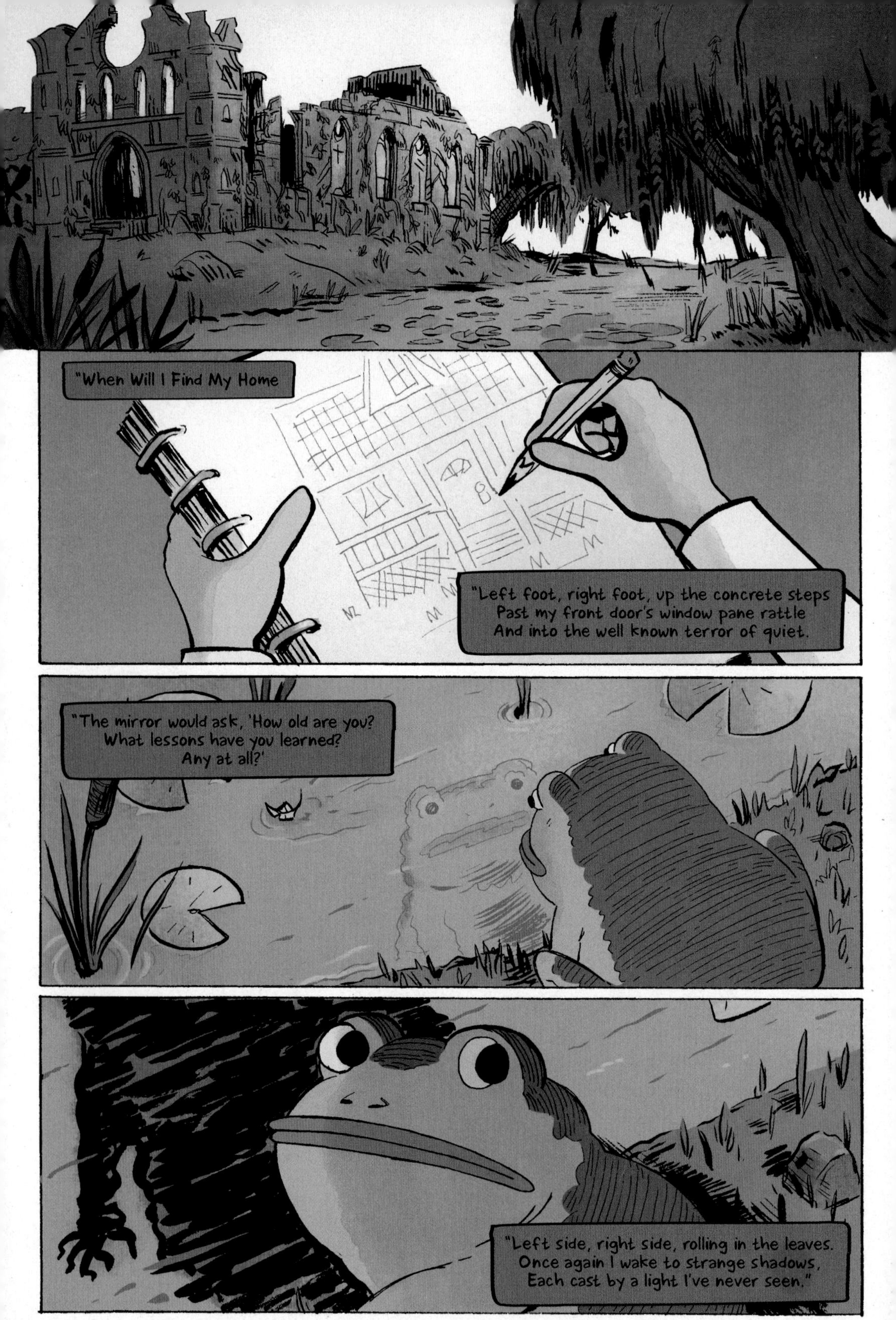
"When Will I Find My Home
"Left foot, right foot, up the concrete steps
Past my front door's window pane rattle
And into the well known terror of quiet.
"The mirror would ask, 'How old are you?
What lessons have you learned?
Any at all?'
"Left side, right side, rolling in the leaves.
Once again I wake to strange shadows,
Each cast by a light I've never seen."

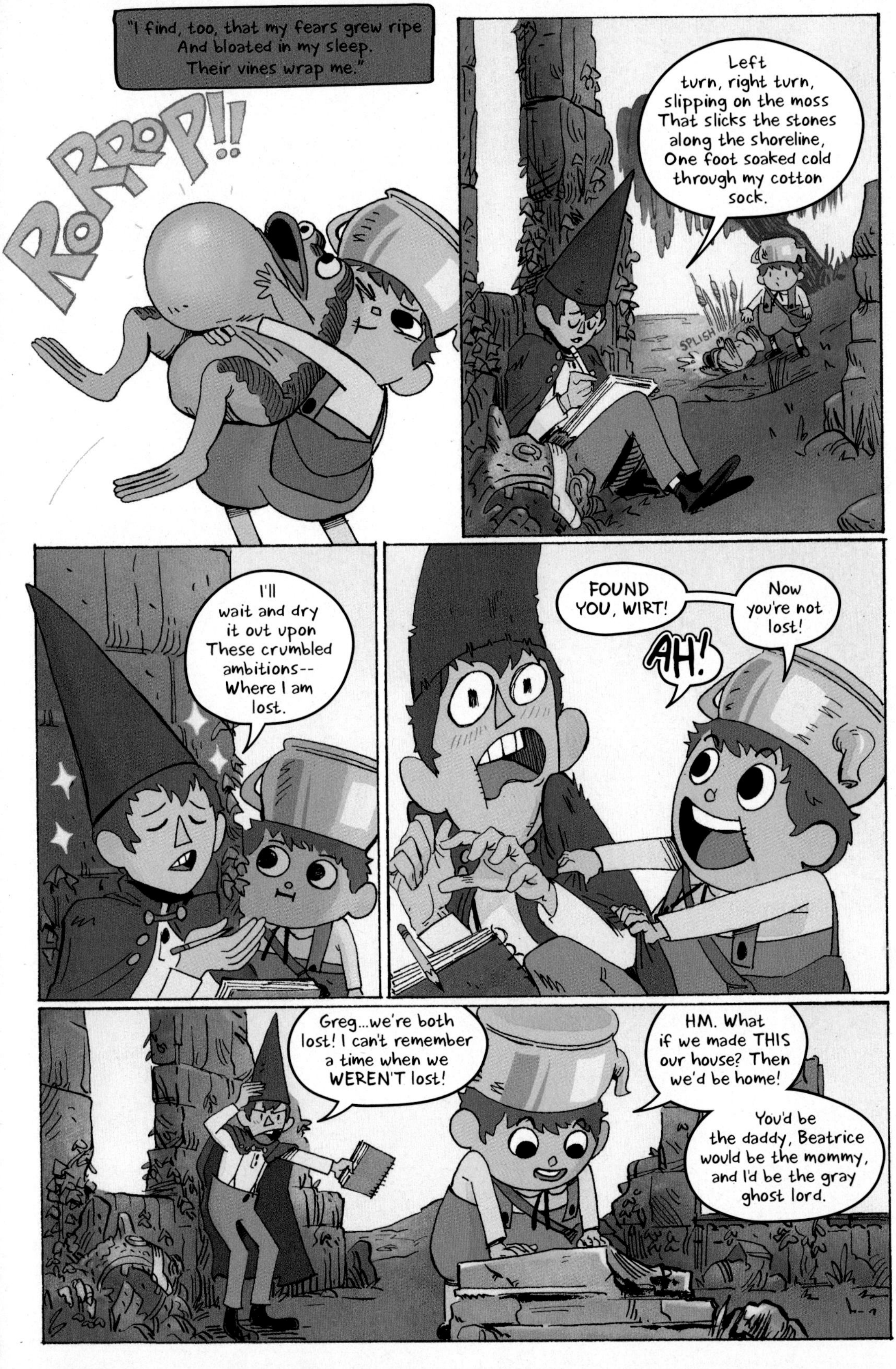
"I find, too, that my fears grew ripe And bloated in my sleep. Their vines wrap me."
RORROOP!!
Left turn, right turn, slipping on the moss That slicks the stones along the shoreline, One foot soaked cold through my cotton sock.
SPLISH
I'll wait and dry it out upon These crumbled ambitions-- Where I am lost.
FOUND YOU, WIRT!
Now you're not lost!
AH!
Greg...we're both lost! I can't remember a time when we WEREN'T lost!
HM. What if we made THIS our house? Then we'd be home!
You'd be the daddy, Beatrice would be the mommy, and I'd be the gray ghost lord.

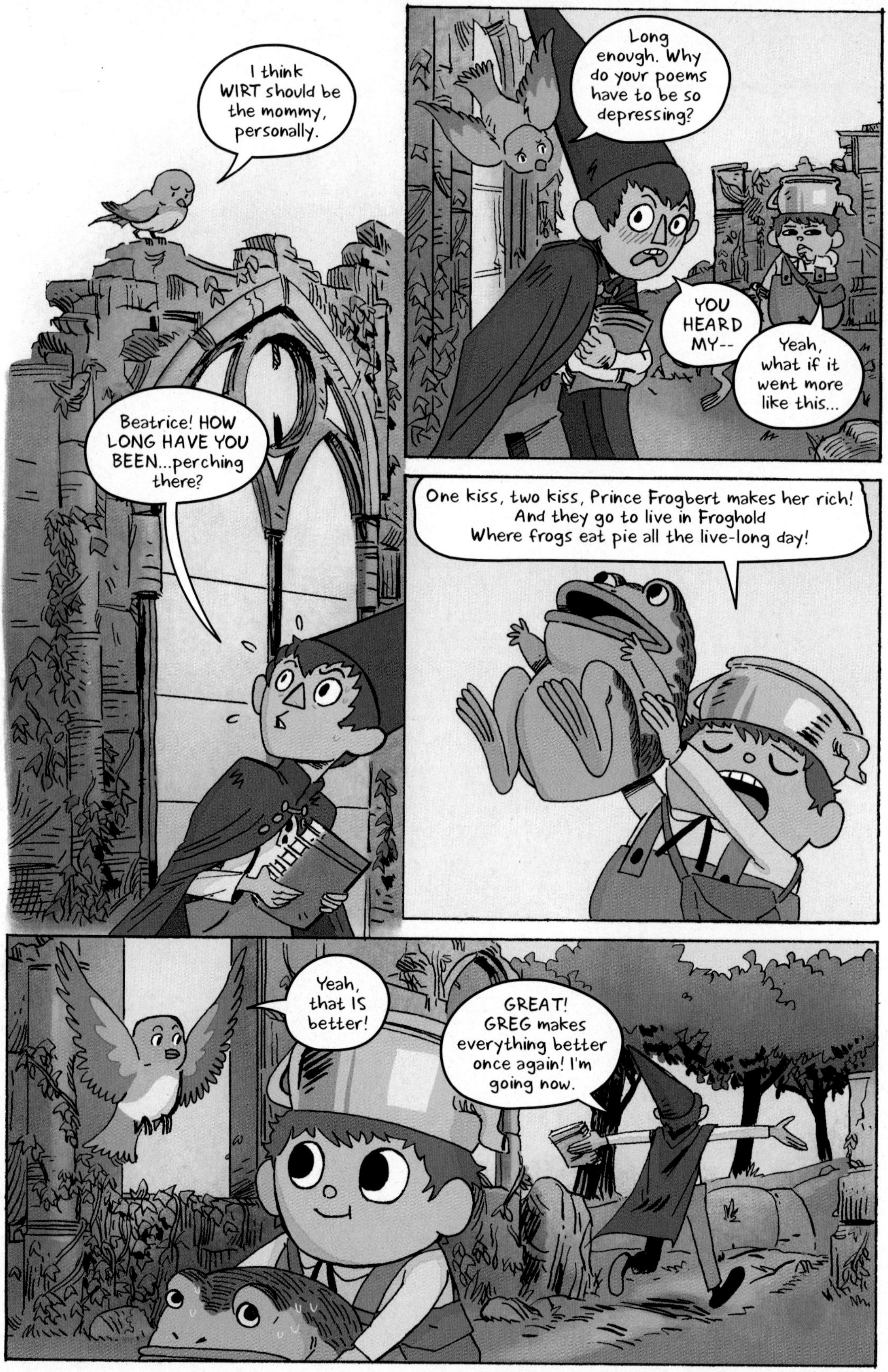
I think WIRT should be the mommy, personally.
Beatrice! HOW LONG HAVE YOU BEEN...perching there?
Long enough. Why do your poems have to be so depressing?
YOU HEARD MY--
Yeah, what if it went more like this...
One kiss, two kiss, Prince Frogbert makes her rich! And they go to live in Froghold Where frogs eat pie all the live-long day!
Yeah, that IS better!
GREAT! GREG makes everything better once again! I'm going now.

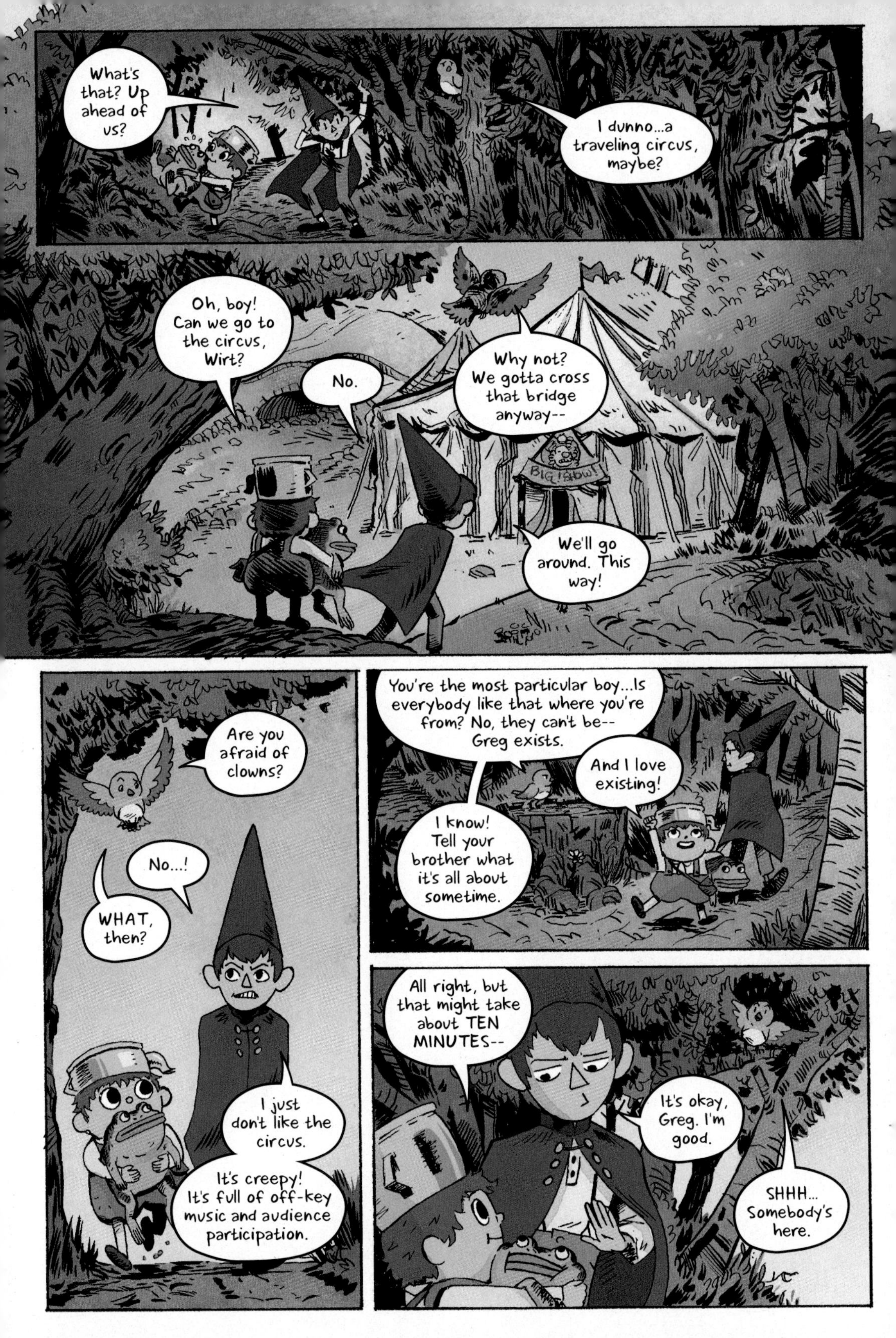
What's that? Up ahead of us?
I dunno...a traveling circus, maybe?
Oh, boy! Can we go to the circus, Wirt?
No.
Why not? We gotta cross that bridge anyway--
BIG! SHOW!
We'll go around. This way!
Are you afraid of clowns?
No...!
WHAT, then?
I just don't like the circus.
It's creepy! It's full of off-key music and audience participation.
You're the most particular boy...Is everybody like that where you're from? No, they can't be-- Greg exists.
And I love existing!
I know! Tell your brother what it's all about sometime.
All right, but that might take about TEN MINUTES--
It's okay, Greg. I'm good.
SHHH... Somebody's here.

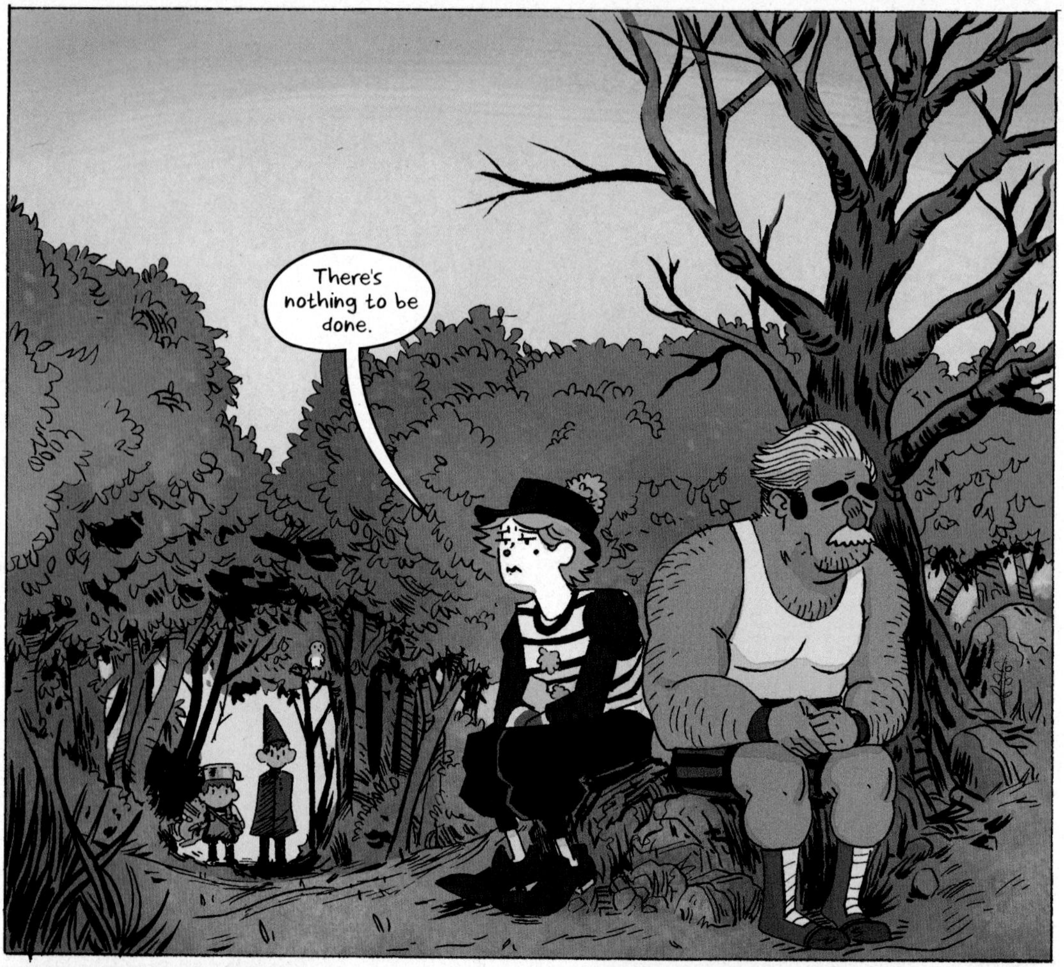
There's nothing to be done.

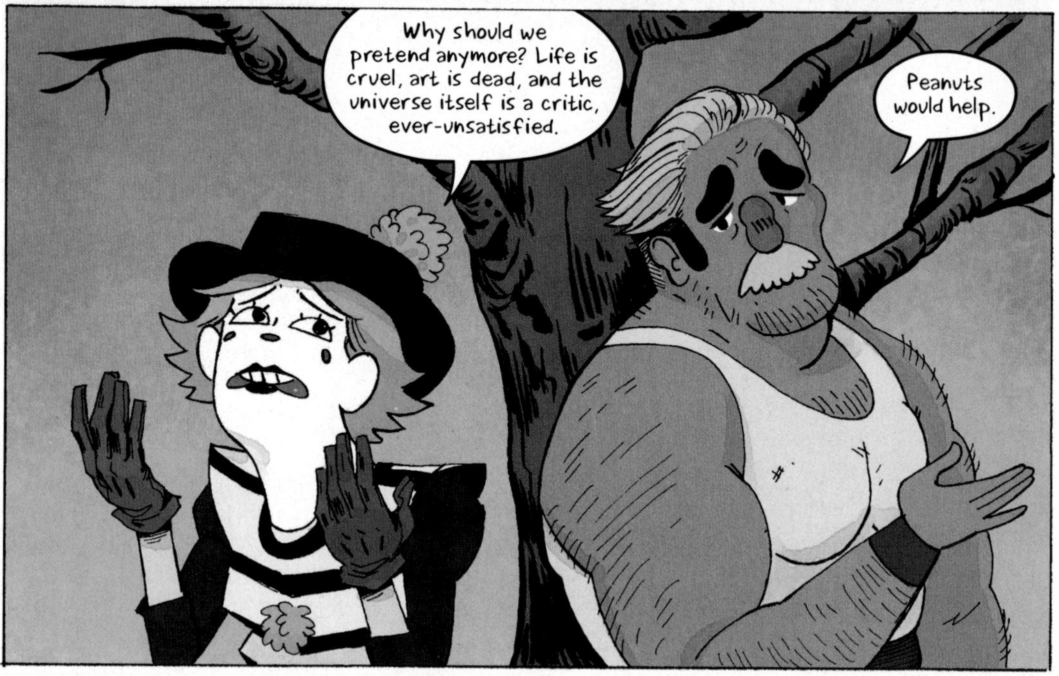
Why should we pretend anymore? Life is cruel, art is dead, and the universe itself is a critic, ever-unsatisfied.
Peanuts would help.

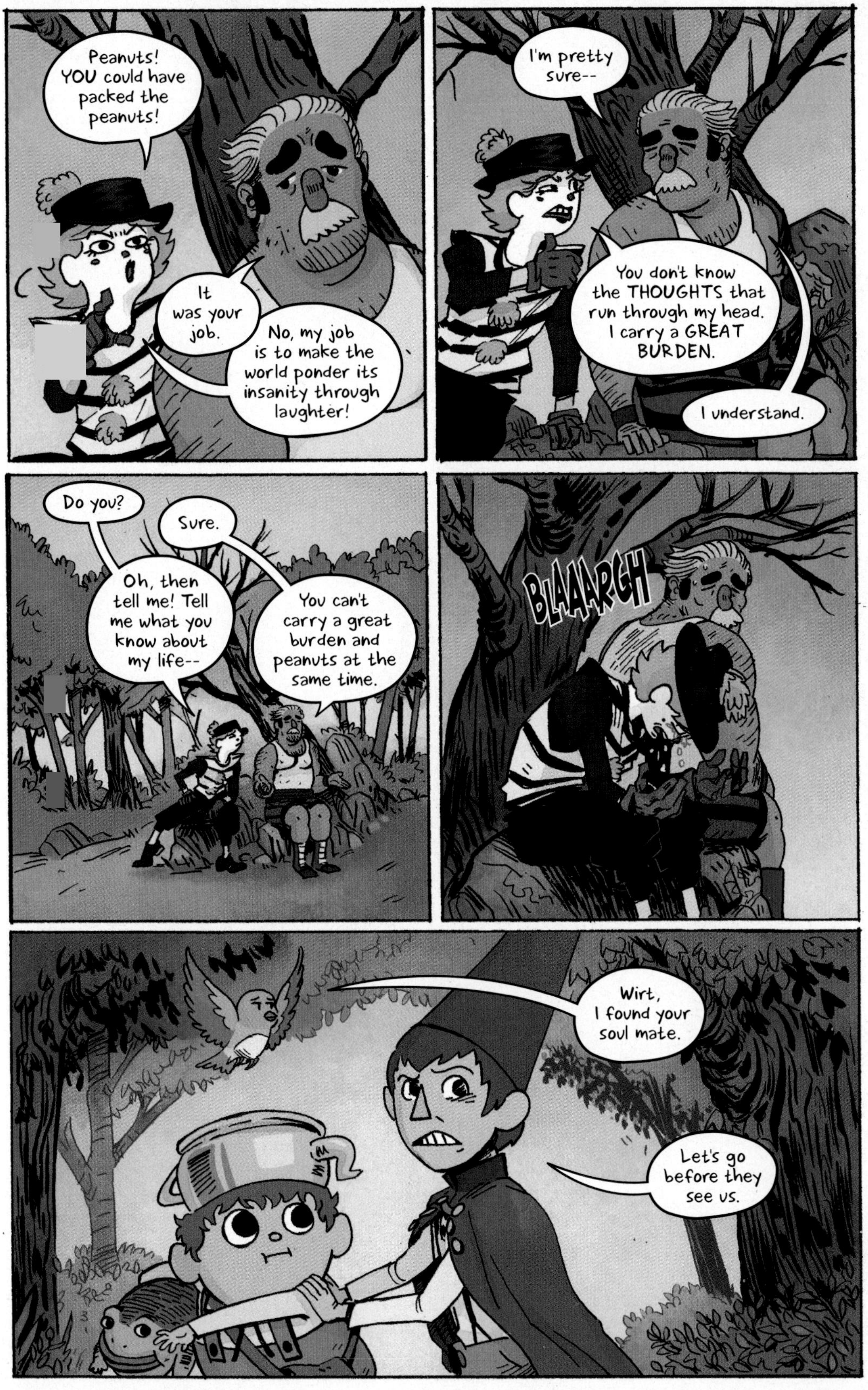
Peanuts! YOU could have packed the peanuts!
It was your job.
No, my job is to make the world ponder its insanity through laughter!
I'm pretty sure--
You don't know the THOUGHTS that run through my head. I carry a GREAT BURDEN.
I understand.
Do you?
Sure.
Oh, then tell me! Tell me what you know about my life--
You can't carry a great burden and peanuts at the same time.
BLAAARGH
Wirt, I found your soul mate.
Let's go before they see us.

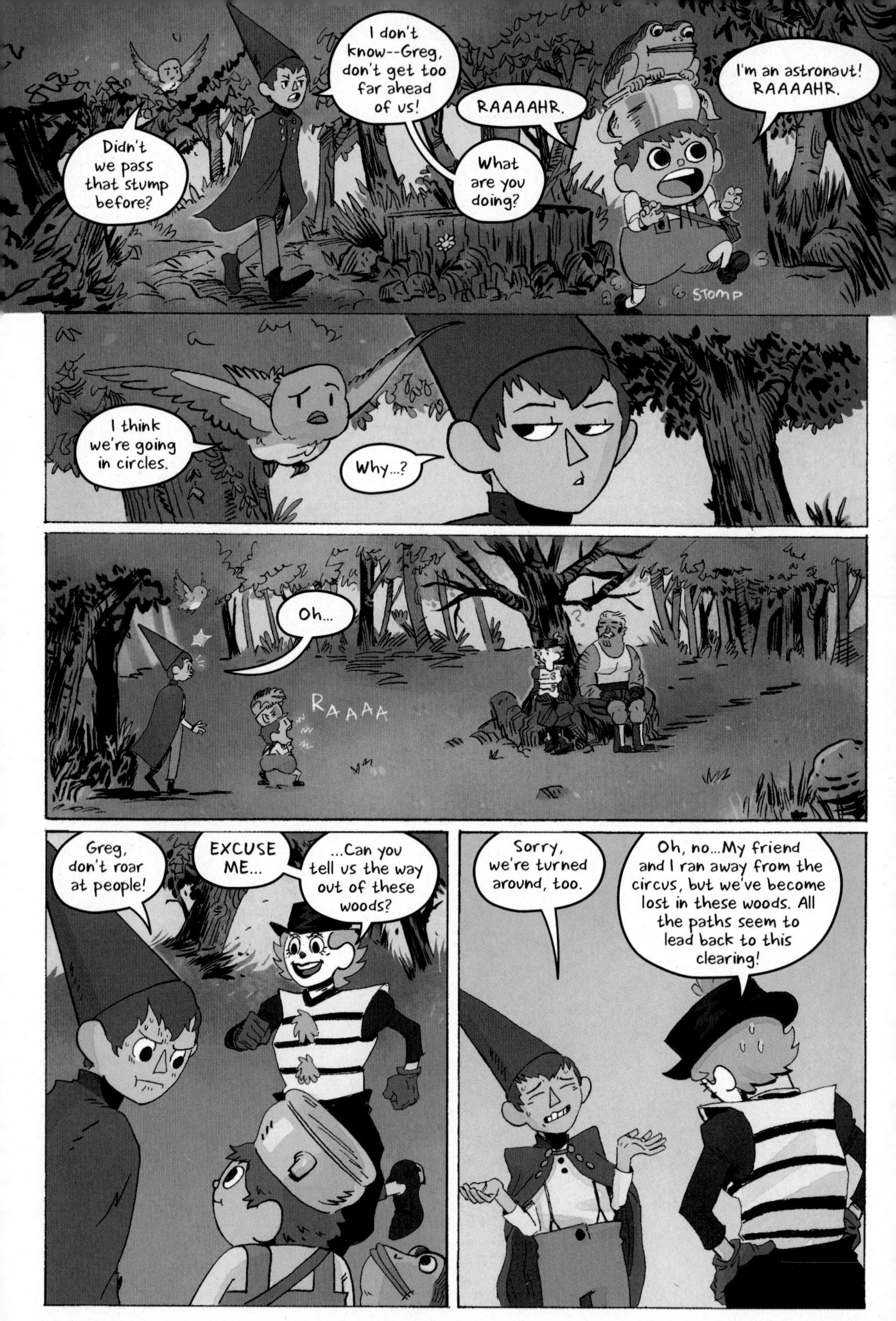
Didn't we pass that stump before?
I don't know--Greg, don't get too far ahead of us!
What are you doing?
RAAAAHR.
I'm an astronaut! RAAAAHR.
STOMP
I think we're going in circles.
Why...?
Oh...
RAAAA
Greg, don't roar at people!
EXCUSE ME...
...Can you tell us the way out of these woods?
Sorry, we're turned around, too.
Oh, no...My friend and I ran away from the circus, but we've become lost in these woods. All the paths seem to lead back to this clearing!

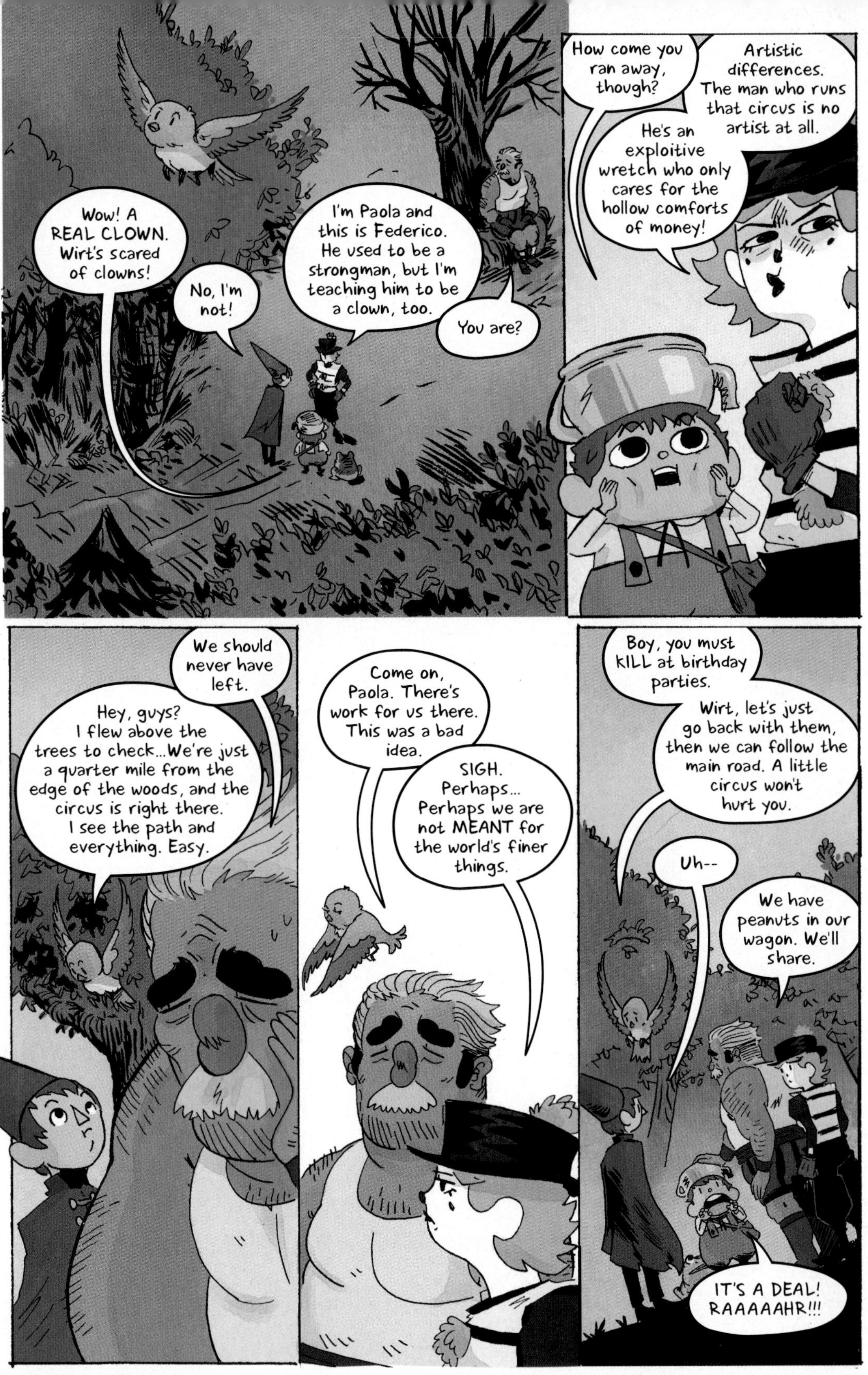
Wow! A REAL CLOWN. Wirt's scared of clowns!
No, I'm not!
I'm Paola and this is Federico. He used to be a strongman, but I'm teaching him to be a clown, too.
You are?
How come you ran away, though?
Artistic differences. The man who runs that circus is no artist at all.
He's an exploitive wretch who only cares for the hollow comforts of money!
We should never have left.
Hey, guys? I flew above the trees to check...We're just a quarter mile from the edge of the woods, and the circus is right there. I see the path and everything. Easy.
Come on, Paola. There's work for us there. This was a bad idea.
SIGH. Perhaps... Perhaps we are not MEANT for the world's finer things.
Boy, you must KILL at birthday parties.
Wirt, let's just go back with them, then we can follow the main road. A little circus won't hurt you.
Uh--
We have peanuts in our wagon. We'll share.
IT'S A DEAL! RAAAAAHR!!!

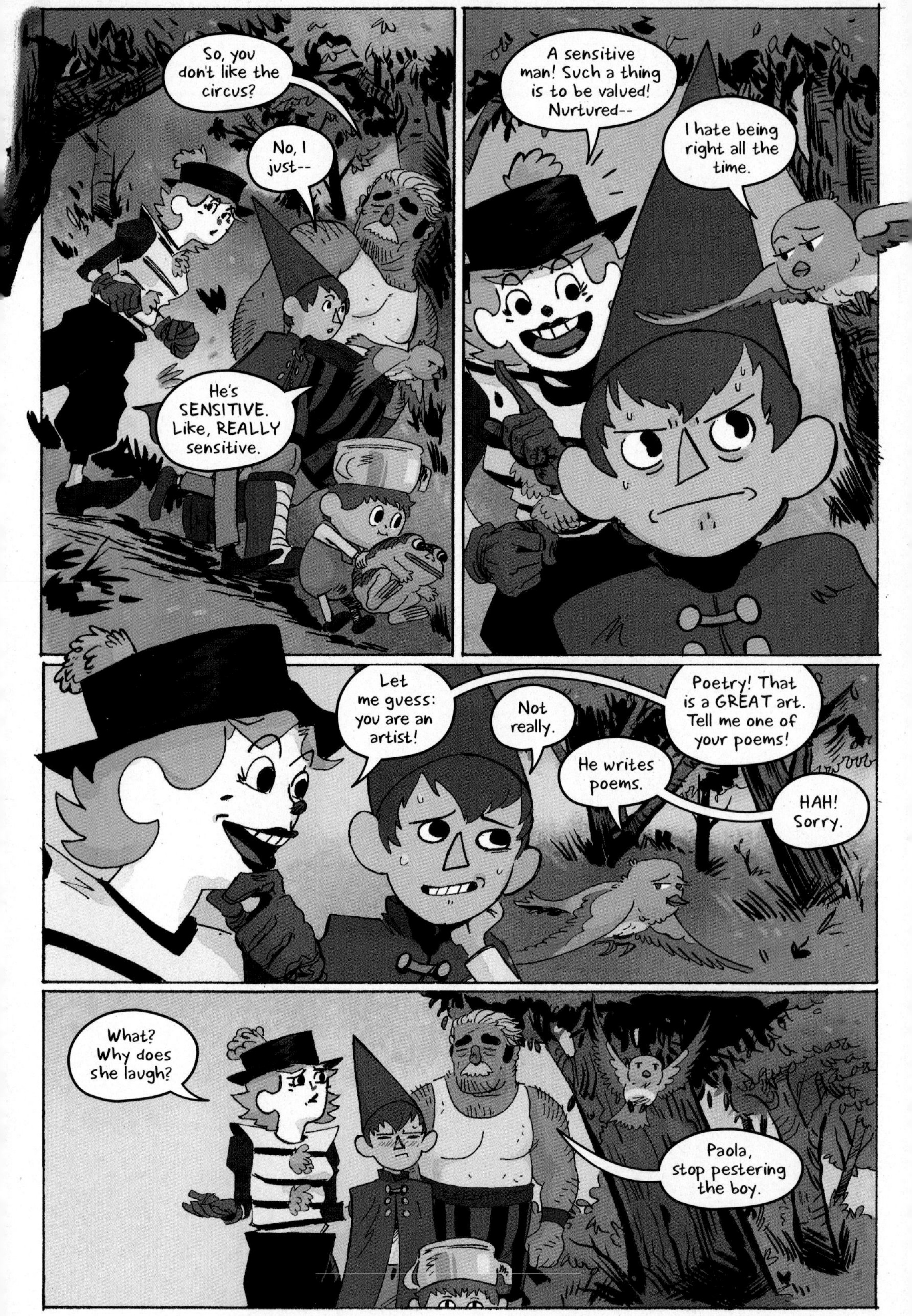
So, you don't like the circus?
No, I just--
He's SENSITIVE. Like, REALLY sensitive.
A sensitive man! Such a thing is to be valued! Nurtured--
I hate being right all the time.
Let me guess: you are an artist!
Not really.
Poetry! That is a GREAT art. Tell me one of your poems!
He writes poems.
HAH! Sorry.
What? Why does she laugh?
Paola, stop pestering the boy.

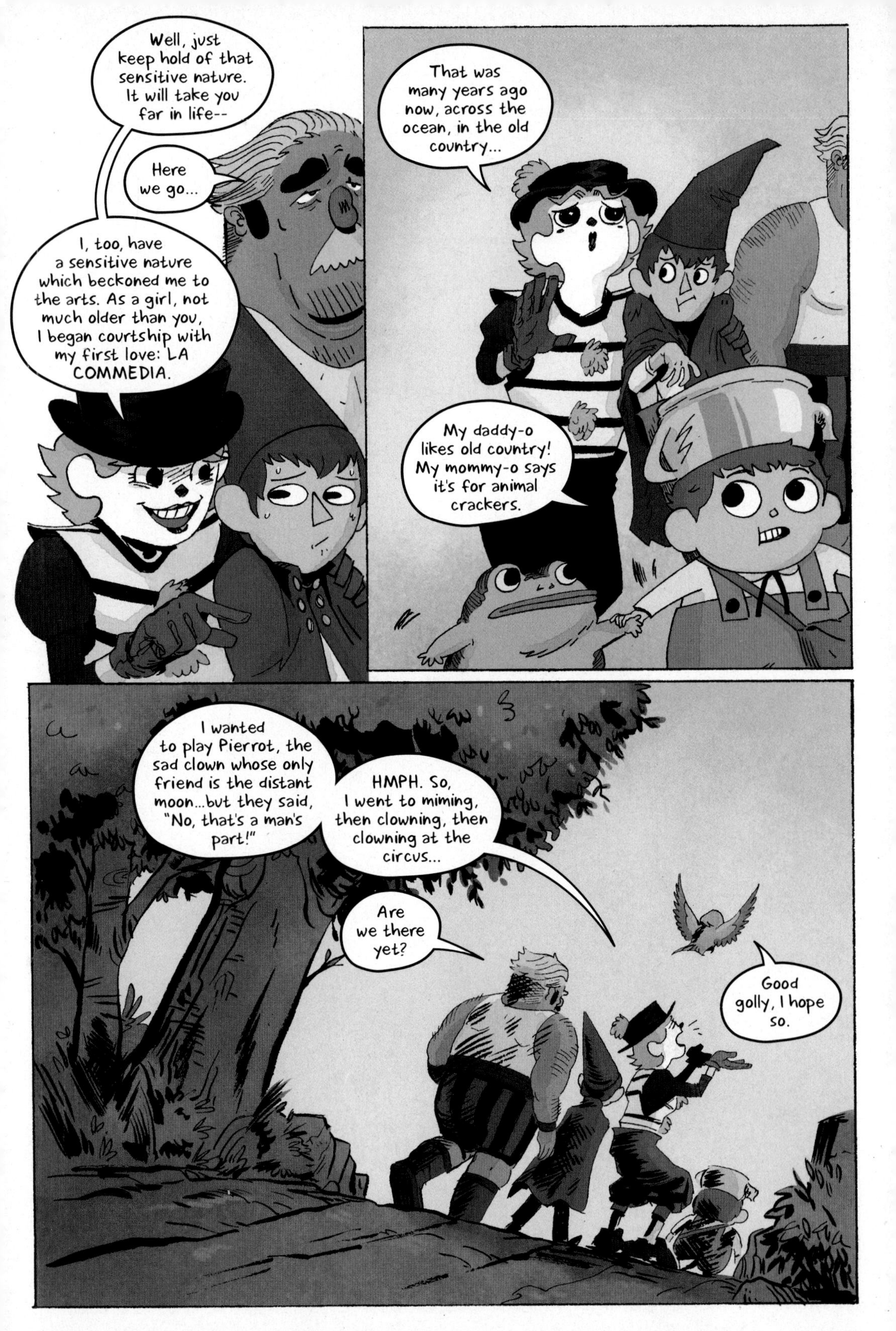
Well, just keep hold of that sensitive nature. It will take you far in life--
Here we go...
I, too, have a sensitive nature which beckoned me to the arts. As a girl, not much older than you, I began courtship with my first love: LA COMMEDIA.
That was many years ago now, across the ocean, in the old country...
My daddy-o likes old country! My mommy-o says it's for animal crackers.
I wanted to play Pierrot, the sad clown whose only friend is the distant moon...but they said, "No, that's a man's part!"
HMPH. So, I went to miming, then clowning, then clowning at the circus...
Are we there yet?
Good golly, I hope so.

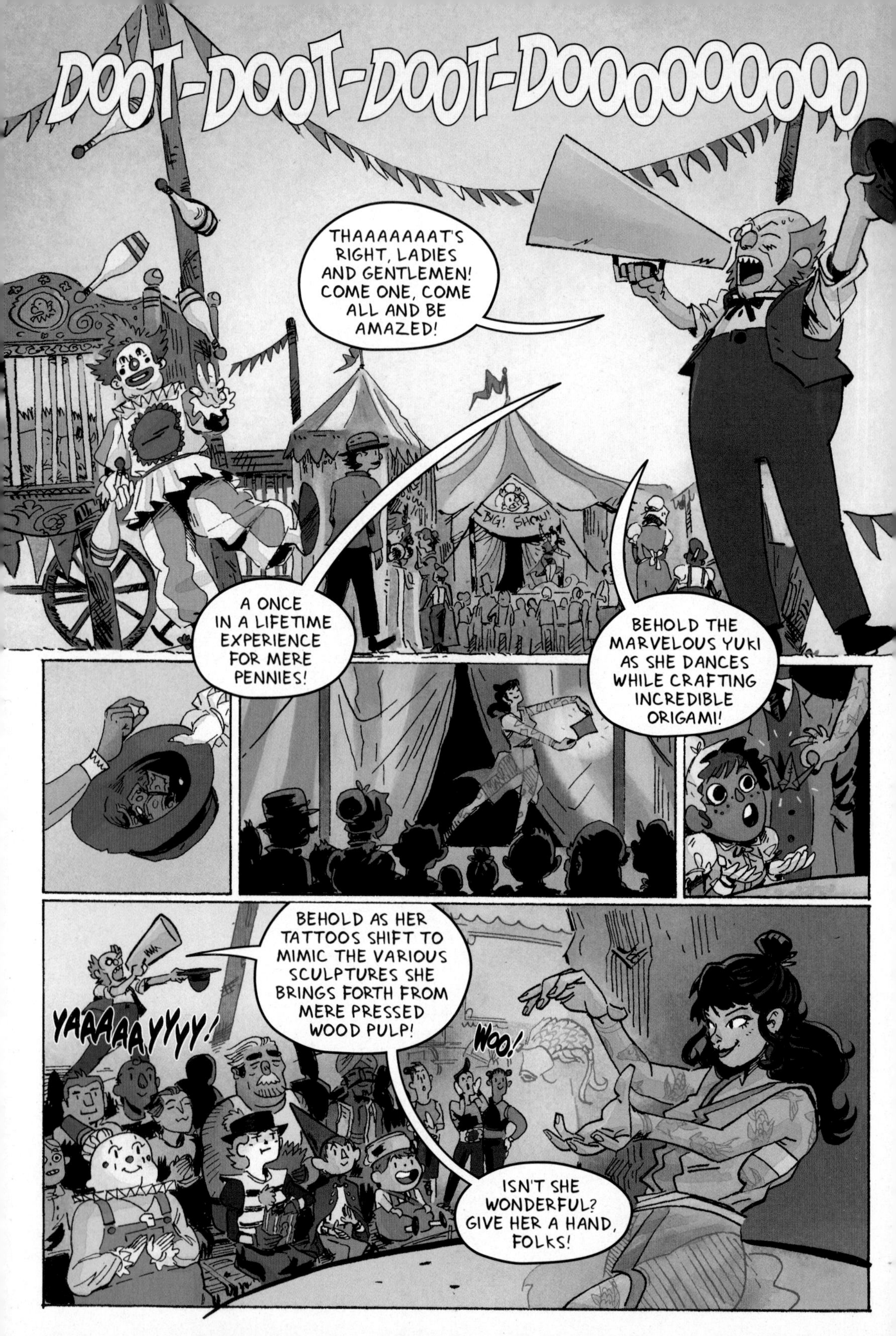
DOOT-DOOT-DOOT-DOOOOOOOOO
THAAAAAAAT'S RIGHT, LADIES AND GENTLEMEN! COME ONE, COME ALL AND BE AMAZED!
BIG! SHOW!
A ONCE IN A LIFETIME EXPERIENCE FOR MERE PENNIES!
BEHOLD THE MARVELOUS YUKI AS SHE DANCES WHILE CRAFTING INCREDIBLE ORIGAMI!
BEHOLD AS HER TATTOOS SHIFT TO MIMIC THE VARIOUS SCULPTURES SHE BRINGS FORTH FROM MERE PRESSED WOOD PULP!
YAAAAAYYYY!
WOO!
ISN'T SHE WONDERFUL? GIVE HER A HAND, FOLKS!

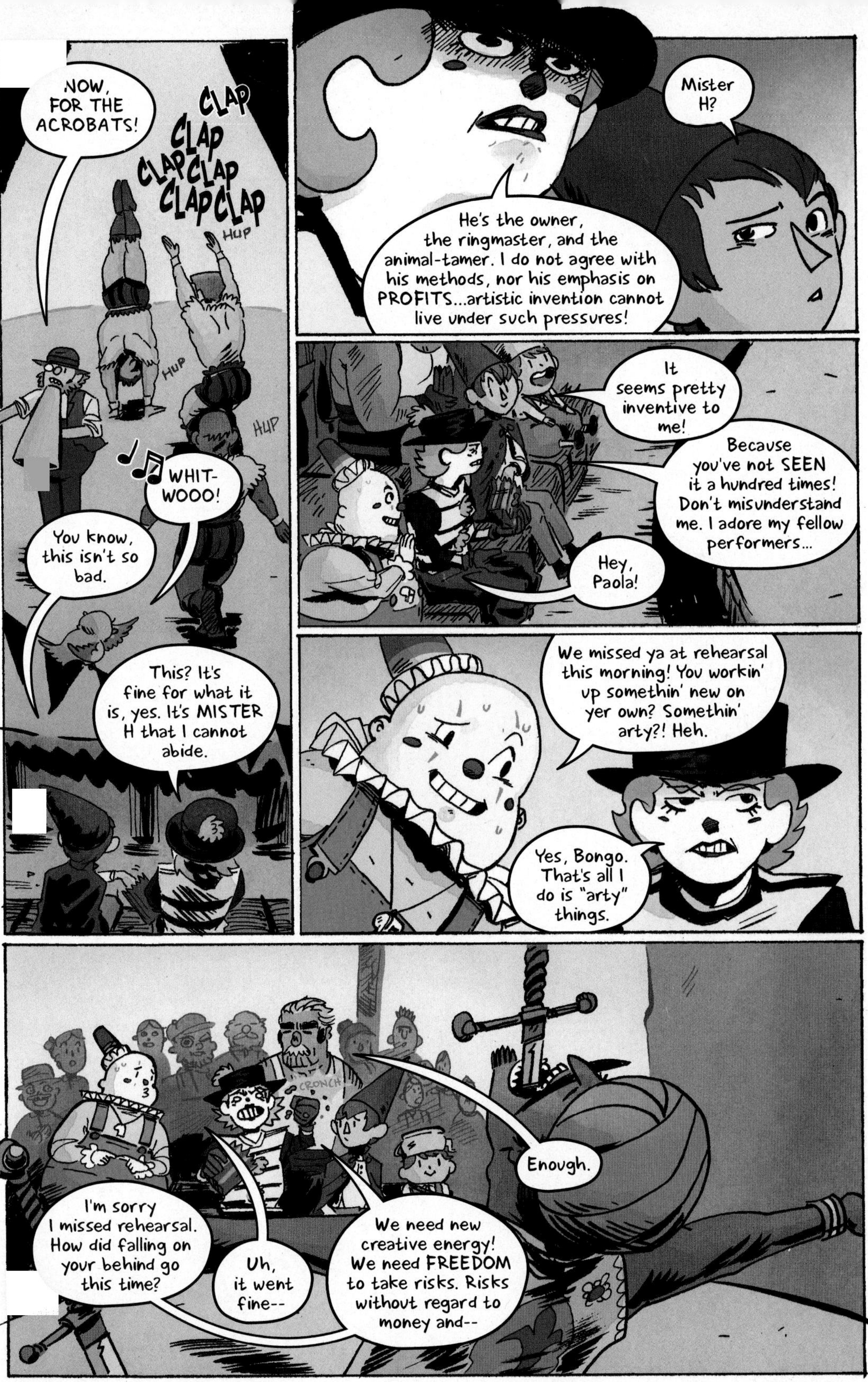
NOW, FOR THE ACROBATS!
CLAP CLAP CLAP CLAP CLAP CLAP
HUP
HUP
HUP
WHIT-WOOO!
You know, this isn't so bad.
This? It's fine for what it is, yes. It's MISTER H that I cannot abide.
Mister H?
He's the owner, the ringmaster, and the animal-tamer. I do not agree with his methods, nor his emphasis on PROFITS...artistic invention cannot live under such pressures!
It seems pretty inventive to me!
Because you've not SEEN it a hundred times! Don't misunderstand me. I adore my fellow performers...
Hey, Paola!
We missed ya at rehearsal this morning! You workin' up somethin' new on yer own? Somethin' arty?! Heh.
Yes, Bongo. That's all I do is "arty" things.
CRONCH
Enough.
I'm sorry I missed rehearsal. How did falling on your behind go this time?
Uh, it went fine--
We need new creative energy! We need FREEDOM to take risks. Risks without regard to money and--

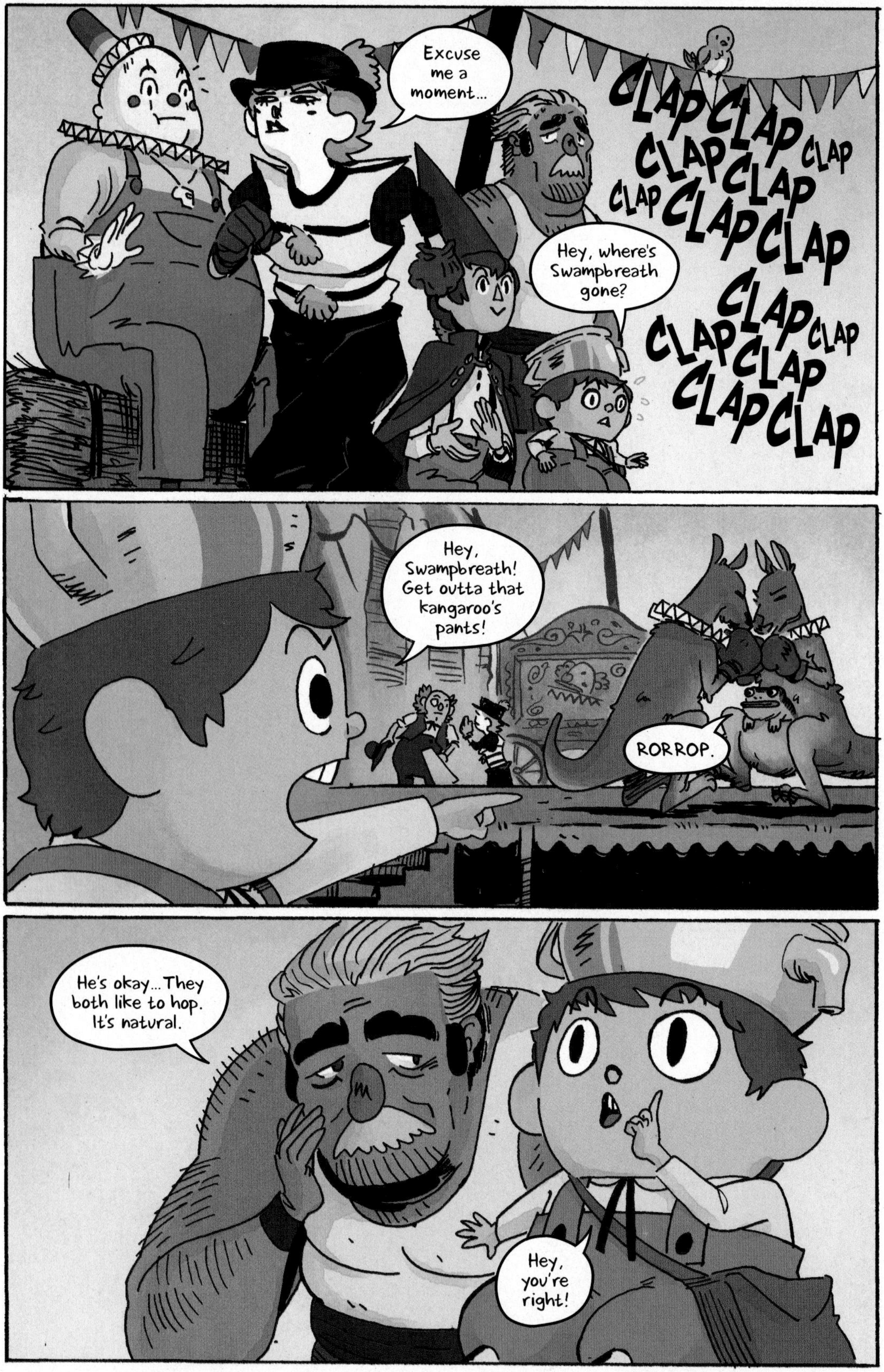
Excuse me a moment...
CLAP CLAP CLAP CLAP CLAP CLAP CLAP CLAP CLAP CLAP CLAP
Hey, where's Swampbreath gone?
CLAP CLAP CLAP CLAP CLAP CLAP CLAP
Hey, Swampbreath! Get outta that kangaroo's pants!
RORROP.
He's okay... They both like to hop. It's natural.
Hey, you're right!

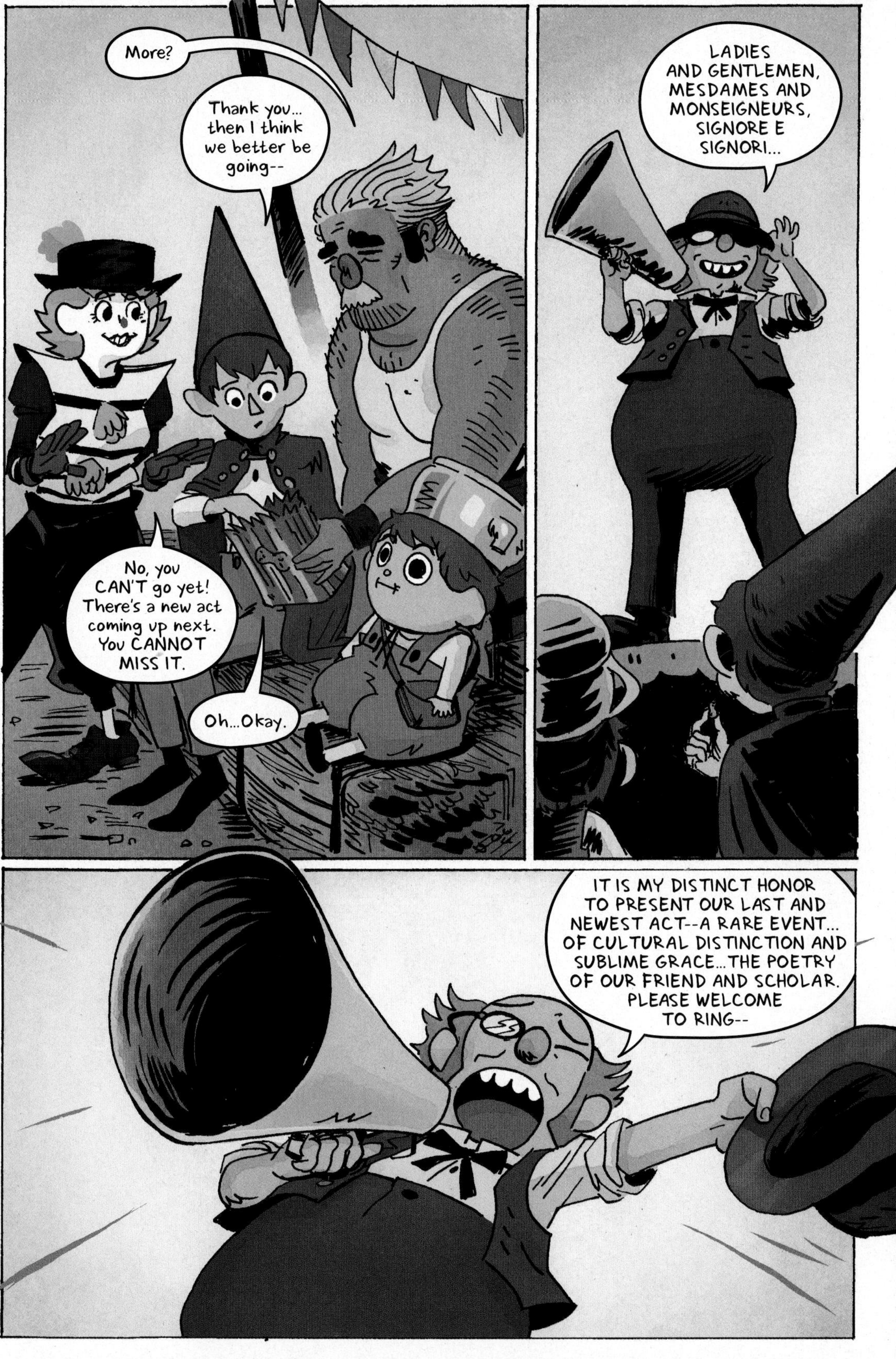
More?
Thank you... then I think we better be going--
No, you CAN'T go yet! There's a new act coming up next. You CANNOT MISS IT.
Oh...Okay.
LADIES AND GENTLEMEN, MESDAMES AND MONSEIGNEURS, SIGNORE E SIGNORI...
IT IS MY DISTINCT HONOR TO PRESENT OUR LAST AND NEWEST ACT--A RARE EVENT... OF CULTURAL DISTINCTION AND SUBLIME GRACE...THE POETRY OF OUR FRIEND AND SCHOLAR. PLEASE WELCOME TO RING--

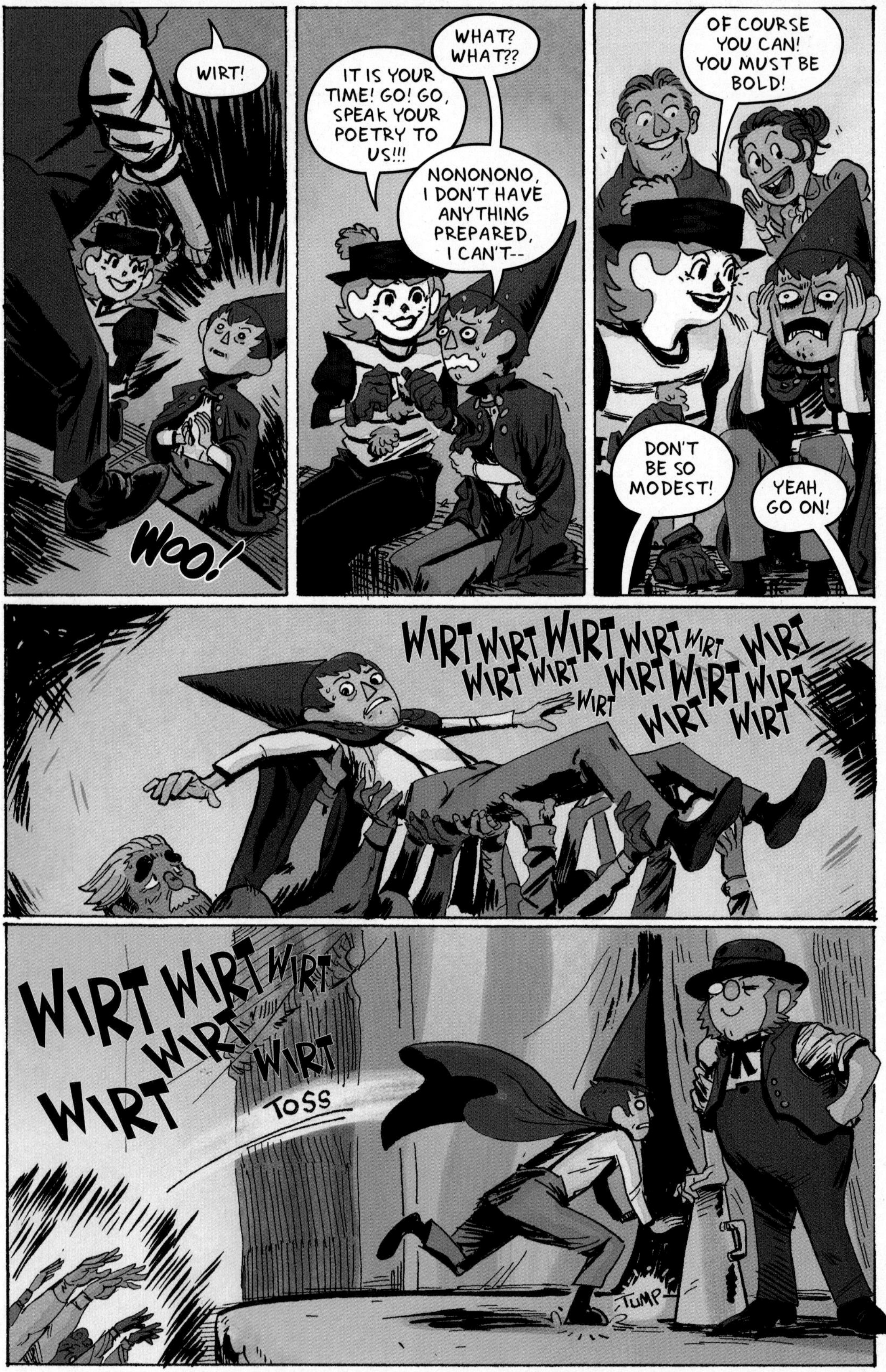
WIRT!
WOO!
WHAT? WHAT??
IT IS YOUR TIME! GO! GO, SPEAK YOUR POETRY TO US!!!
NONONONO, I DON'T HAVE ANYTHING PREPARED, I CAN'T--
OF COURSE YOU CAN! YOU MUST BE BOLD!
DON'T BE SO MODEST!
YEAH, GO ON!
WIRT WIRT WIRT WIRT WIRT WIRT WIRT WIRT WIRT WIRT WIRT WIRT WIRT WIRT WIRT
WIRT WIRT WIRT WIRT WIRT WIRT
TOSS
TUMP

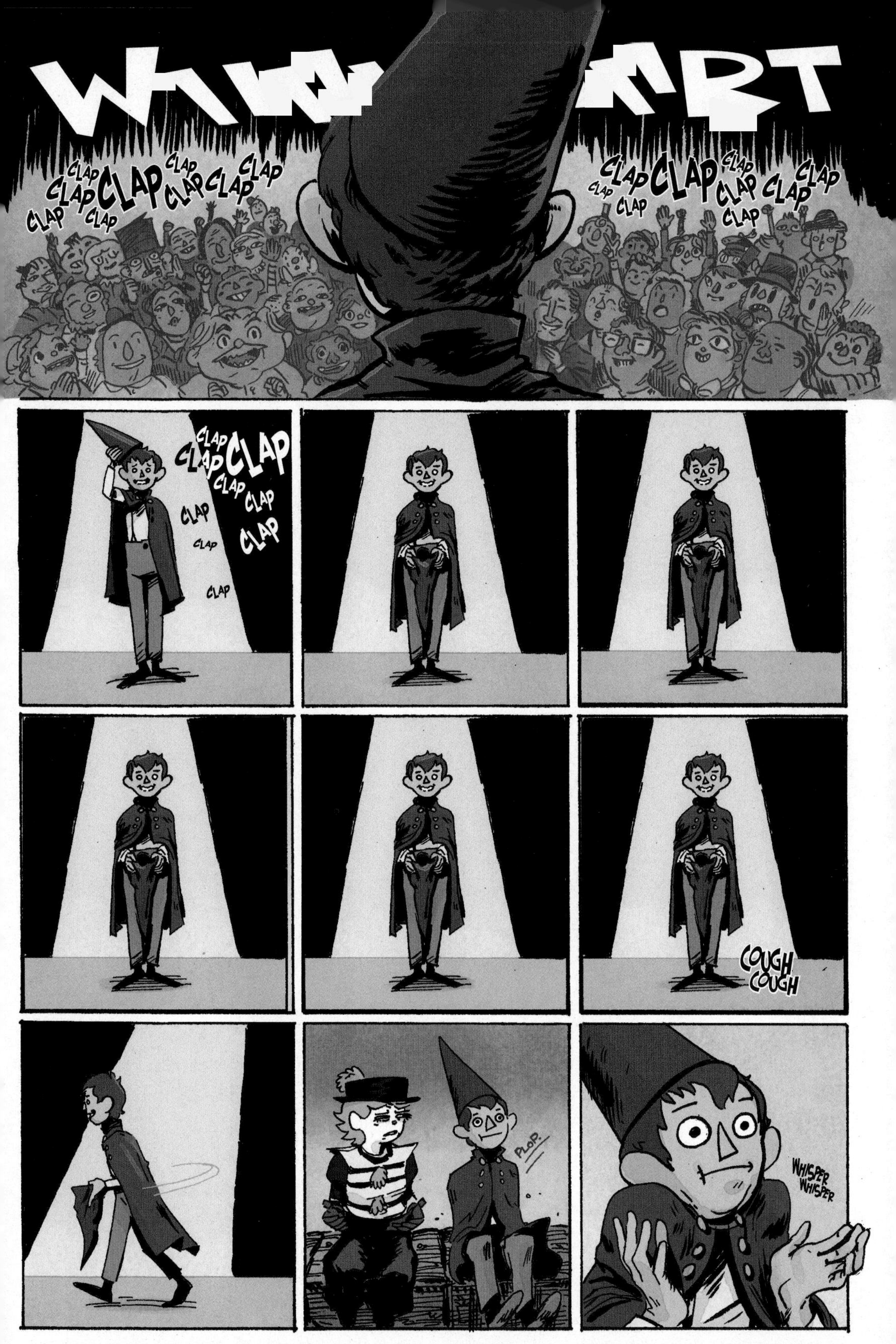
CLAP CLAP CLAP CLAP CLAP CLAP CLAP CLAP CLAP
CLAP CLAP CLAP CLAP CLAP CLAP CLAP CLAP CLAP
CLAP CLAP CLAP CLAP CLAP CLAP CLAP CLAP
COUGH COUGH
PLOP.
WHISPER WHISPER

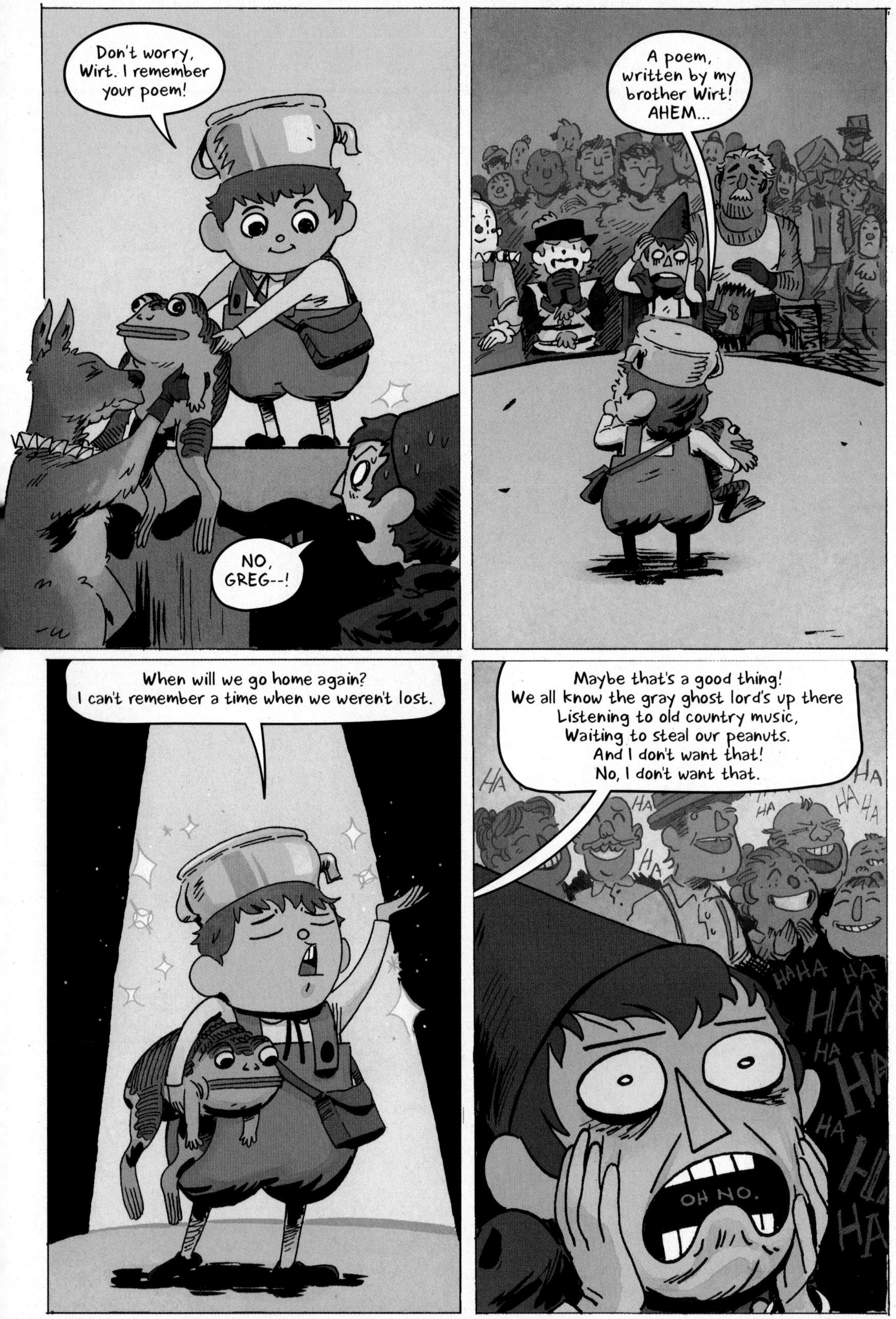

Don't worry, Wirt. I remember your poem!
NO, GREG--!
A poem, written by my brother Wirt! AHEM...
When will we go home again? I can't remember a time when we weren't lost.
Maybe that's a good thing! We all know the gray ghost lord's up there Listening to old country music, Waiting to steal our peanuts. And I don't want that! No, I don't want that.
HA HA HA HA HA HA HA
HAHA HA HA HA HA HA HA HA
OH NO.

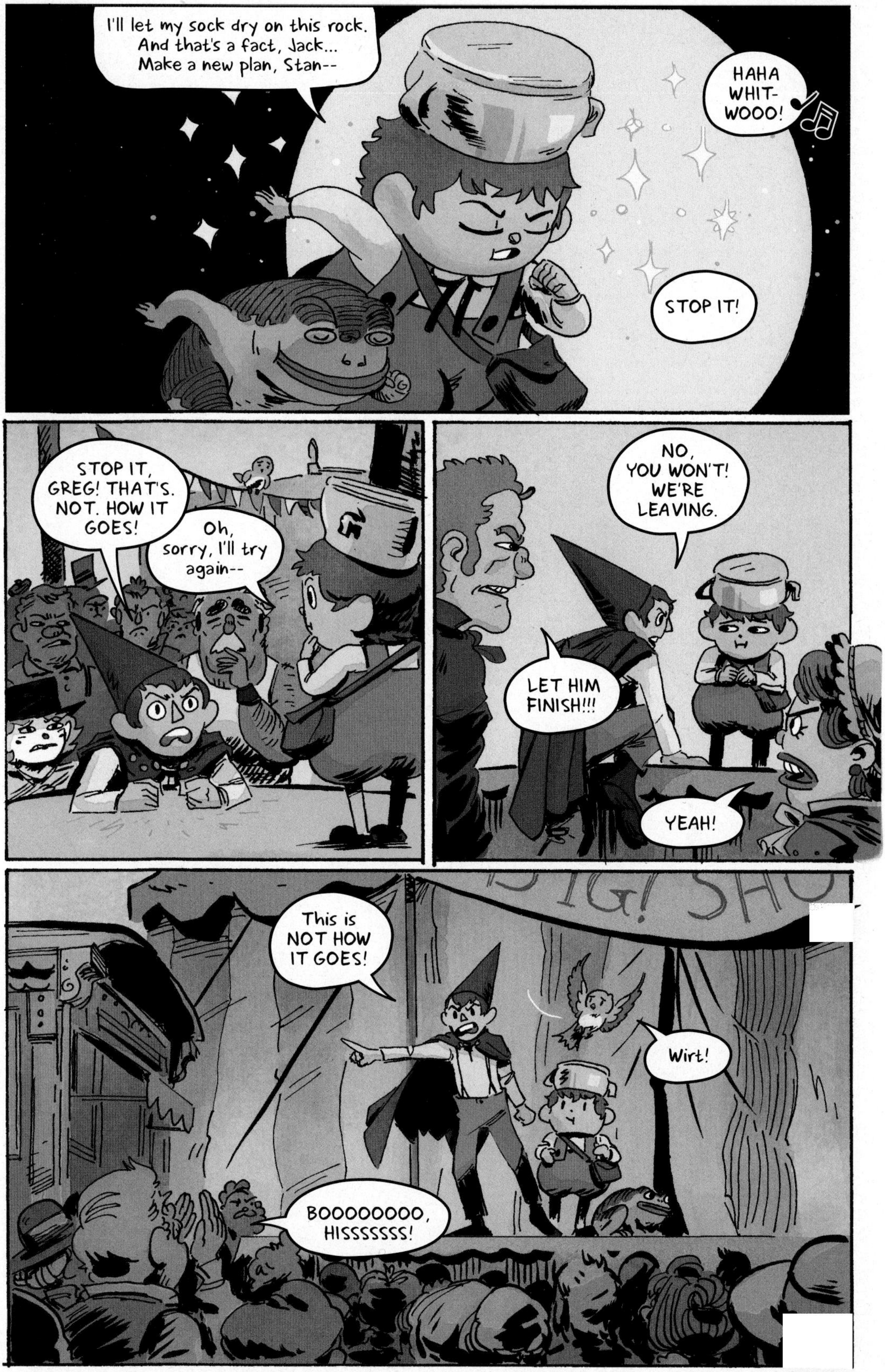
I'll let my sock dry on this rock. And that's a fact, Jack... Make a new plan, Stan--
HAHA WHIT-WOOO!
STOP IT!
STOP IT, GREG! THAT'S. NOT. HOW IT GOES!
Oh, sorry, I'll try again--
NO, YOU WON'T! WE'RE LEAVING.
LET HIM FINISH!!!
YEAH!
This is NOT HOW IT GOES!
Wirt!
BOOOOOOOO, HISSSSSSS!

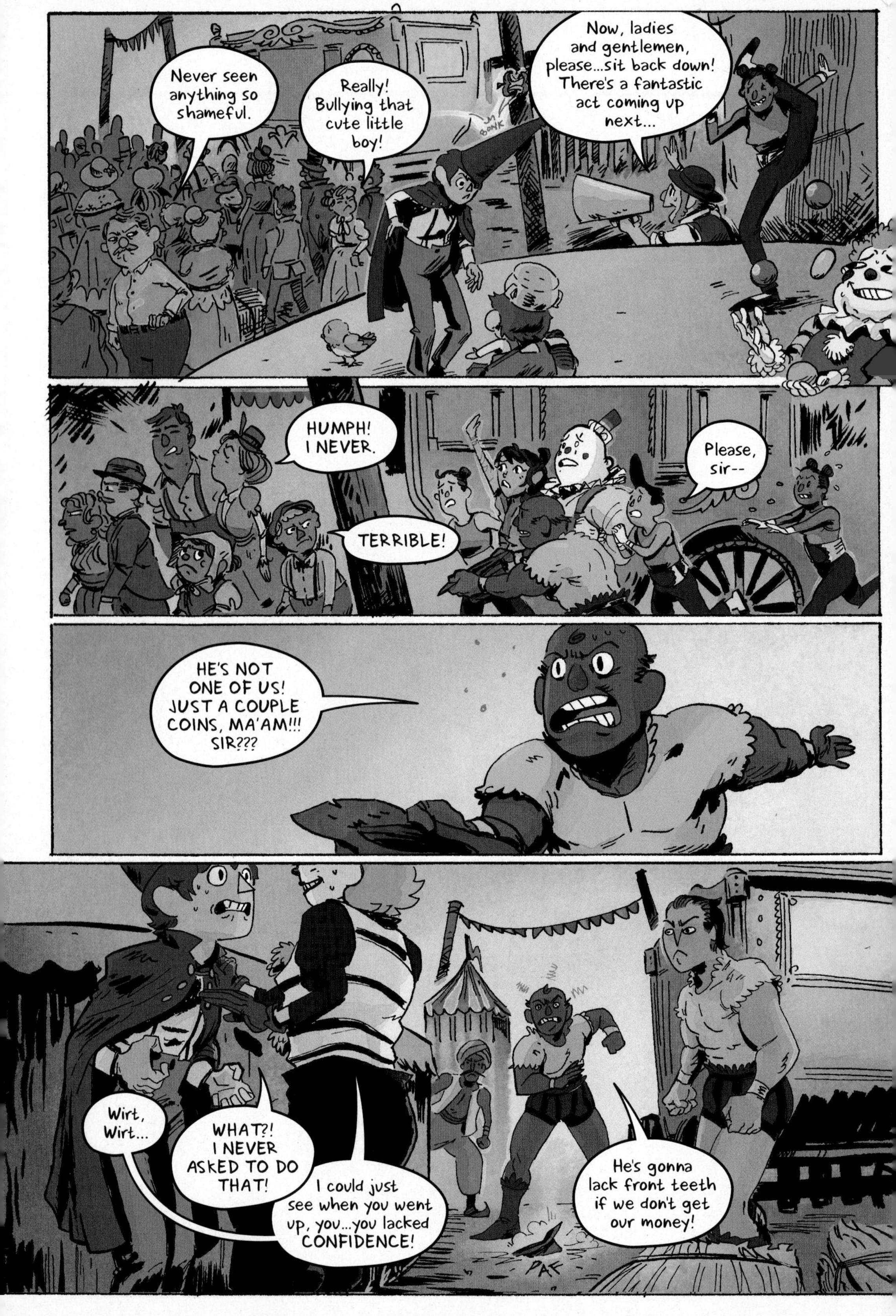

Never seen anything so shameful.
Really! Bullying that cute little boy!
BONK
Now, ladies and gentlemen, please...sit back down! There's a fantastic act coming up next...
HUMPH! I NEVER.
TERRIBLE!
Please, sir--
HE'S NOT ONE OF US! JUST A COUPLE COINS, MA'AM!!! SIR???
Wirt, Wirt...
WHAT?! I NEVER ASKED TO DO THAT!
I could just see when you went up, you...you lacked CONFIDENCE!
He's gonna lack front teeth if we don't get our money!
PAF

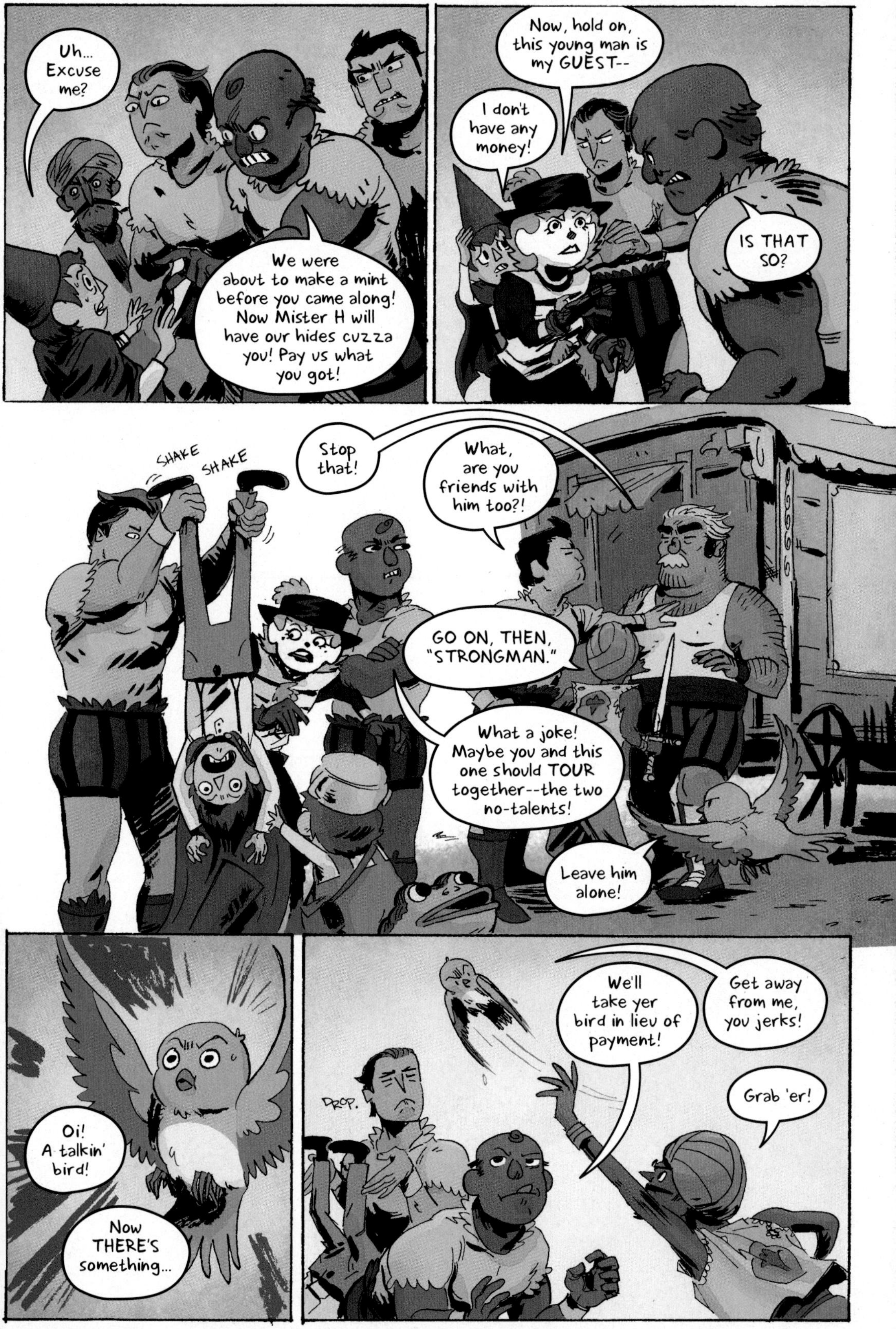

Uh... Excuse me?
We were about to make a mint before you came along! Now Mister H will have our hides cuzza you! Pay us what you got!
Now, hold on, this young man is my GUEST--
I don't have any money!
IS THAT SO?
SHAKE SHAKE
Stop that!
What, are you friends with him too?!
GO ON, THEN, "STRONGMAN."
What a joke! Maybe you and this one should TOUR together--the two no-talents!
Leave him alone!
Oi! A talkin' bird!
Now THERE'S something...
Get away from me, you jerks!
We'll take yer bird in lieu of payment!
DROP.
Grab 'er!

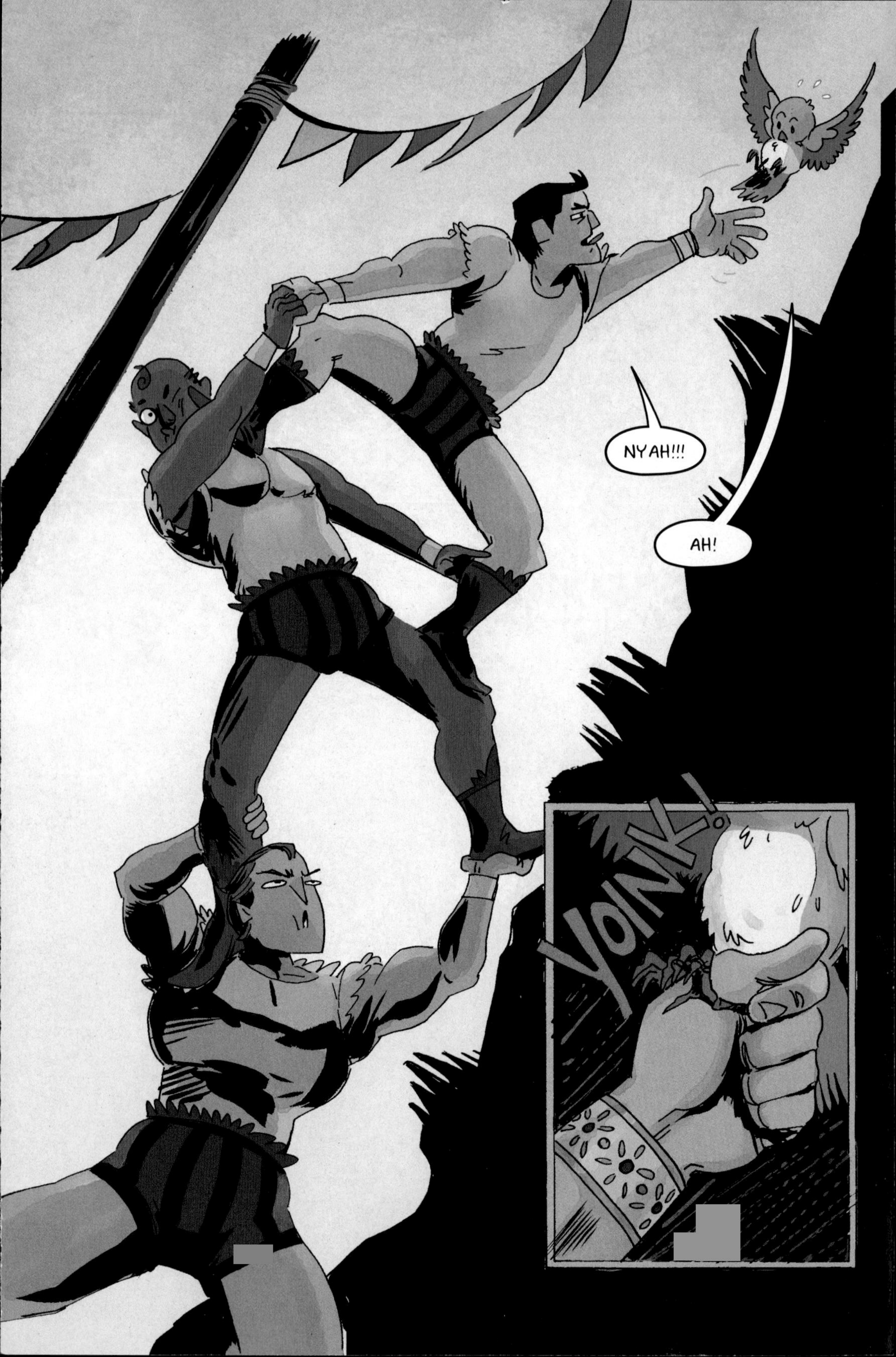
NYAH!!!
AH!
YOINK!

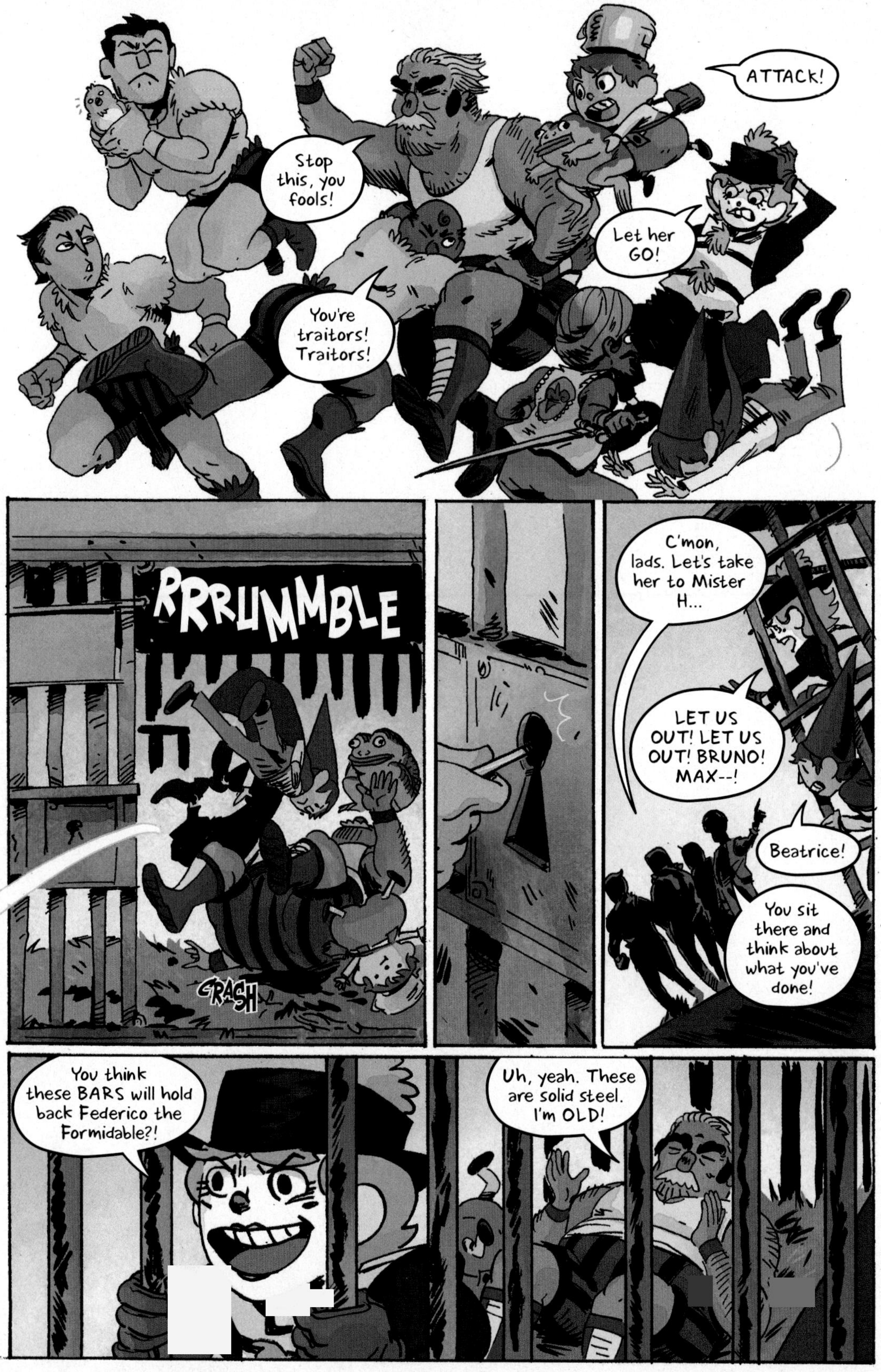
Stop this, you fools!
ATTACK!
Let her GO!
You're traitors! Traitors!
RRRUMMBLE
CRASH
C'mon, lads. Let's take her to Mister H...
LET US OUT! LET US OUT! BRUNO! MAX--!
Beatrice!
You sit there and think about what you've done!
You think these BARS will hold back Federico the Formidable?!
Uh, yeah. These are solid steel. I'm OLD!

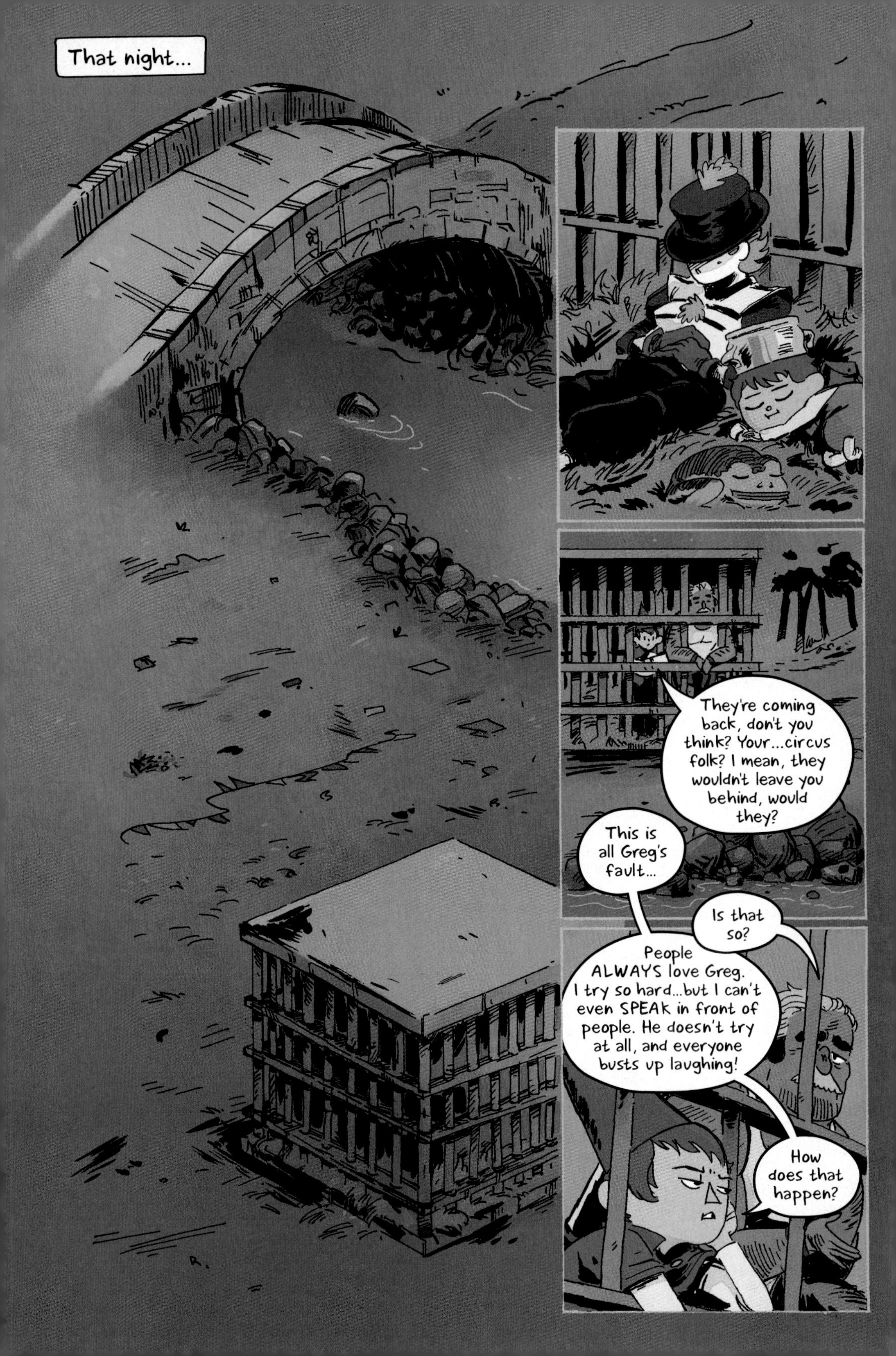

That night...
They're coming back, don't you think? Your...circus folk? I mean, they wouldn't leave you behind, would they?
This is all Greg's fault...
Is that so?
People ALWAYS love Greg. I try so hard...but I can't even SPEAK in front of people. He doesn't try at all, and everyone busts up laughing!
How does that happen?

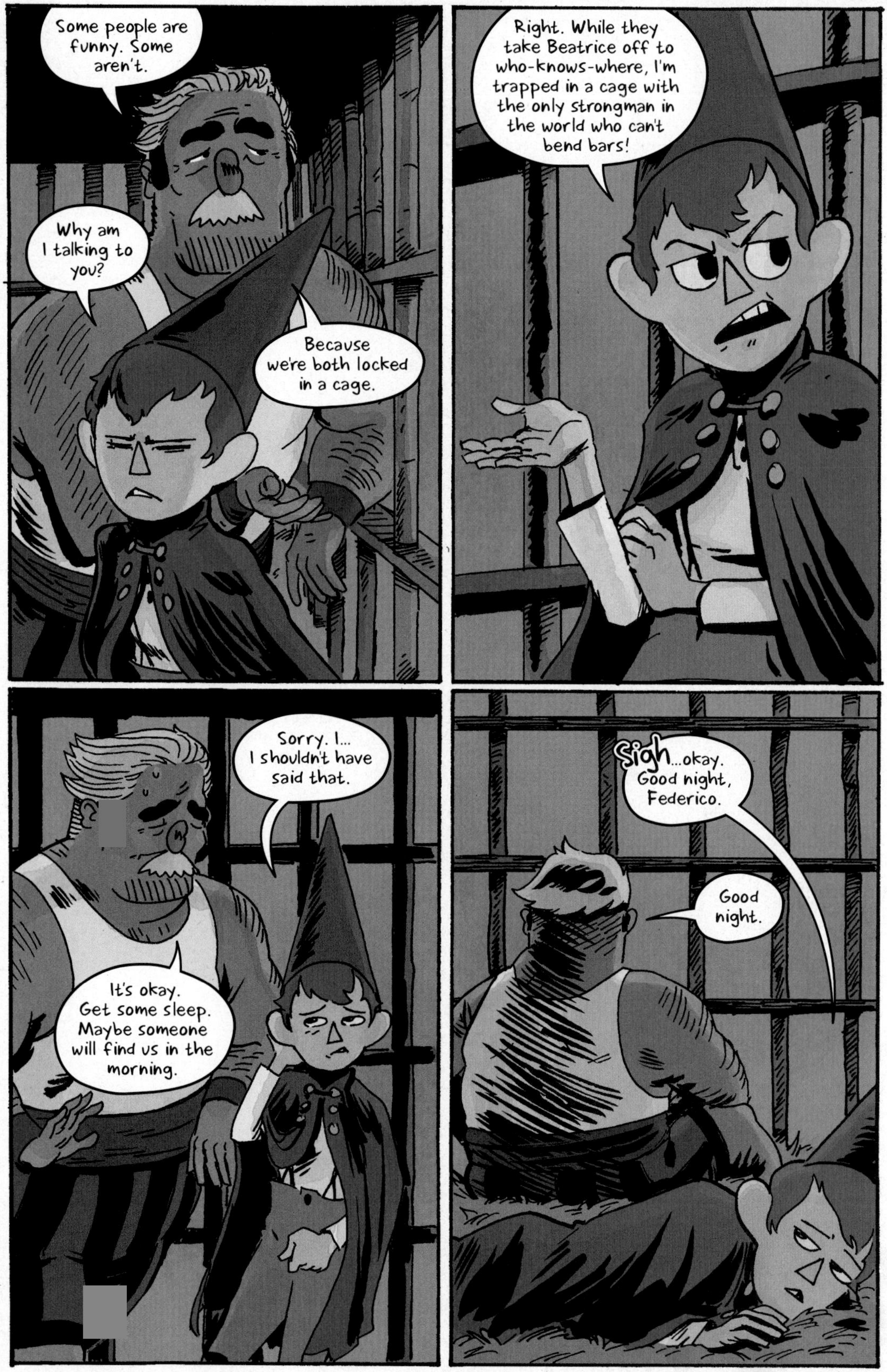
Some people are funny. Some aren't.
Why am I talking to you?
Because we're both locked in a cage.
Right. While they take Beatrice off to who-knows-where, I'm trapped in a cage with the only strongman in the world who can't bend bars!
Sorry. I... I shouldn't have said that.
It's okay. Get some sleep. Maybe someone will find us in the morning.
Sigh...okay. Good night, Federico.
Good night.

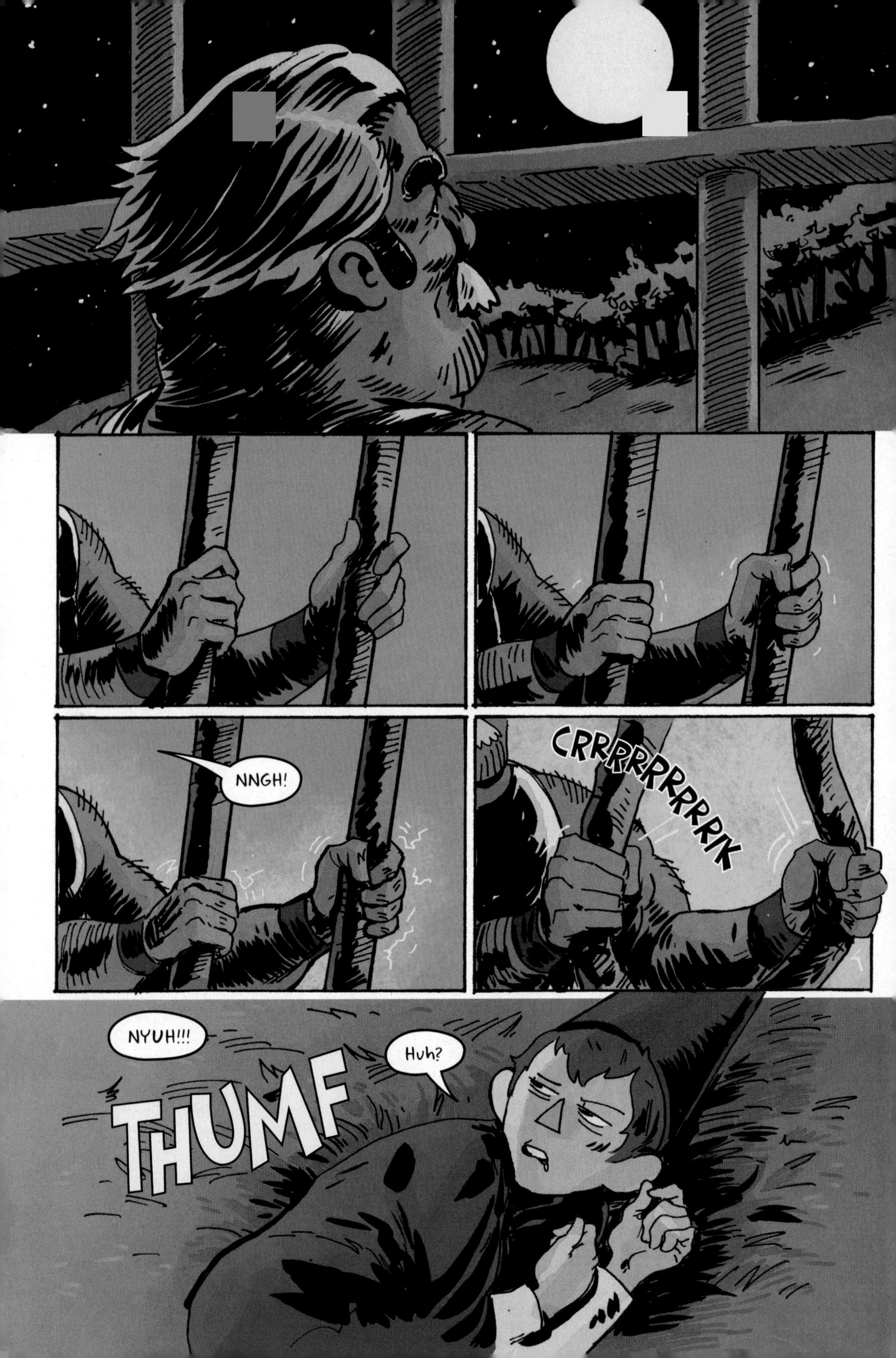
NNGH!
CRRRRRRRRRIK
NYUH!!!
THUMF
Huh?

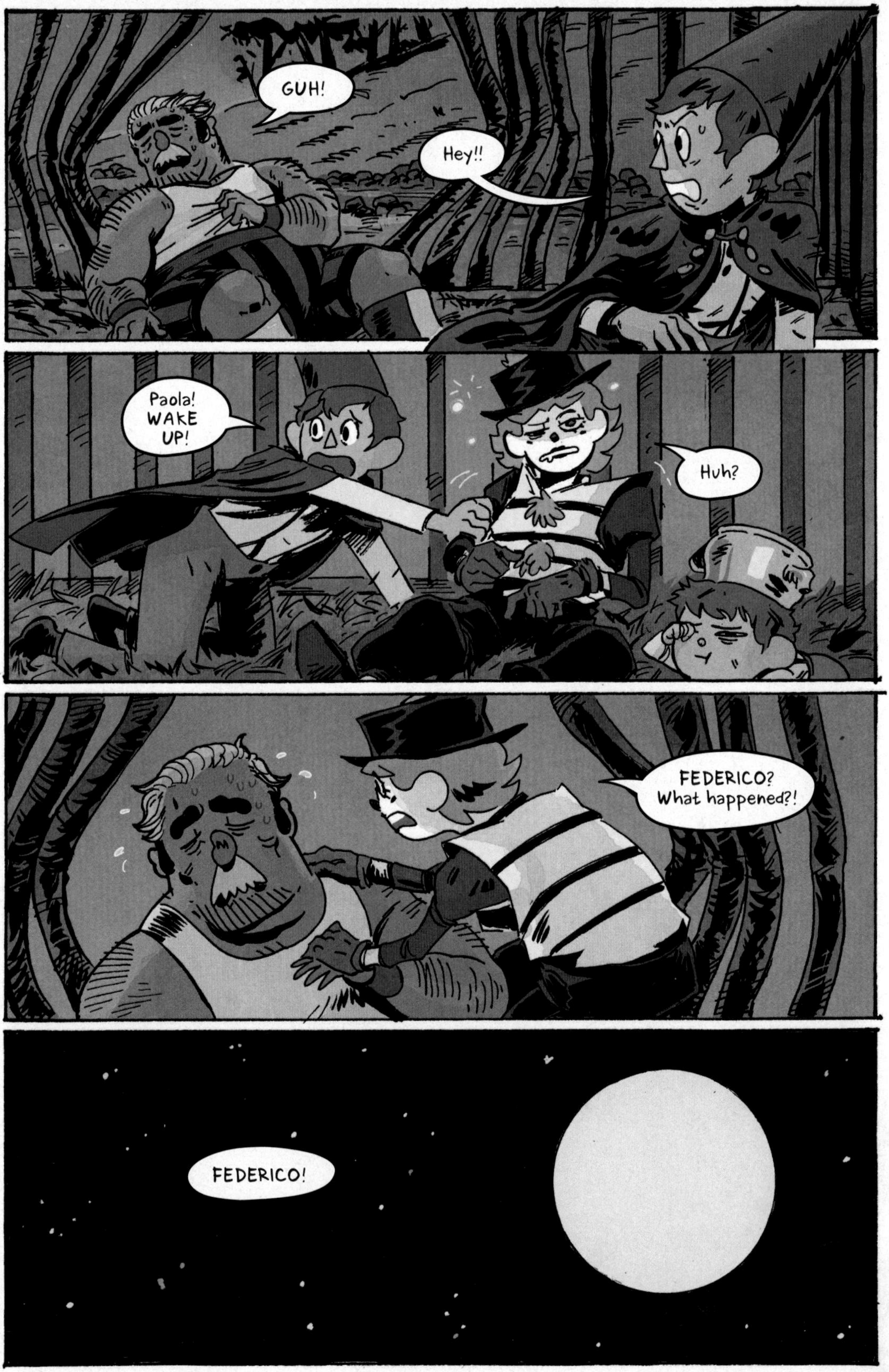
GUH!
Hey!!
Paola! WAKE UP!
Huh?
FEDERICO? What happened?!
FEDERICO!

ACT TWO

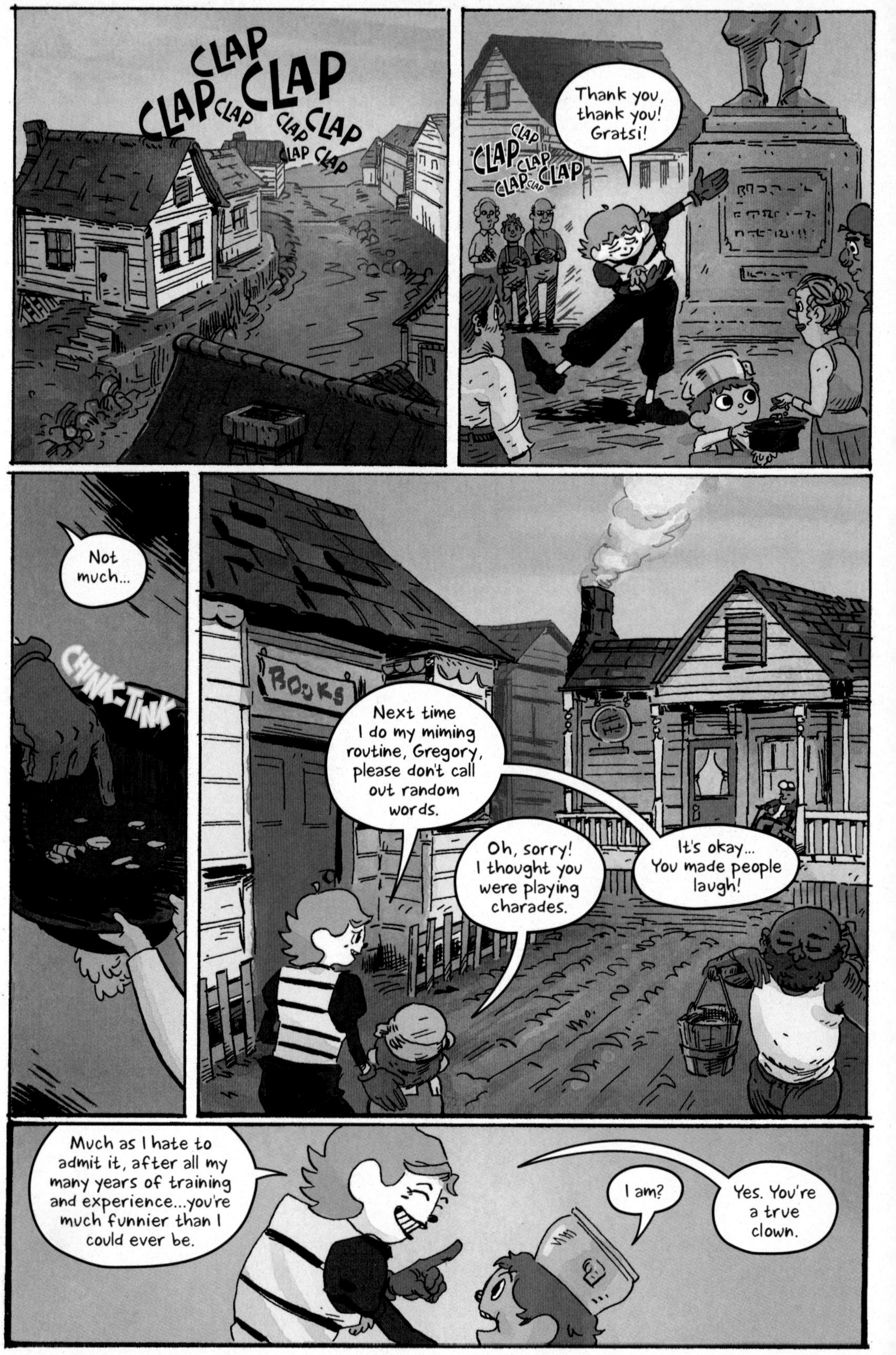
CLAP CLAP CLAP CLAP CLAP CLAP CLAP CLAP CLAP
CLAP CLAP CLAP CLAP CLAP CLAP
Thank you, thank you! Gratsi!
Not much...
CHINK-TINK
BOOKS
Next time I do my miming routine, Gregory, please don't call out random words.
Oh, sorry! I thought you were playing charades.
It's okay... You made people laugh!
Much as I hate to admit it, after all my many years of training and experience...you're much funnier than I could ever be.
I am?
Yes. You're a true clown.

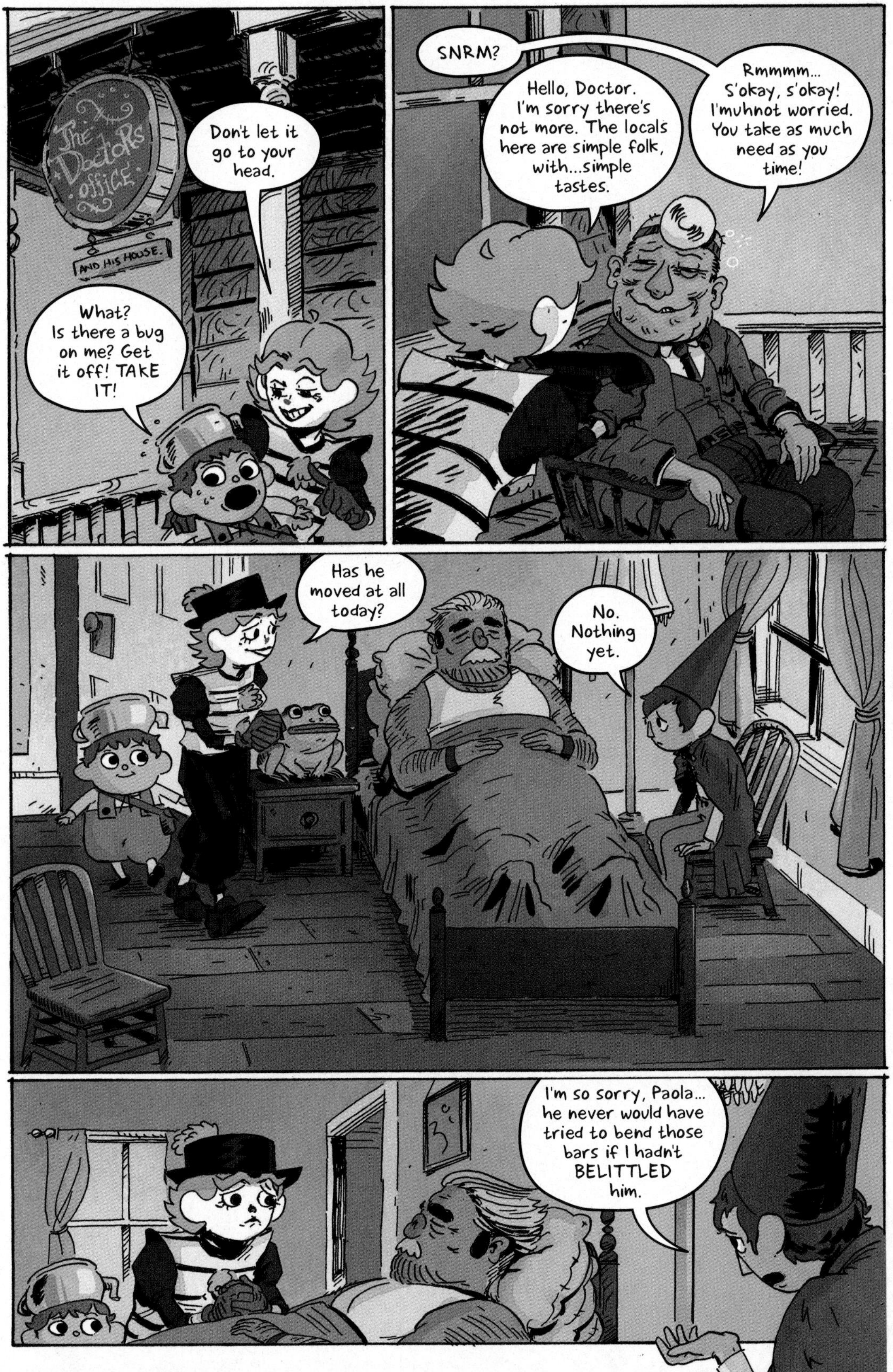
THE DOCTOR'S OFFICE
AND HIS HOUSE.
Don't let it go to your head.
What? Is there a bug on me? Get it off! TAKE IT!
SNRM?
Hello, Doctor. I'm sorry there's not more. The locals here are simple folk, with...simple tastes.
Rmmmm... S'okay, s'okay! I'muhnot worried. You take as much need as you time!
Has he moved at all today?
No. Nothing yet.
I'm so sorry, Paola... he never would have tried to bend those bars if I hadn't BELITTLED him.

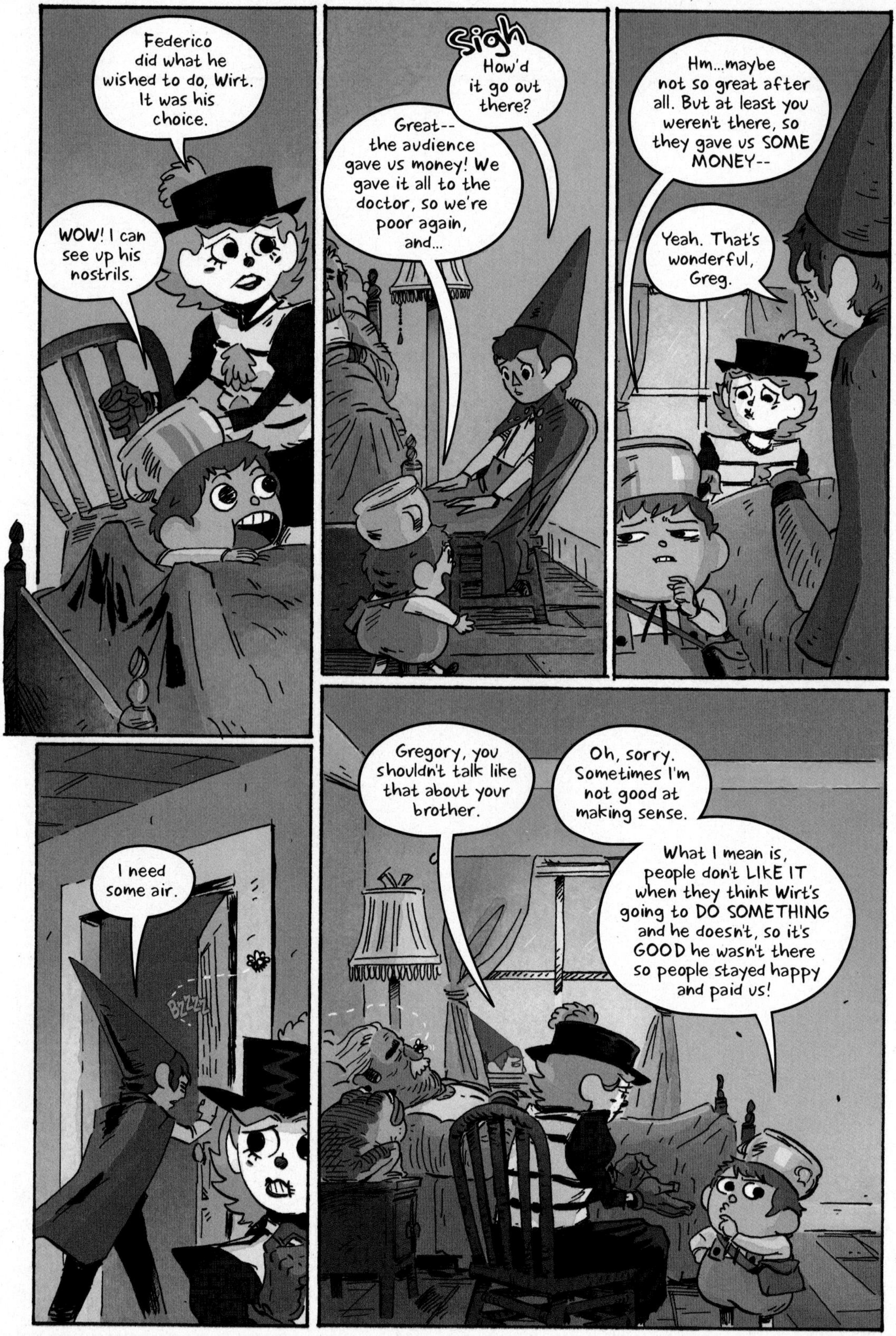
Federico did what he wished to do, Wirt. It was his choice.
WOW! I can see up his nostrils.
Sigh
How'd it go out there?
Great-- the audience gave us money! We gave it all to the doctor, so we're poor again, and...
Hm...maybe not so great after all. But at least you weren't there, so they gave us SOME MONEY--
Yeah. That's wonderful, Greg.
I need some air.
Bzzzz
Gregory, you shouldn't talk like that about your brother.
Oh, sorry. Sometimes I'm not good at making sense.
What I mean is, people don't LIKE IT when they think Wirt's going to DO SOMETHING and he doesn't, so it's GOOD he wasn't there so people stayed happy and paid us!

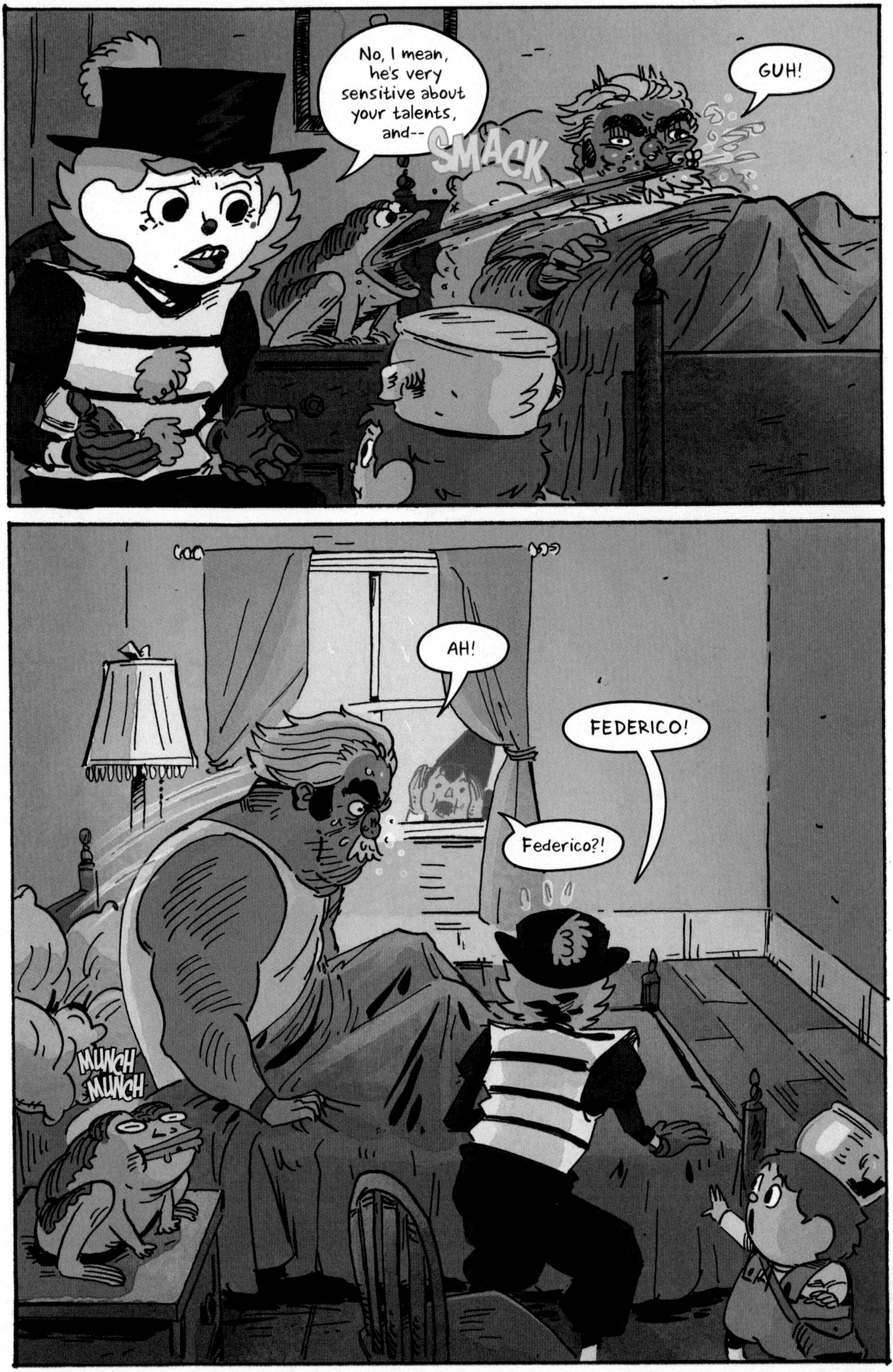
No, I mean, he's very sensitive about your talents, and--
SMACK
GUH!
AH!
FEDERICO!
Federico?!
MUNCH MUNCH

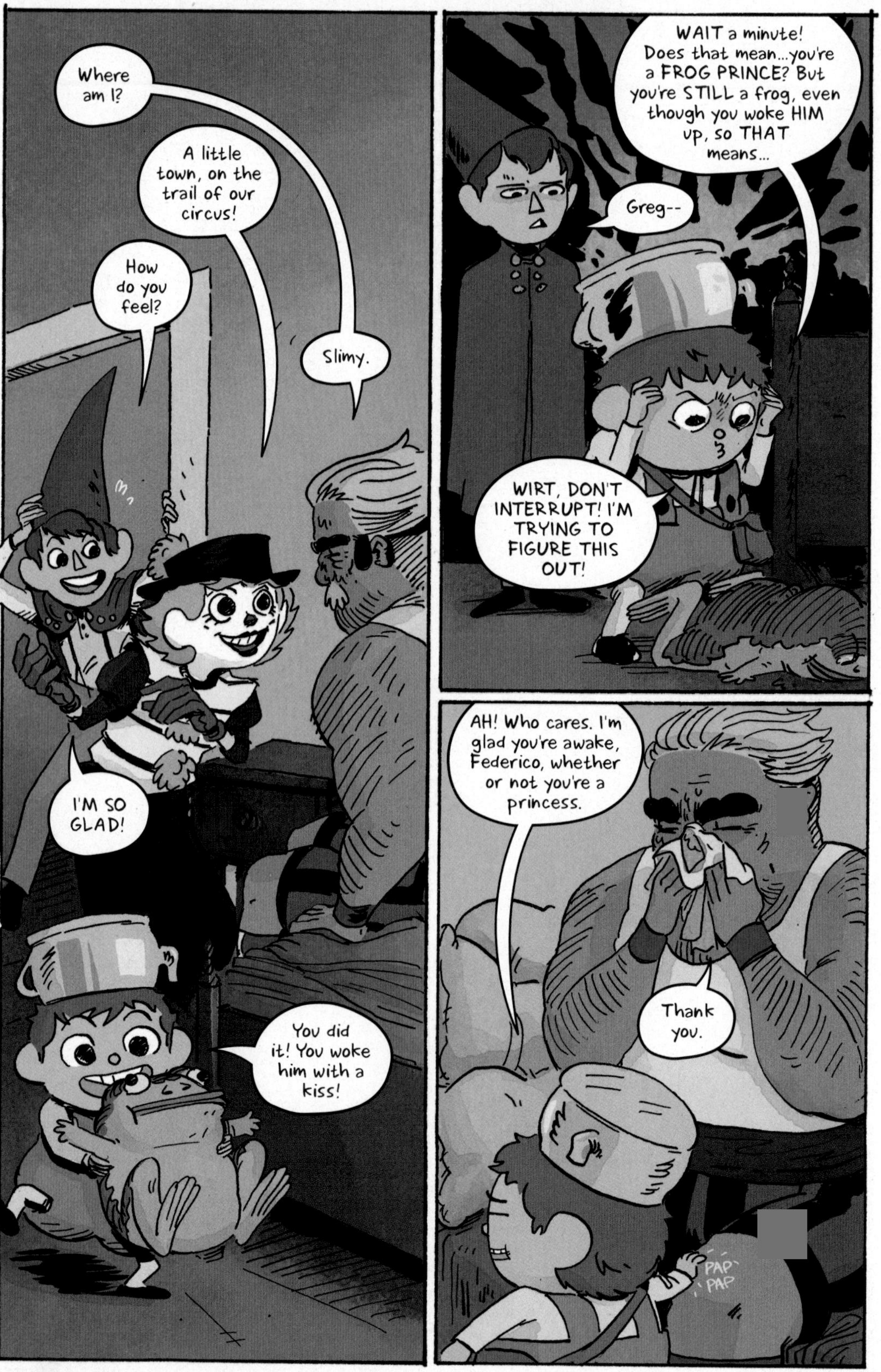
Where am I?
A little town, on the trail of our circus!
How do you feel?
Slimy.
I'M SO GLAD!
You did it! You woke him with a kiss!
WAIT a minute! Does that mean...you're a FROG PRINCE? But you're STILL a frog, even though you woke HIM up, so THAT means...
Greg--
WIRT, DON'T INTERRUPT! I'M TRYING TO FIGURE THIS OUT!
AH! Who cares. I'm glad you're awake, Federico, whether or not you're a princess.
Thank you.
PAP PAP

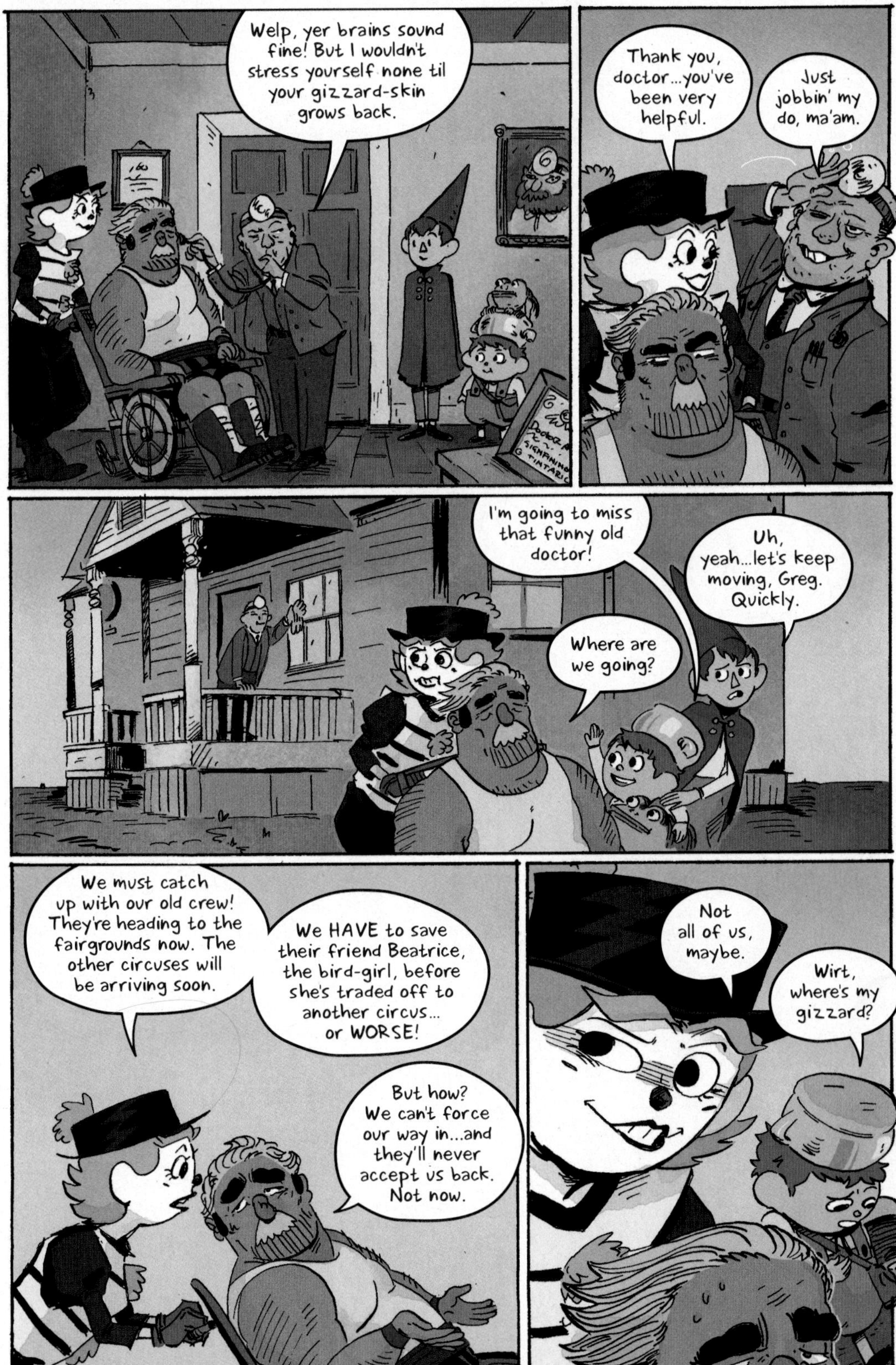
Welp, yer brains sound fine! But I wouldn't stress yourself none til your gizzard-skin grows back.
Thank you, doctor...you've been very helpful.
Just jobbin' my do, ma'am.
I'm going to miss that funny old doctor!
Uh, yeah...let's keep moving, Greg. Quickly.
Where are we going?
We must catch up with our old crew! They're heading to the fairgrounds now. The other circuses will be arriving soon.
We HAVE to save their friend Beatrice, the bird-girl, before she's traded off to another circus... or WORSE!
But how? We can't force our way in...and they'll never accept us back. Not now.
Not all of us, maybe.
Wirt, where's my gizzard?

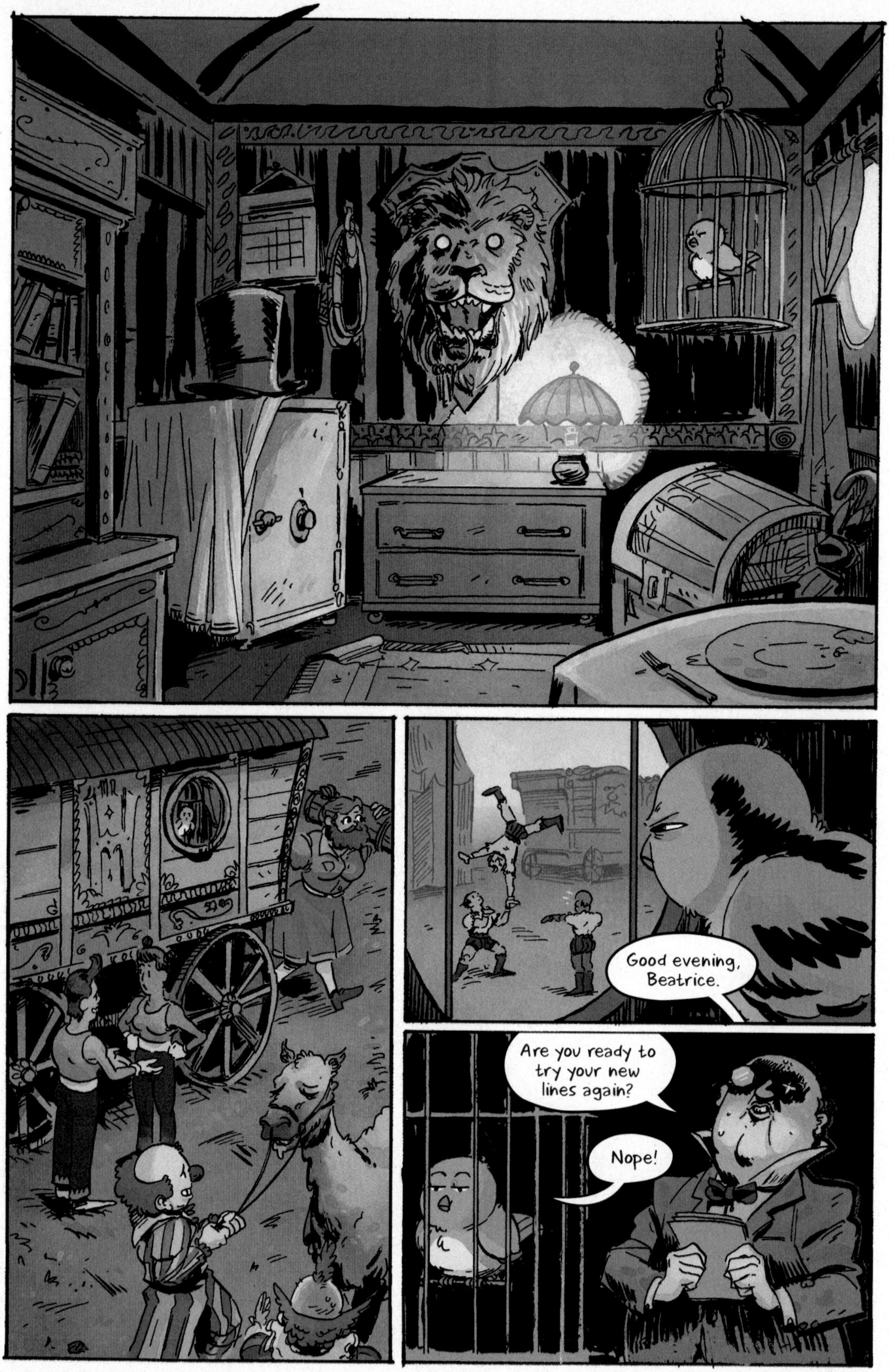
Good evening, Beatrice.
Are you ready to try your new lines again?
Nope!

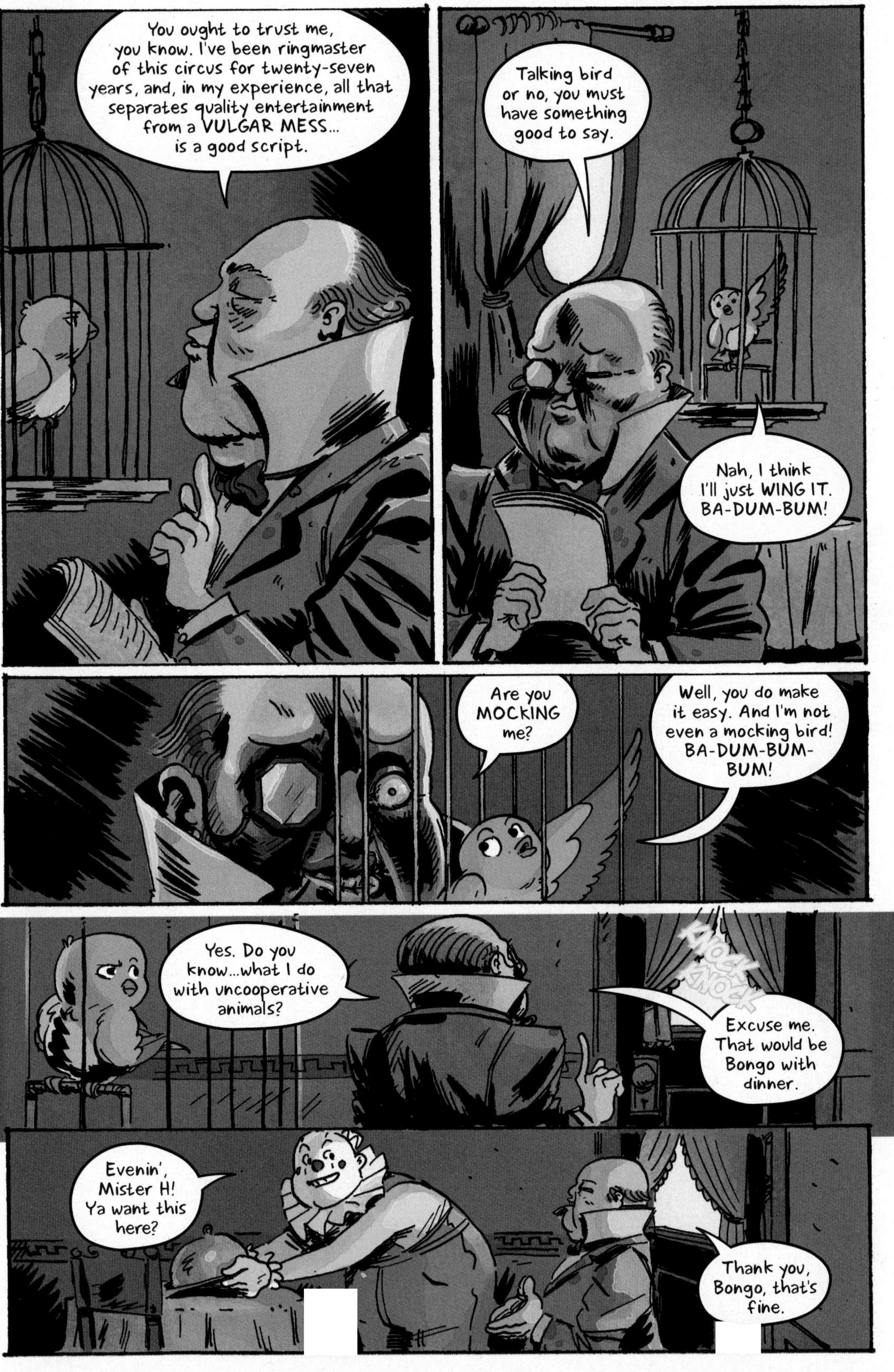
You ought to trust me, you know. I've been ringmaster of this circus for twenty-seven years, and, in my experience, all that separates quality entertainment from a VULGAR MESS... is a good script.
Talking bird or no, you must have something good to say.
Nah, I think I'll just WING IT. BA-DUM-BUM!
Are you MOCKING me?
Well, you do make it easy. And I'm not even a mocking bird! BA-DUM-BUM-BUM!
Yes. Do you know...what I do with uncooperative animals?
KNOCK KNOCK
Excuse me. That would be Bongo with dinner.
Evenin', Mister H! Ya want this here?
Thank you, Bongo, that's fine.

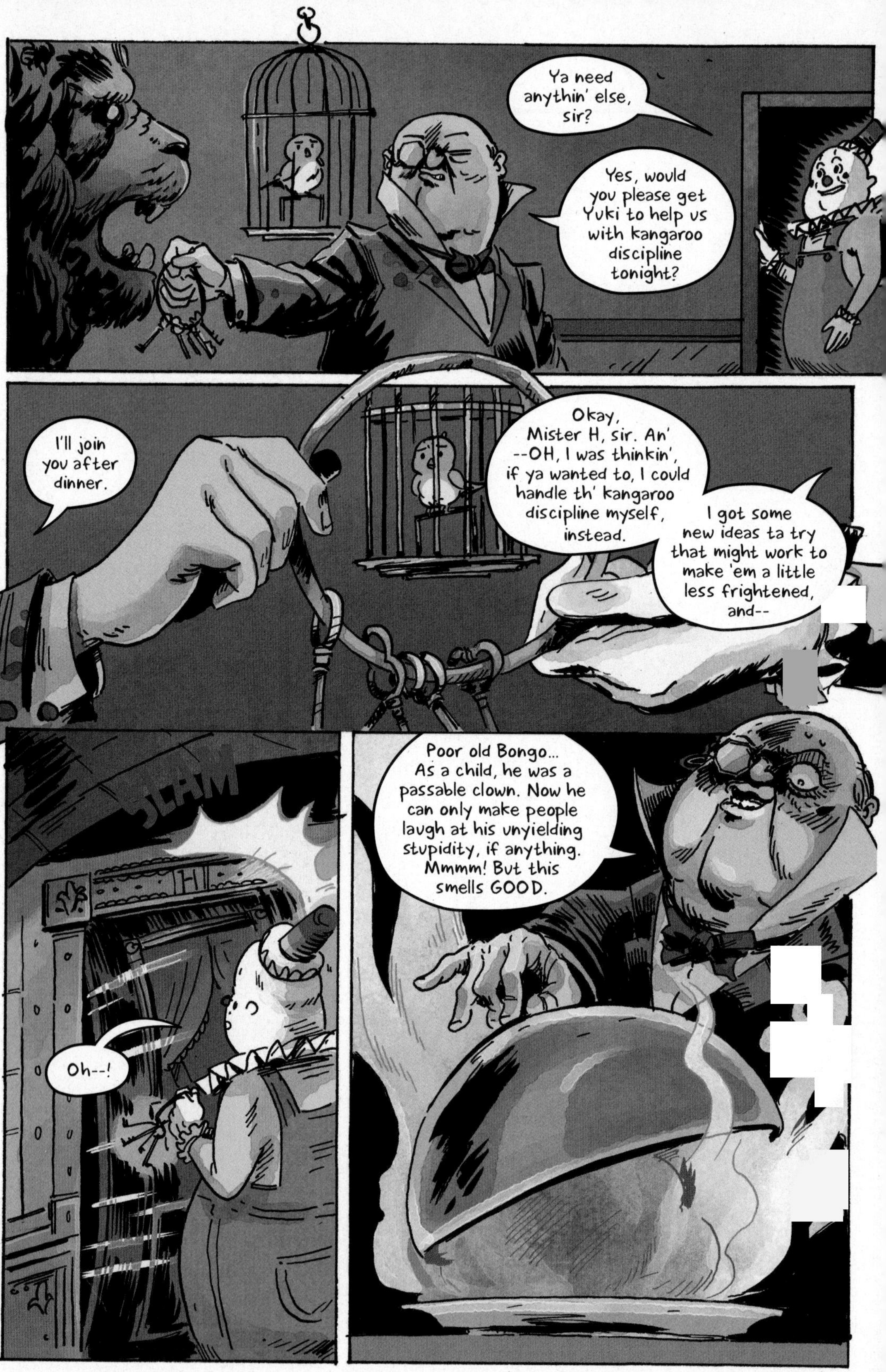
Ya need anythin' else, sir?
Yes, would you please get Yuki to help us with kangaroo discipline tonight?
I'll join you after dinner.
Okay, Mister H, sir. An' --OH, I was thinkin', if ya wanted to, I could handle th' kangaroo discipline myself, instead.
I got some new ideas ta try that might work to make 'em a little less frightened, and--
SLAM
Oh--!
Poor old Bongo... As a child, he was a passable clown. Now he can only make people laugh at his unyielding stupidity, if anything. Mmmm! But this smells GOOD.

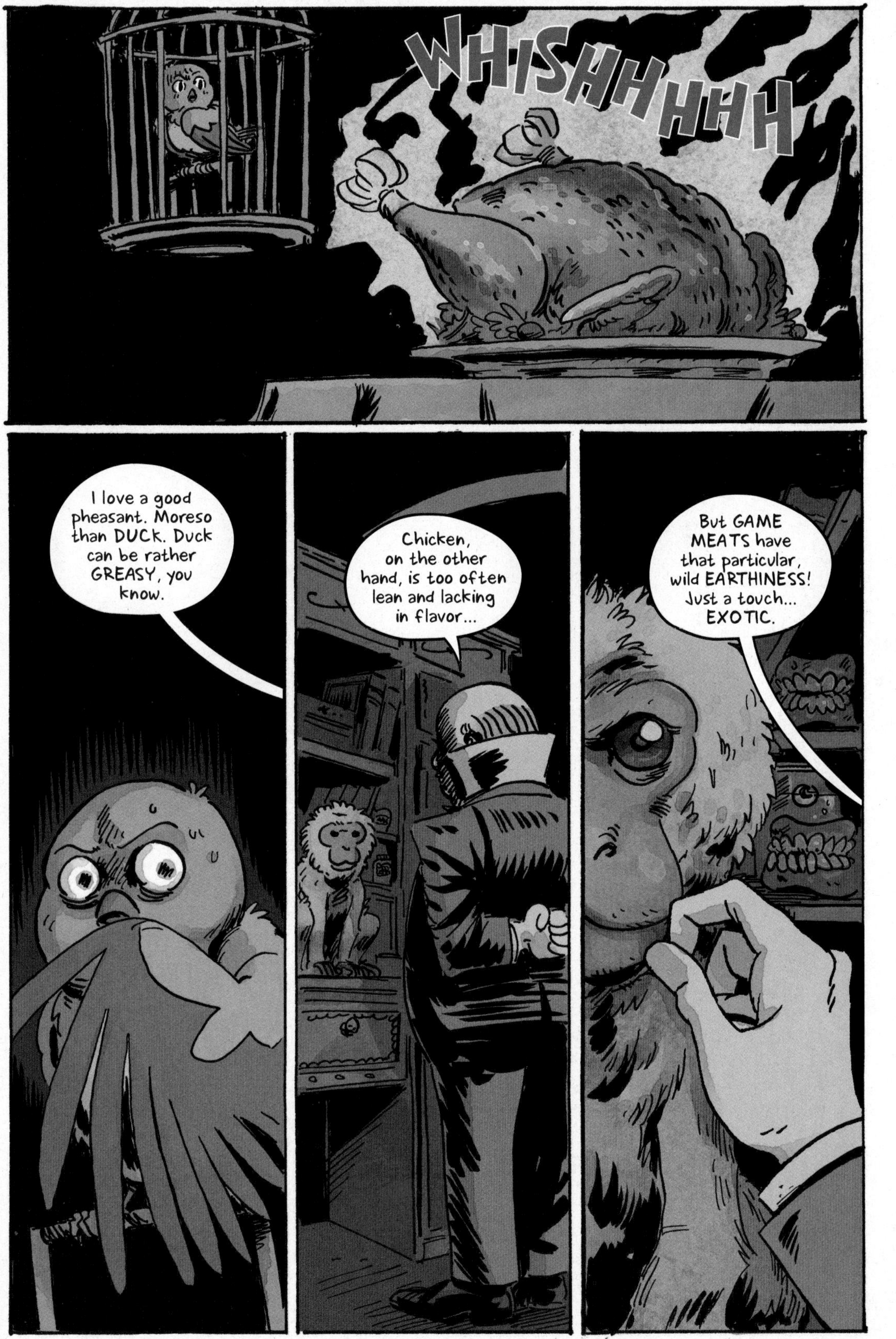
WHISHHHHH
I love a good pheasant. Moreso than DUCK. Duck can be rather GREASY, you know.
Chicken, on the other hand, is too often lean and lacking in flavor...
But GAME MEATS have that particular, wild EARTHINESS! Just a touch... EXOTIC.

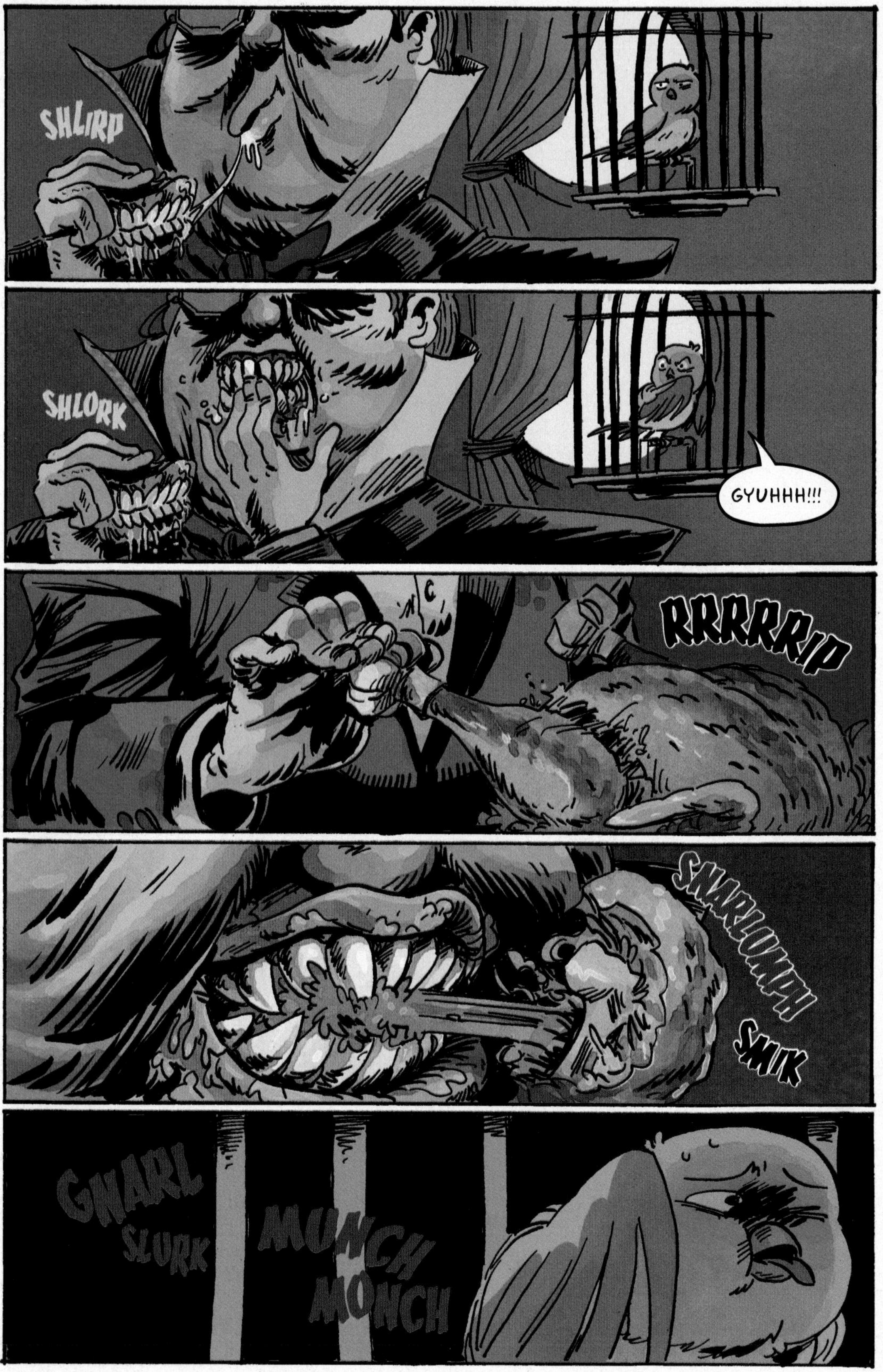
SHLIRP
SHLORK
GYUHHH!!!
RRRRRIP
SNARLUMPH
SMIK
GNARL
SLURK
MUNCH
MONCH

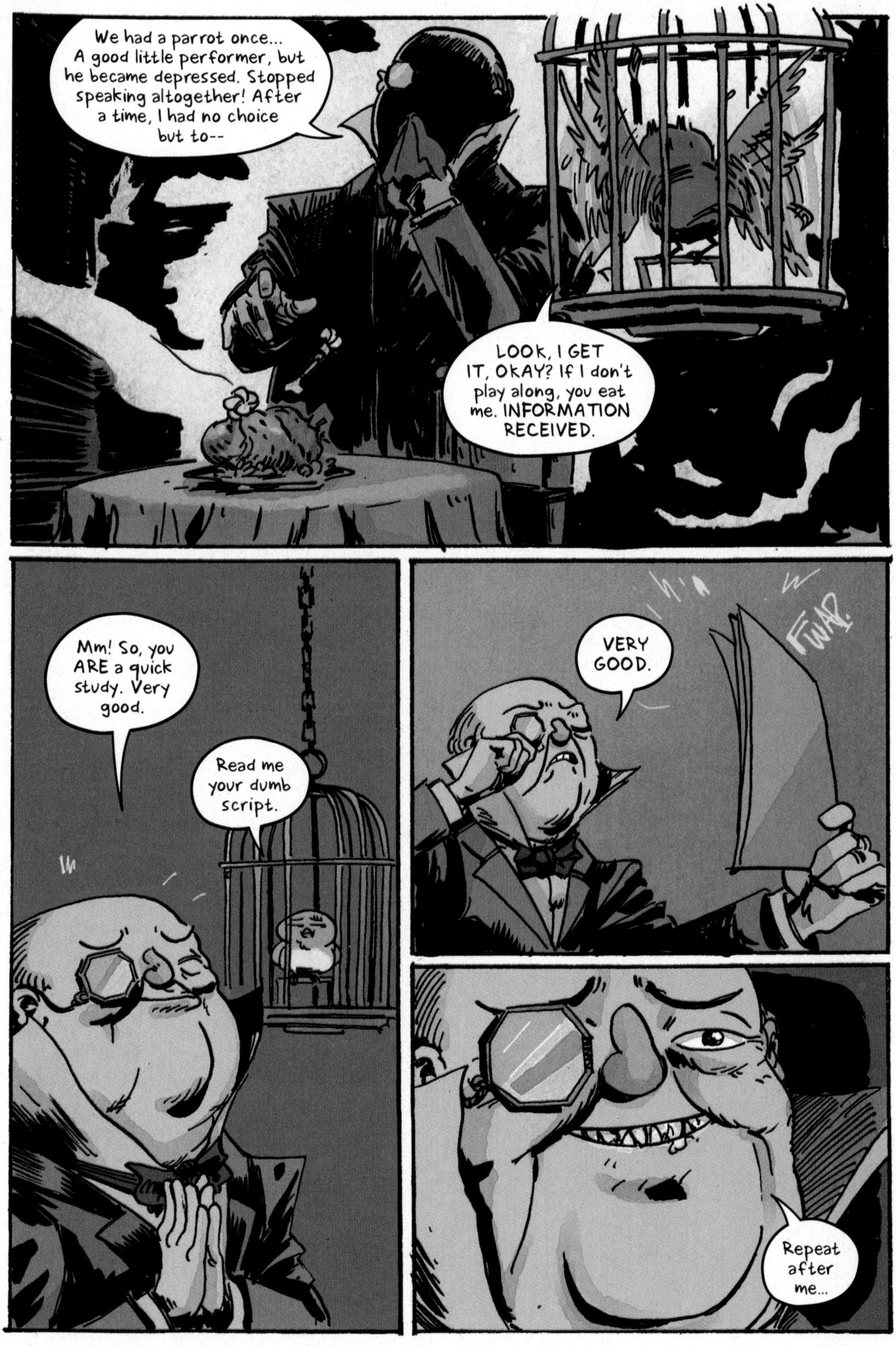

We had a parrot once... A good little performer, but he became depressed. Stopped speaking altogether! After a time, I had no choice but to--
LOOK, I GET IT, OKAY? If I don't play along, you eat me. INFORMATION RECEIVED.
Mm! So, you ARE a quick study. Very good.
Read me your dumb script.
VERY GOOD.
FWAP!
Repeat after me...

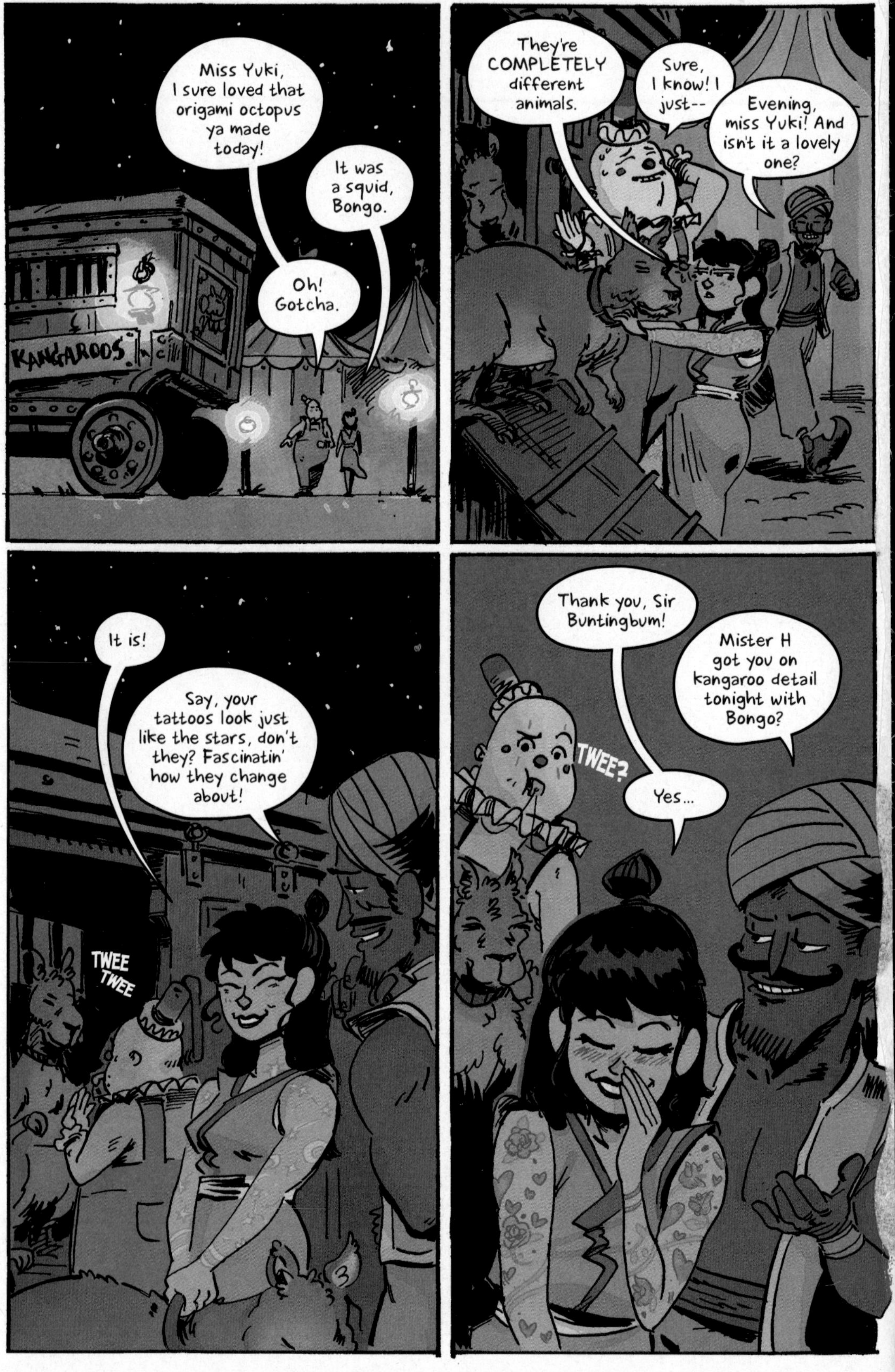
Miss Yuki, I sure loved that origami octopus ya made today!
It was a squid, Bongo.
Oh! Gotcha.
KANGAROOS
They're COMPLETELY different animals.
Sure, I know! I just--
Evening, miss Yuki! And isn't it a lovely one?
It is!
Say, your tattoos look just like the stars, don't they? Fascinatin' how they change about!
TWEE TWEE
Thank you, Sir Buntingbum!
Mister H got you on kangaroo detail tonight with Bongo?
TWEE?
Yes...

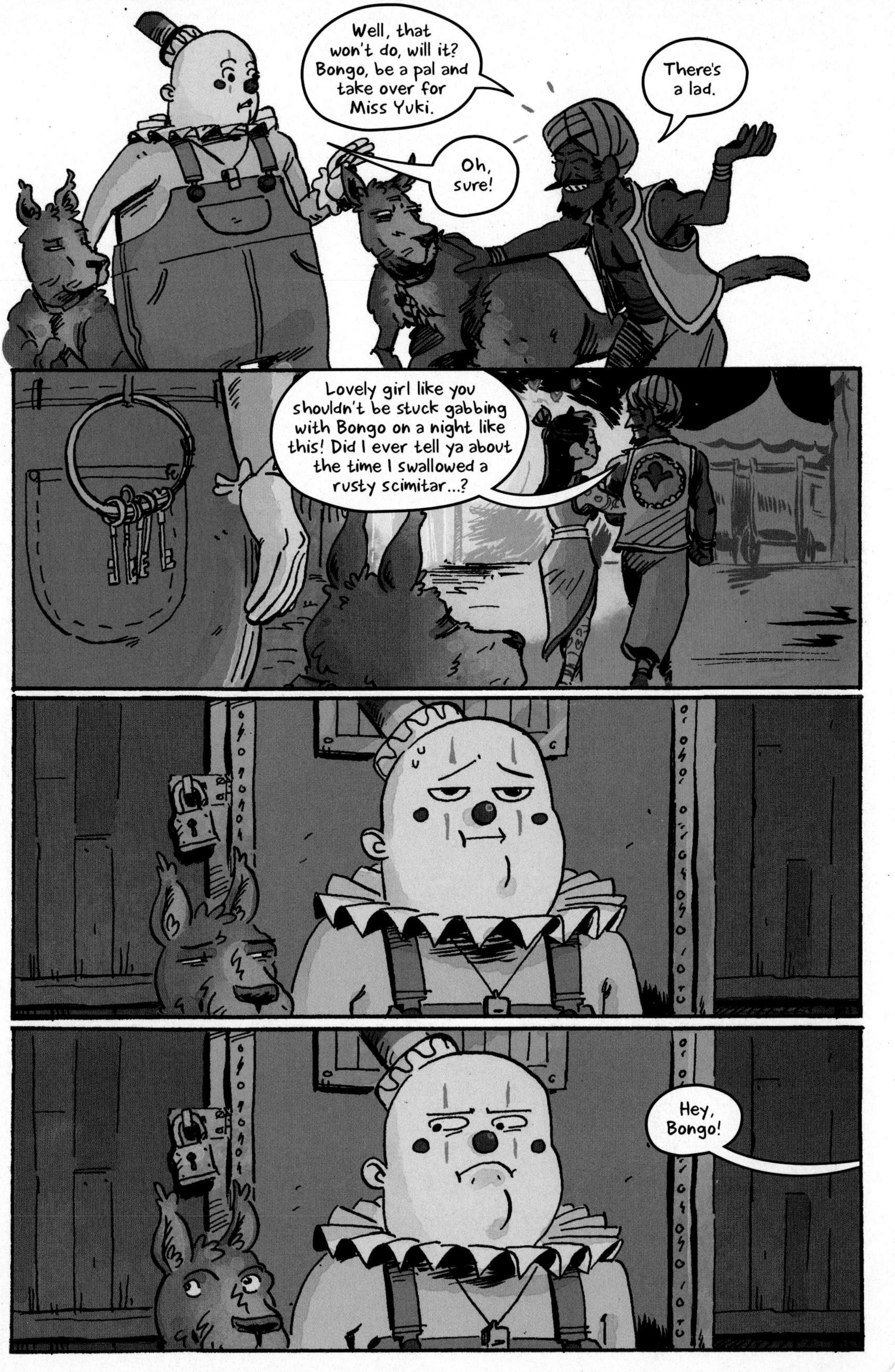
Well, that won't do, will it? Bongo, be a pal and take over for Miss Yuki.
Oh, sure!
There's a lad.
Lovely girl like you shouldn't be stuck gabbing with Bongo on a night like this! Did I ever tell ya about the time I swallowed a rusty scimitar...?
Hey, Bongo!

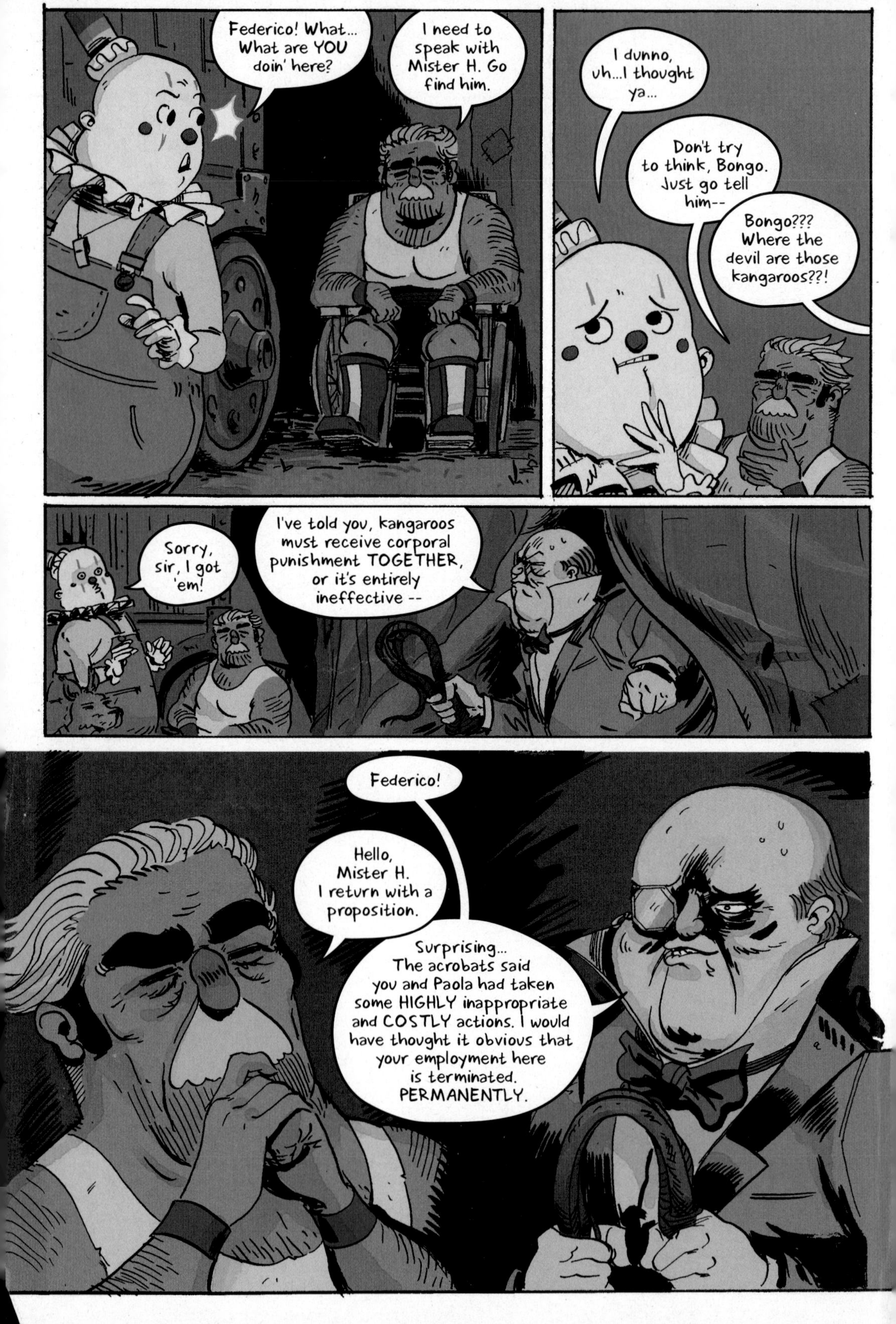
Federico! What... What are YOU doin' here?
I need to speak with Mister H. Go find him.
I dunno, uh...I thought ya...
Don't try to think, Bongo. Just go tell him--
Bongo??? Where the devil are those kangaroos??!
Sorry, sir, I got 'em!
I've told you, kangaroos must receive corporal punishment TOGETHER, or it's entirely ineffective --
Federico!
Hello, Mister H. I return with a proposition.
Surprising... The acrobats said you and Paola had taken some HIGHLY inappropriate and COSTLY actions. I would have thought it obvious that your employment here is terminated. PERMANENTLY.

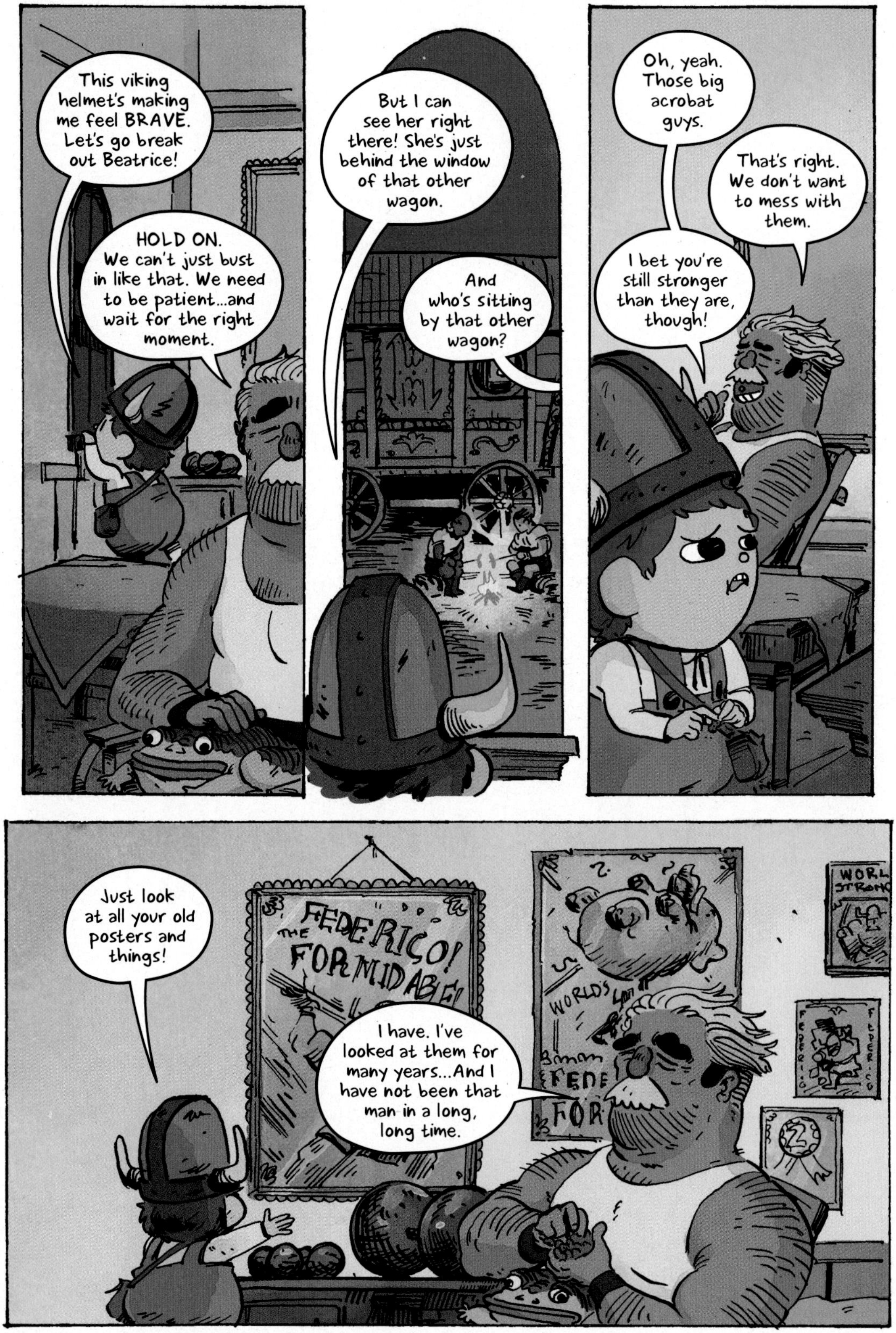
This viking helmet's making me feel BRAVE. Let's go break out Beatrice!
HOLD ON. We can't just bust in like that. We need to be patient...and wait for the right moment.
But I can see her right there! She's just behind the window of that other wagon.
And who's sitting by that other wagon?
Oh, yeah. Those big acrobat guys.
That's right. We don't want to mess with them.
I bet you're still stronger than they are, though!
Just look at all your old posters and things!
THE FEDERICO! FORMIDABLE!
WORLD'S
I have. I've looked at them for many years...And I have not been that man in a long, long time.

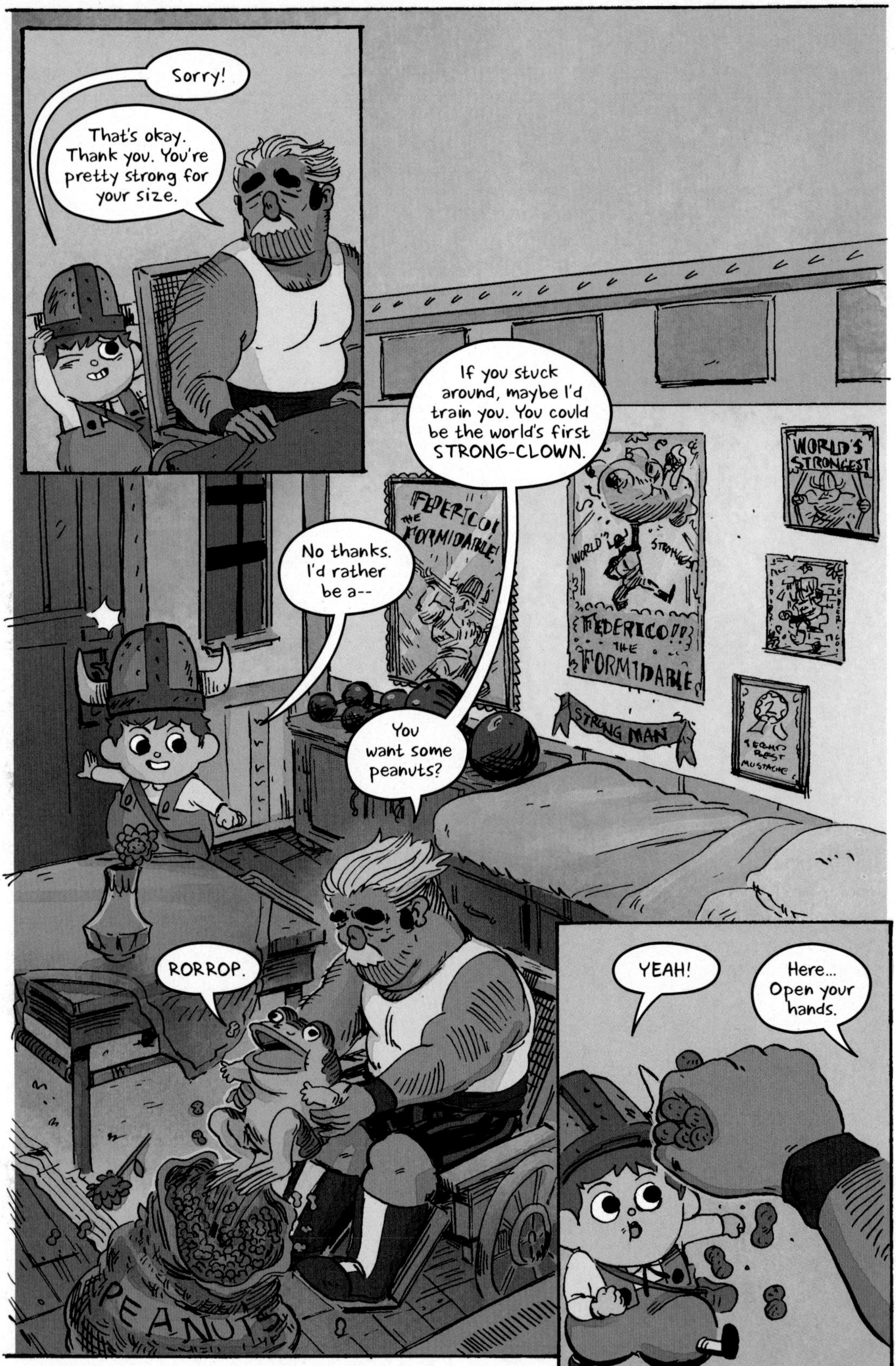

Sorry!
That's okay. Thank you. You're pretty strong for your size.
If you stuck around, maybe I'd train you. You could be the world's first STRONG-CLOWN.
FEDERICO! THE FORMIDABLE!
WORLD'S STRONGEST
FEDERICO!!! THE FORMIDABLE
WORLD'S STRONGEST
No thanks. I'd rather be a--
STRONG MAN
You want some peanuts?
RORROP.
PEANUTS
YEAH!
Here... Open your hands.

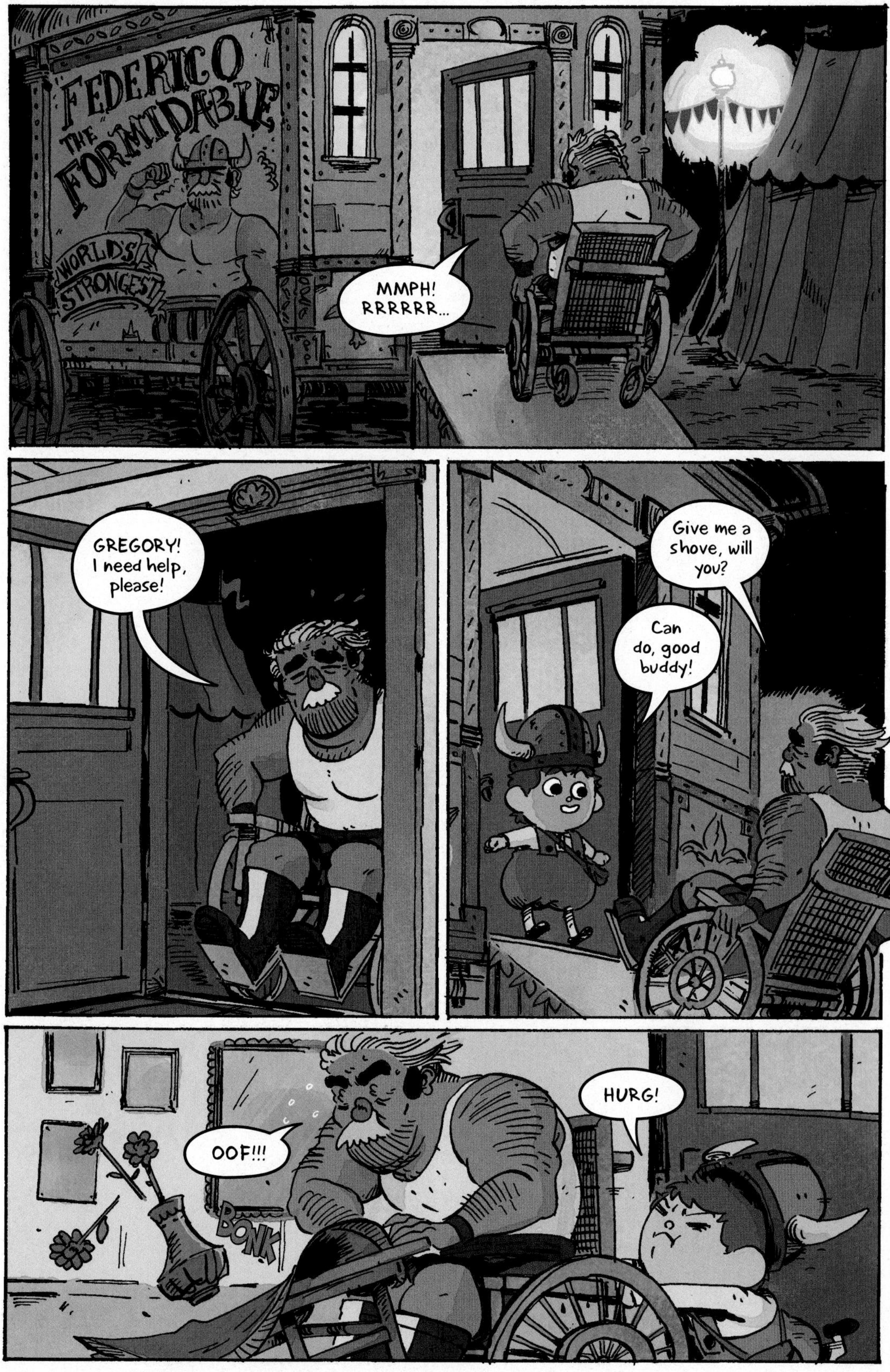
FEDERICO THE FORMIDABLE
WORLD'S STRONGEST
MMPH! RRRRRR...
GREGORY! I need help, please!
Give me a shove, will you?
Can do, good buddy!
HURG!
OOF!!!
BONK

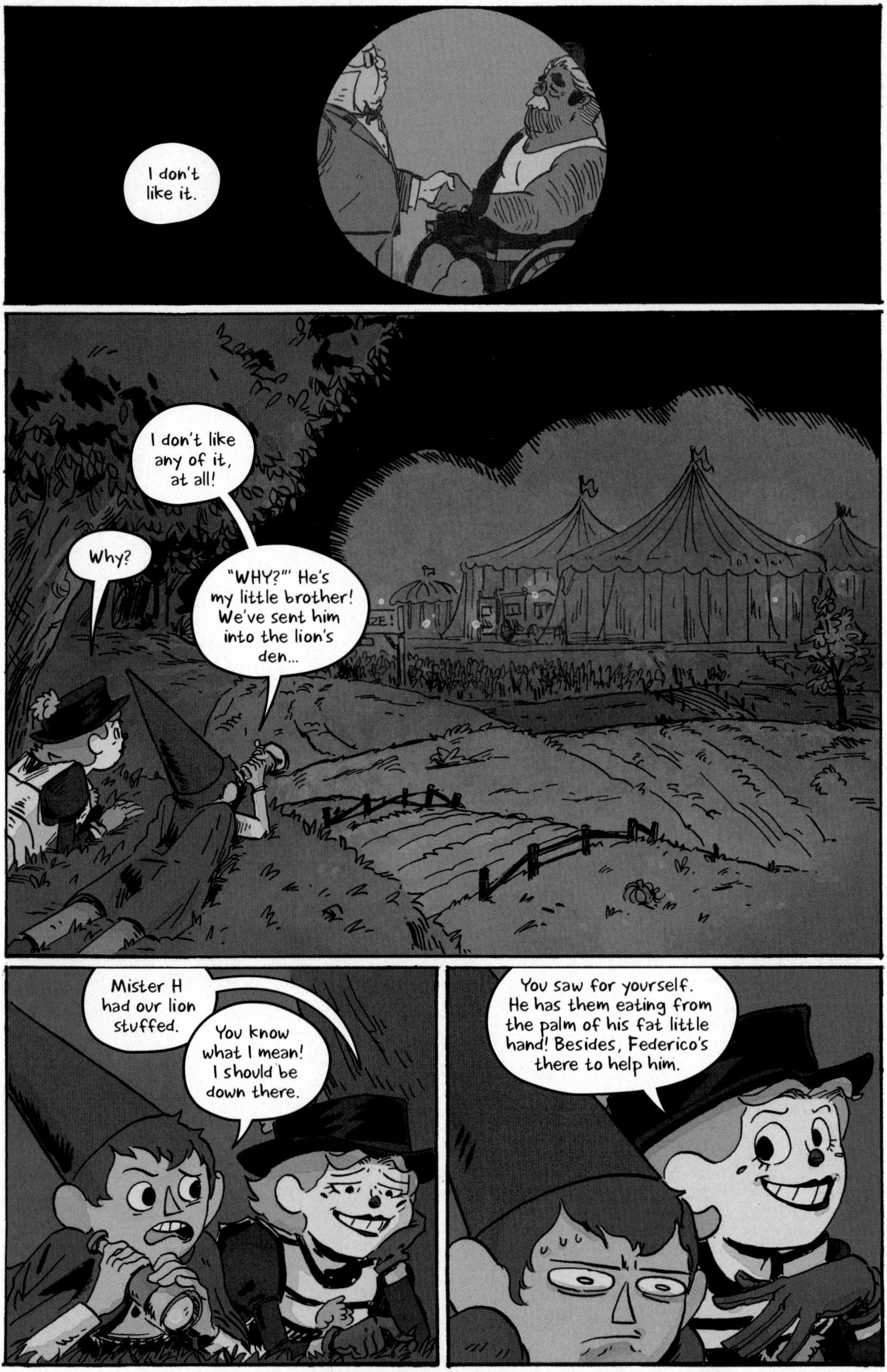
I don't like it.
I don't like any of it, at all!
Why?
"WHY?" He's my little brother! We've sent him into the lion's den...
Mister H had our lion stuffed.
You know what I mean! I should be down there.
You saw for yourself. He has them eating from the palm of his fat little hand! Besides, Federico's there to help him.

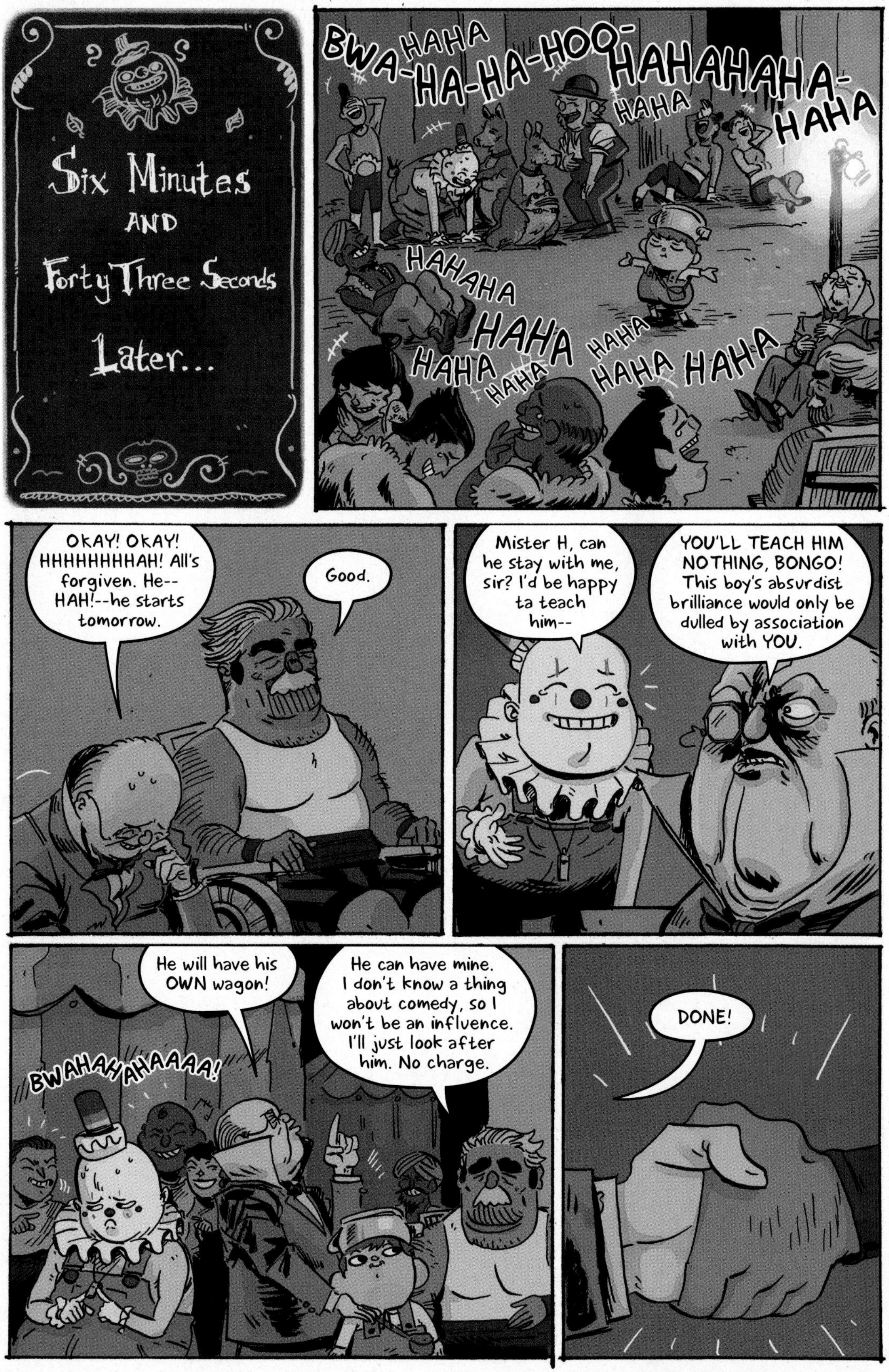
Six Minutes AND Forty Three Seconds Later...
BWA-HAHA-HA-HA-HOO-HAHAHAHA-HAHA
HAHA
HAHAHA
HAHA
HAHA
HAHA
HAHA
HAHA HAHA
OKAY! OKAY! HHHHHHHHAH! All's forgiven. He--HAH!--he starts tomorrow.
Good.
Mister H, can he stay with me, sir? I'd be happy ta teach him--
YOU'LL TEACH HIM NOTHING, BONGO! This boy's absurdist brilliance would only be dulled by association with YOU.
He will have his OWN wagon!
He can have mine. I don't know a thing about comedy, so I won't be an influence. I'll just look after him. No charge.
BWAHAHAHAAAA!
DONE!

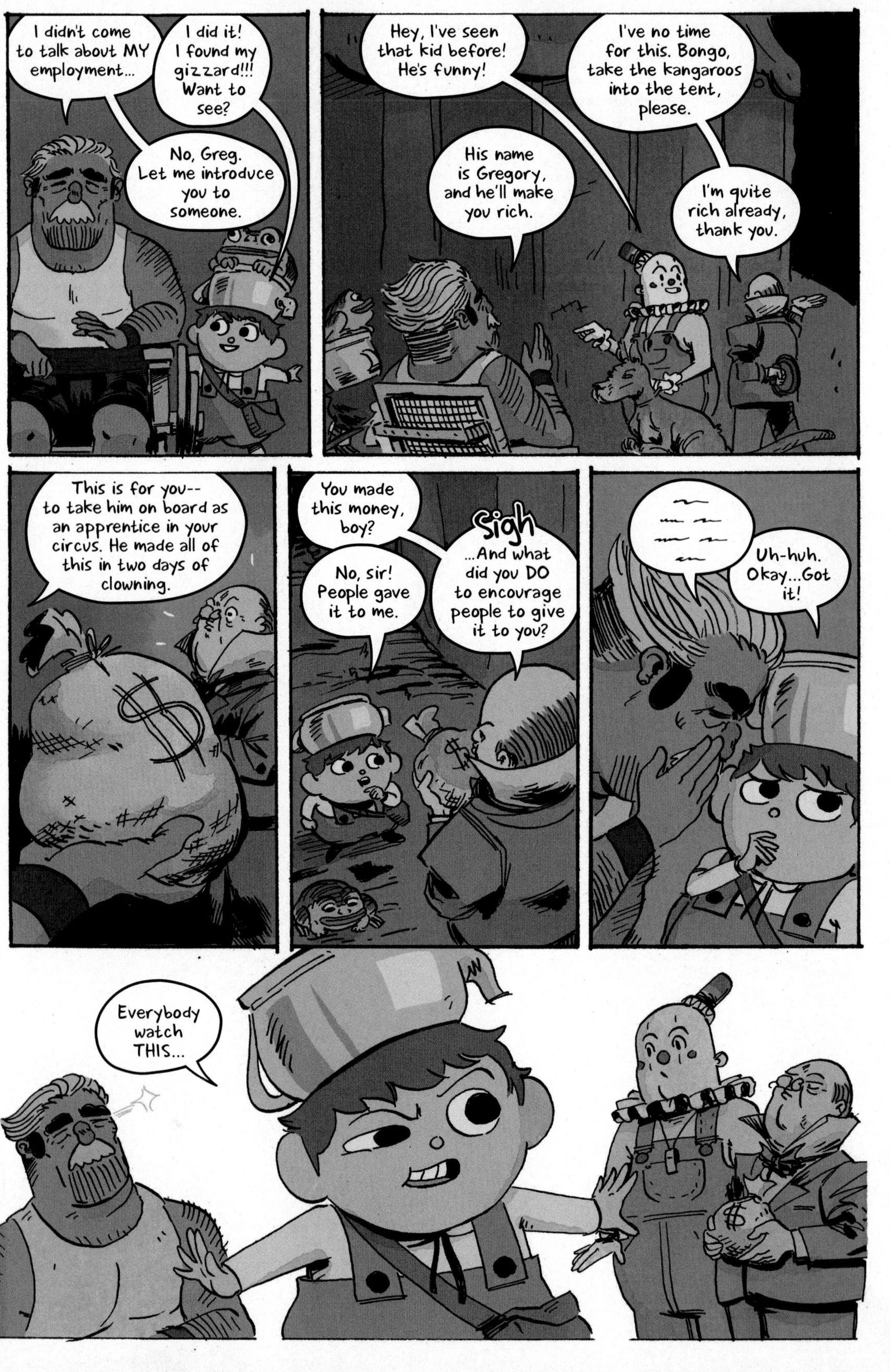

I didn't come to talk about MY employment...
I did it! I found my gizzard!!! Want to see?
No, Greg. Let me introduce you to someone.
Hey, I've seen that kid before! He's funny!
I've no time for this. Bongo, take the kangaroos into the tent, please.
His name is Gregory, and he'll make you rich.
I'm quite rich already, thank you.
This is for you-- to take him on board as an apprentice in your circus. He made all of this in two days of clowning.
You made this money, boy?
No, sir! People gave it to me.
Sigh
...And what did you DO to encourage people to give it to you?
Uh-huh. Okay...Got it!
Everybody watch THIS...

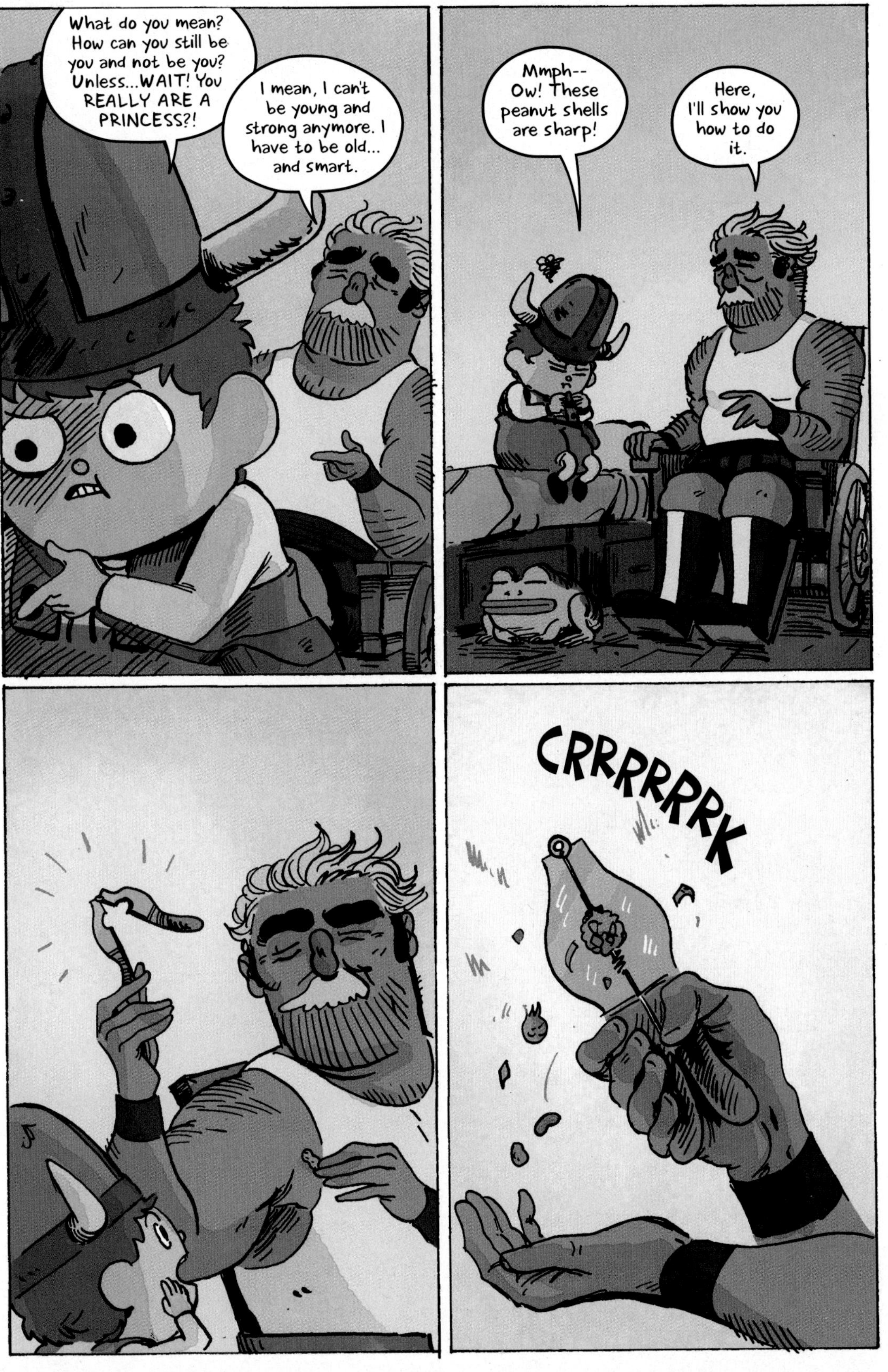
What do you mean? How can you still be you and not be you? Unless...WAIT! You REALLY ARE A PRINCESS?!
I mean, I can't be young and strong anymore. I have to be old... and smart.
Mmph-- Ow! These peanut shells are sharp!
Here, I'll show you how to do it.
CRRRRRRK

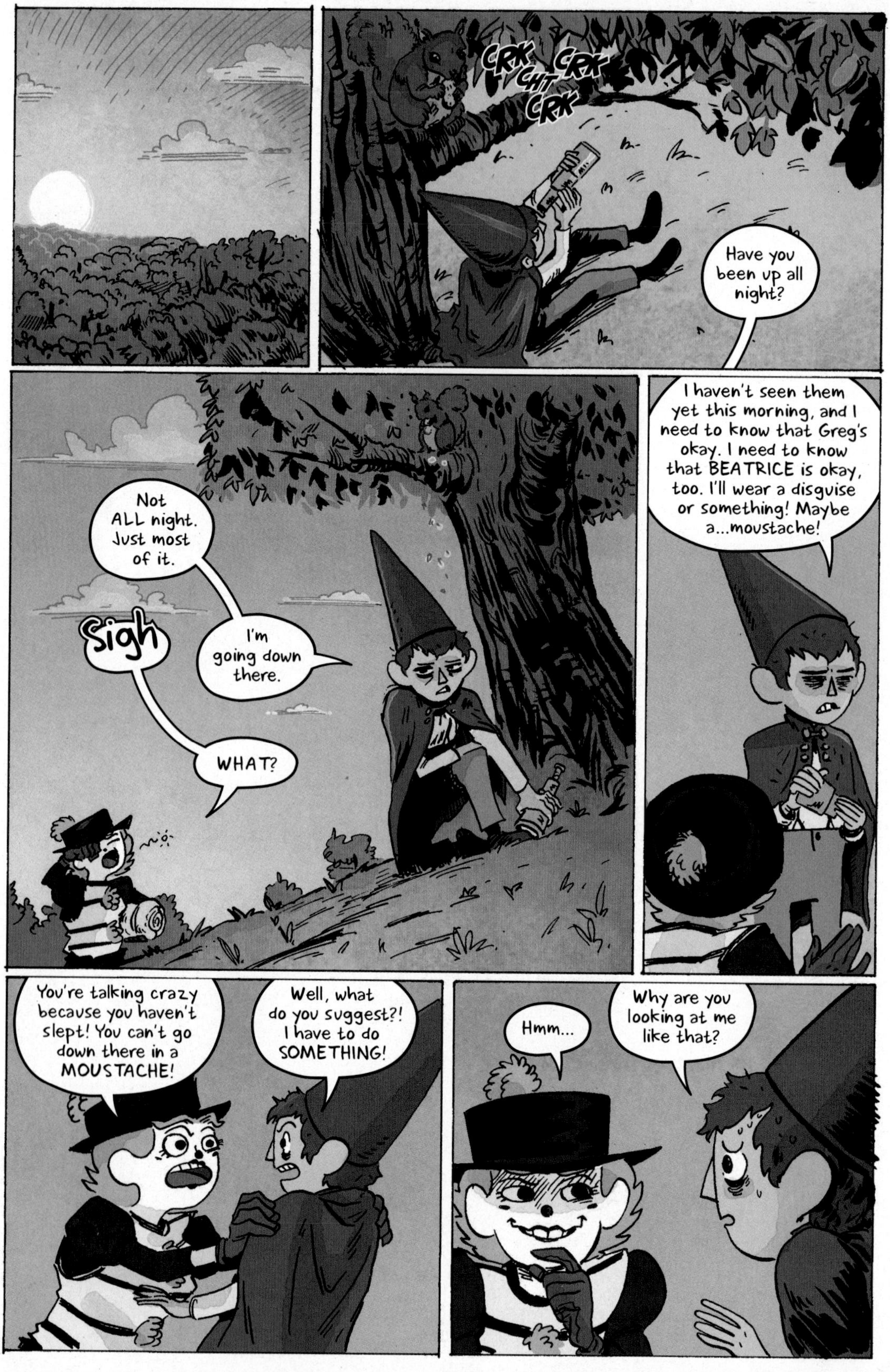
CRK CHT CRK CRK
Have you been up all night?
Not ALL night. Just most of it.
I'm going down there.
Sigh
WHAT?
I haven't seen them yet this morning, and I need to know that Greg's okay. I need to know that BEATRICE is okay, too. I'll wear a disguise or something! Maybe a...moustache!
You're talking crazy because you haven't slept! You can't go down there in a MOUSTACHE!
Well, what do you suggest?! I have to do SOMETHING!
Hmm...
Why are you looking at me like that?

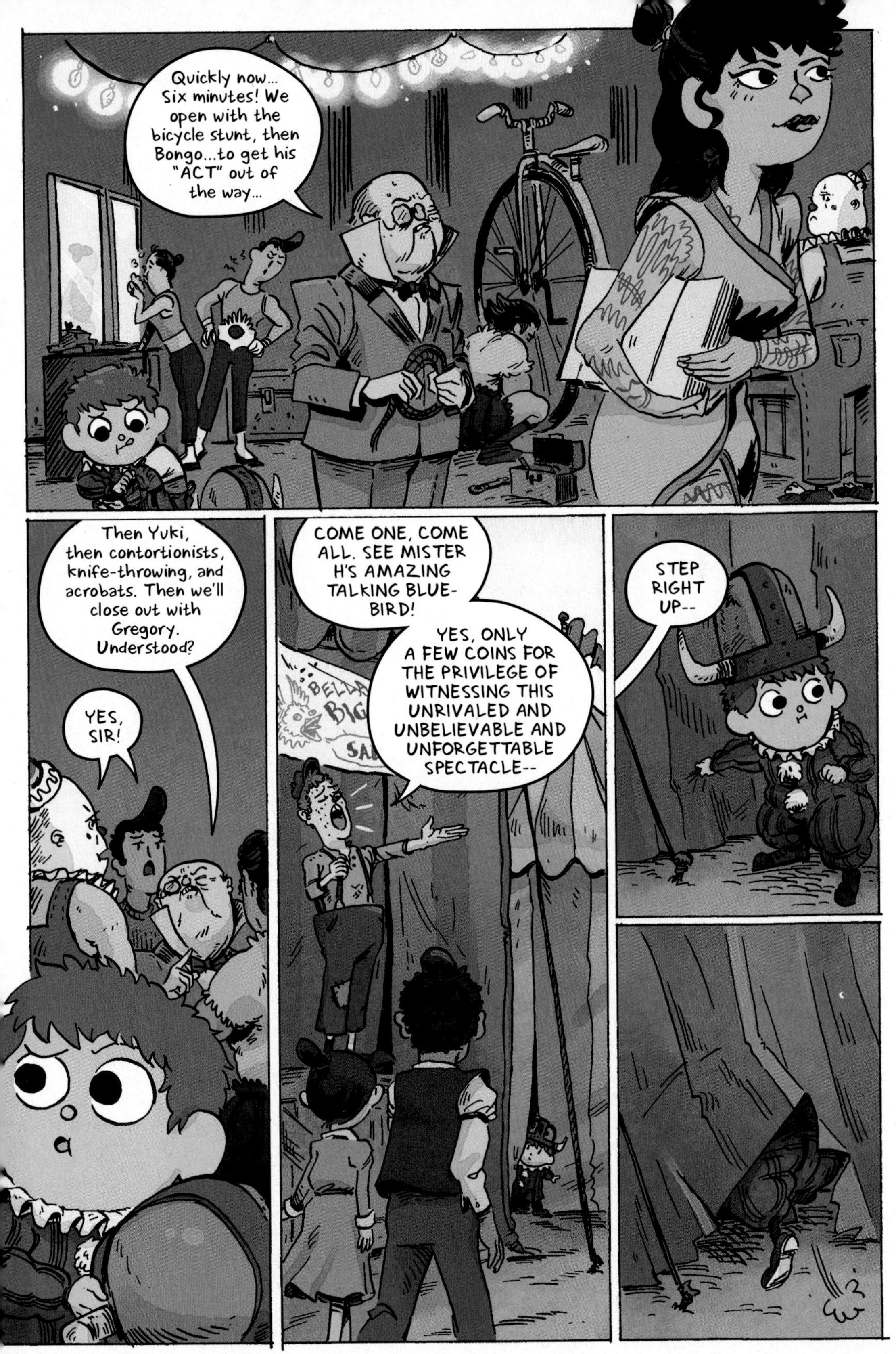
Quickly now... Six minutes! We open with the bicycle stunt, then Bongo...to get his "ACT" out of the way...
Then Yuki, then contortionists, knife-throwing, and acrobats. Then we'll close out with Gregory. Understood?
YES, SIR!
COME ONE, COME ALL. SEE MISTER H'S AMAZING TALKING BLUE-BIRD!
YES, ONLY A FEW COINS FOR THE PRIVILEGE OF WITNESSING THIS UNRIVALED AND UNBELIEVABLE AND UNFORGETTABLE SPECTACLE--
STEP RIGHT UP--

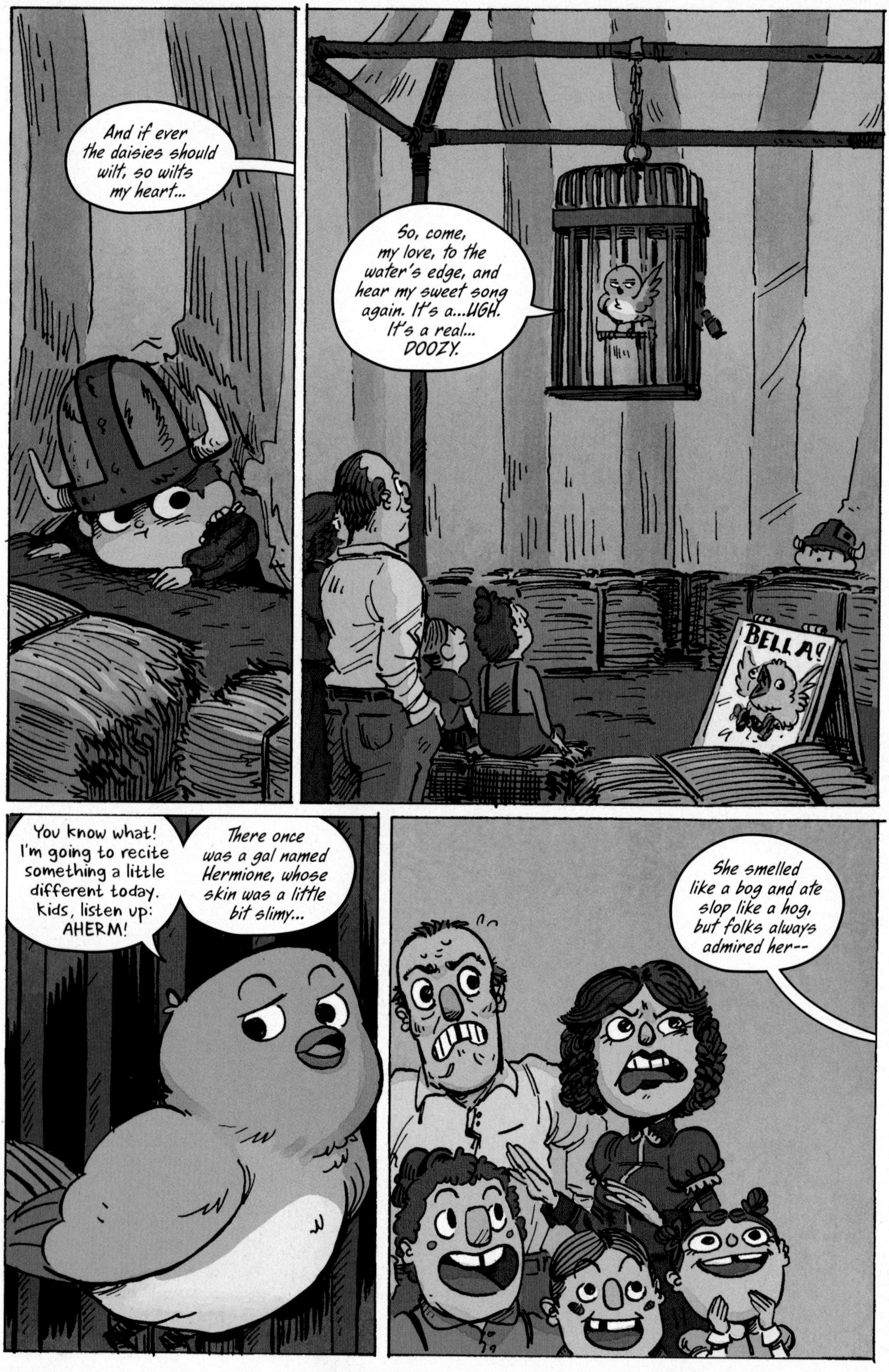

And if ever the daisies should wilt, so wilts my heart...
So, come, my love, to the water's edge, and hear my sweet song again. It's a...UGH. It's a real... DOOZY.
BELLA!
You know what! I'm going to recite something a little different today. kids, listen up: AHERM!
There once was a gal named Hermione, whose skin was a little bit slimy...
She smelled like a bog and ate slop like a hog, but folks always admired her--

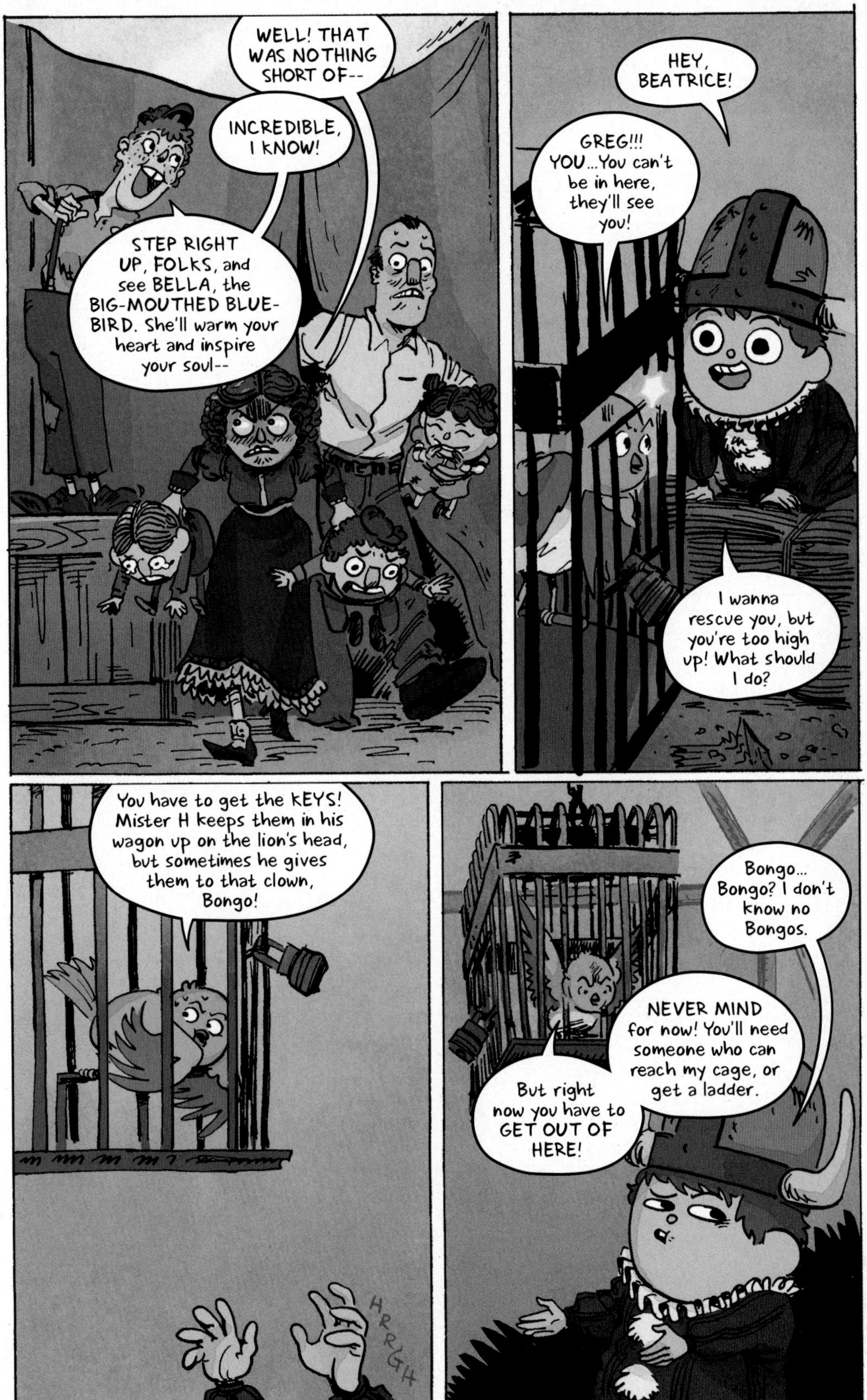
WELL! THAT WAS NOTHING SHORT OF--
INCREDIBLE, I KNOW!
STEP RIGHT UP, FOLKS, and see BELLA, the BIG-MOUTHED BLUE-BIRD. She'll warm your heart and inspire your soul--
HEY, BEATRICE!
GREG!!! YOU...You can't be in here, they'll see you!
I wanna rescue you, but you're too high up! What should I do?
You have to get the KEYS! Mister H keeps them in his wagon up on the lion's head, but sometimes he gives them to that clown, Bongo!
HRRGH
Bongo... Bongo? I don't know no Bongos.
NEVER MIND for now! You'll need someone who can reach my cage, or get a ladder.
But right now you have to GET OUT OF HERE!

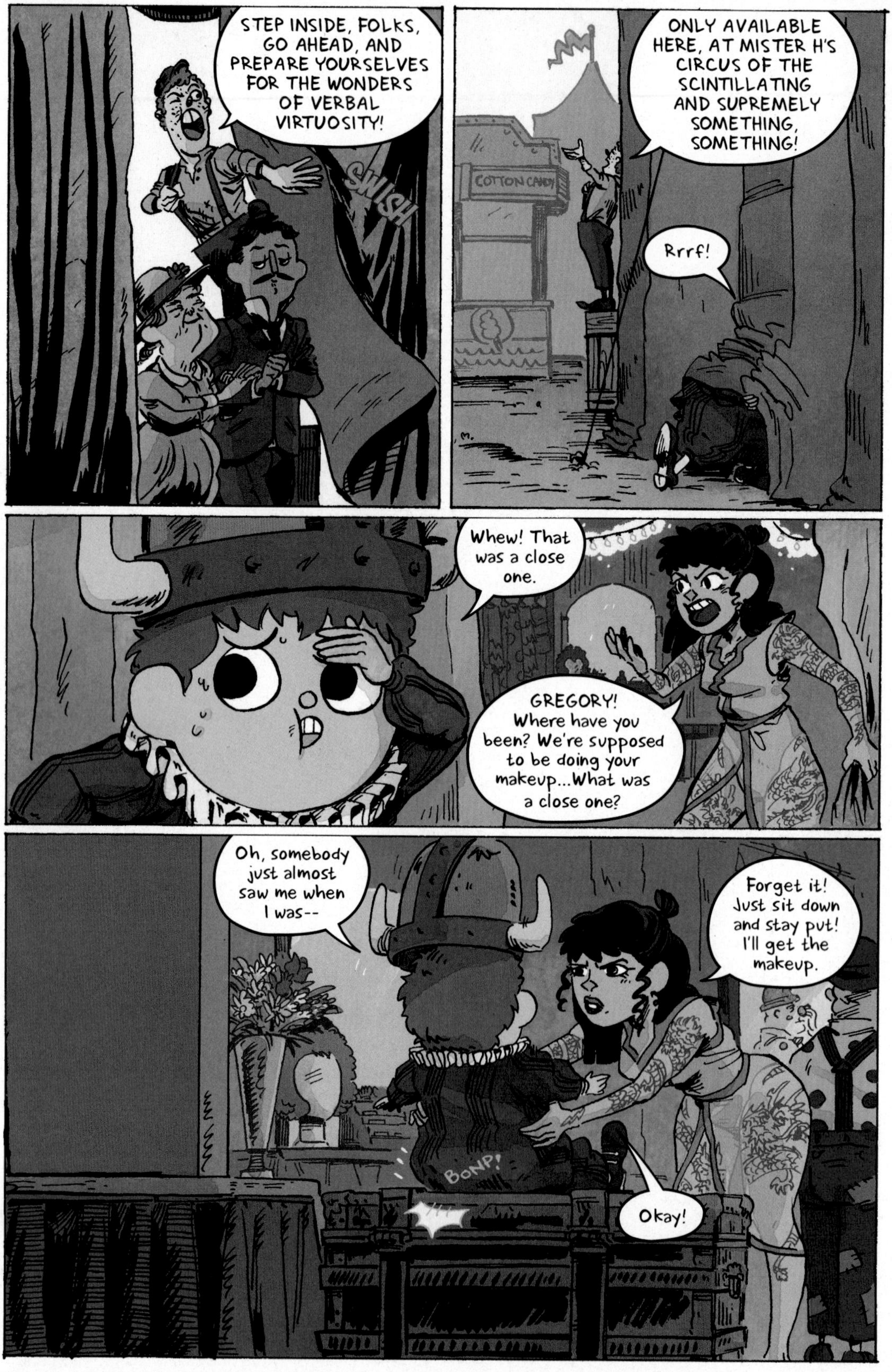
STEP INSIDE, FOLKS, GO AHEAD, AND PREPARE YOURSELVES FOR THE WONDERS OF VERBAL VIRTUOSITY!
SWISH
ONLY AVAILABLE HERE, AT MISTER H'S CIRCUS OF THE SCINTILLATING AND SUPREMELY SOMETHING, SOMETHING!
COTTON CANDY
Rrrf!
Whew! That was a close one.
GREGORY! Where have you been? We're supposed to be doing your makeup...What was a close one?
Oh, somebody just almost saw me when I was--
Forget it! Just sit down and stay put! I'll get the makeup.
BONP!
Okay!

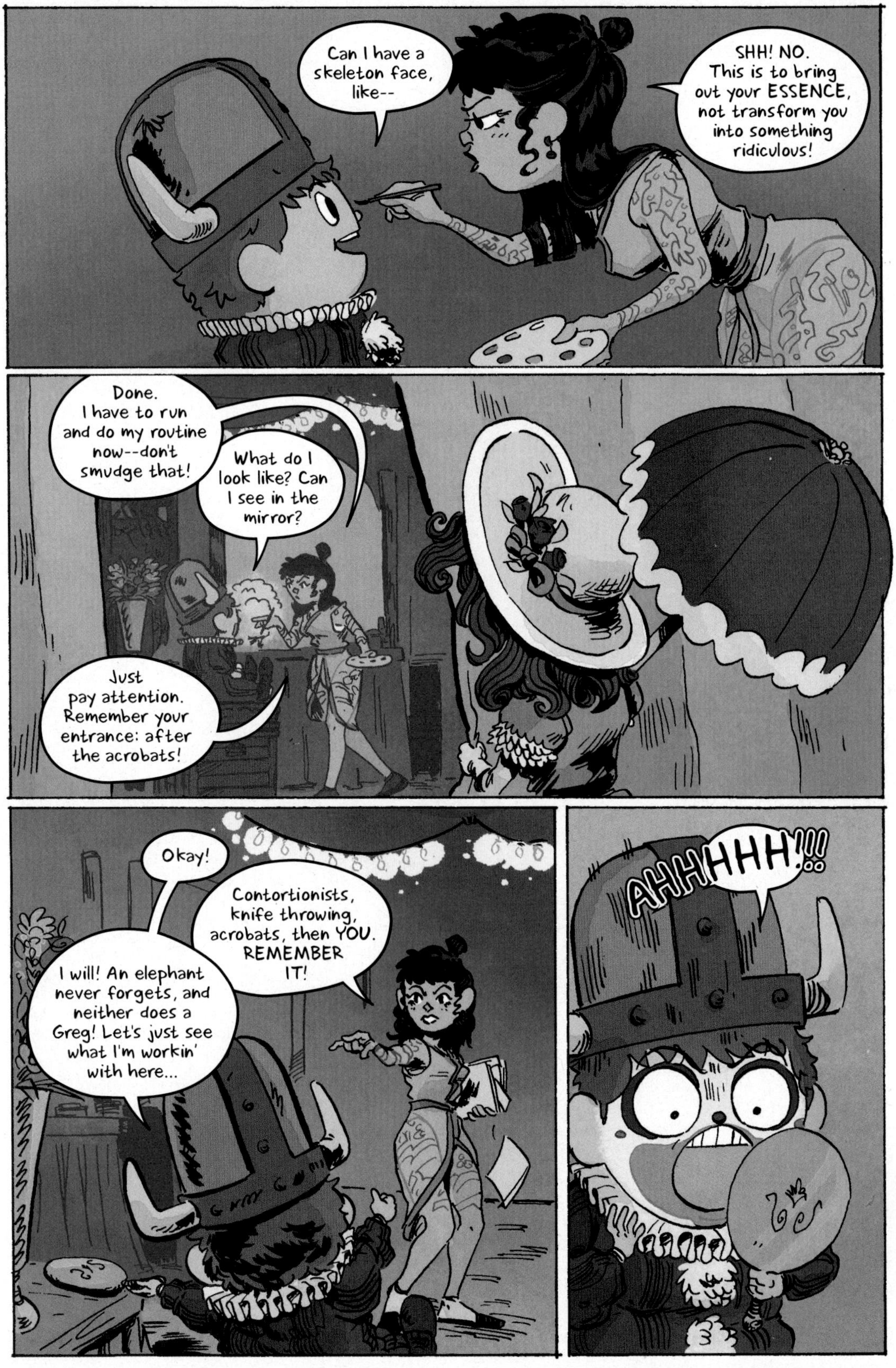
Can I have a skeleton face, like--
SHH! NO. This is to bring out your ESSENCE, not transform you into something ridiculous!
Done. I have to run and do my routine now--don't smudge that!
What do I look like? Can I see in the mirror?
Just pay attention. Remember your entrance: after the acrobats!
Okay!
Contortionists, knife throwing, acrobats, then YOU. REMEMBER IT!
I will! An elephant never forgets, and neither does a Greg! Let's just see what I'm workin' with here...
AHHHHH!!!

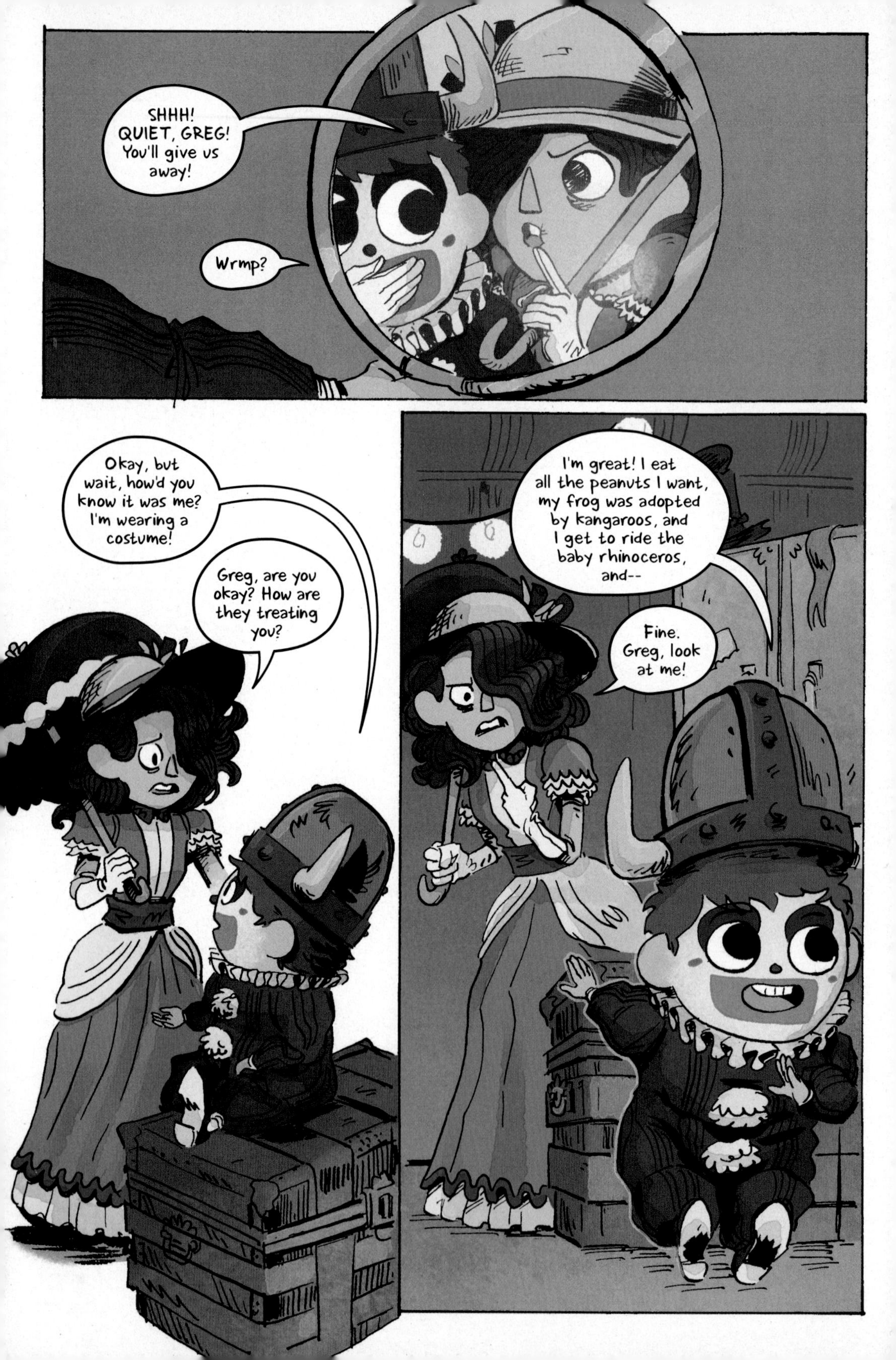
SHHH! QUIET, GREG! You'll give us away!
Wrmp?
Okay, but wait, how'd you know it was me? I'm wearing a costume!
Greg, are you okay? How are they treating you?
I'm great! I eat all the peanuts I want, my frog was adopted by kangaroos, and I get to ride the baby rhinoceros, and--
Fine. Greg, look at me!

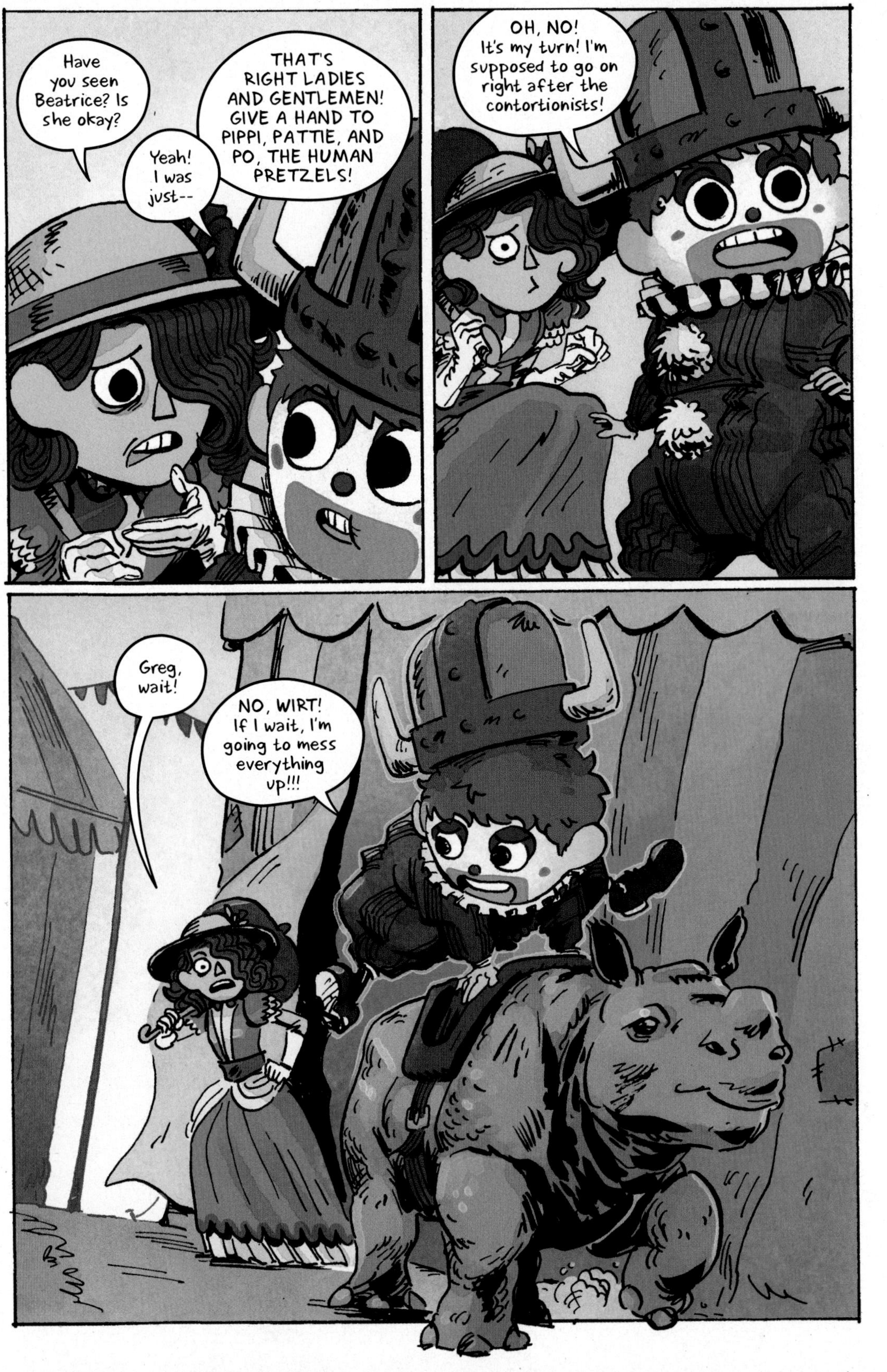
Have you seen Beatrice? Is she okay?
Yeah! I was just--
THAT'S RIGHT LADIES AND GENTLEMEN! GIVE A HAND TO PIPPI, PATTIE, AND PO, THE HUMAN PRETZELS!
OH, NO! It's my turn! I'm supposed to go on right after the contortionists!
Greg, wait!
NO, WIRT! If I wait, I'm going to mess everything up!!!

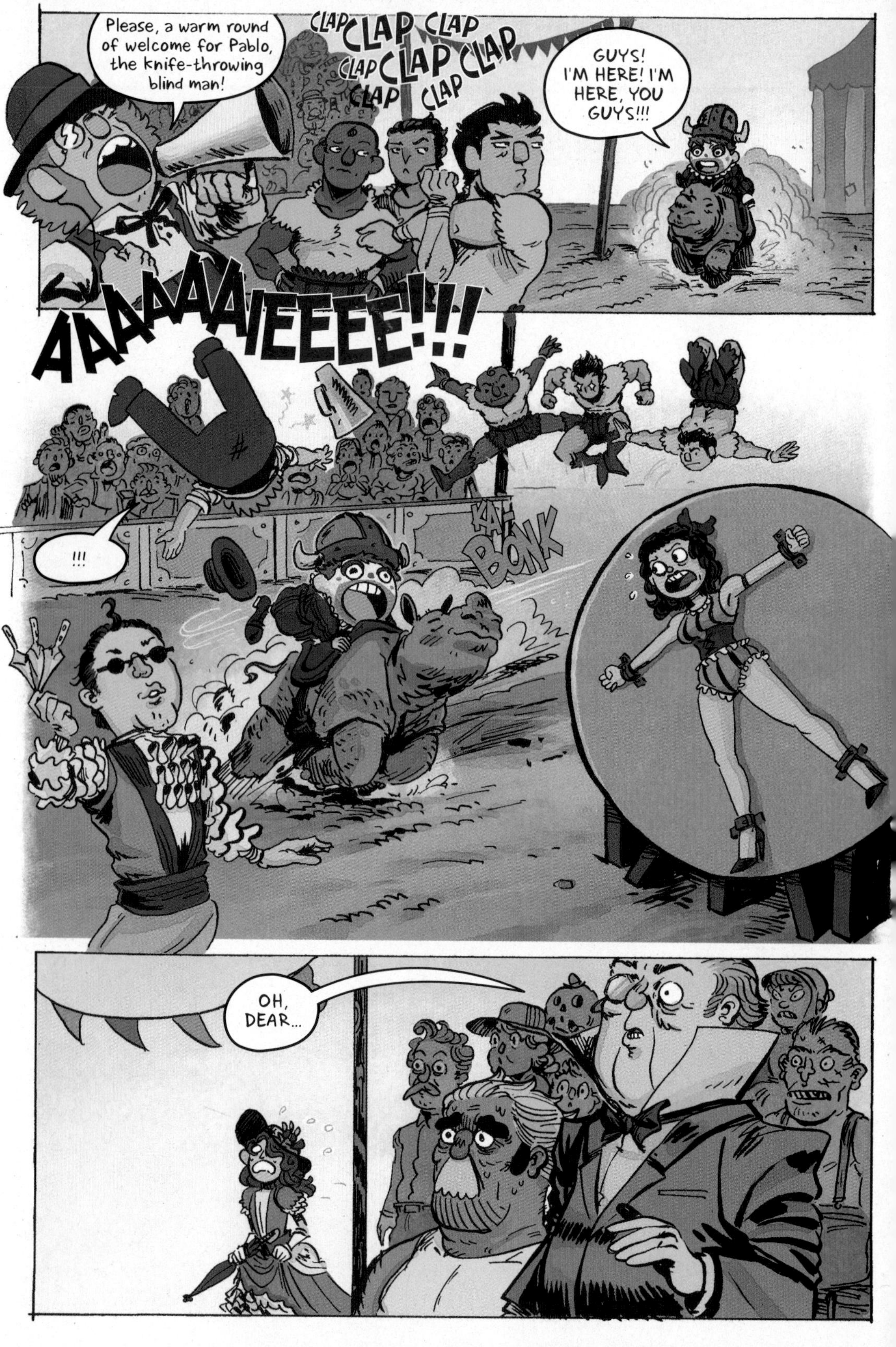

Please, a warm round of welcome for Pablo, the knife-throwing blind man!
CLAP CLAP CLAP CLAP CLAP CLAP CLAP CLAP CLAP
GUYS! I'M HERE! I'M HERE, YOU GUYS!!!
AAAAAAIEEEEE!!!!
!!!
KA-BONK
OH, DEAR...

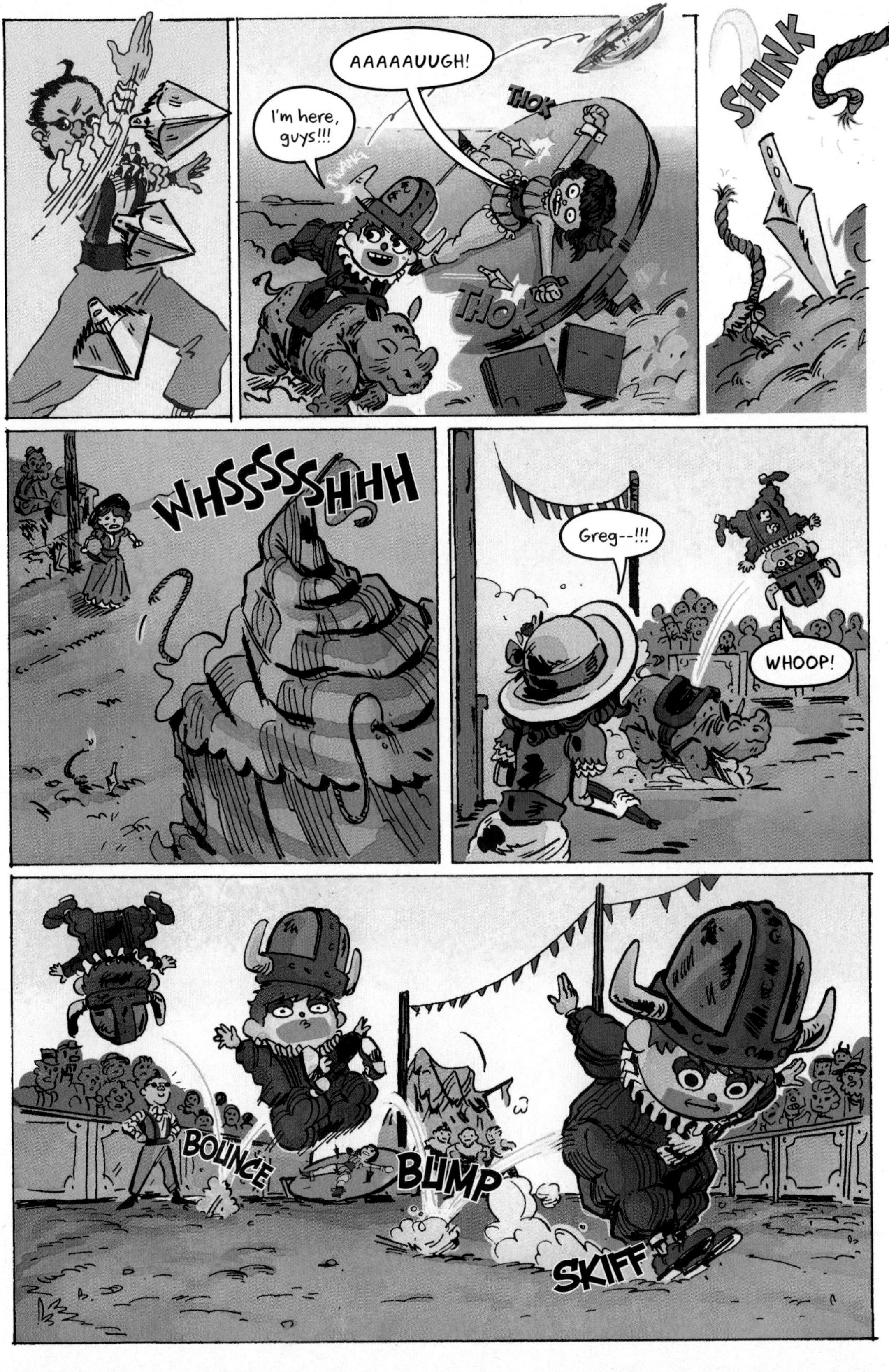
AAAAAUUGH!
I'm here, guys!!!
PWANG
THOK
THOK
SHINK
WHSSSSSHHH
Greg--!!!
WHOOP!
BOUNCE
BUMP
SKIFF

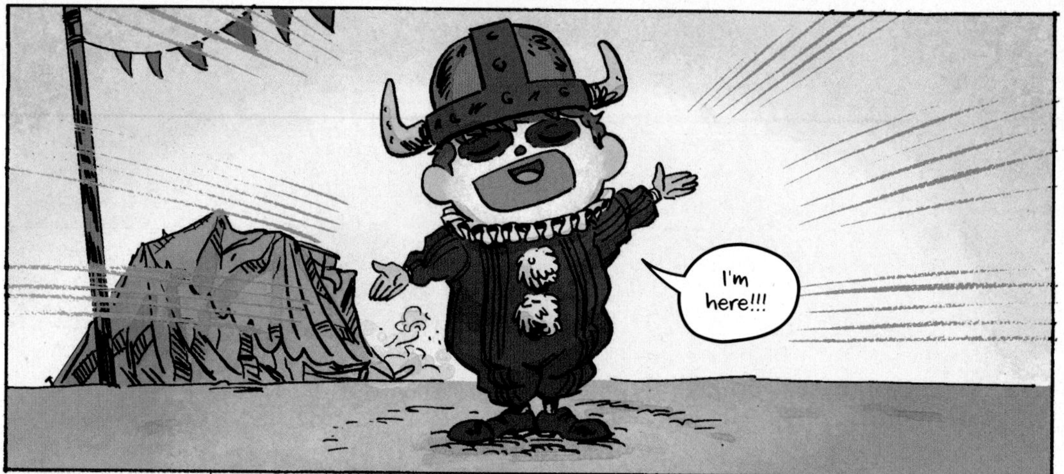
I'm here!!!

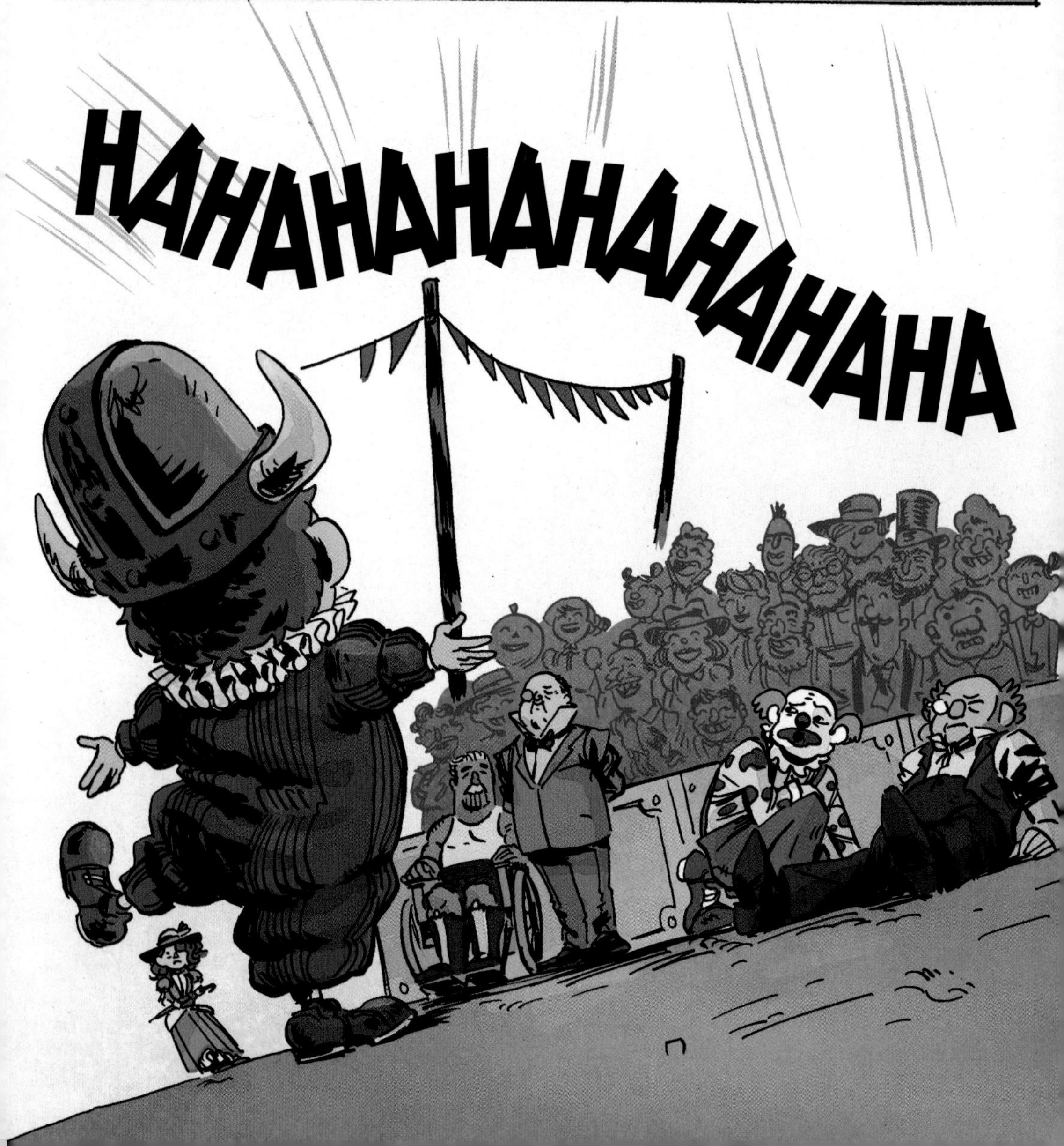
HAHAHAHAHAHAHAHAHAHA

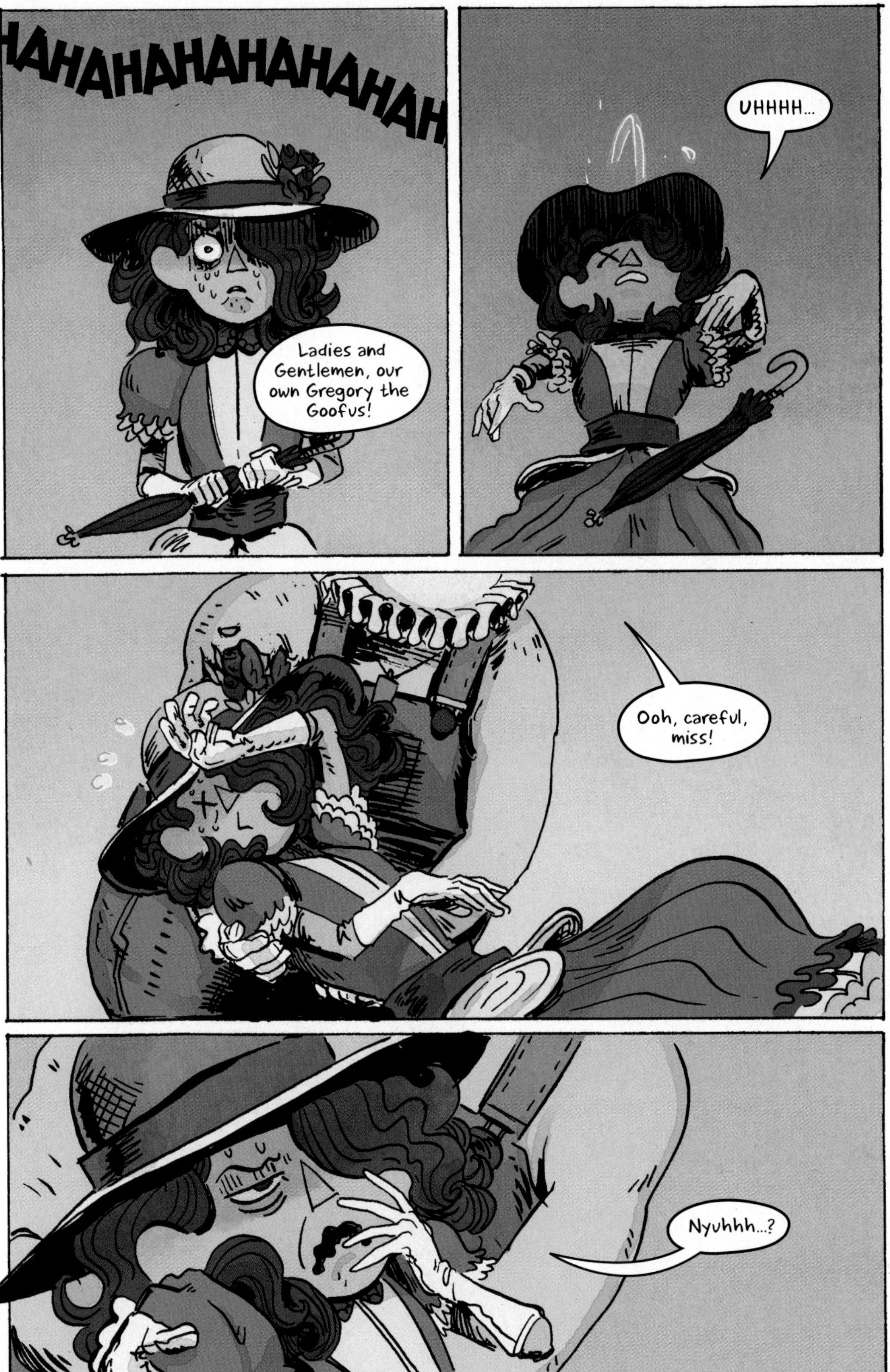
HAHAHAHAHAHAHAHAH
Ladies and Gentlemen, our own Gregory the Goofus!
UHHHH...
Ooh, careful, miss!
Nyuhhh...?

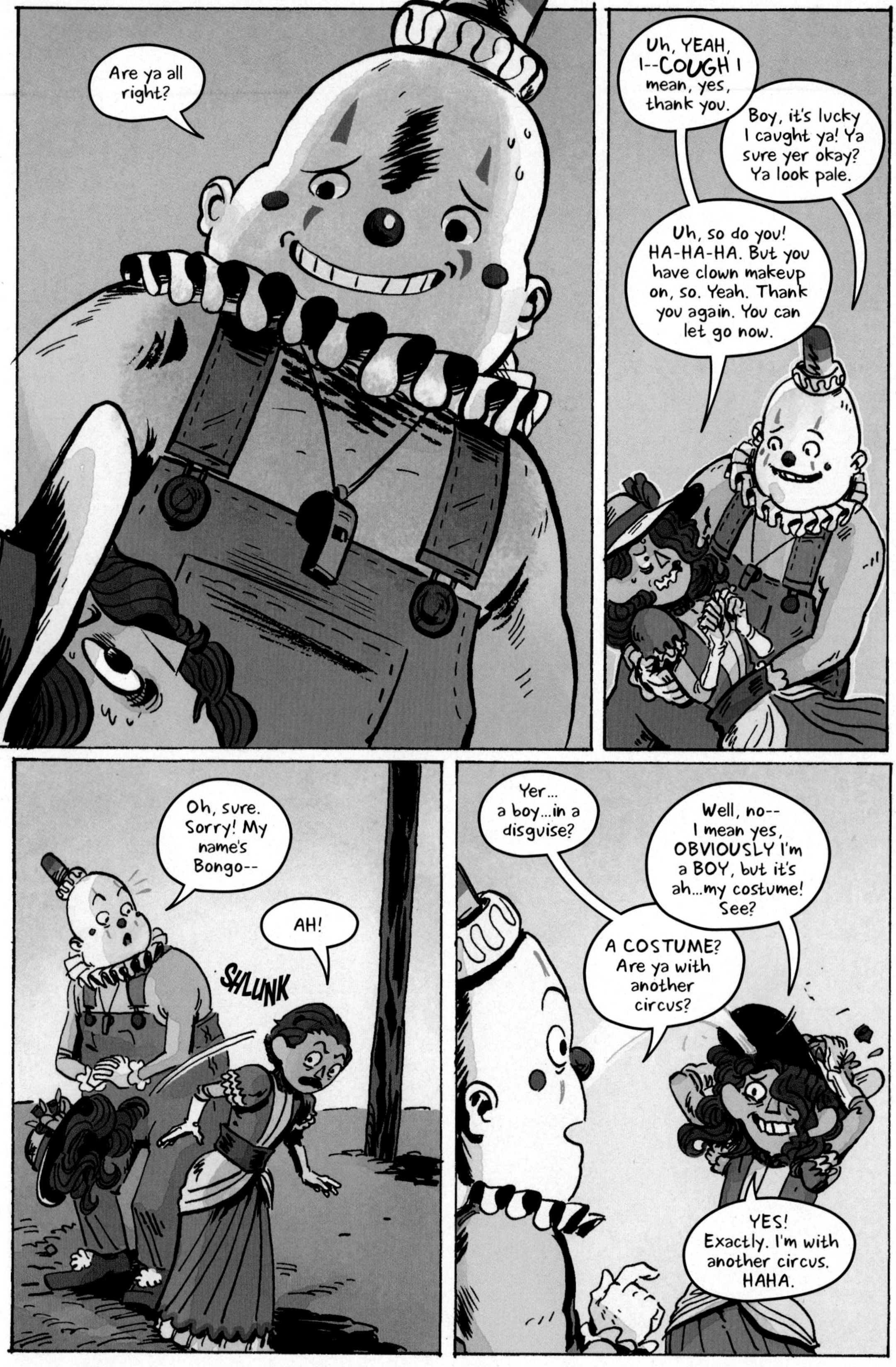
Are ya all right?
Uh, YEAH, I--COUGH I mean, yes, thank you.
Boy, it's lucky I caught ya! Ya sure yer okay? Ya look pale.
Uh, so do you! HA-HA-HA. But you have clown makeup on, so. Yeah. Thank you again. You can let go now.
Oh, sure. Sorry! My name's Bongo--
SHLUNK
AH!
Yer... a boy...in a disguise?
Well, no-- I mean yes, OBVIOUSLY I'm a BOY, but it's ah...my costume! See?
A COSTUME? Are ya with another circus?
YES! Exactly. I'm with another circus. HAHA.

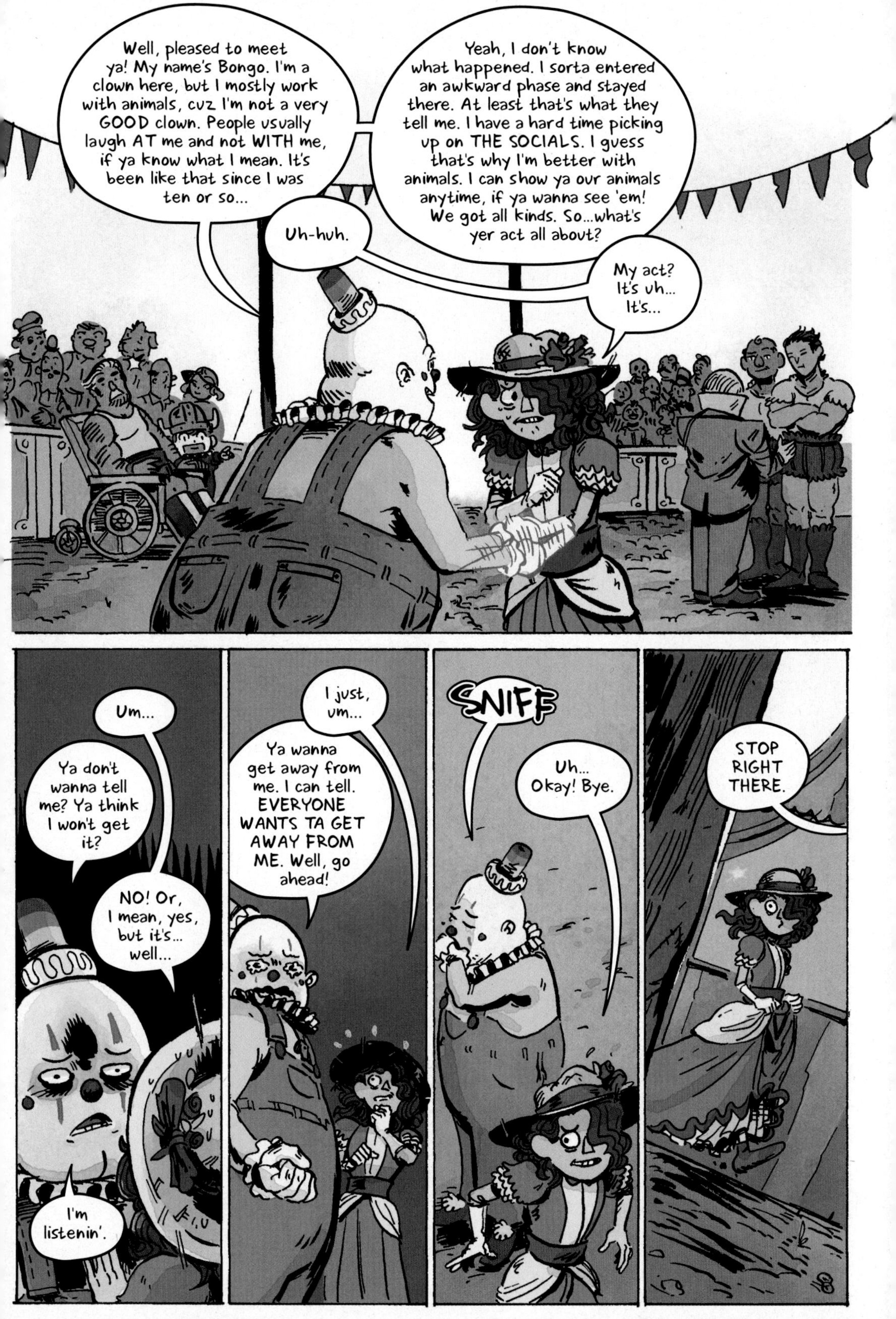
Well, pleased to meet ya! My name's Bongo. I'm a clown here, but I mostly work with animals, cuz I'm not a very GOOD clown. People usually laugh AT me and not WITH me, if ya know what I mean. It's been like that since I was ten or so...
Uh-huh.
Yeah, I don't know what happened. I sorta entered an awkward phase and stayed there. At least that's what they tell me. I have a hard time picking up on THE SOCIALS. I guess that's why I'm better with animals. I can show ya our animals anytime, if ya wanna see 'em! We got all kinds. So...what's yer act all about?
My act? It's uh... It's...
Um...
Ya don't wanna tell me? Ya think I won't get it?
NO! Or, I mean, yes, but it's... well...
I'm listenin'.
I just, um...
Ya wanna get away from me. I can tell. EVERYONE WANTS TA GET AWAY FROM ME. Well, go ahead!
SNIFF
Uh... Okay! Bye.
STOP RIGHT THERE.

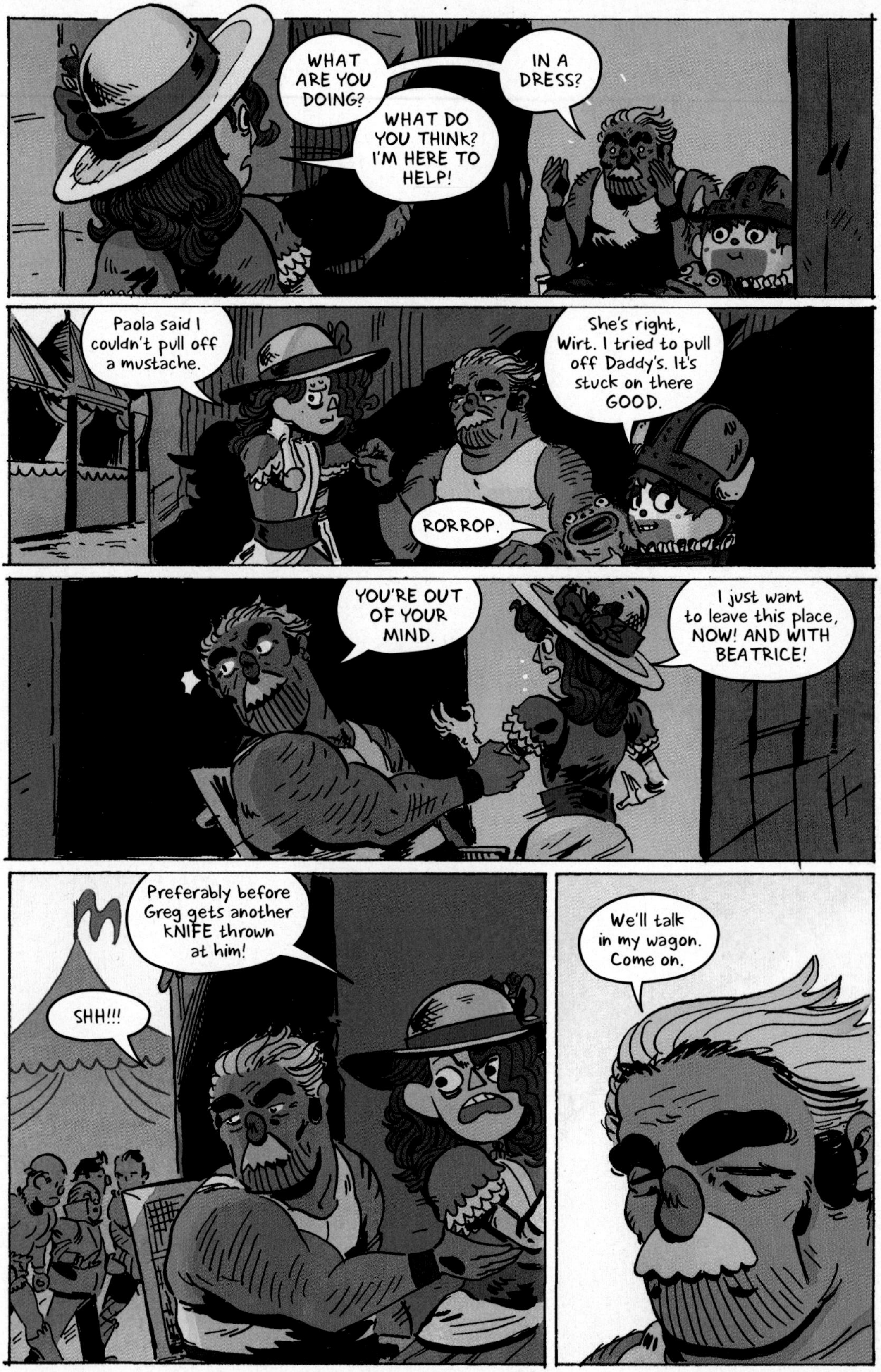
WHAT ARE YOU DOING?
IN A DRESS?
WHAT DO YOU THINK? I'M HERE TO HELP!
Paola said I couldn't pull off a mustache.
She's right, Wirt. I tried to pull off Daddy's. It's stuck on there GOOD.
RORROP.
YOU'RE OUT OF YOUR MIND.
I just want to leave this place, NOW! AND WITH BEATRICE!
Preferably before Greg gets another KNIFE thrown at him!
SHH!!!
We'll talk in my wagon. Come on.

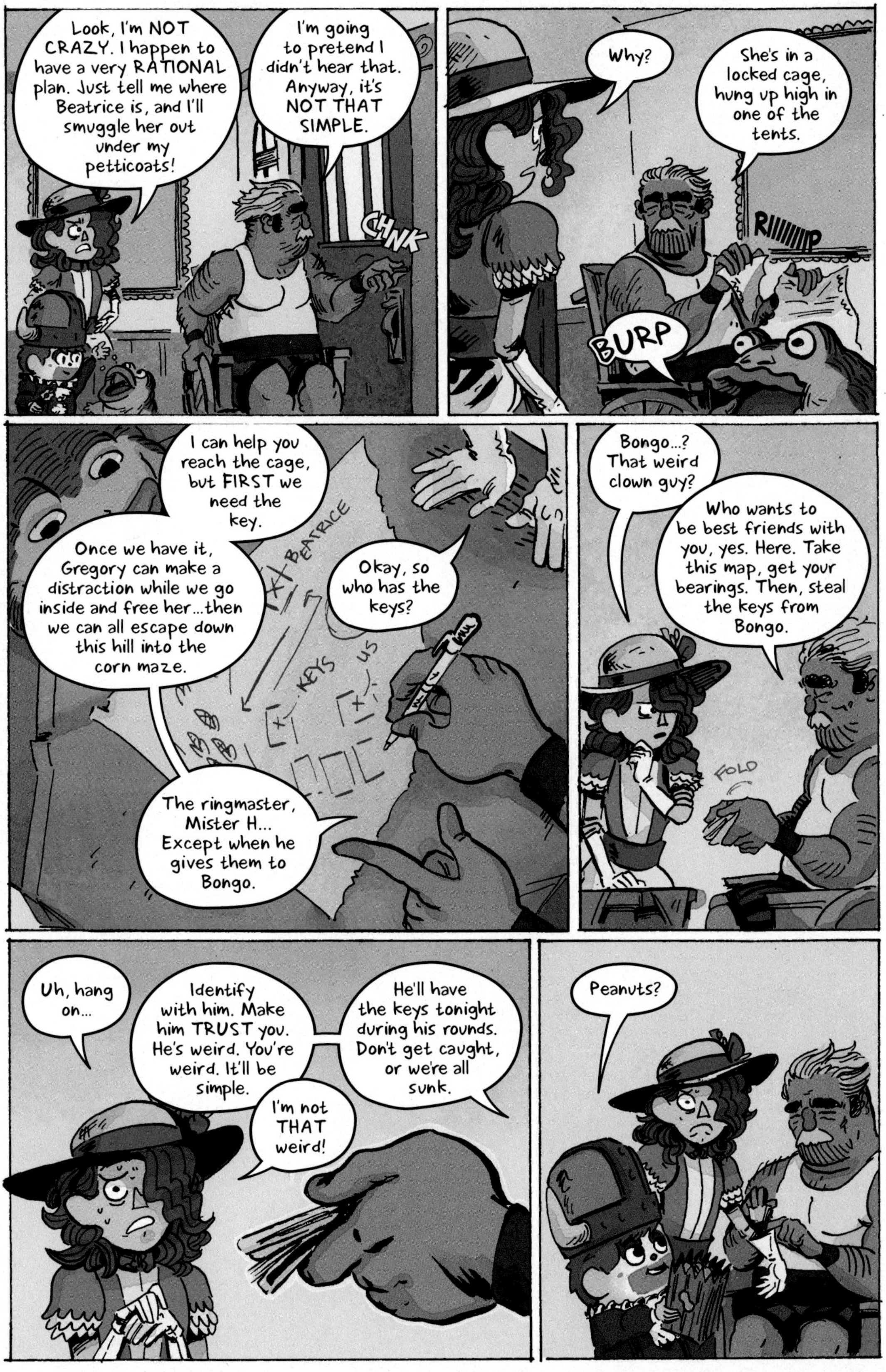
Look, I'm NOT CRAZY. I happen to have a very RATIONAL plan. Just tell me where Beatrice is, and I'll smuggle her out under my petticoats!
I'm going to pretend I didn't hear that. Anyway, it's NOT THAT SIMPLE.
CHNK
Why?
She's in a locked cage, hung up high in one of the tents.
RIIIIIIP
BURP
I can help you reach the cage, but FIRST we need the key.
Once we have it, Gregory can make a distraction while we go inside and free her...then we can all escape down this hill into the corn maze.
BEATRICE
KEYS
US
Okay, so who has the keys?
The ringmaster, Mister H... Except when he gives them to Bongo.
Bongo...? That weird clown guy?
Who wants to be best friends with you, yes. Here. Take this map, get your bearings. Then, steal the keys from Bongo.
FOLD
Uh, hang on...
Identify with him. Make him TRUST you. He's weird. You're weird. It'll be simple.
He'll have the keys tonight during his rounds. Don't get caught, or we're all sunk.
I'm not THAT weird!
Peanuts?

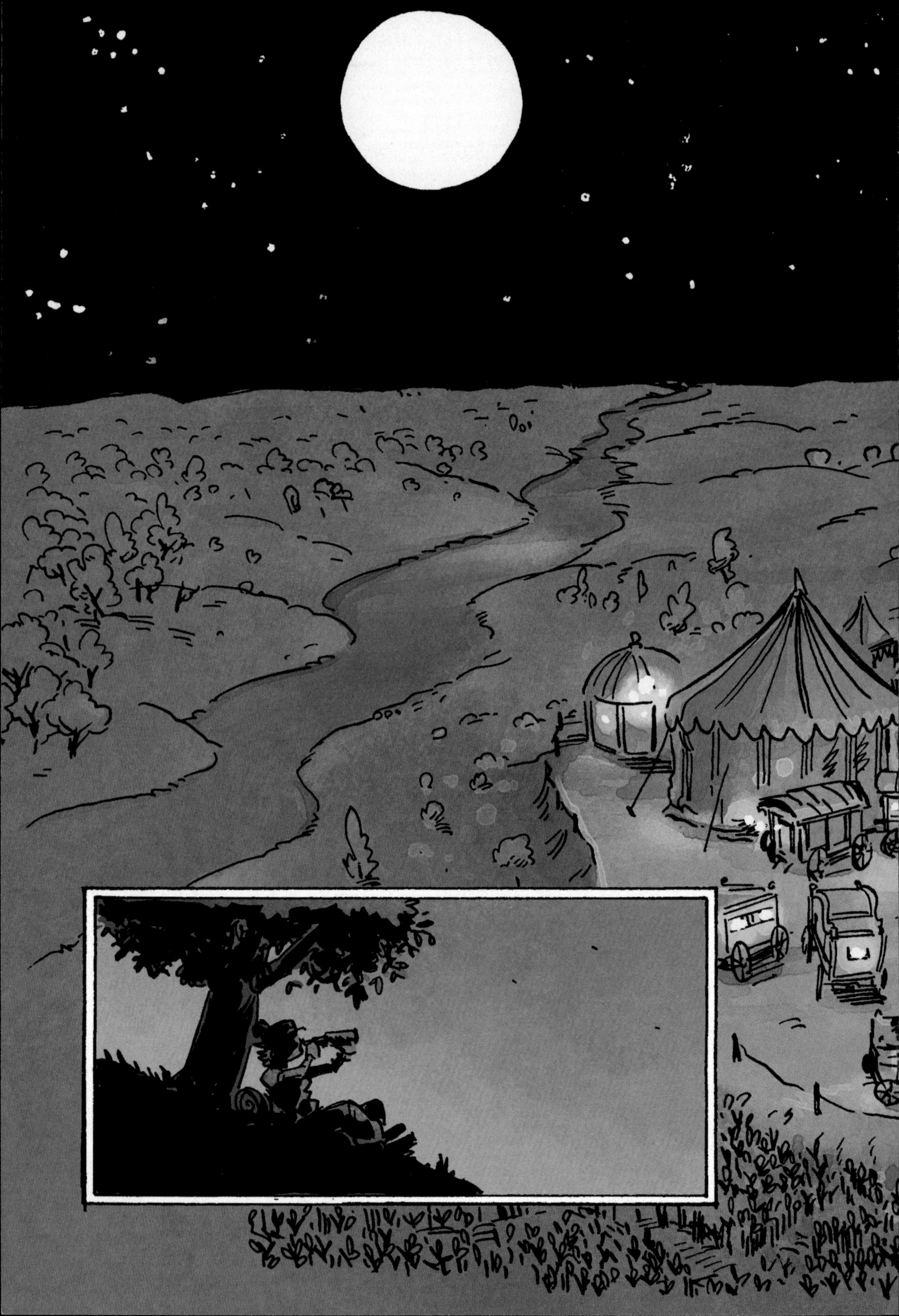

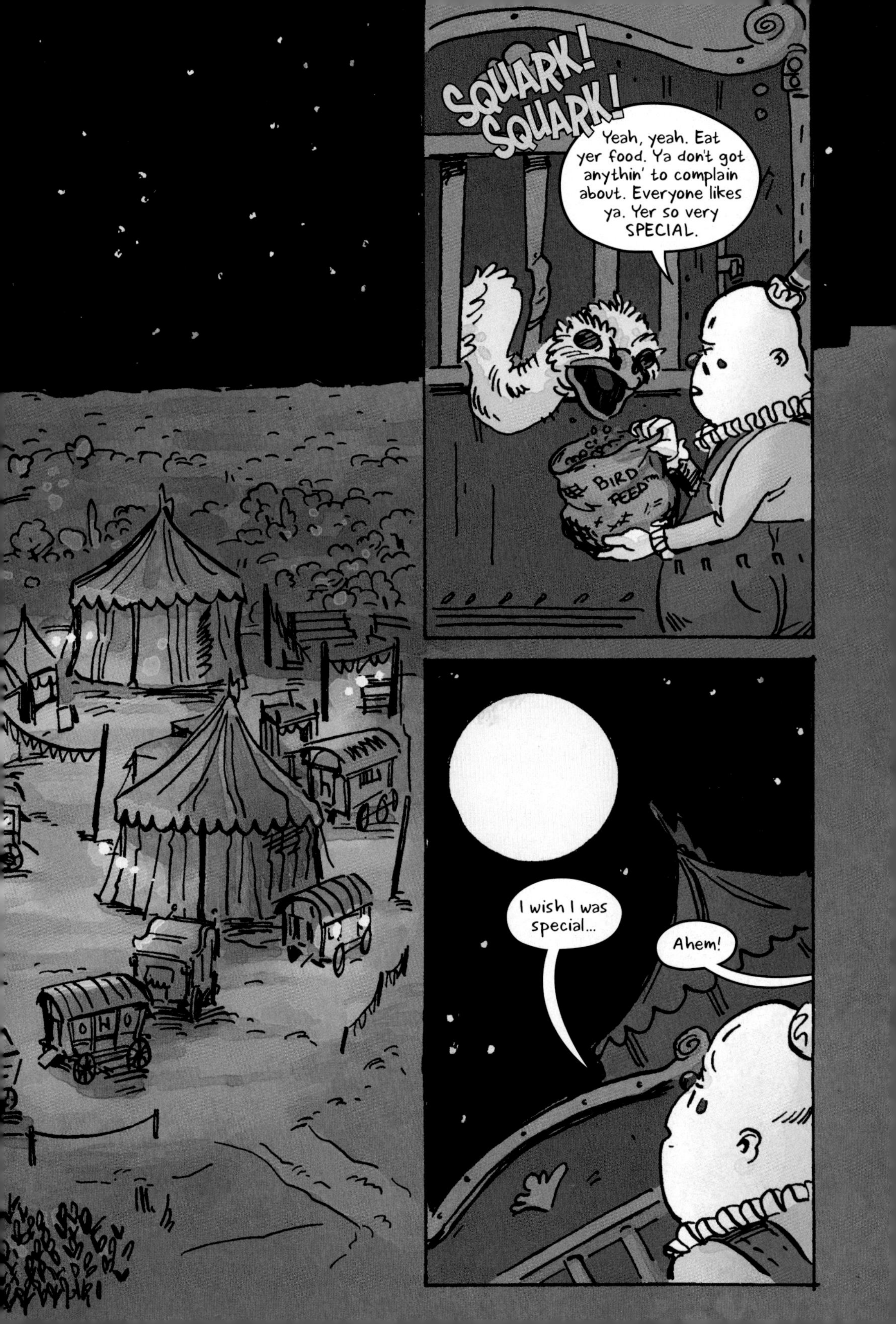
SQUARK! SQUARK!
Yeah, yeah. Eat yer food. Ya don't got anythin' to complain about. Everyone likes ya. Yer so very SPECIAL.
BIRD FEED™
I wish I was special...
Ahem!

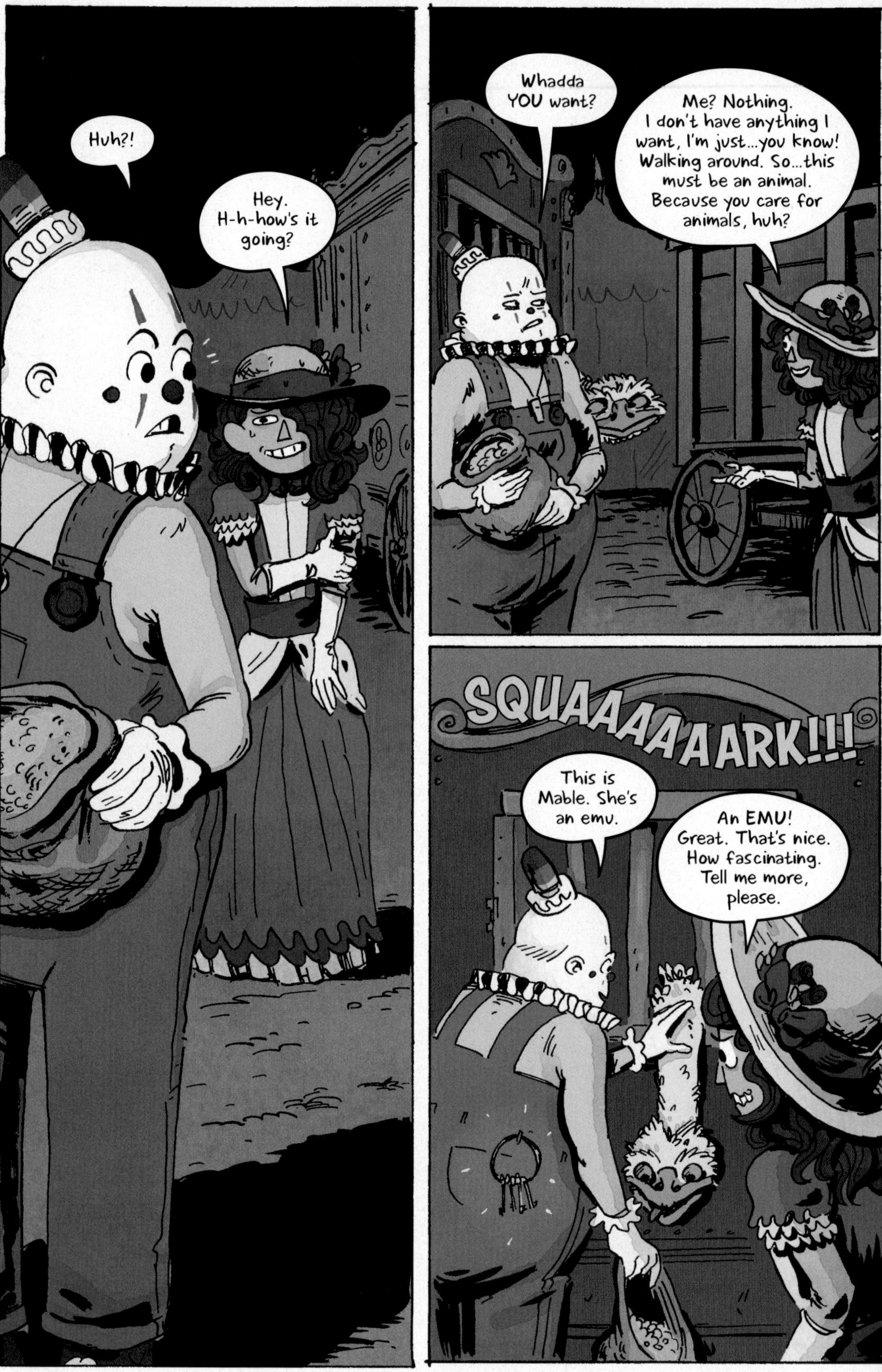
Huh?!
Hey. H-h-how's it going?
Whadda YOU want?
Me? Nothing. I don't have anything I want, I'm just...you know! Walking around. So...this must be an animal. Because you care for animals, huh?
SQUAAAAAAARK!!!
This is Mable. She's an emu.
An EMU! Great. That's nice. How fascinating. Tell me more, please.

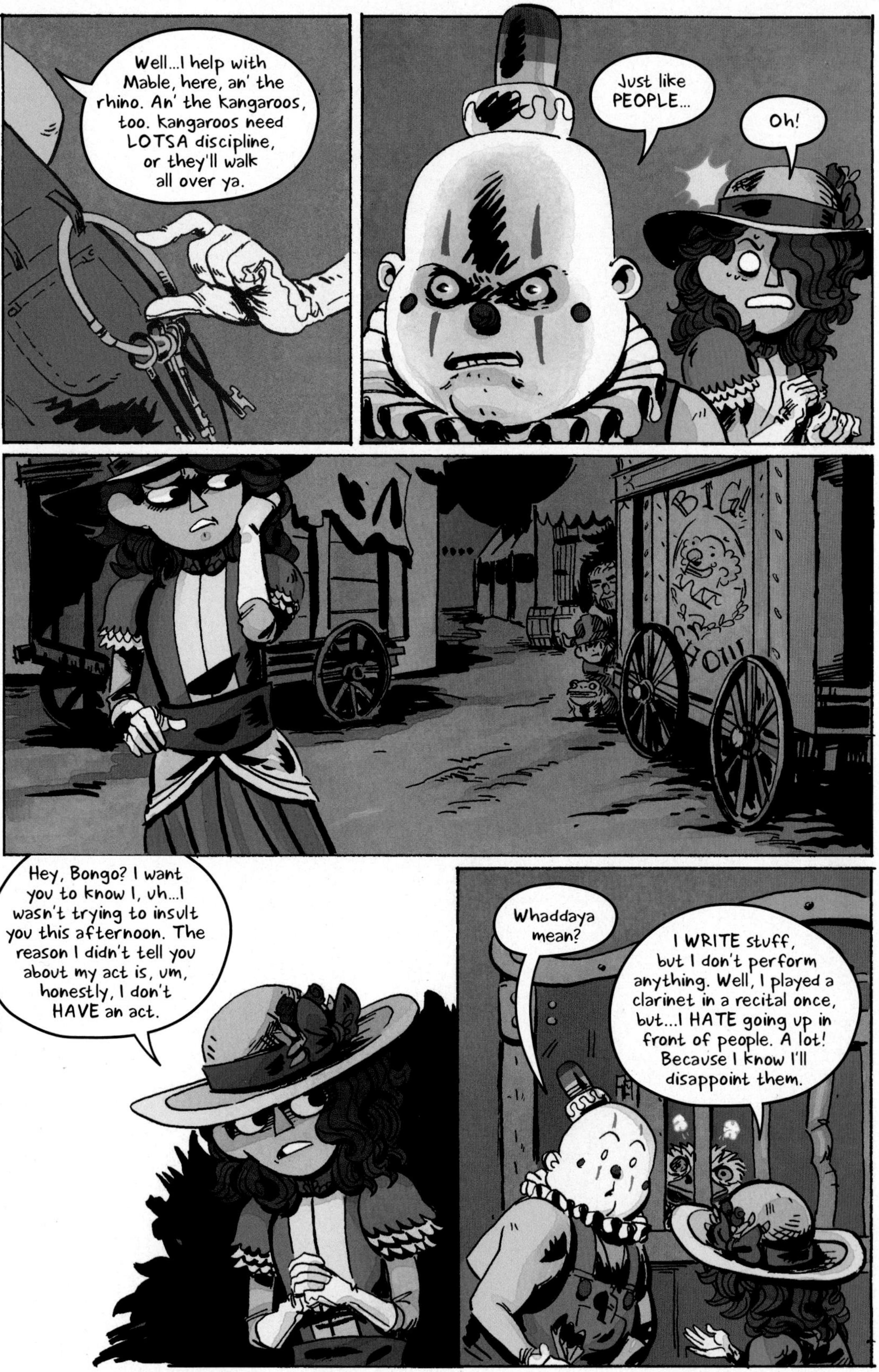
Well...I help with Mable, here, an' the rhino. An' the kangaroos, too. kangaroos need LOTSA discipline, or they'll walk all over ya.
Just like PEOPLE...
Oh!
BIG!! SHOW
Hey, Bongo? I want you to know I, uh...I wasn't trying to insult you this afternoon. The reason I didn't tell you about my act is, um, honestly, I don't HAVE an act.
Whaddaya mean?
I WRITE stuff, but I don't perform anything. Well, I played a clarinet in a recital once, but...I HATE going up in front of people. A lot! Because I know I'll disappoint them.

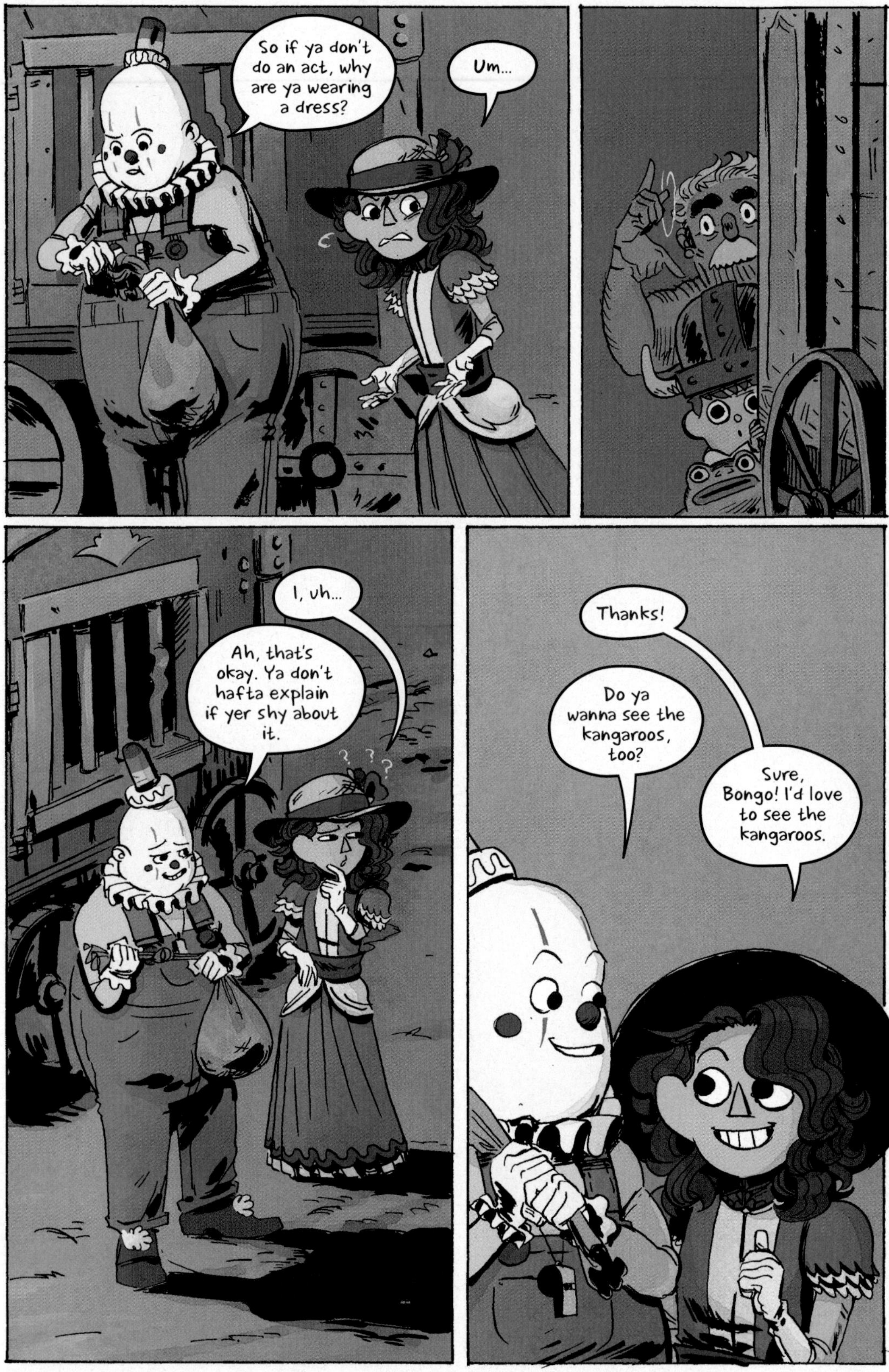
So if ya don't do an act, why are ya wearing a dress?
Um...
I, uh...
Ah, that's okay. Ya don't hafta explain if yer shy about it.
? ? ?
Do ya wanna see the kangaroos, too?
Sure, Bongo! I'd love to see the kangaroos.
Thanks!

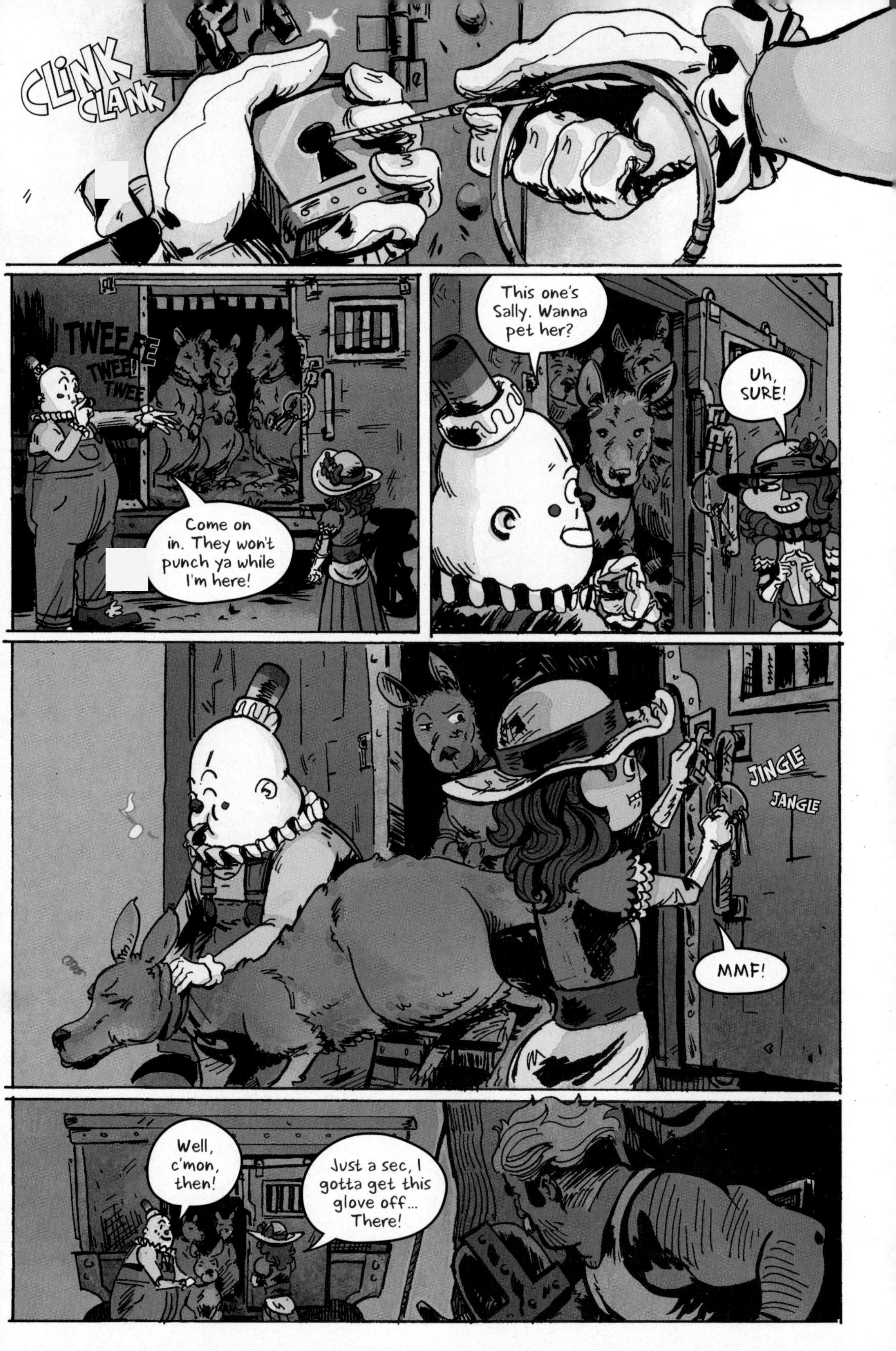
CLINK
CLANK
TWEEEE
TWEE!
TWEE
Come on in. They won't punch ya while I'm here!
This one's Sally. Wanna pet her?
Uh, SURE!
JINGLE
JANGLE
MMF!
Well, c'mon, then!
Just a sec, I gotta get this glove off... There!

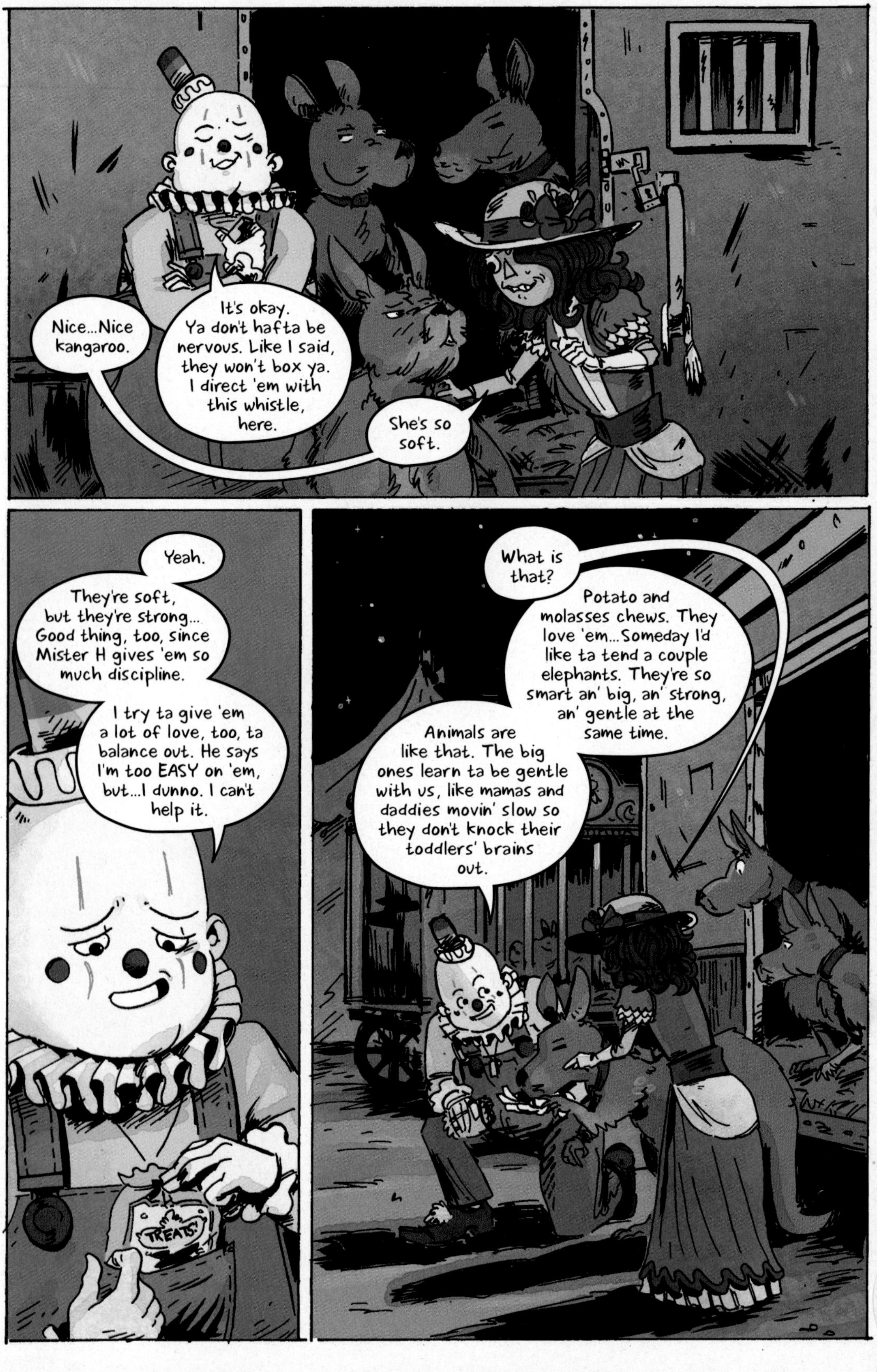
Nice...Nice kangaroo.
It's okay. Ya don't hafta be nervous. Like I said, they won't box ya. I direct 'em with this whistle, here.
She's so soft.
Yeah.
They're soft, but they're strong... Good thing, too, since Mister H gives 'em so much discipline.
I try ta give 'em a lot of love, too, ta balance out. He says I'm too EASY on 'em, but...I dunno. I can't help it.
TREATS!
What is that?
Potato and molasses chews. They love 'em...Someday I'd like ta tend a couple elephants. They're so smart an' big, an' strong, an' gentle at the same time.
Animals are like that. The big ones learn ta be gentle with us, like mamas and daddies movin' slow so they don't knock their toddlers' brains out.

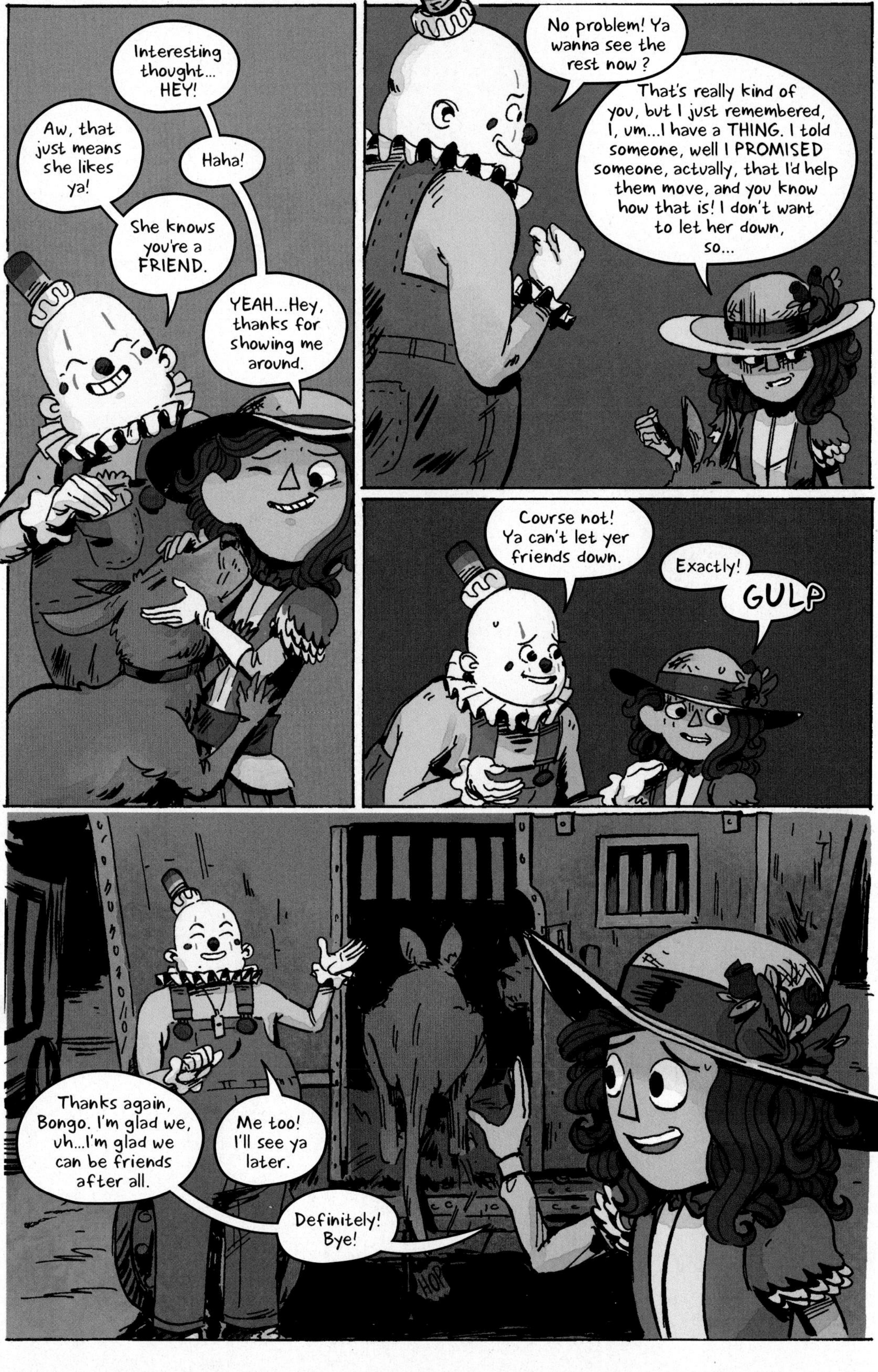
Interesting thought... HEY!
Aw, that just means she likes ya!
Haha!
She knows you're a FRIEND.
YEAH...Hey, thanks for showing me around.
No problem! Ya wanna see the rest now?
That's really kind of you, but I just remembered, I, um...I have a THING. I told someone, well I PROMISED someone, actually, that I'd help them move, and you know how that is! I don't want to let her down, so...
Course not! Ya can't let yer friends down.
Exactly!
GULP
Thanks again, Bongo. I'm glad we, uh...I'm glad we can be friends after all.
Me too! I'll see ya later.
Definitely! Bye!
HOP

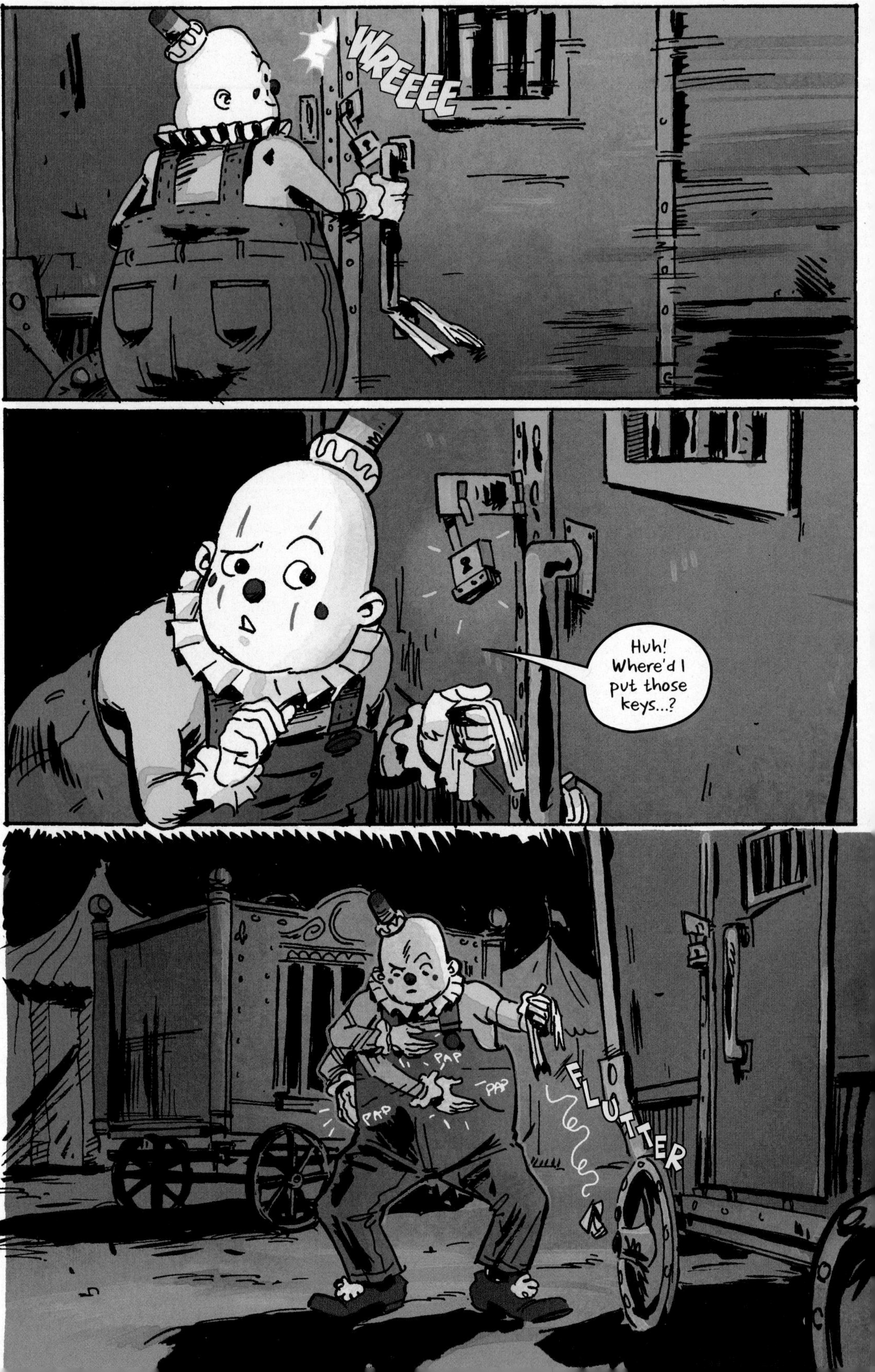
WREEEEE
Huh! Where'd I put those keys...?
PAP
PAP
PAP
PAP
FLUTTER

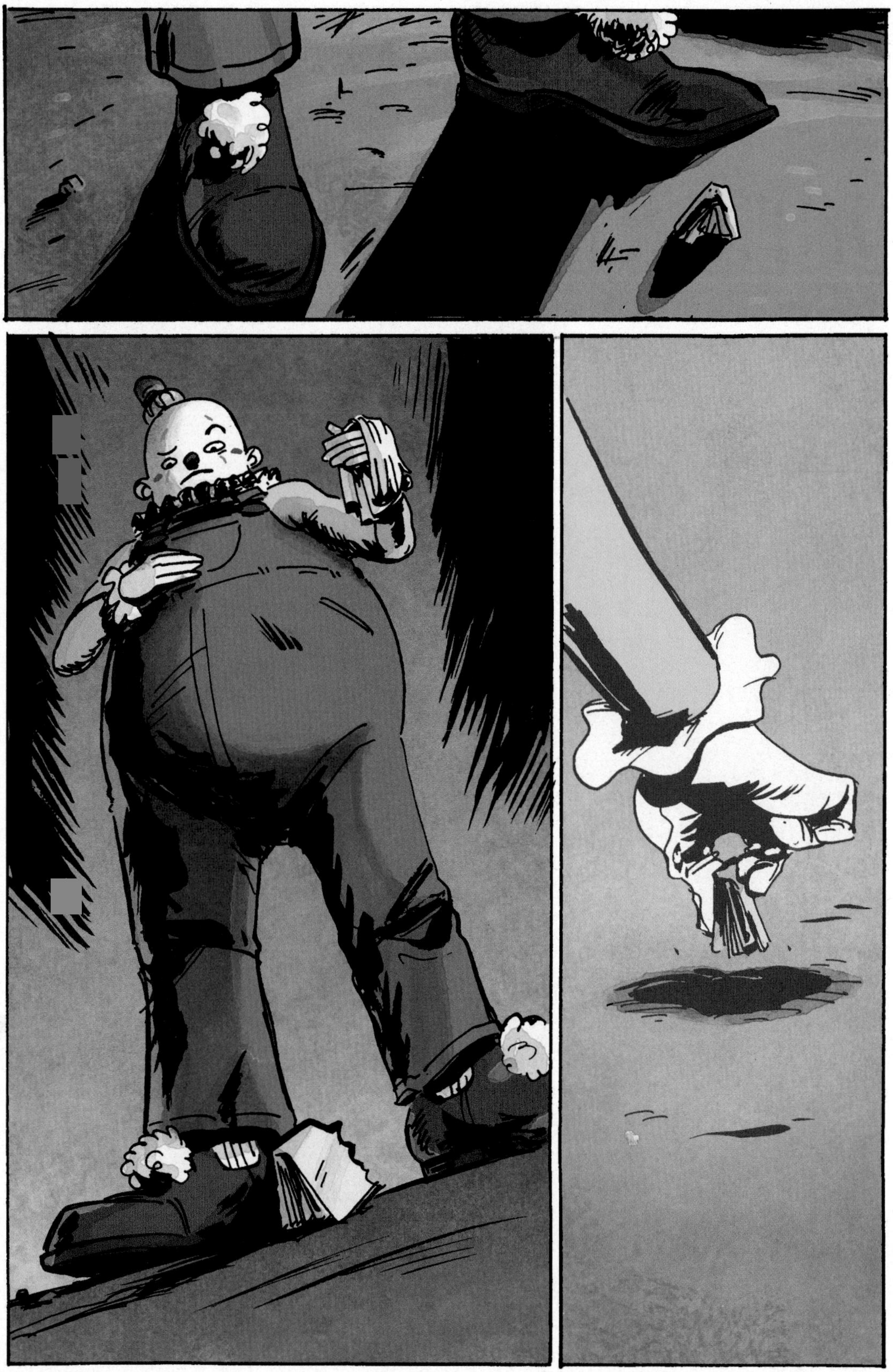

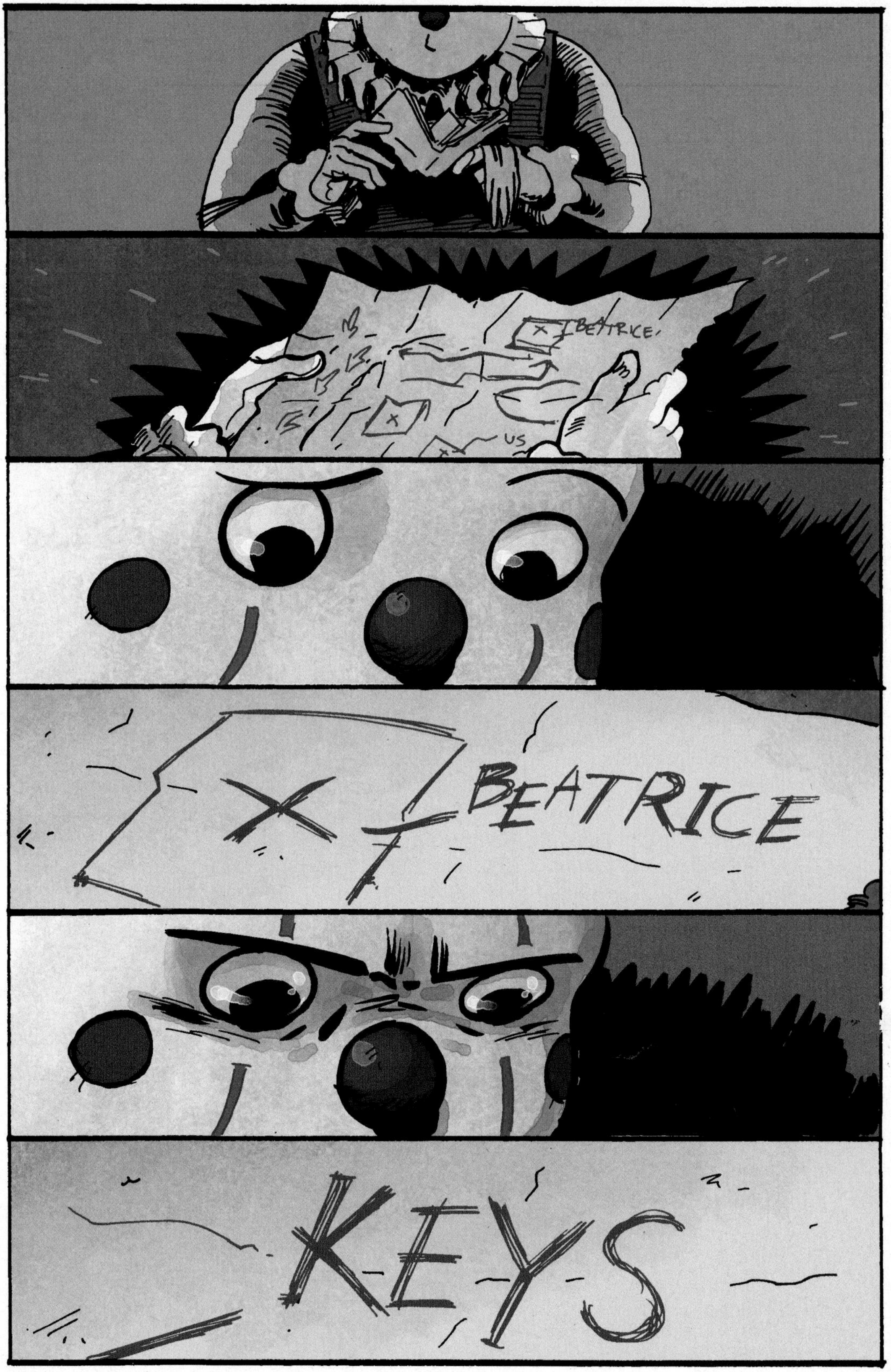

BEATRICE
US
BEATRICE
KEYS

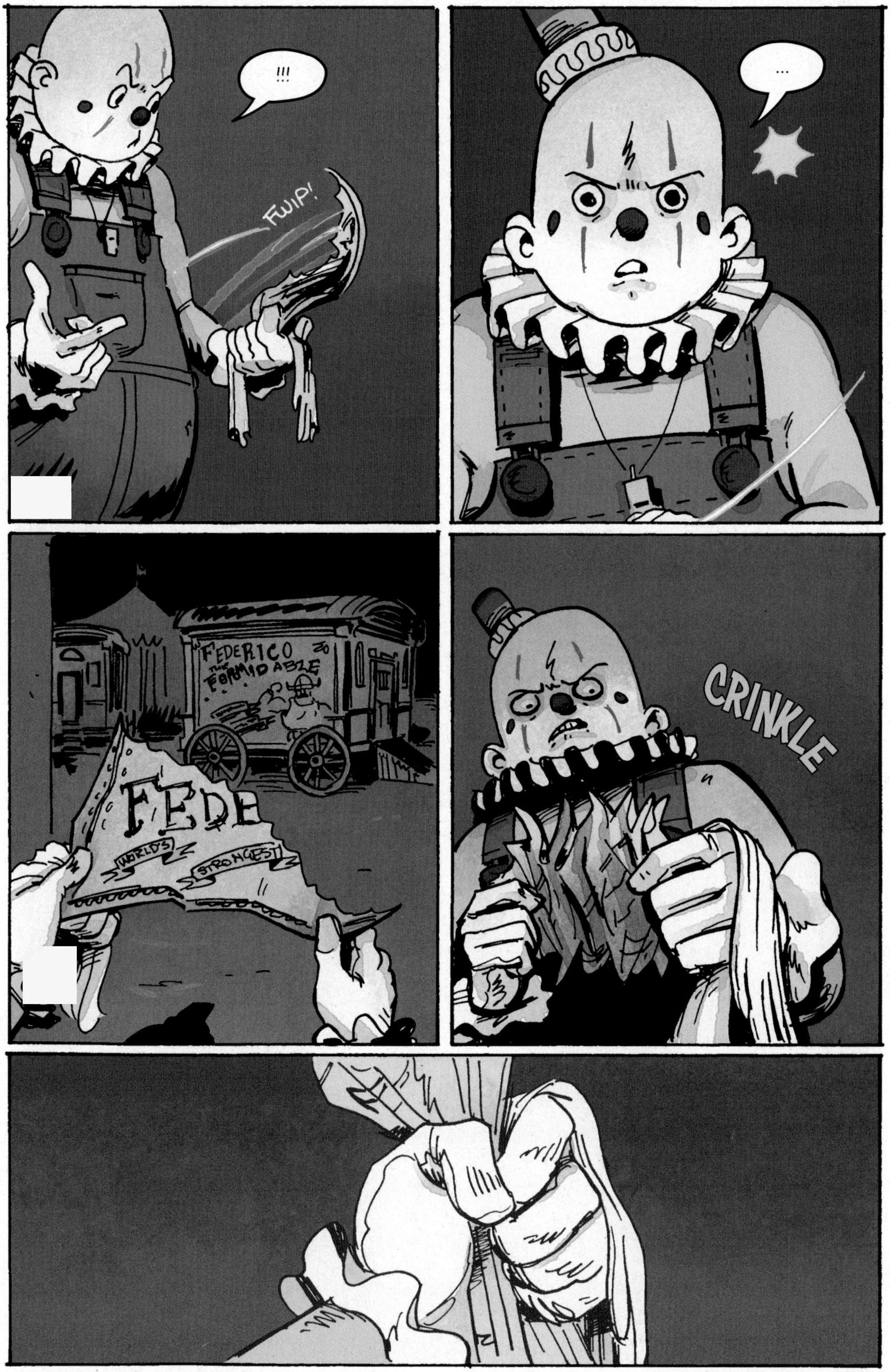
!!!
FWIP!
...
FEDERICO THE FORMIDABLE
FEDE
WORLD'S
STRONGEST
CRINKLE

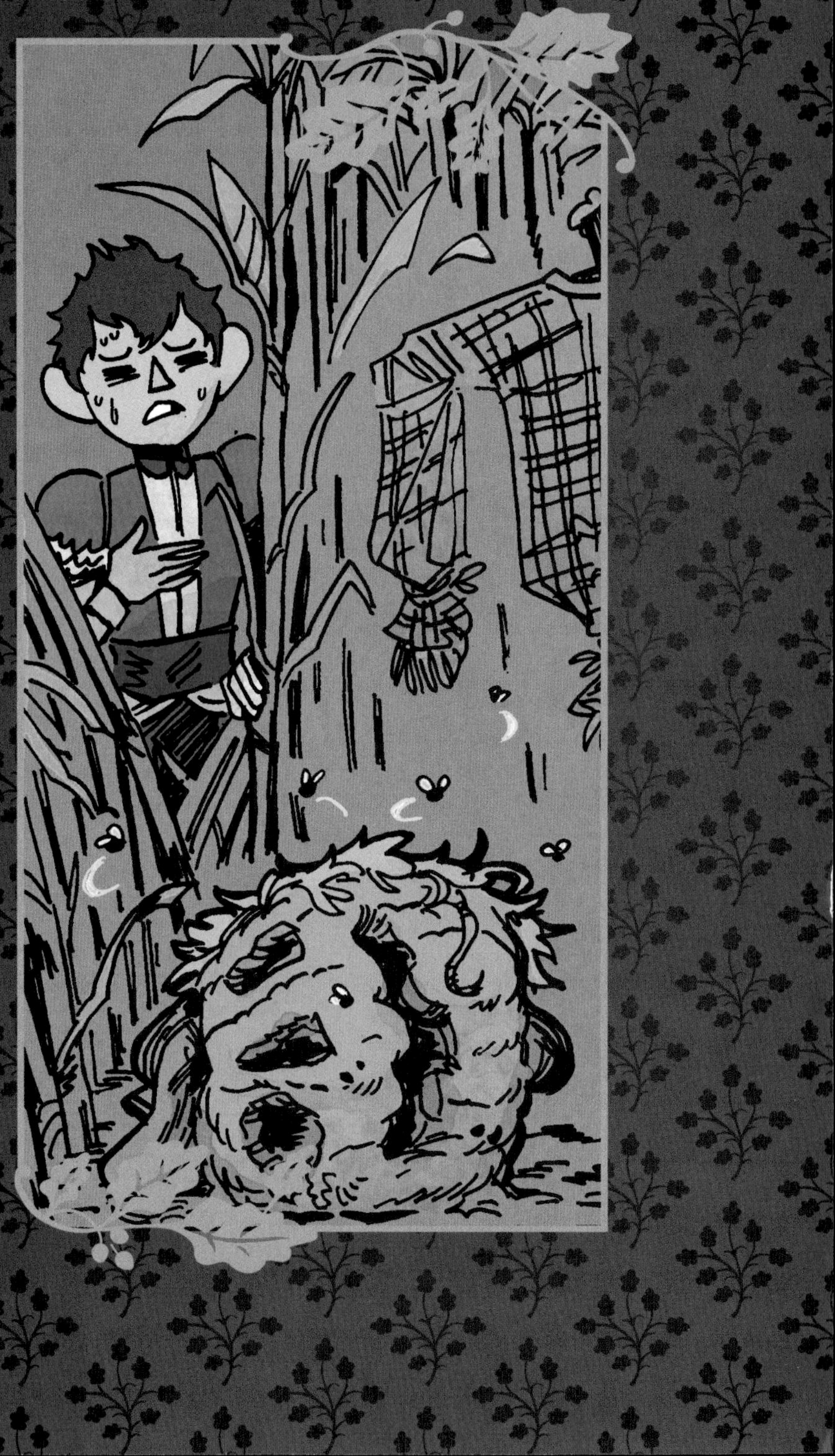

ACT THREE

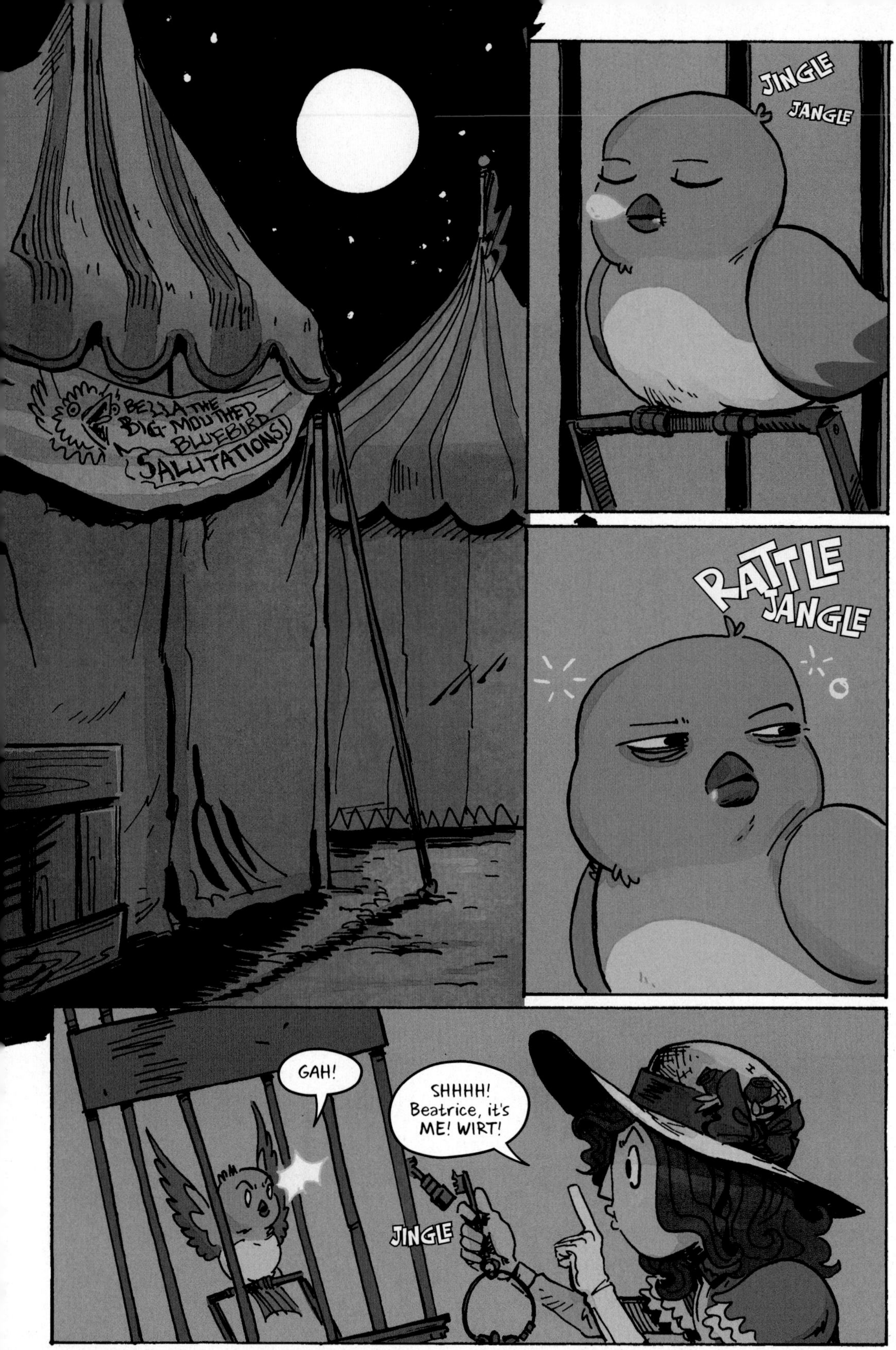

BELLA THE BIG-MOUTHED BLUEBIRD
SALUTATIONS!
JINGLE
JANGLE
RATTLE
JANGLE
GAH!
SHHHH! Beatrice, it's ME! WIRT!
JINGLE

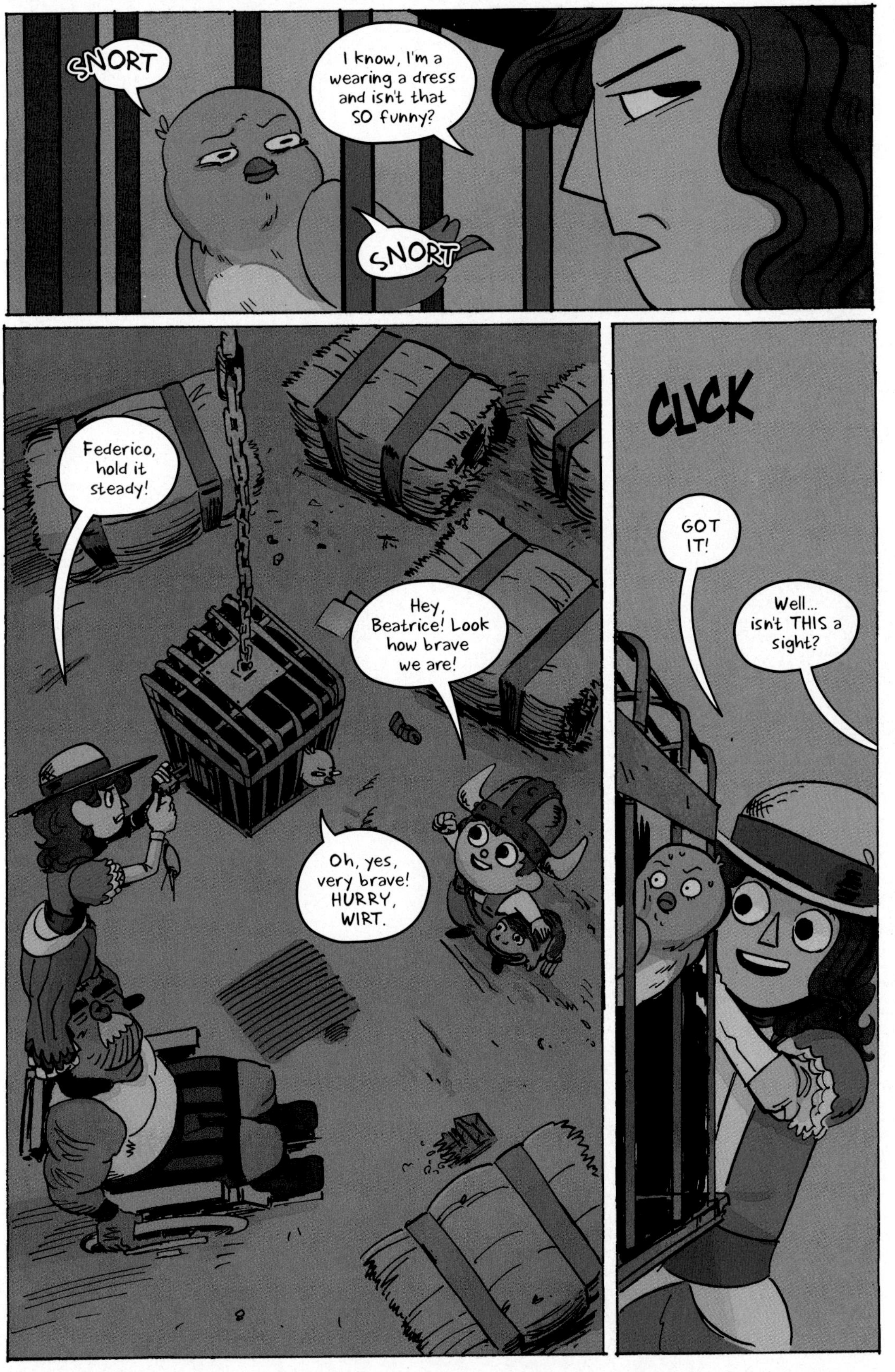
SNORT
I know, I'm a wearing a dress and isn't that SO funny?
SNORT
Federico, hold it steady!
Hey, Beatrice! Look how brave we are!
Oh, yes, very brave! HURRY, WIRT.
CLICK
GOT IT!
Well... isn't THIS a sight?

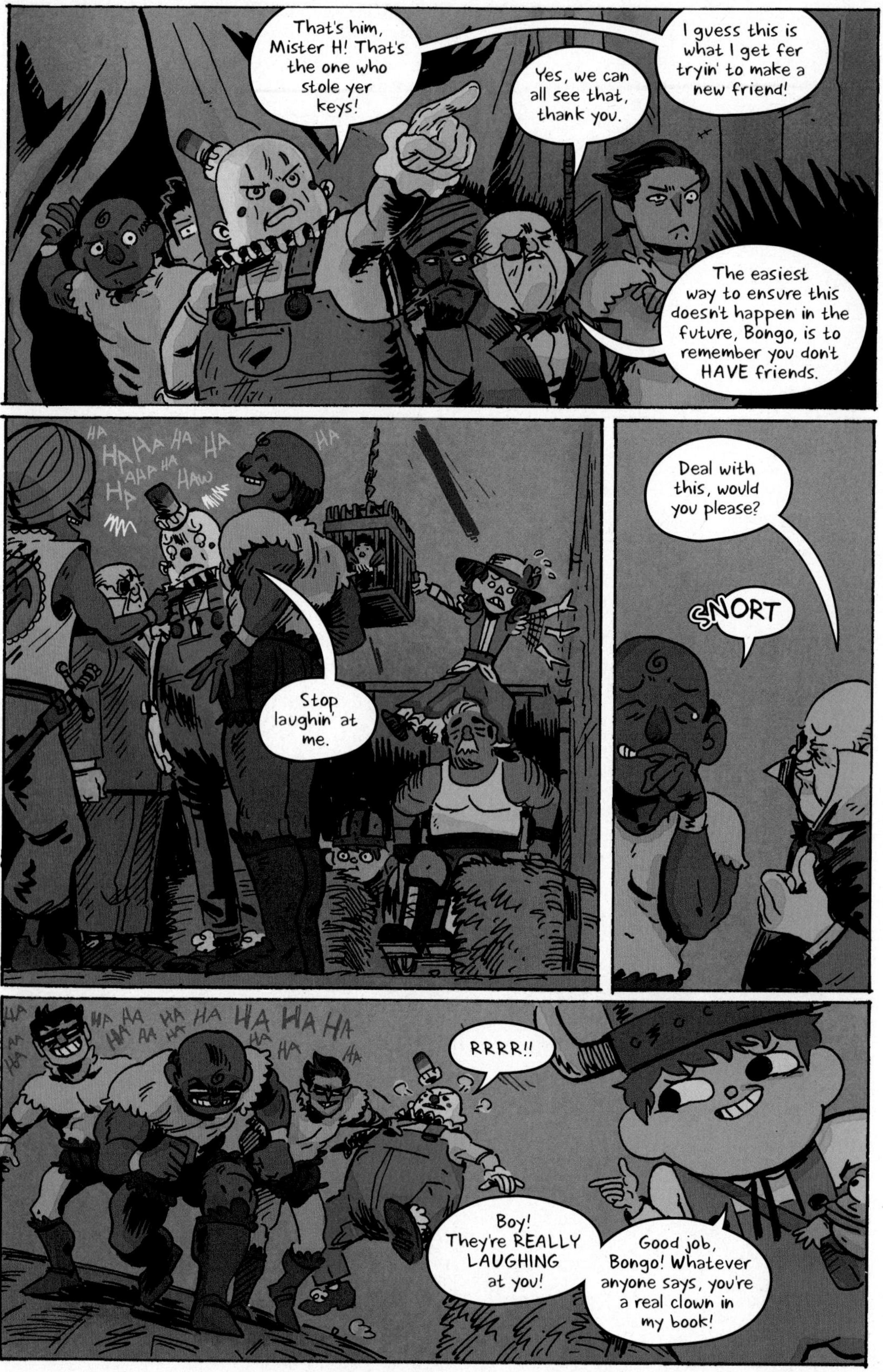
That's him, Mister H! That's the one who stole yer keys!
Yes, we can all see that, thank you.
I guess this is what I get fer tryin' to make a new friend!
The easiest way to ensure this doesn't happen in the future, Bongo, is to remember you don't HAVE friends.
HA HA HA HA HA HA HA AHA HA HAW
Stop laughin' at me.
Deal with this, would you please?
SNORT
HA HA HA HA HA HA HA HA HA HA HA HA HA HA
RRRR!!
Boy! They're REALLY LAUGHING at you!
Good job, Bongo! Whatever anyone says, you're a real clown in my book!

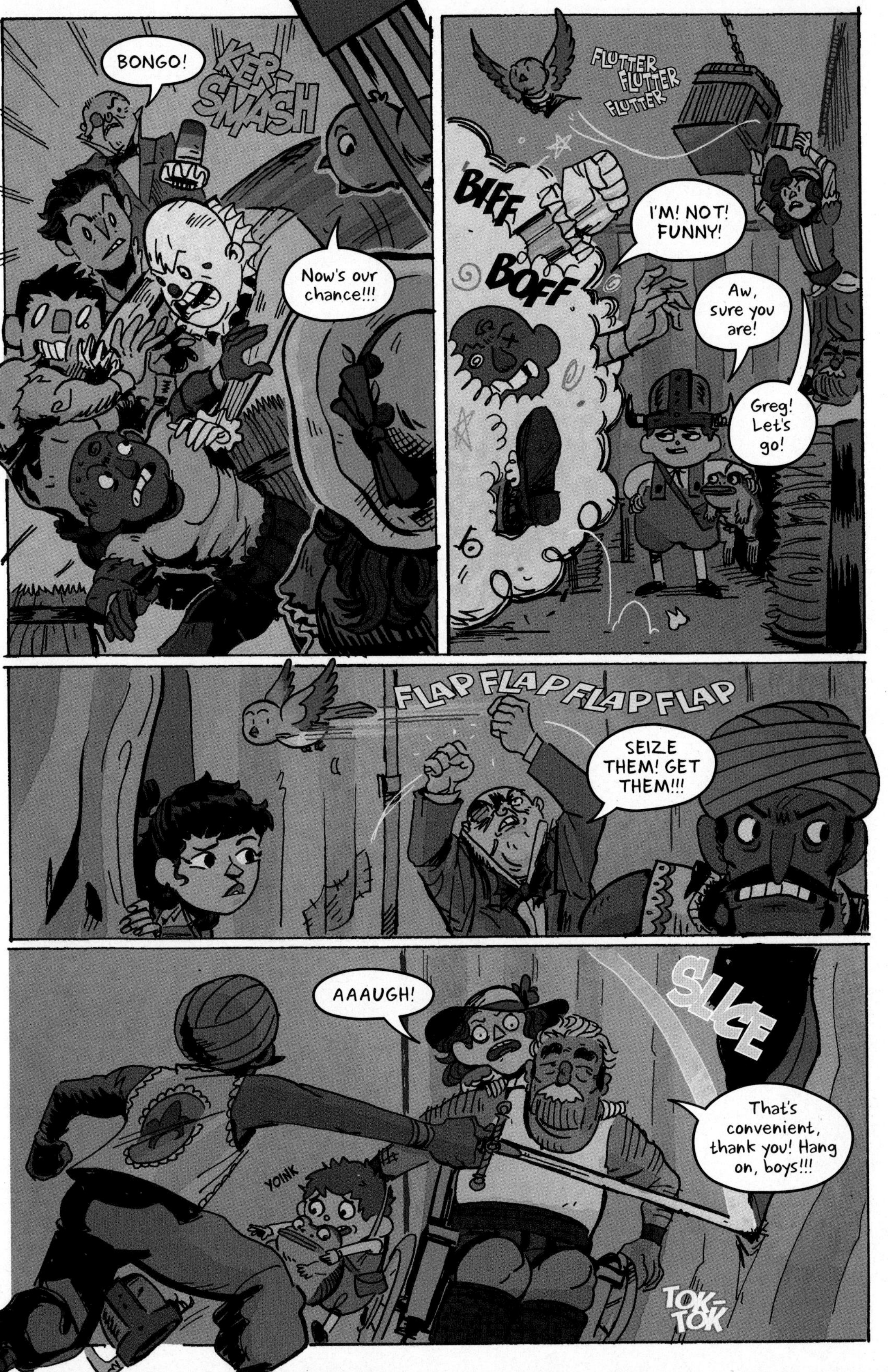

BONGO!
KER-SMASH
Now's our chance!!!
FLUTTER FLUTTER FLUTTER
BIFF
BOFF
I'M! NOT! FUNNY!
Aw, sure you are!
Greg! Let's go!
FLAP FLAP FLAP FLAP
SEIZE THEM! GET THEM!!!
AAAUGH!
SLICE
YOINK
That's convenient, thank you! Hang on, boys!!!
TOK-TOK

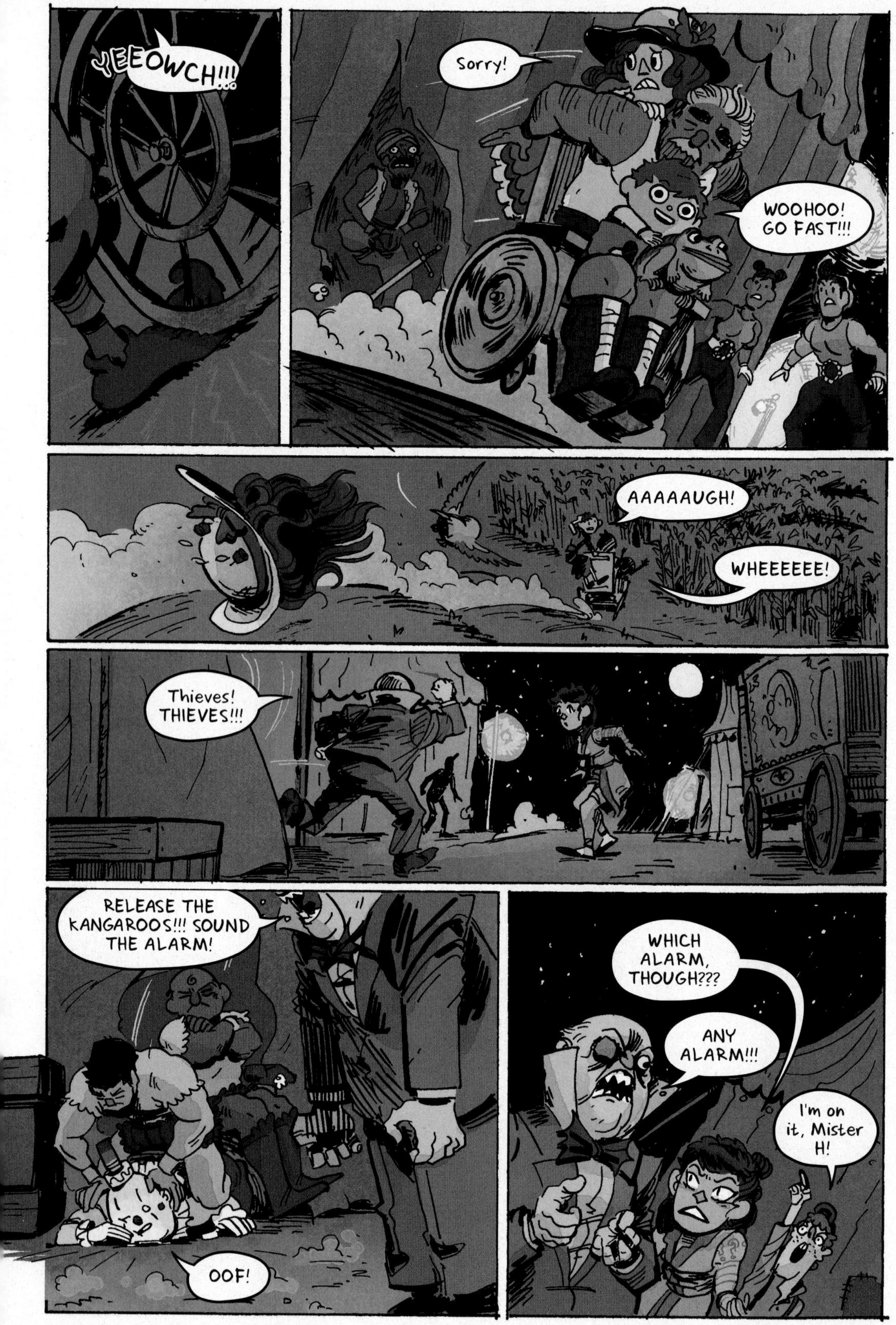
YEEOWCH!!!
Sorry!
WOOHOO! GO FAST!!!
AAAAAUGH!
WHEEEEEE!
Thieves! THIEVES!!!
RELEASE THE KANGAROOS!!! SOUND THE ALARM!
OOF!
WHICH ALARM, THOUGH???
ANY ALARM!!!
I'm on it, Mister H!

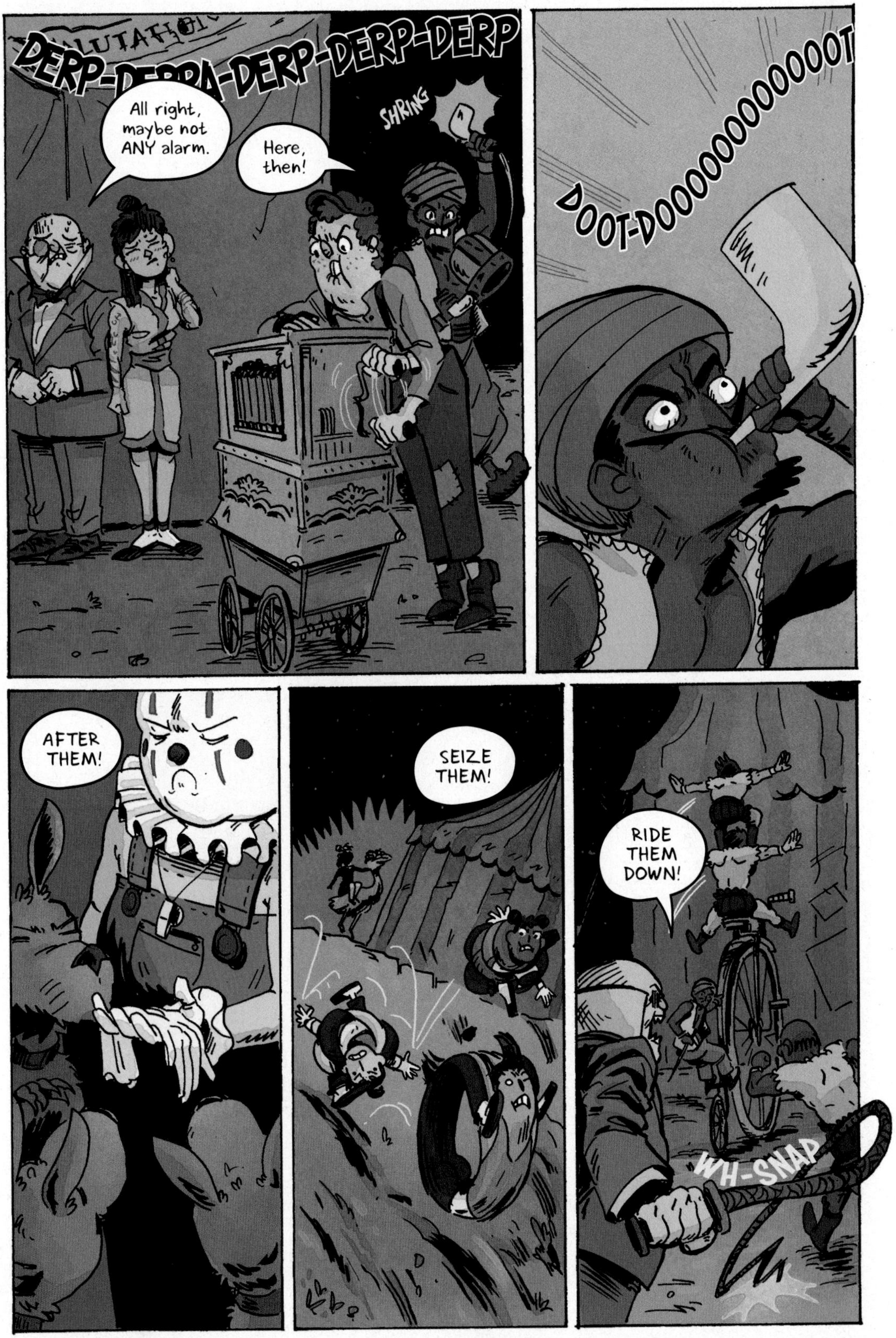
DERP-DERRA-DERP-DERP-DERP
All right, maybe not ANY alarm.
Here, then!
SHRING
DOOT-DOOOOOOOOOOOOOT
AFTER THEM!
SEIZE THEM!
RIDE THEM DOWN!
WH-SNAP

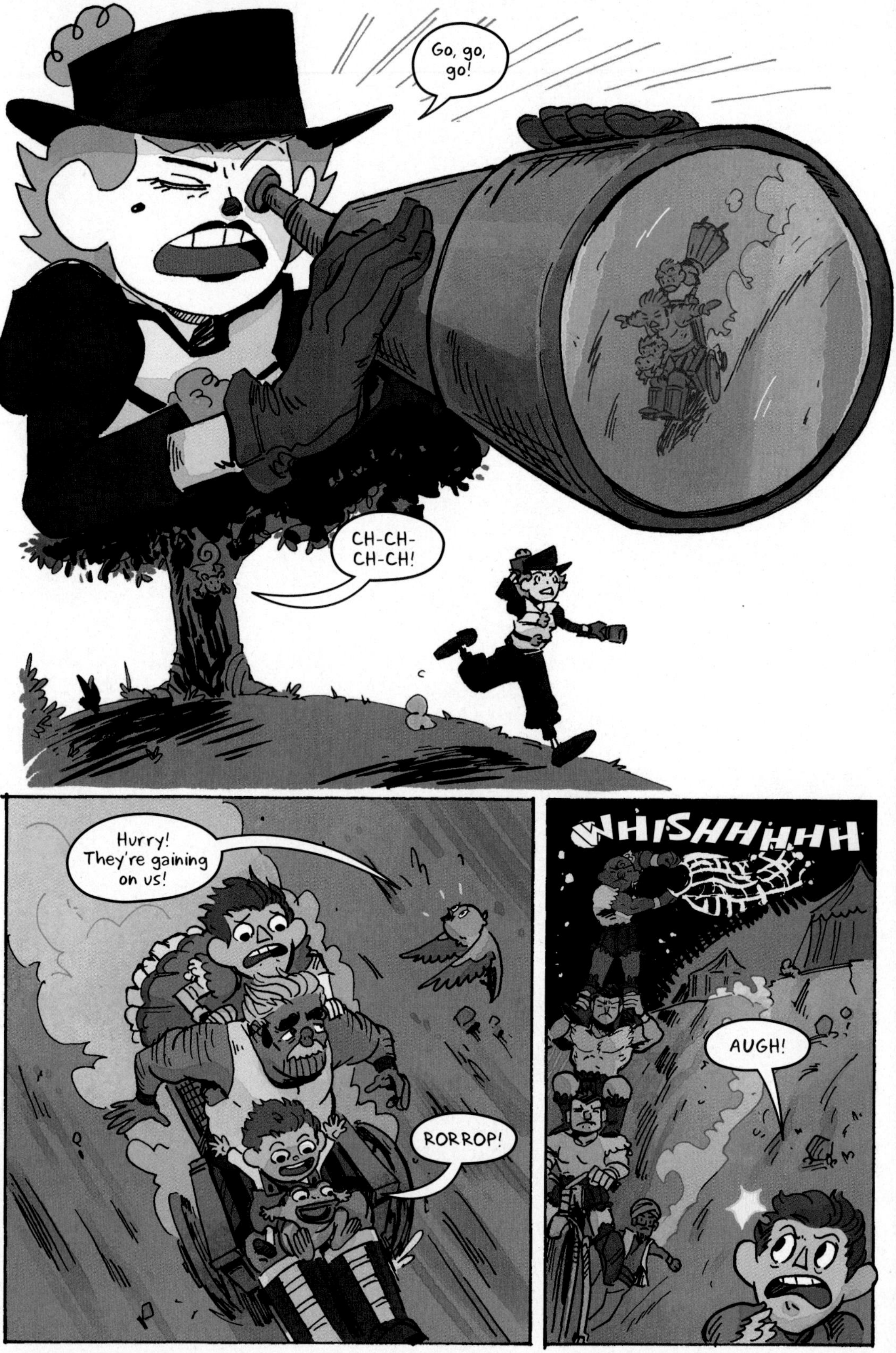
Go, go, go!
CH-CH-CH-CH!
Hurry! They're gaining on us!
RORROP!
WHISHHHHH
AUGH!

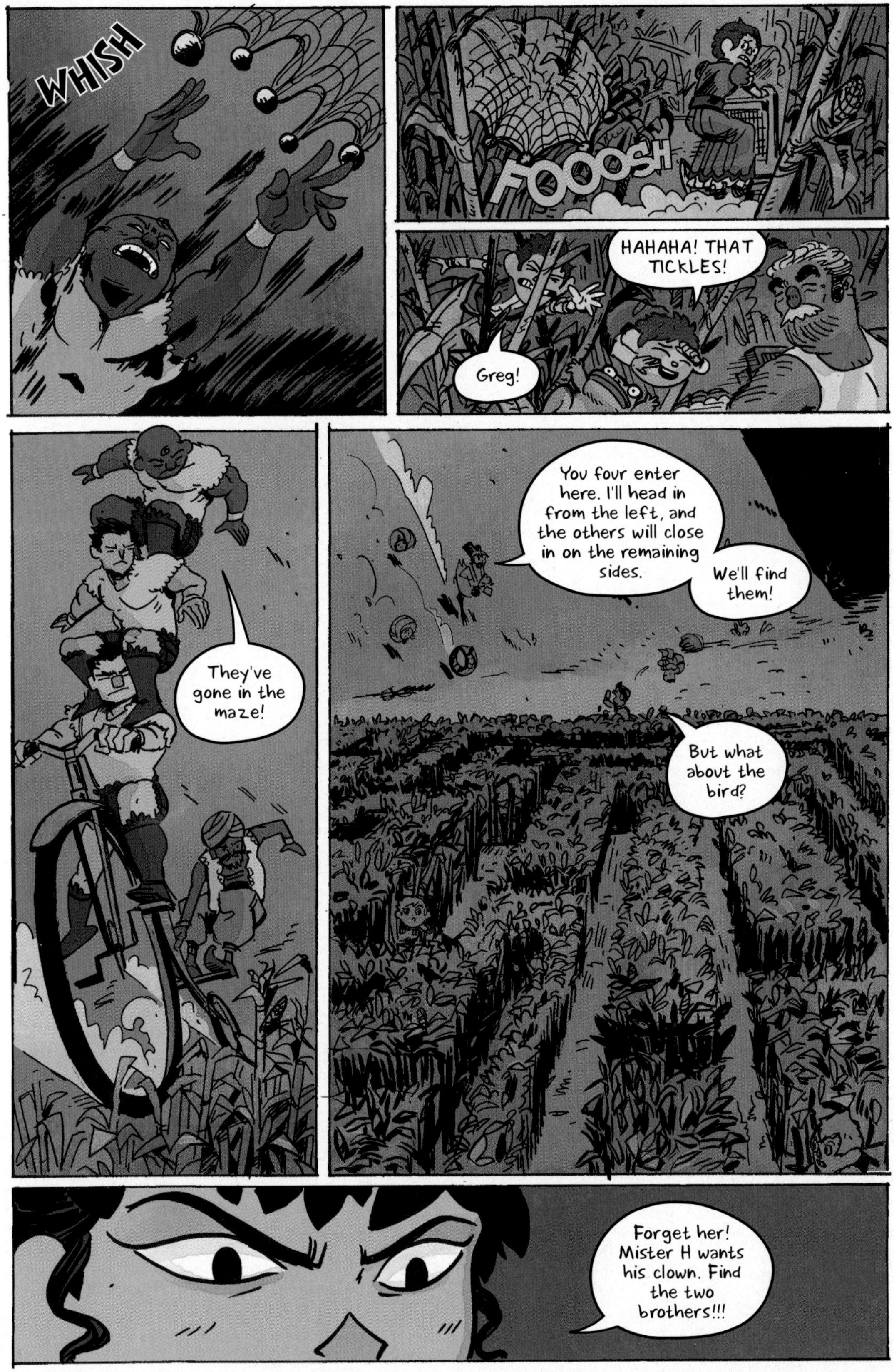
WHISH
FOOOSH
HAHAHA! THAT TICKLES!
Greg!
They've gone in the maze!
You four enter here. I'll head in from the left, and the others will close in on the remaining sides.
We'll find them!
But what about the bird?
Forget her! Mister H wants his clown. Find the two brothers!!!

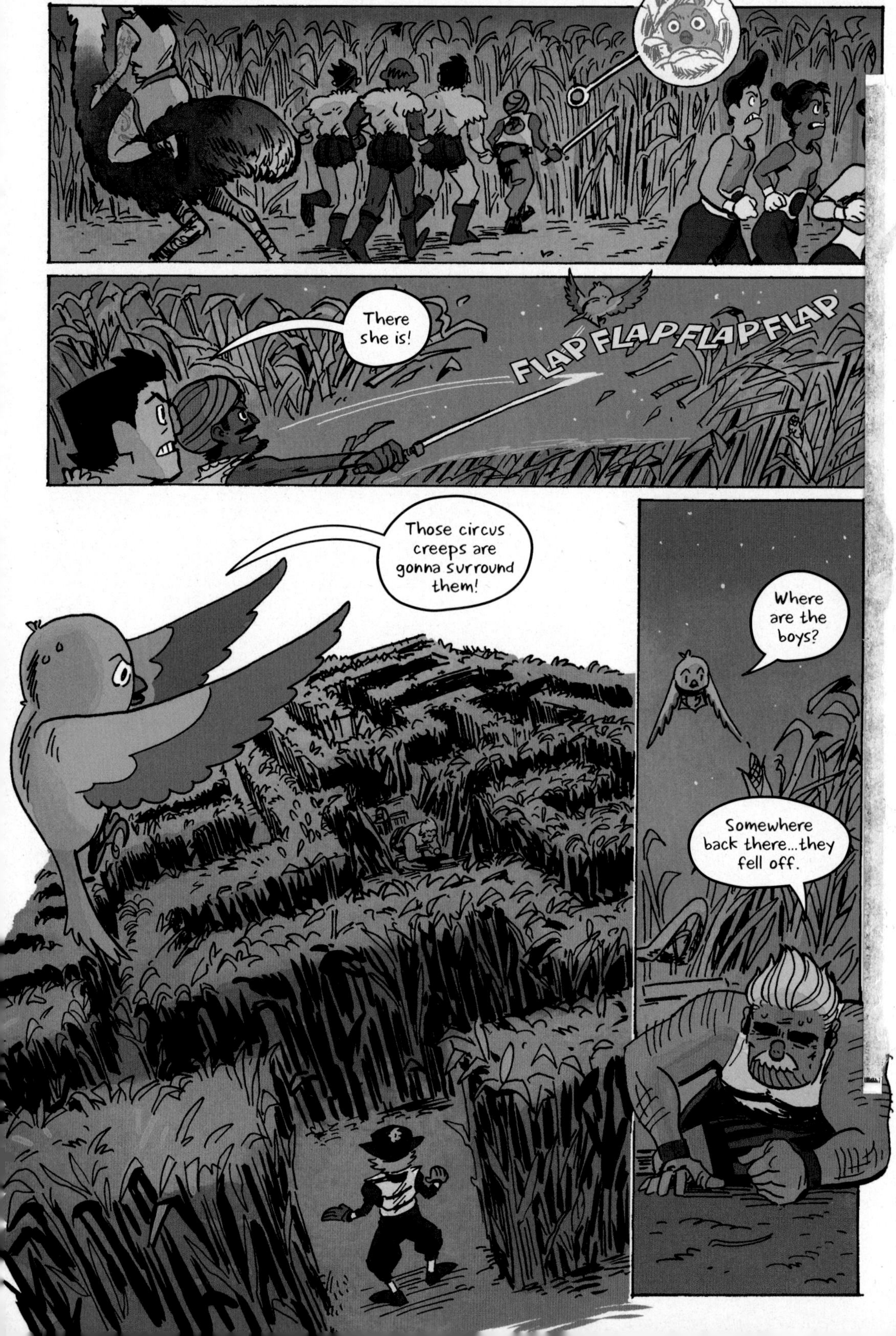
There she is!
FLAP FLAP FLAP FLAP FLAP
Those circus creeps are gonna surround them!
Where are the boys?
Somewhere back there...they fell off.

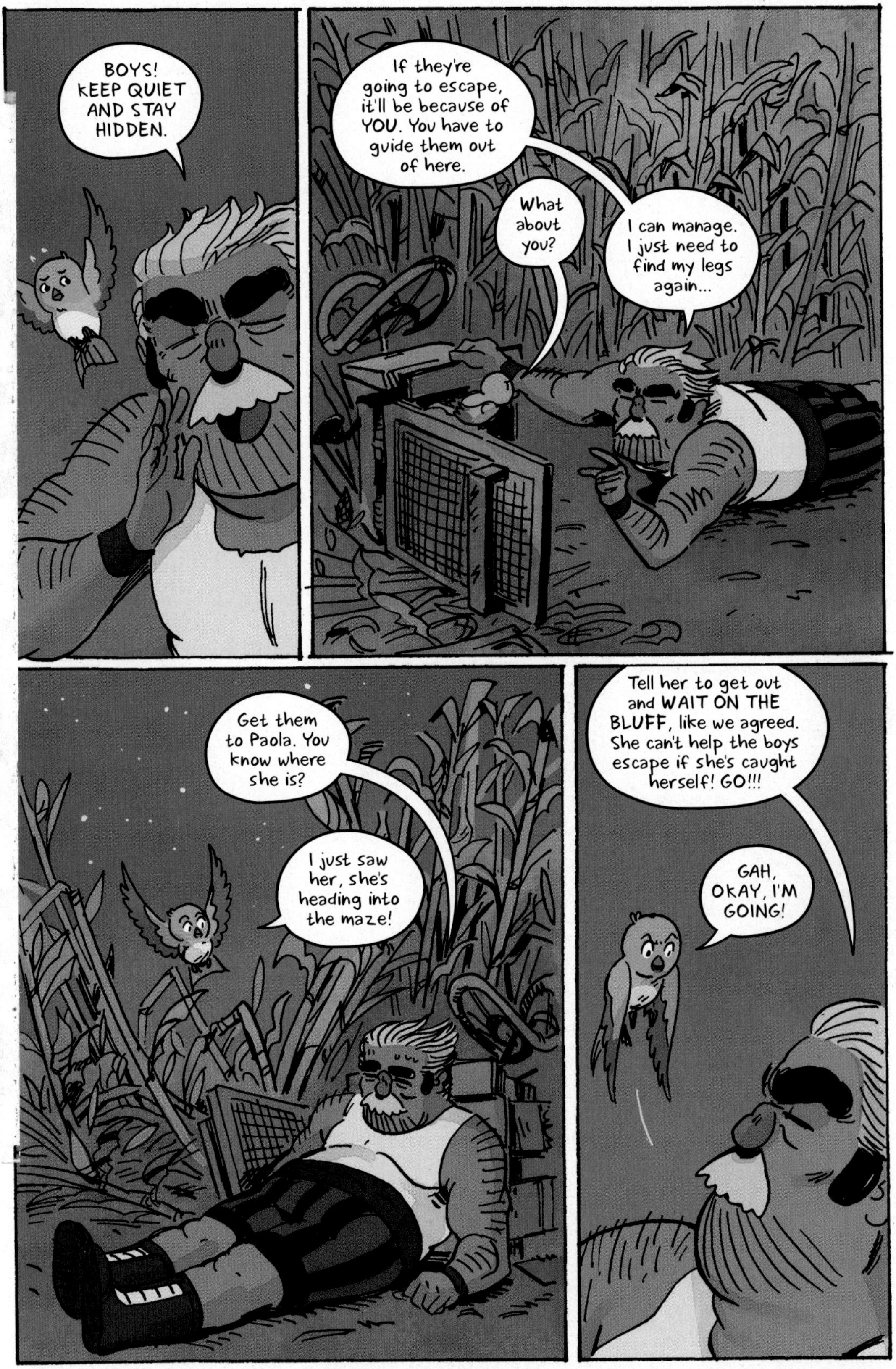
BOYS! KEEP QUIET AND STAY HIDDEN.
If they're going to escape, it'll be because of YOU. You have to guide them out of here.
What about you?
I can manage. I just need to find my legs again...
Get them to Paola. You know where she is?
I just saw her, she's heading into the maze!
Tell her to get out and WAIT ON THE BLUFF, like we agreed. She can't help the boys escape if she's caught herself! GO!!!
GAH, OKAY, I'M GOING!

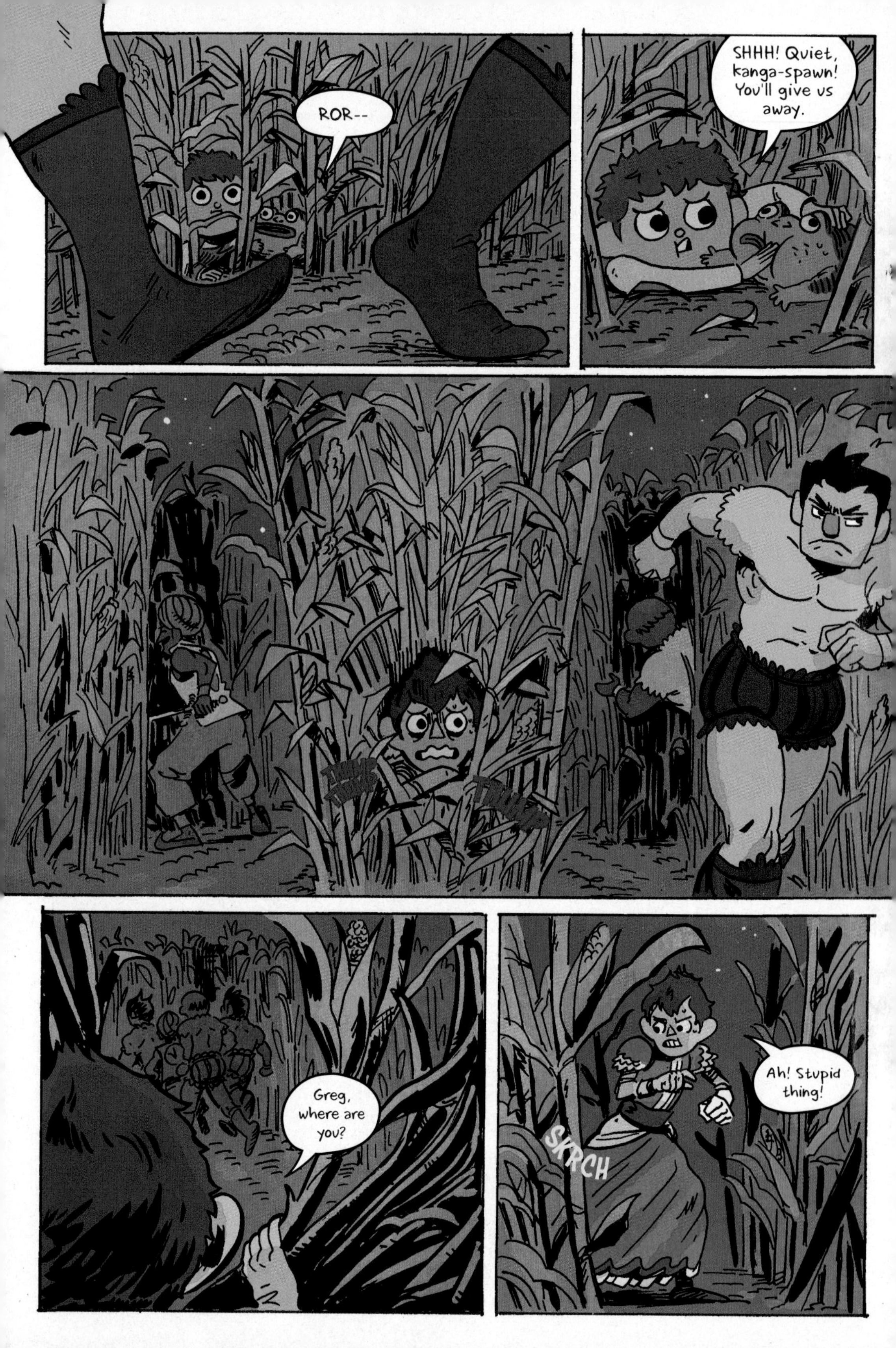
ROR--
SHHH! Quiet, kanga-spawn! You'll give us away.
Greg, where are you?
SKRCH
Ah! Stupid thing!

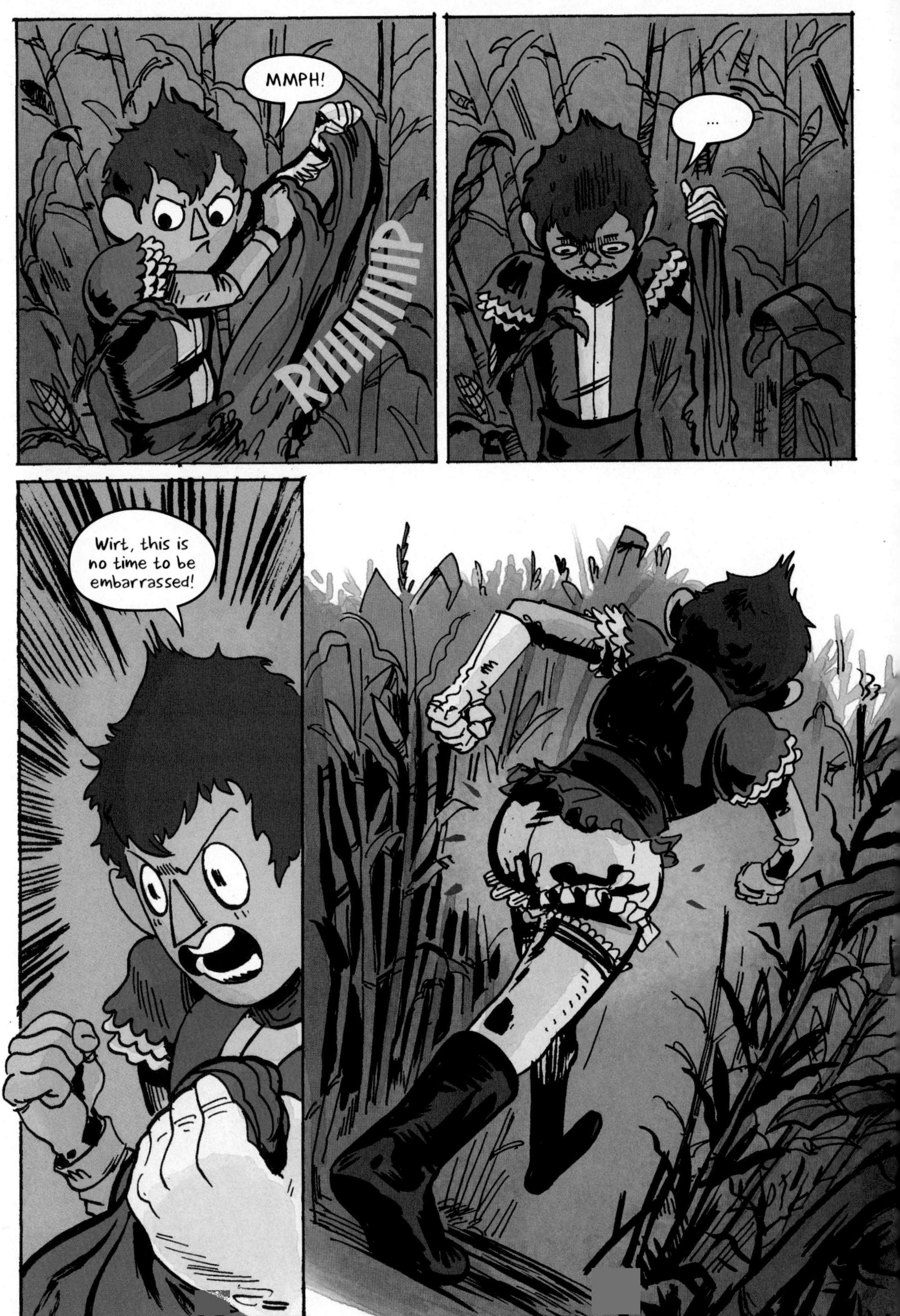
MMPH!
RIIIIIIIP
...
Wirt, this is no time to be embarrassed!

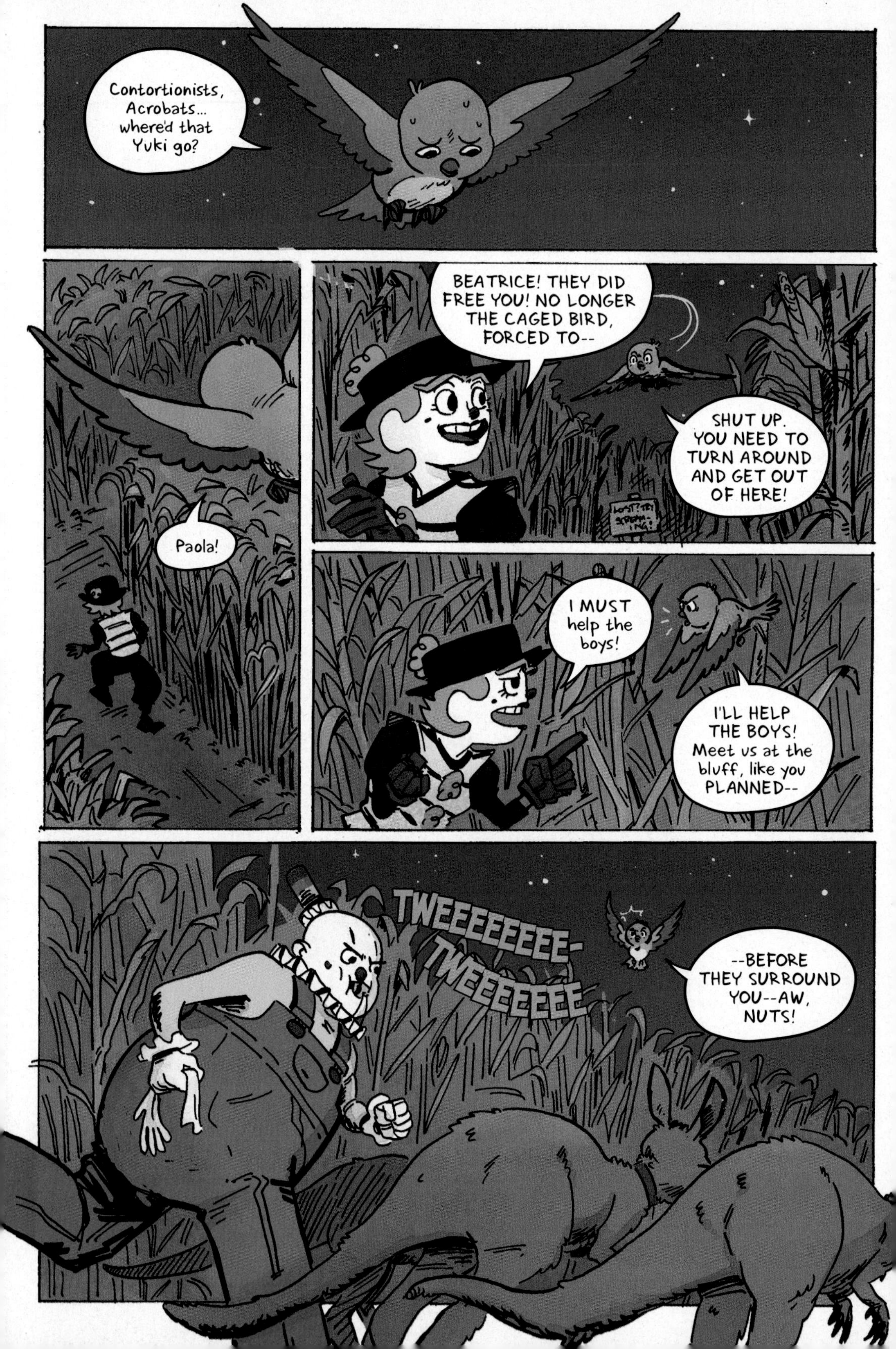

Contortionists, Acrobats... where'd that Yuki go?
Paola!
BEATRICE! THEY DID FREE YOU! NO LONGER THE CAGED BIRD, FORCED TO--
SHUT UP. YOU NEED TO TURN AROUND AND GET OUT OF HERE!
LOST? TRY SCREAM-ING!
I MUST help the boys!
I'LL HELP THE BOYS! Meet us at the bluff, like you PLANNED--
TWEEEEEEEE-TWEEEEEEE
--BEFORE THEY SURROUND YOU--AW, NUTS!

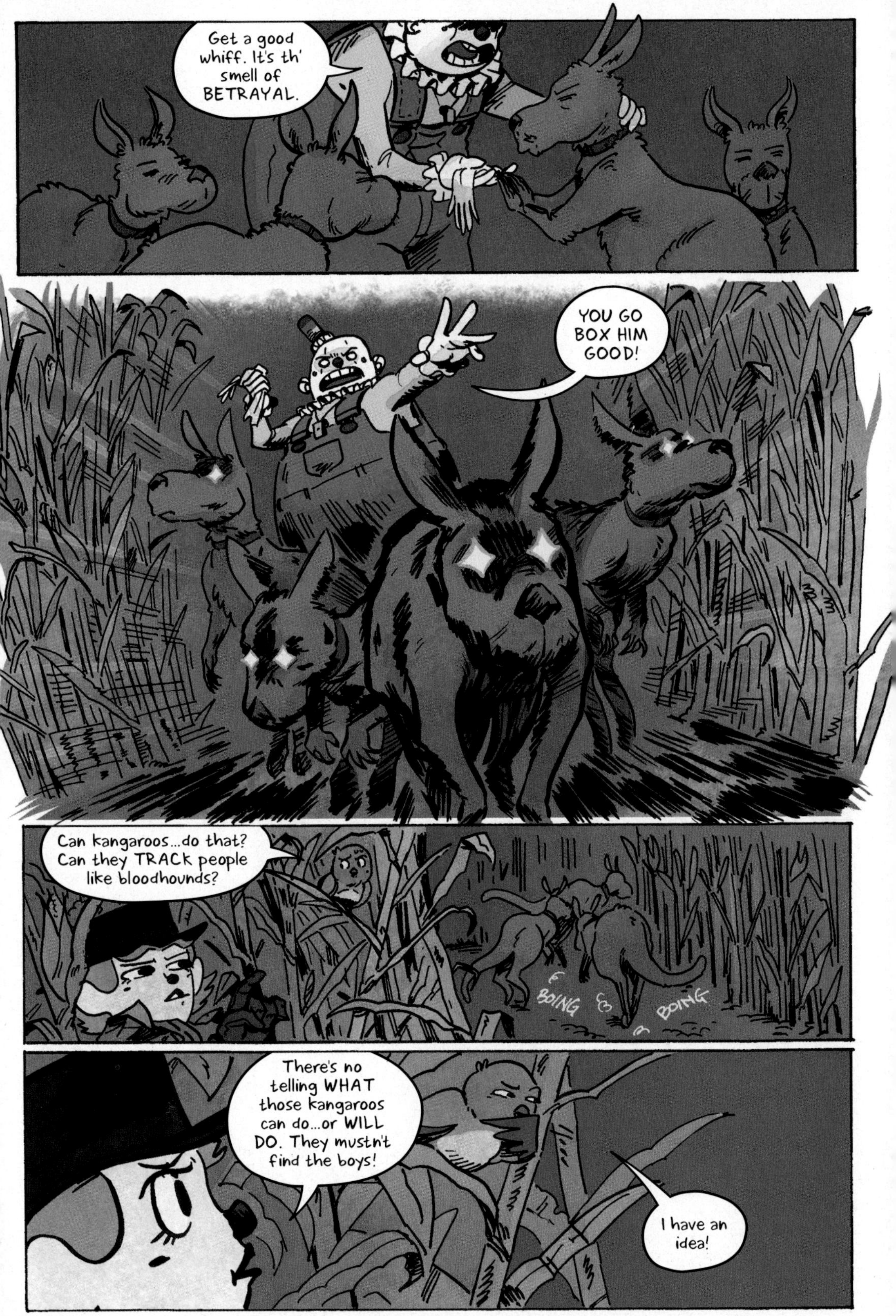
Get a good whiff. It's th' smell of BETRAYAL.
YOU GO BOX HIM GOOD!
Can kangaroos...do that? Can they TRACK people like bloodhounds?
BOING
BOING
There's no telling WHAT those kangaroos can do...or WILL DO. They mustn't find the boys!
I have an idea!

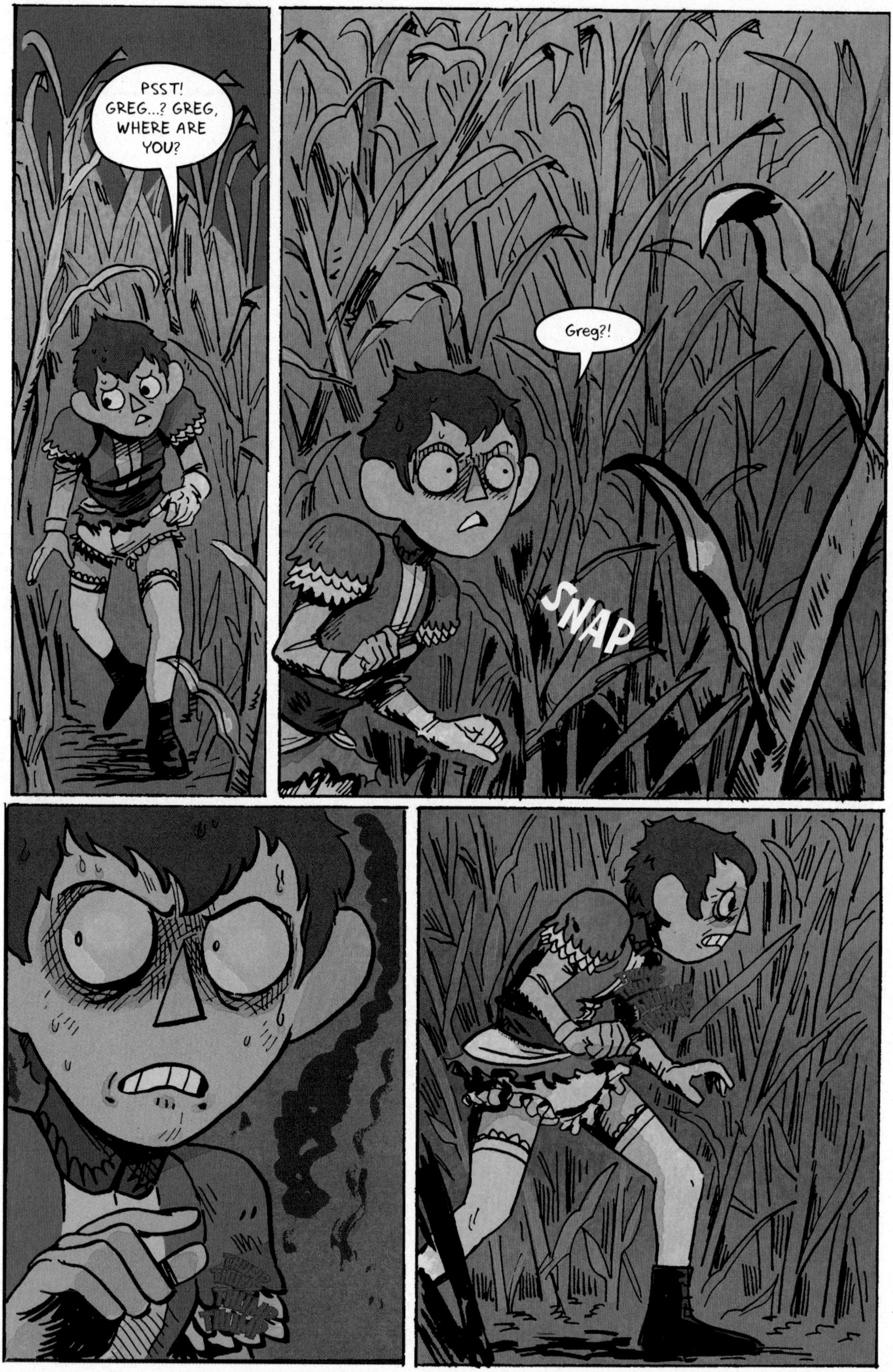
PSST! GREG...? GREG, WHERE ARE YOU?
Greg?!
SNAP

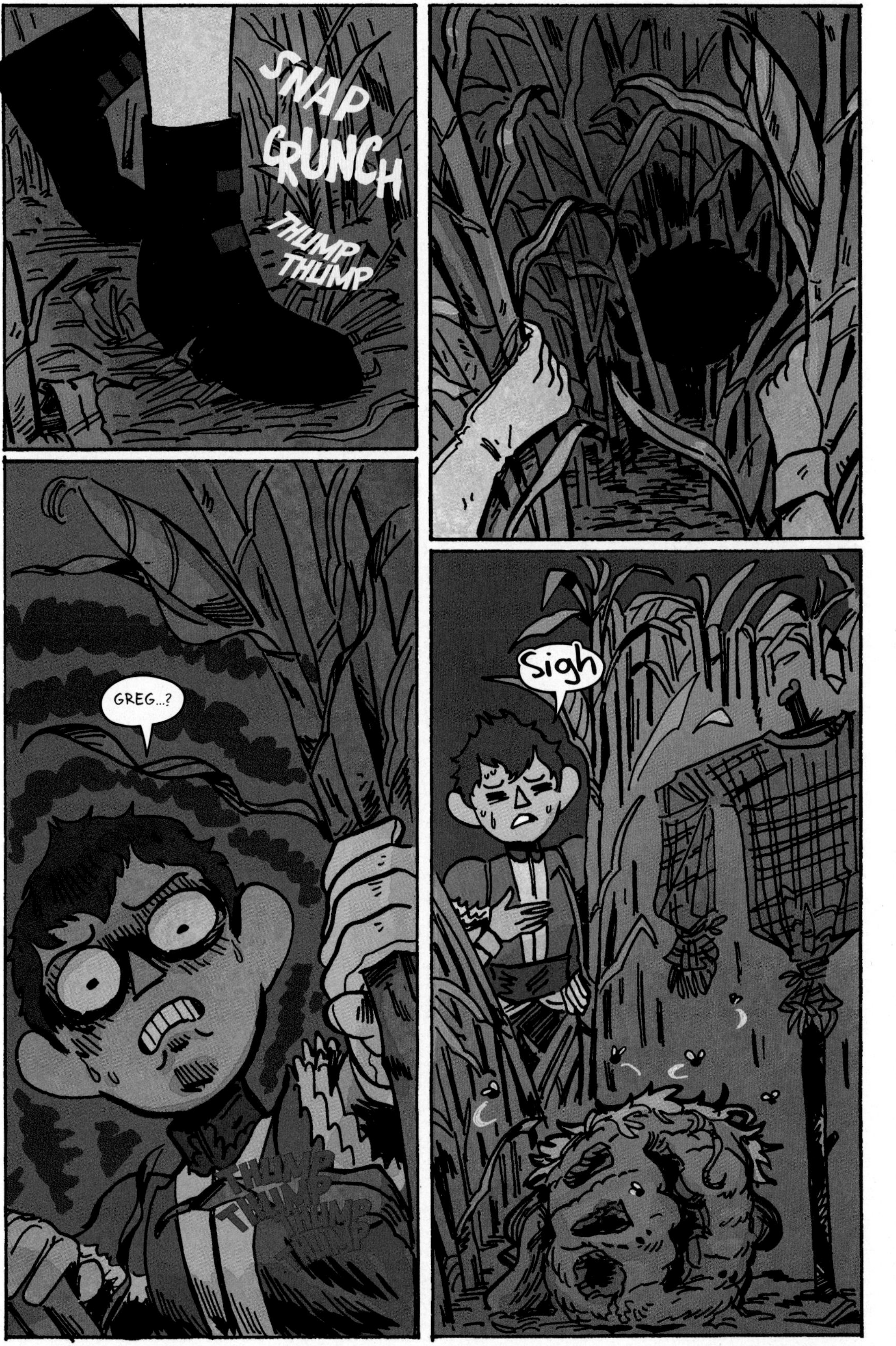
SNAP
CRUNCH
THUMP THUMP
GREG...?
THUMP THUMP THUMP THUMP
Sigh

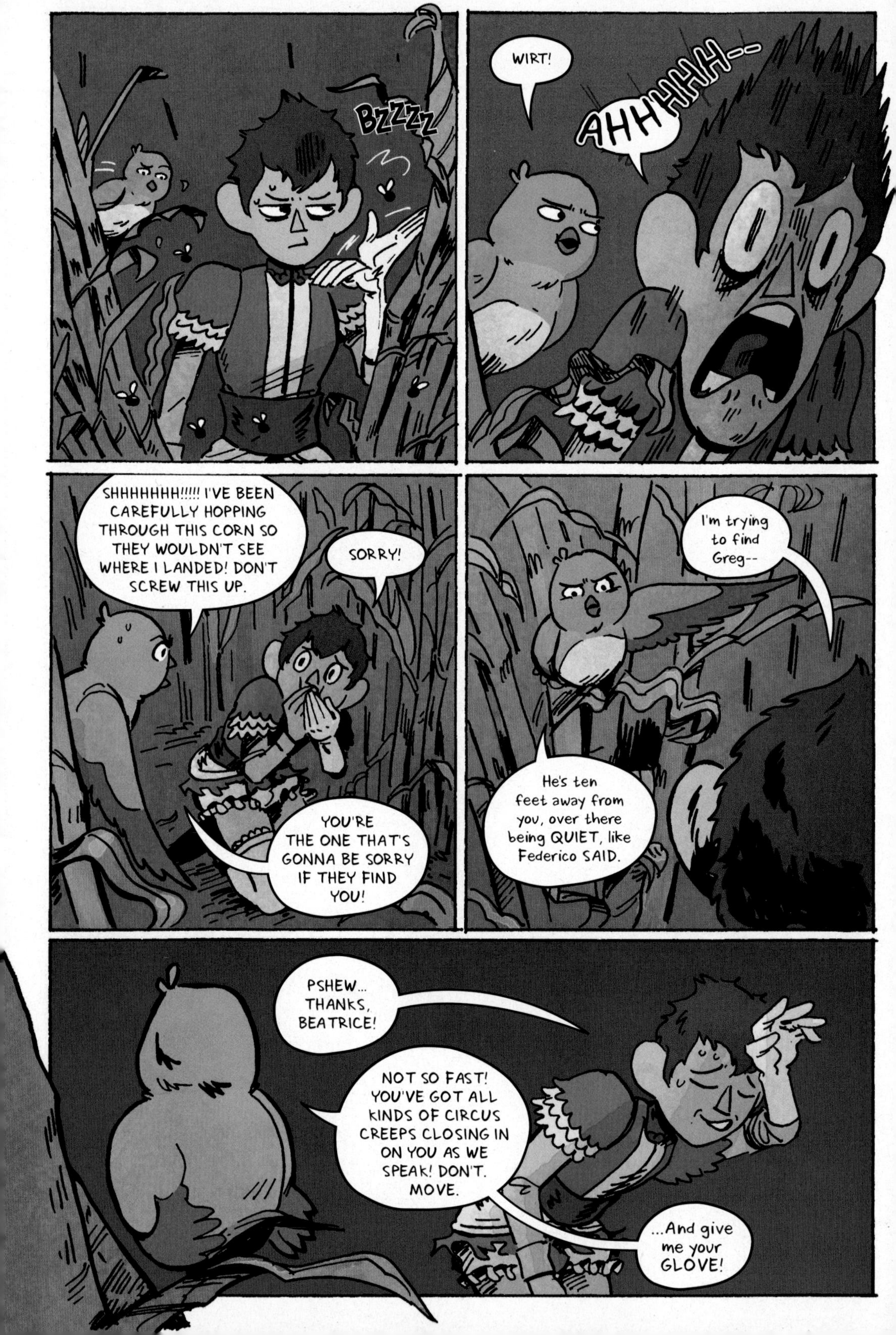
BZZZZ
WIRT!
AHHHHHH--
SHHHHHHH!!!!! I'VE BEEN CAREFULLY HOPPING THROUGH THIS CORN SO THEY WOULDN'T SEE WHERE I LANDED! DON'T SCREW THIS UP.
SORRY!
YOU'RE THE ONE THAT'S GONNA BE SORRY IF THEY FIND YOU!
I'm trying to find Greg--
He's ten feet away from you, over there being QUIET, like Federico SAID.
PSHEW... THANKS, BEATRICE!
NOT SO FAST! YOU'VE GOT ALL KINDS OF CIRCUS CREEPS CLOSING IN ON YOU AS WE SPEAK! DON'T. MOVE.
...And give me your GLOVE!

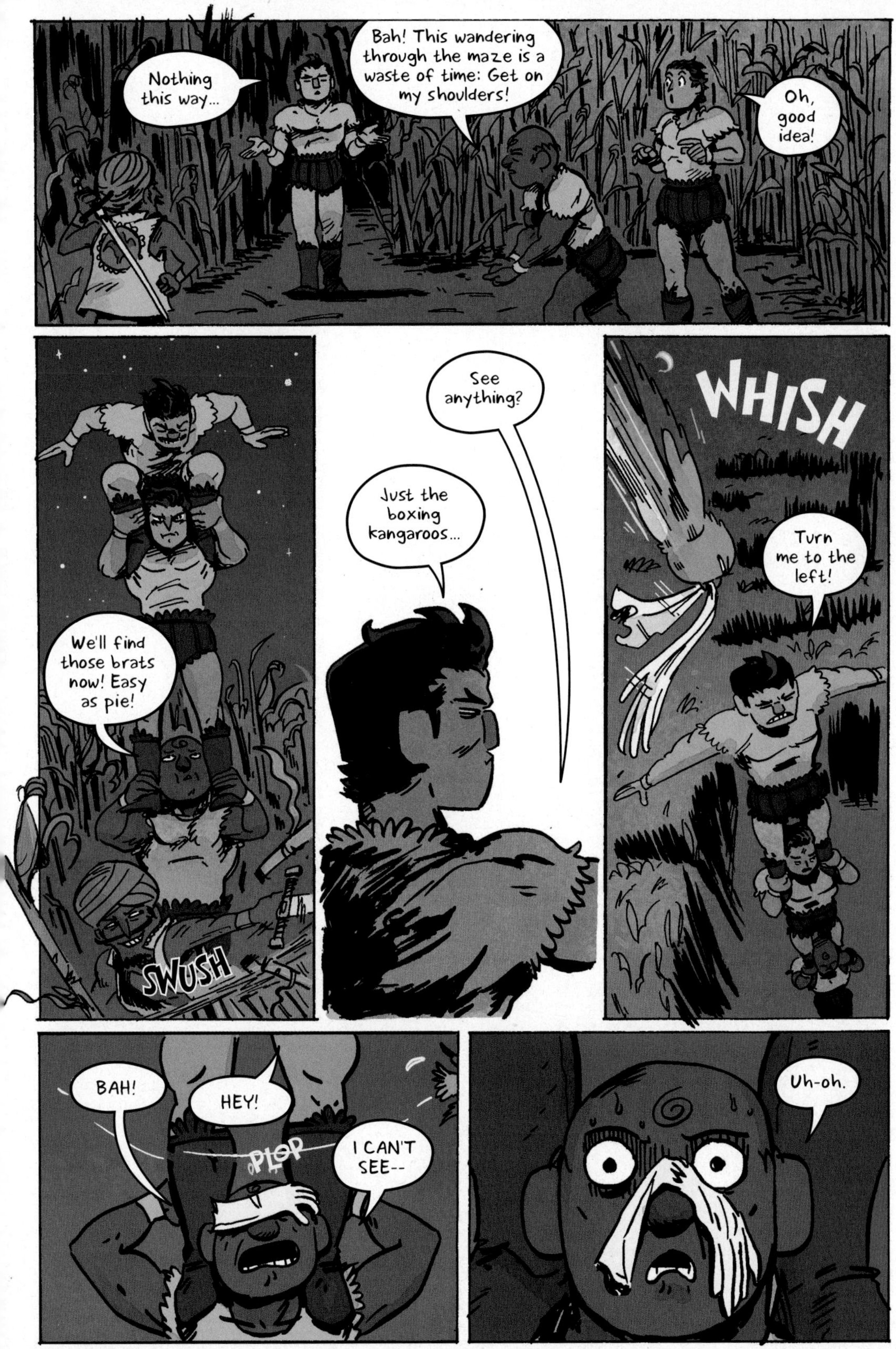

Nothing this way...
Bah! This wandering through the maze is a waste of time: Get on my shoulders!
Oh, good idea!
We'll find those brats now! Easy as pie!
SWUSH
See anything?
Just the boxing kangaroos...
WHISH
Turn me to the left!
BAH!
HEY!
PLOP
I CAN'T SEE--
Uh-oh.

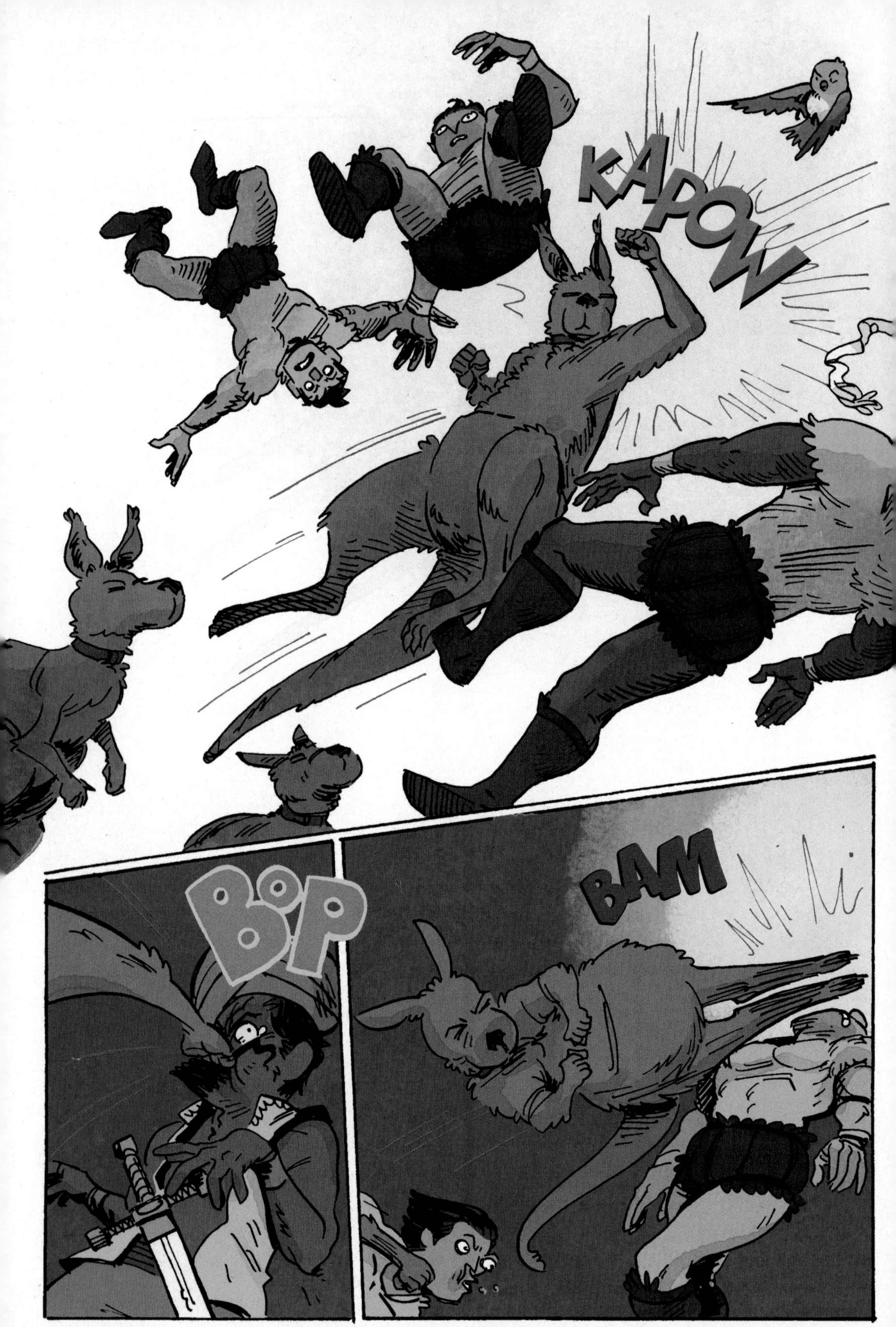
KAPOW
BOP
BAM

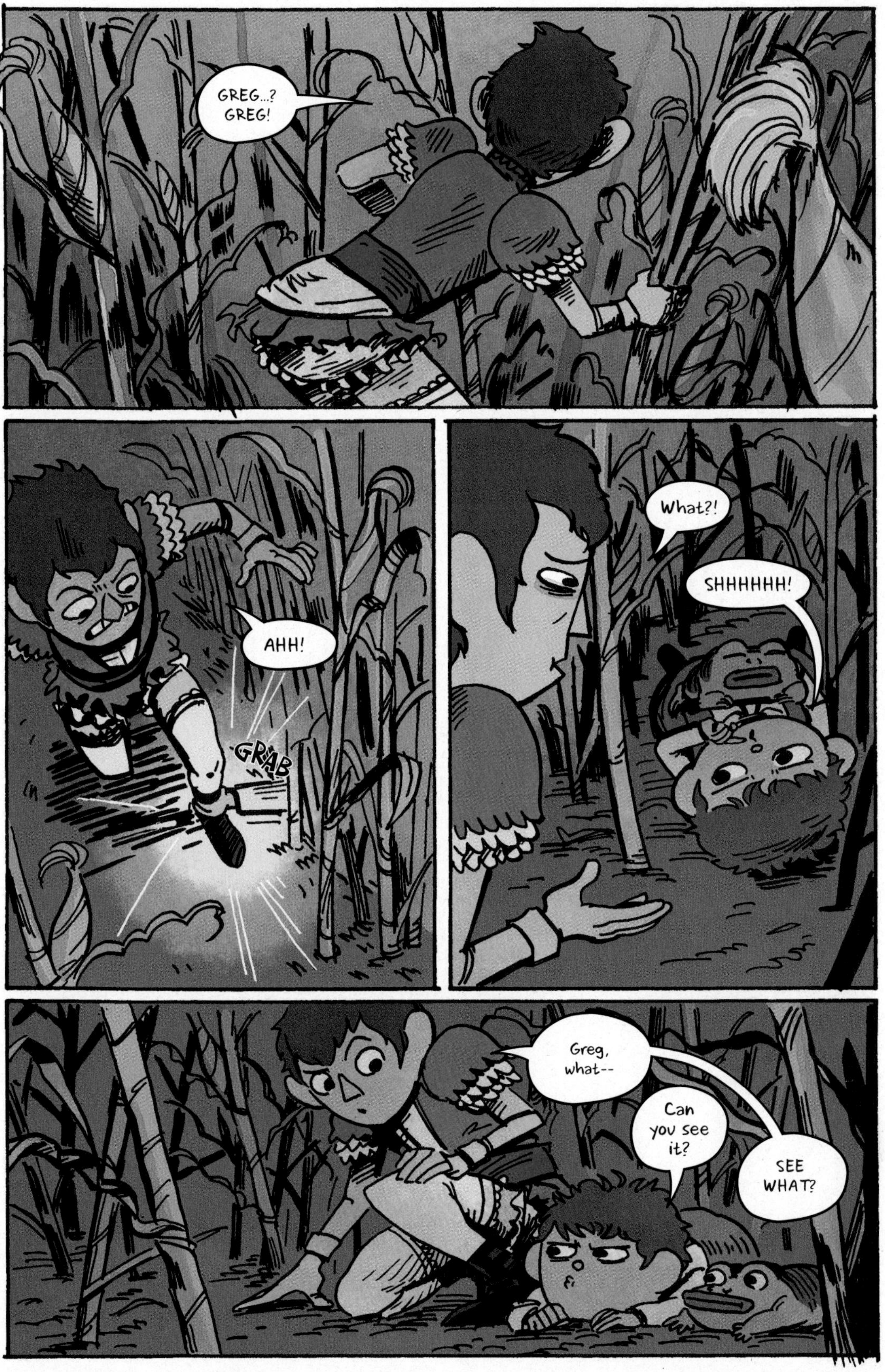
GREG...?
GREG!
AHH!
GRAB
What?!
SHHHHHH!
Greg, what--
Can you see it?
SEE WHAT?

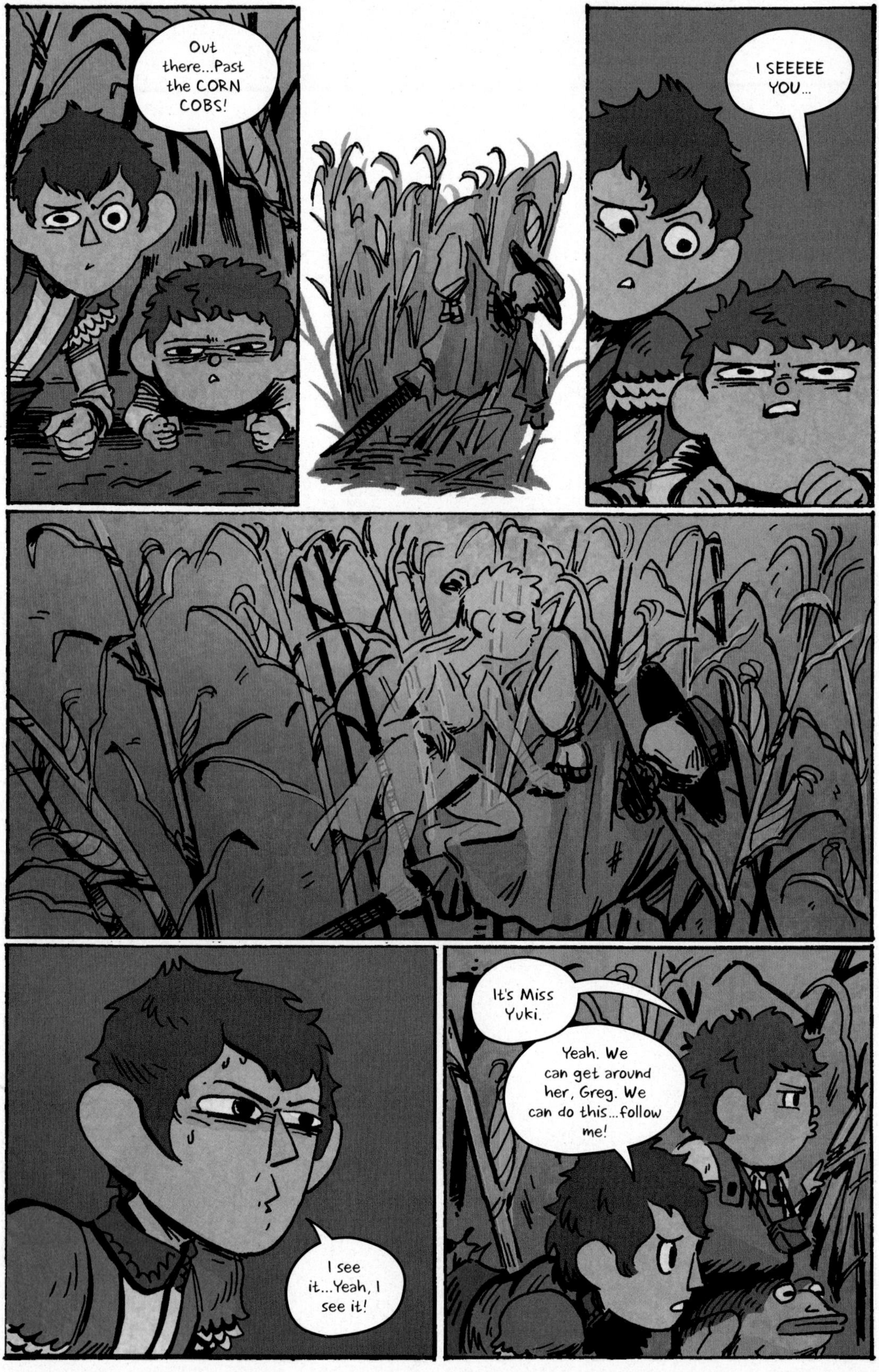
Out there...Past the CORN COBS!
I SEEEEE YOU...
I see it...Yeah, I see it!
It's Miss Yuki.
Yeah. We can get around her, Greg. We can do this...follow me!

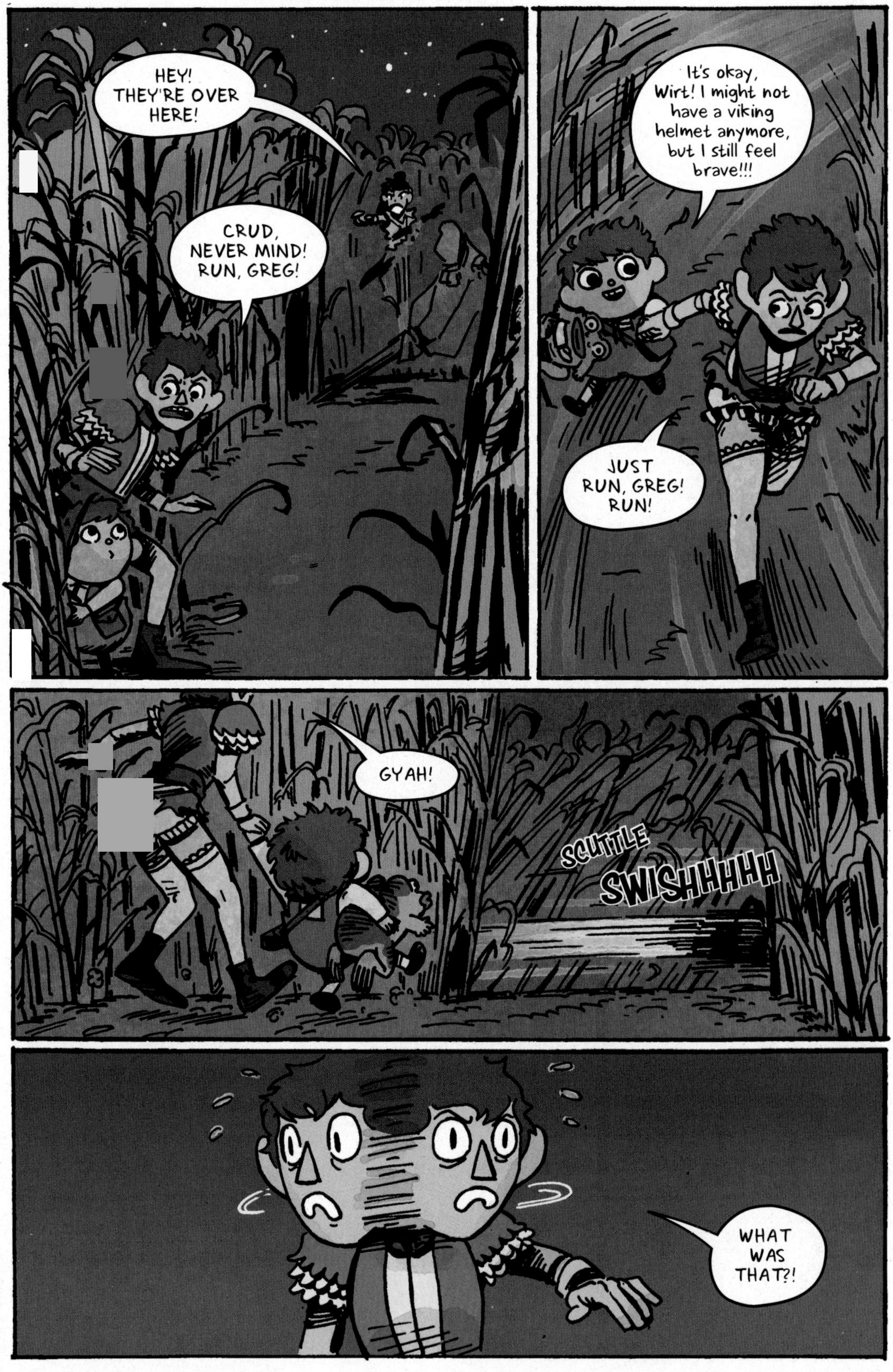
HEY! THEY'RE OVER HERE!
CRUD, NEVER MIND! RUN, GREG!
It's okay, Wirt! I might not have a viking helmet anymore, but I still feel brave!!!
JUST RUN, GREG! RUN!
GYAH!
SCUTTLE
SWISHHHHH
WHAT WAS THAT?!

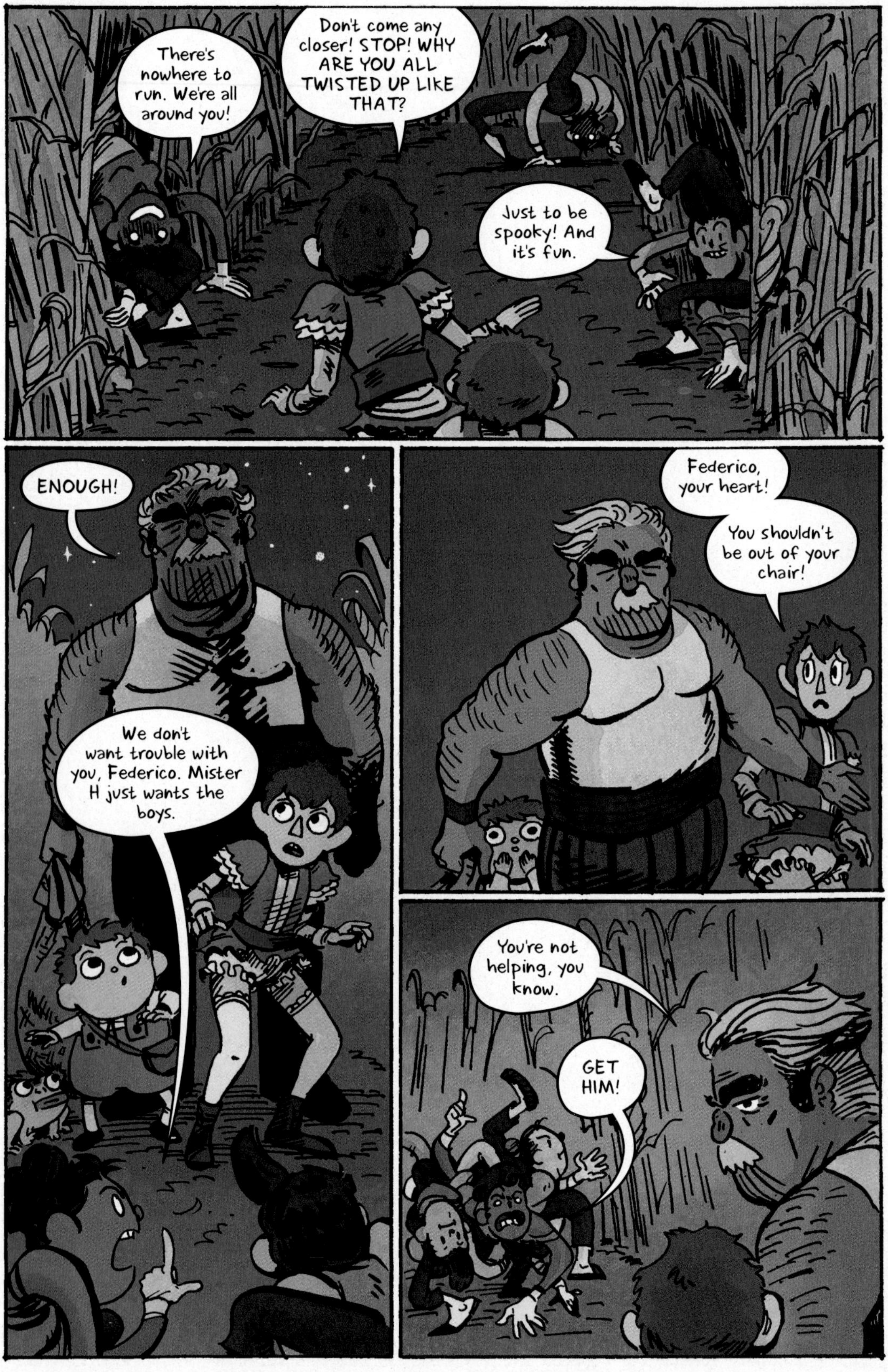
There's nowhere to run. We're all around you!
Don't come any closer! STOP! WHY ARE YOU ALL TWISTED UP LIKE THAT?
Just to be spooky! And it's fun.
ENOUGH!
We don't want trouble with you, Federico. Mister H just wants the boys.
Federico, your heart!
You shouldn't be out of your chair!
You're not helping, you know.
GET HIM!

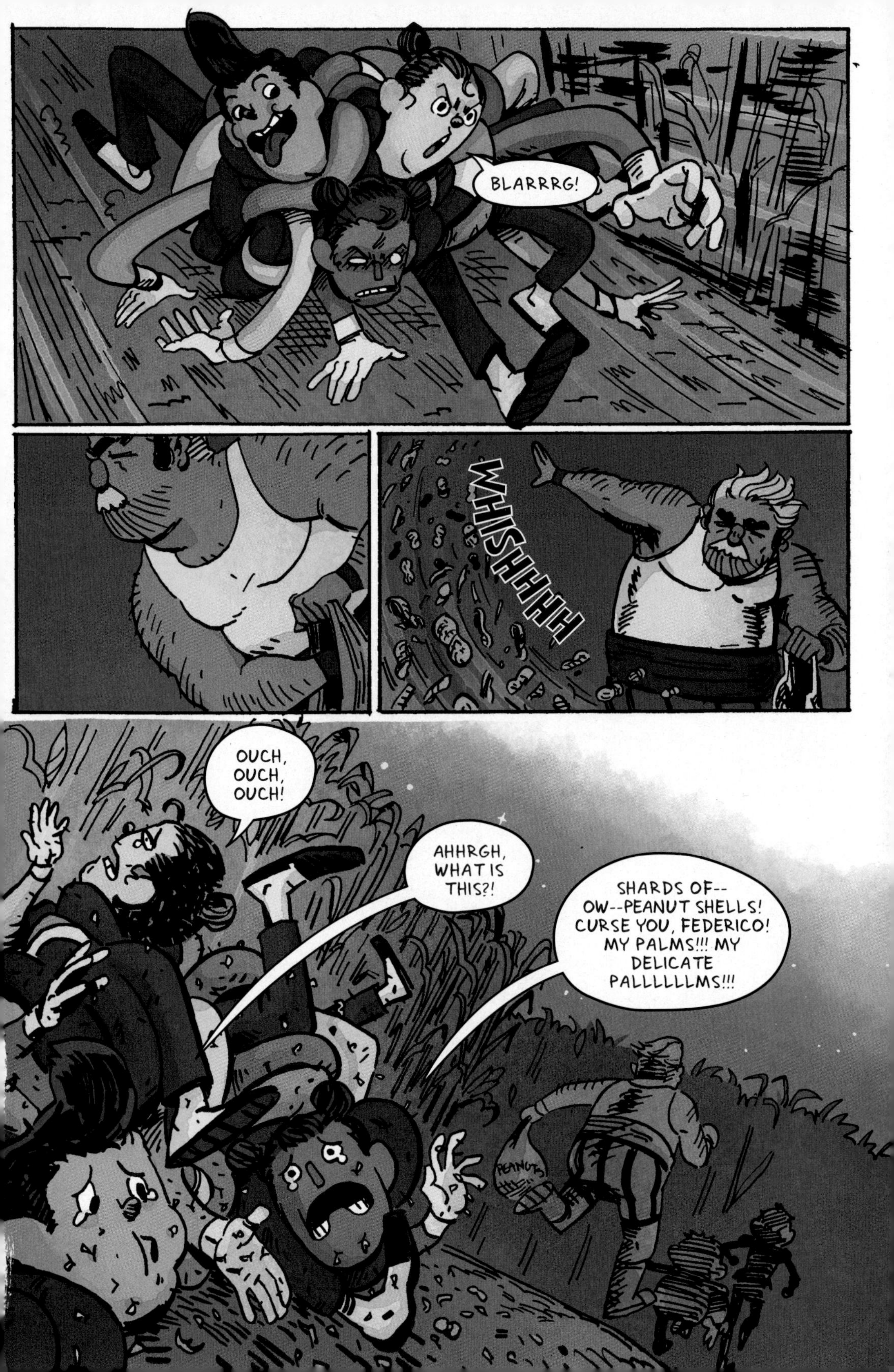
BLARRRG!
WHISHHHH
OUCH, OUCH, OUCH!
AHHRGH, WHAT IS THIS?!
SHARDS OF-- OW--PEANUT SHELLS! CURSE YOU, FEDERICO! MY PALMS!!! MY DELICATE PALLLLLLMS!!!
PEANUTS

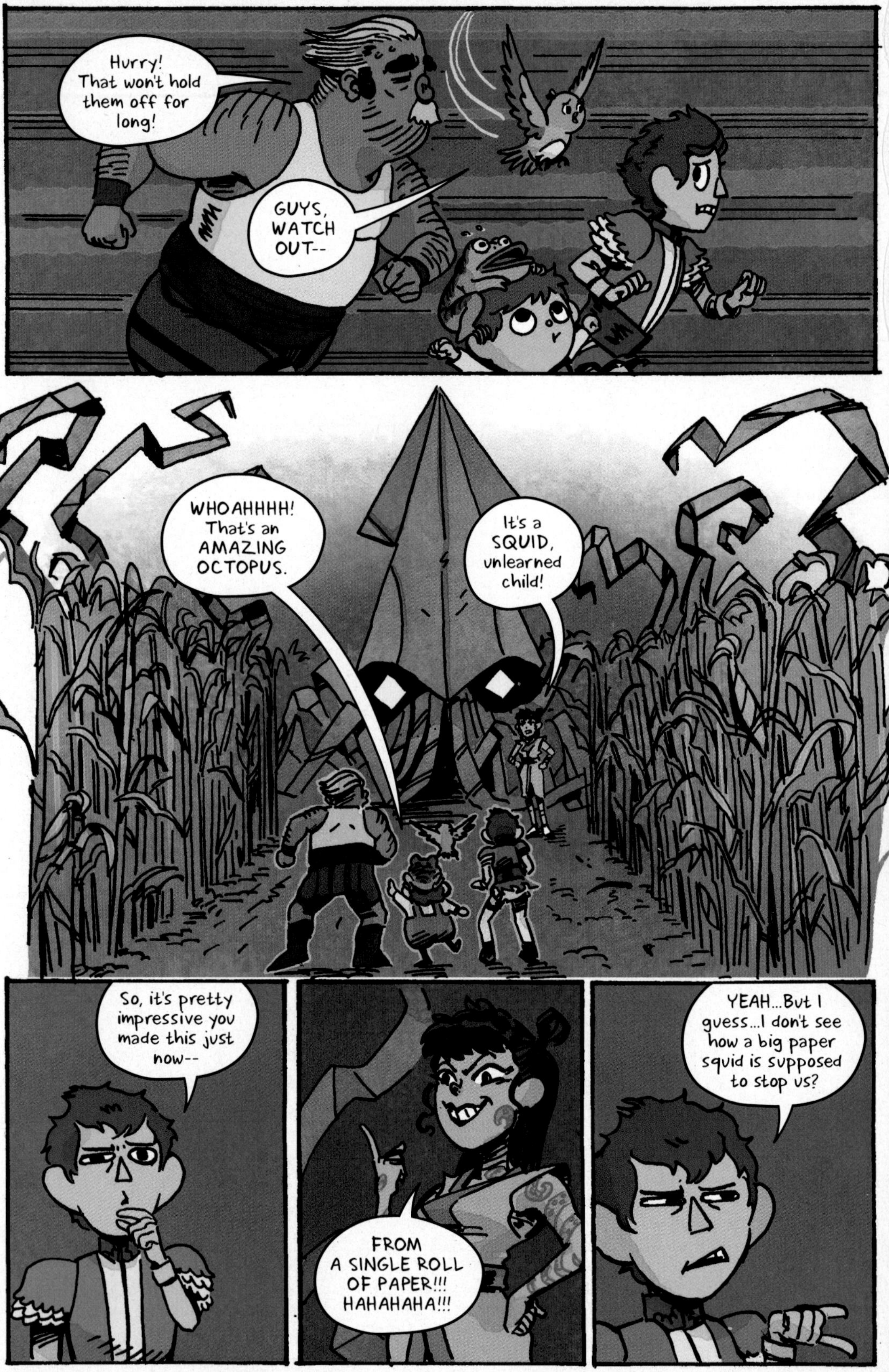
Hurry! That won't hold them off for long!
GUYS, WATCH OUT--
WHOAHHHH! That's an AMAZING OCTOPUS.
It's a SQUID, unlearned child!
So, it's pretty impressive you made this just now--
FROM A SINGLE ROLL OF PAPER!!! HAHAHAHA!!!
YEAH...But I guess...I don't see how a big paper squid is supposed to stop us?

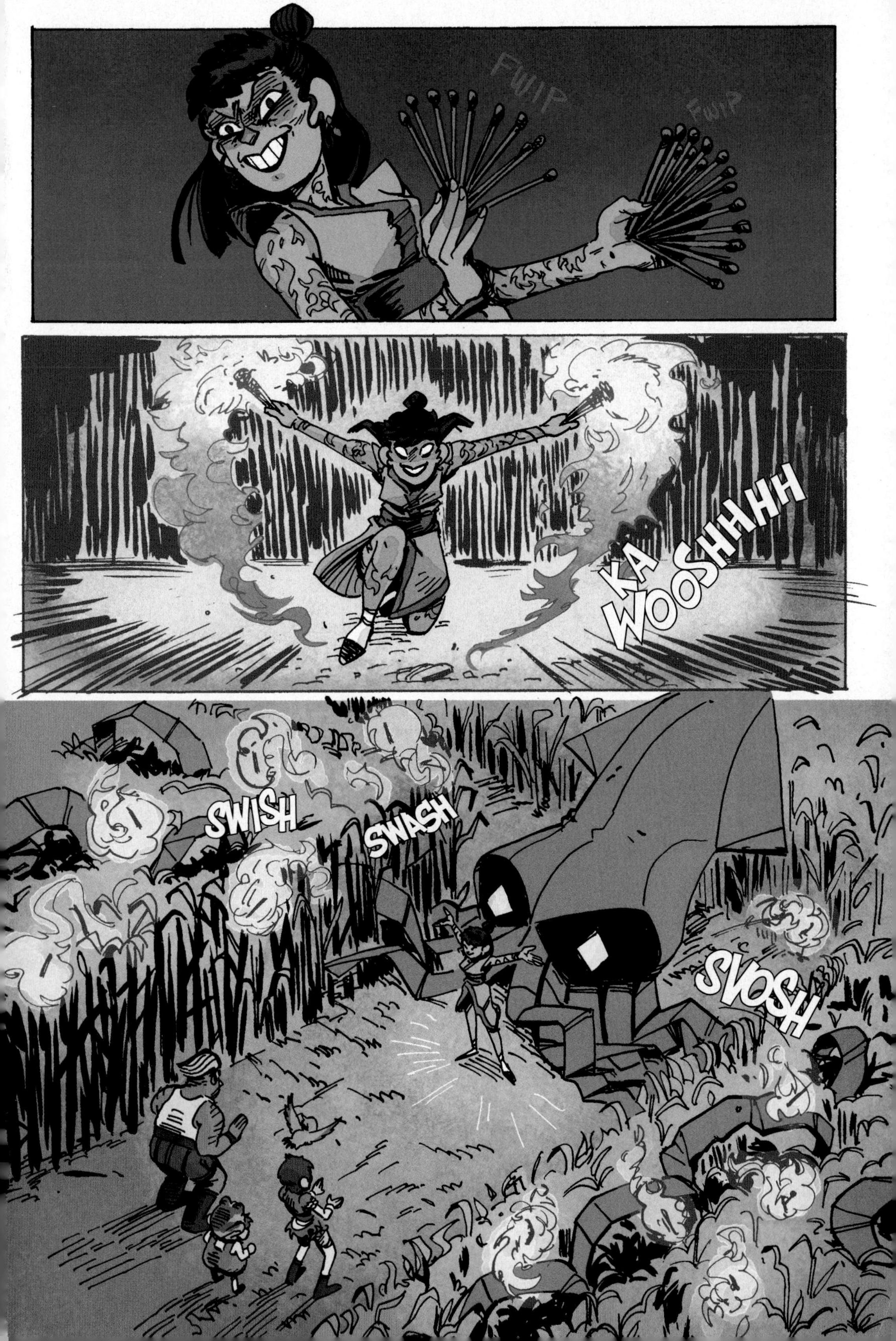
FWIP
FWIP
KA WOOSHHHH
SWISH
SWASH
SVOSH

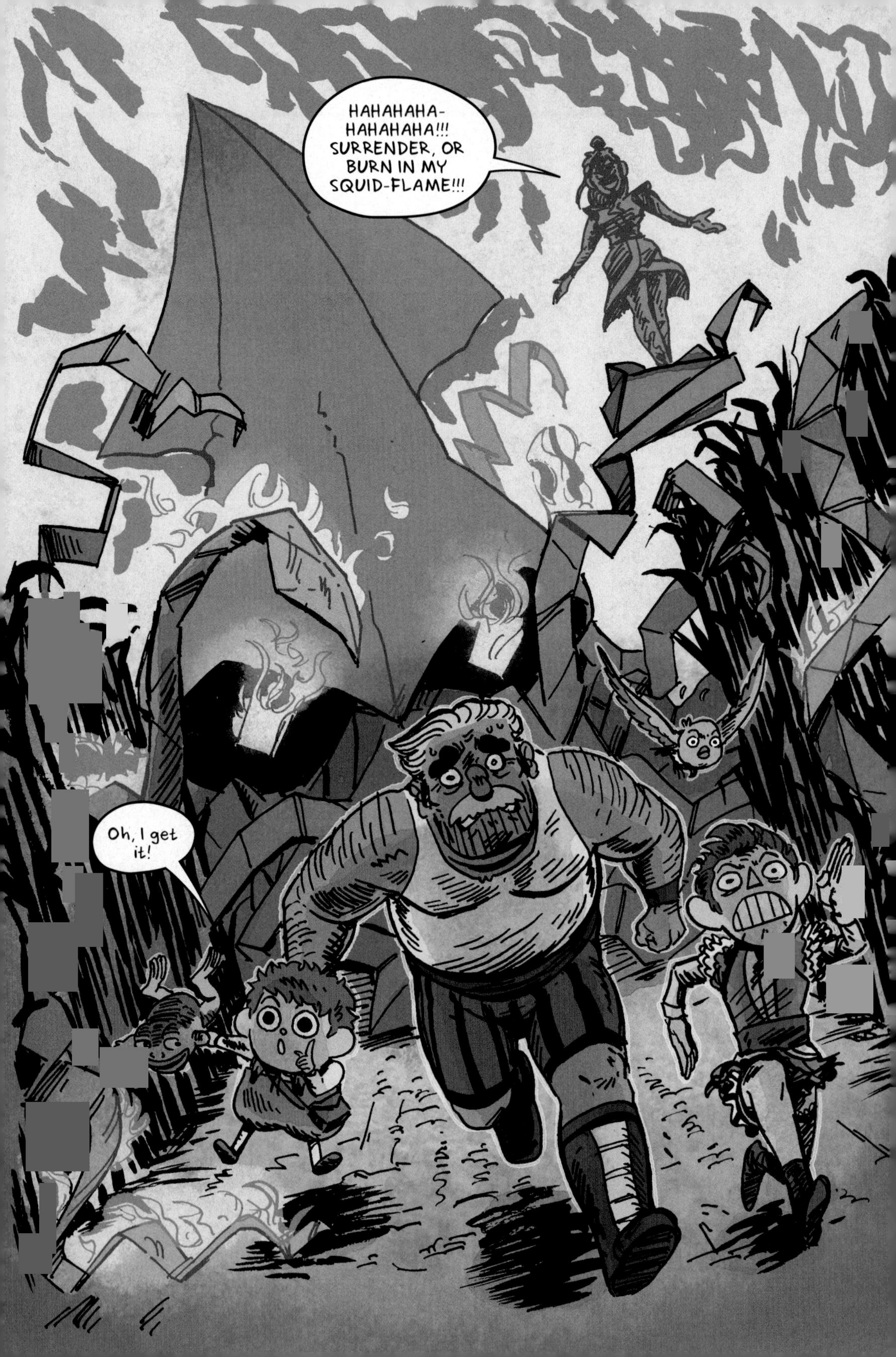
HAHAHAHA-
HAHAHAHA!!!
SURRENDER, OR
BURN IN MY
SQUID-FLAME!!!
Oh, I get it!

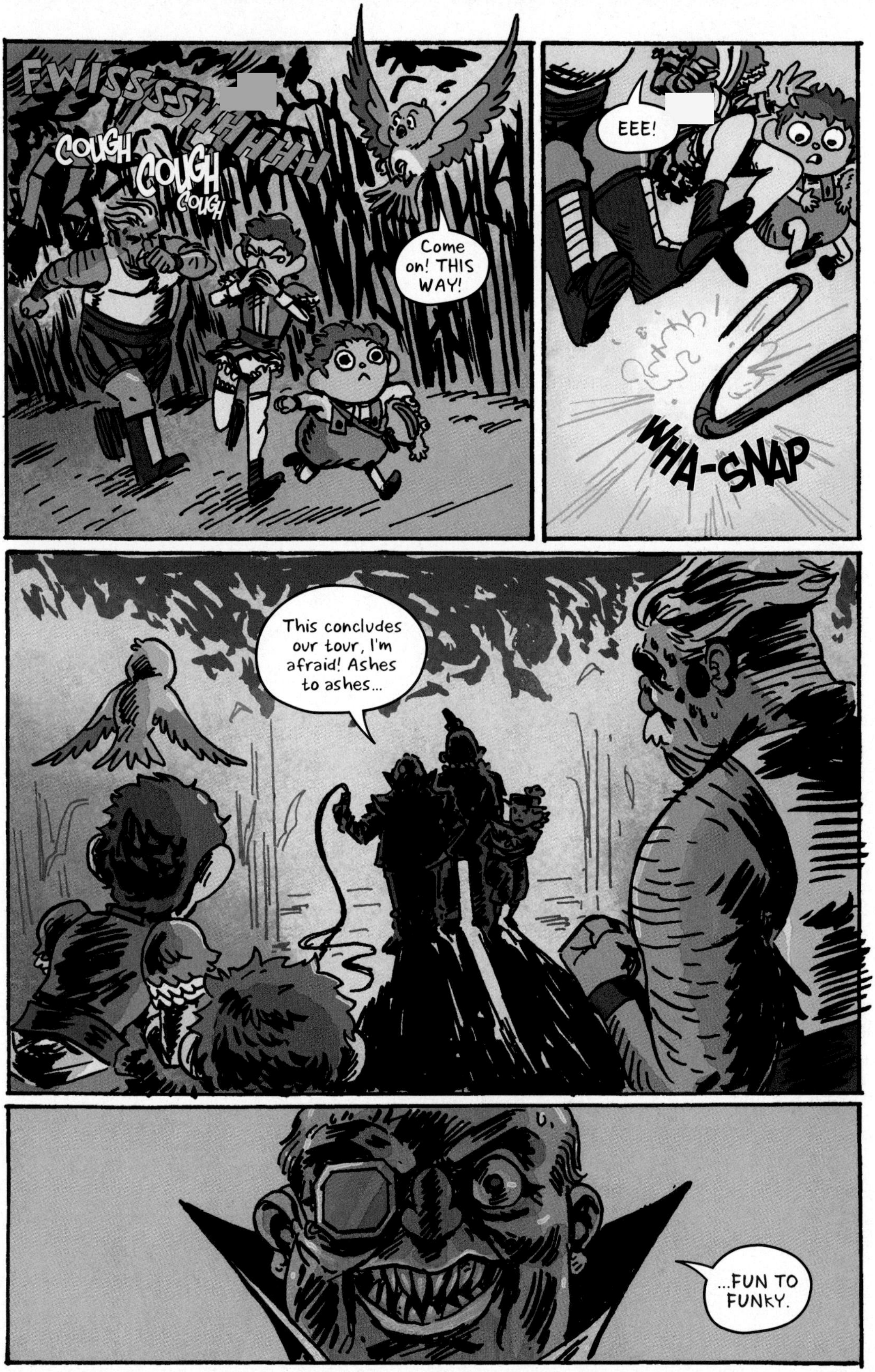
FWISSSSHHHHH
COUGH
COUGH
COUGH
Come on! THIS WAY!
EEE!
WHA-SNAP
This concludes our tour, I'm afraid! Ashes to ashes...
...FUN TO FUNKY.

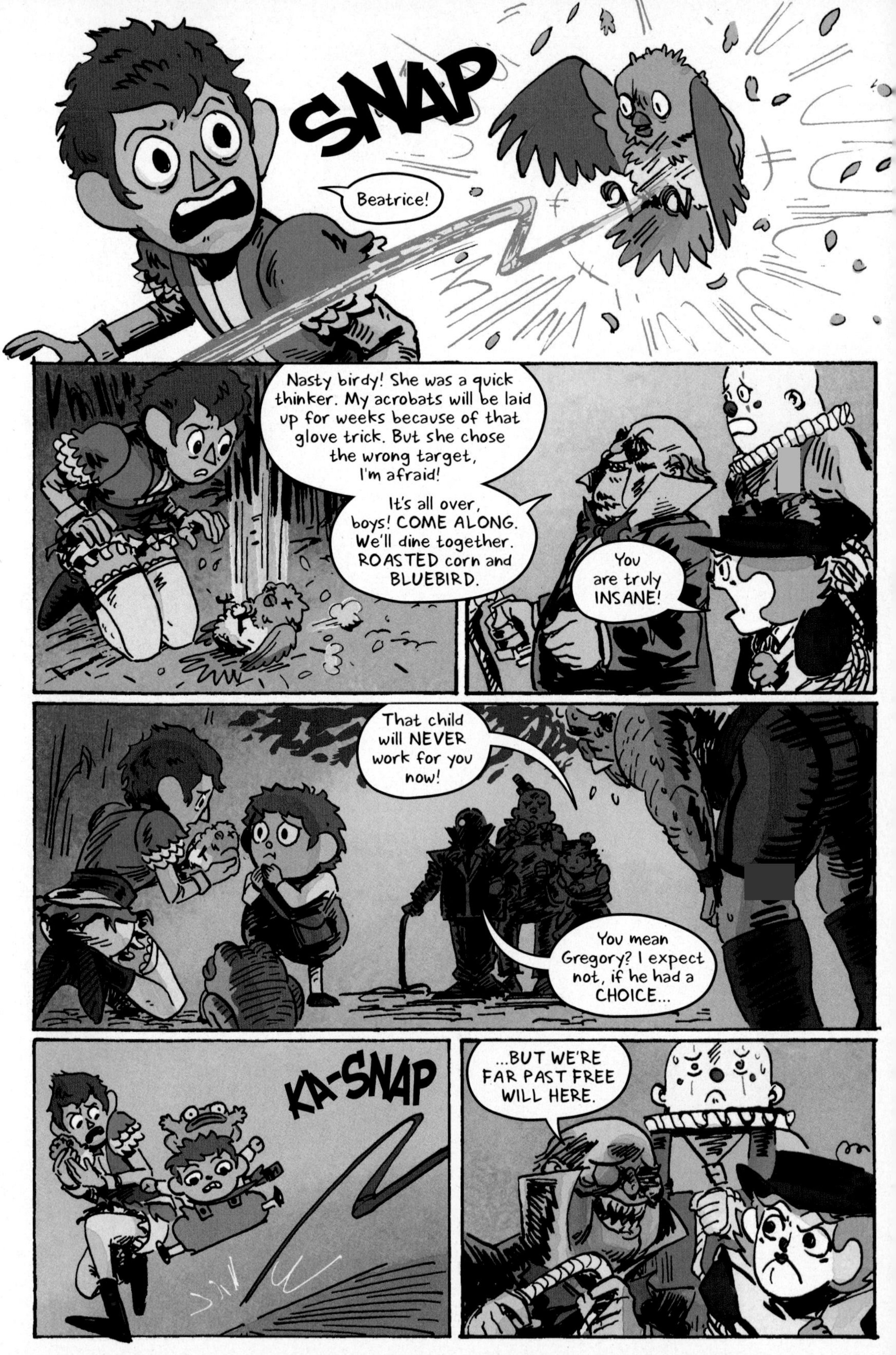
SNAP
Beatrice!
Nasty birdy! She was a quick thinker. My acrobats will be laid up for weeks because of that glove trick. But she chose the wrong target, I'm afraid!
It's all over, boys! COME ALONG. We'll dine together. ROASTED corn and BLUEBIRD.
You are truly INSANE!
That child will NEVER work for you now!
You mean Gregory? I expect not, if he had a CHOICE...
KA-SNAP
...BUT WE'RE FAR PAST FREE WILL HERE.

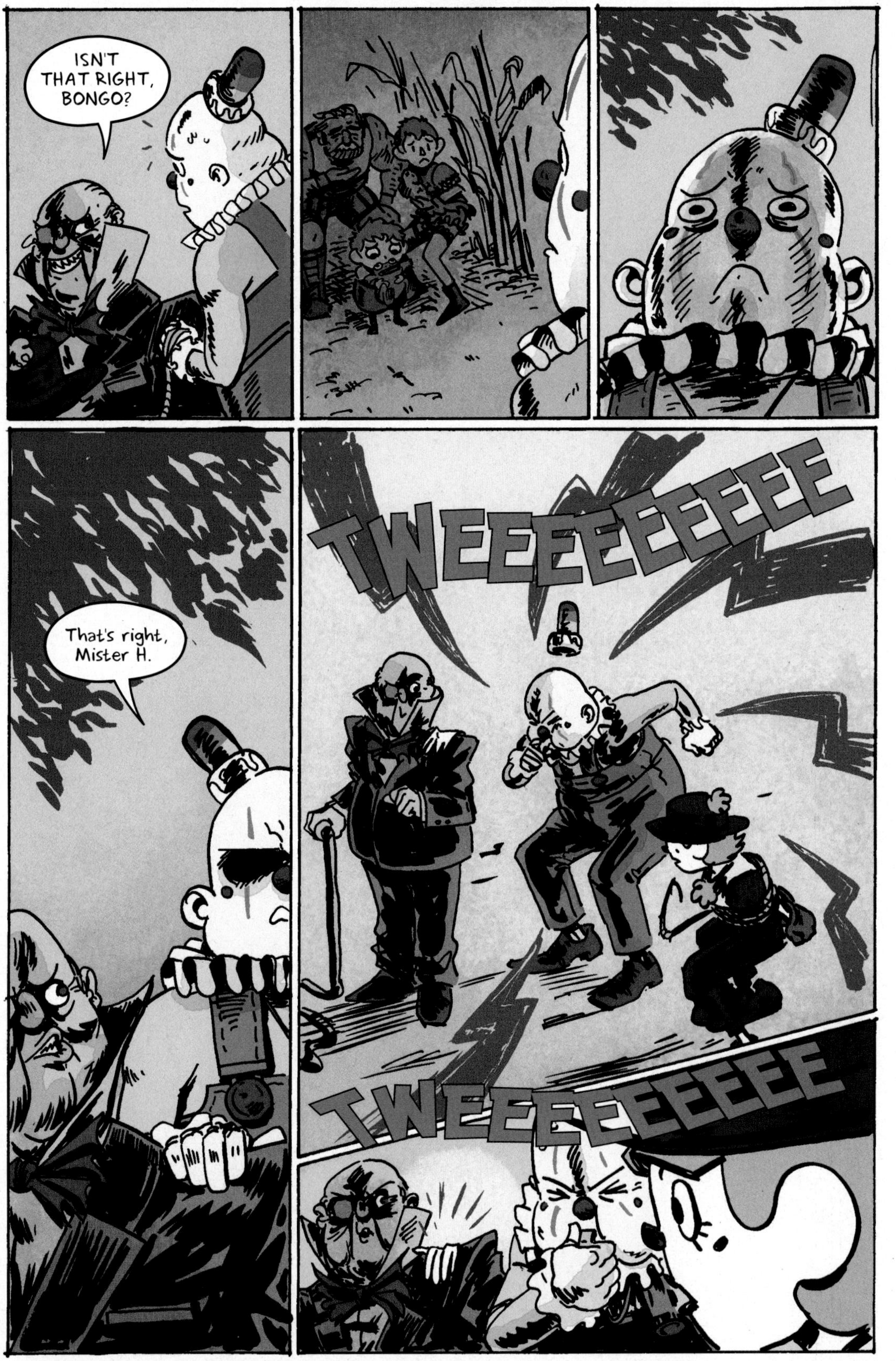
ISN'T THAT RIGHT, BONGO?
That's right, Mister H.
TWEEEEEEEEE
TWEEEEEEEEE

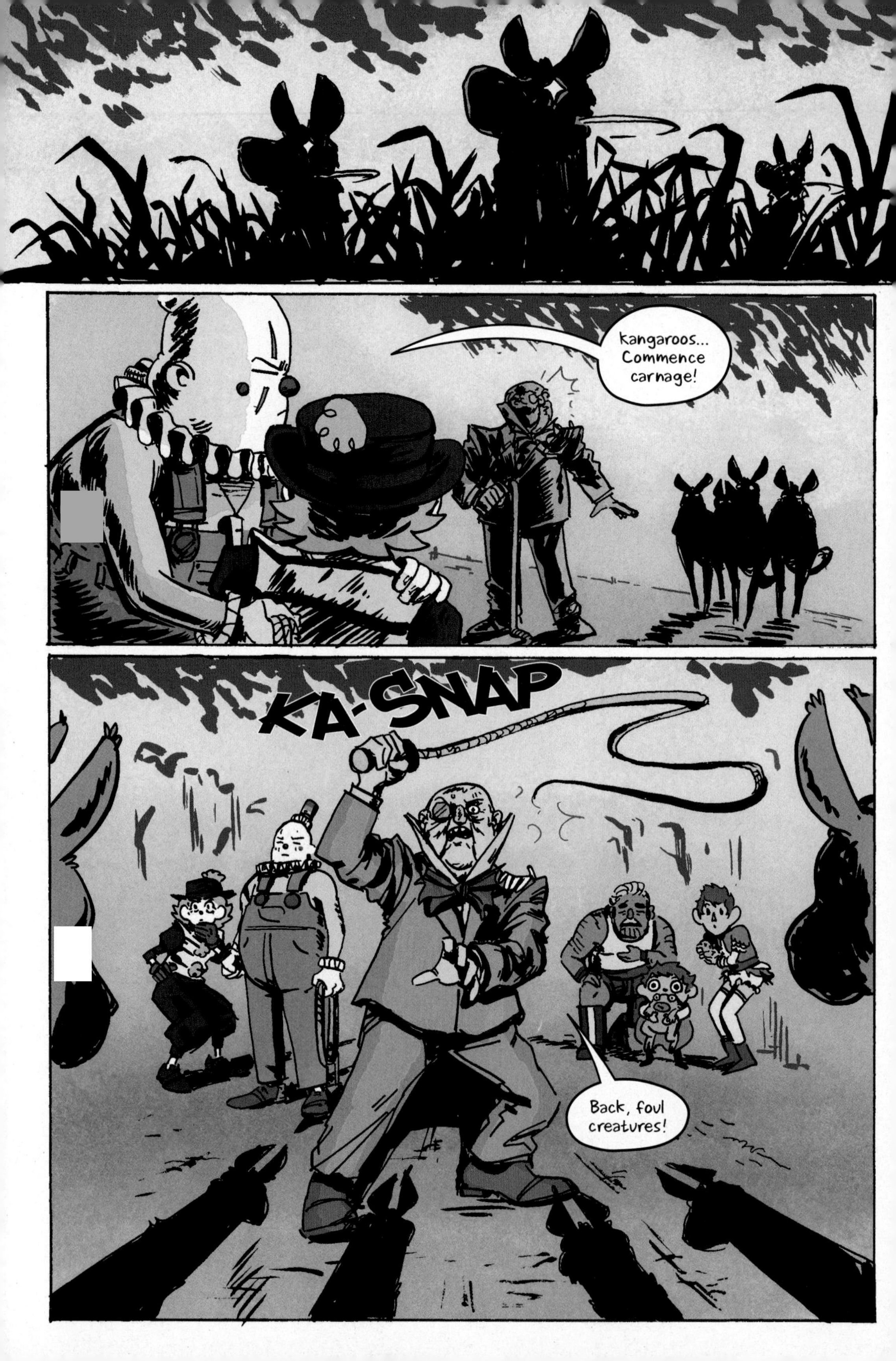
Kangaroos... Commence carnage!
KA-SNAP
Back, foul creatures!

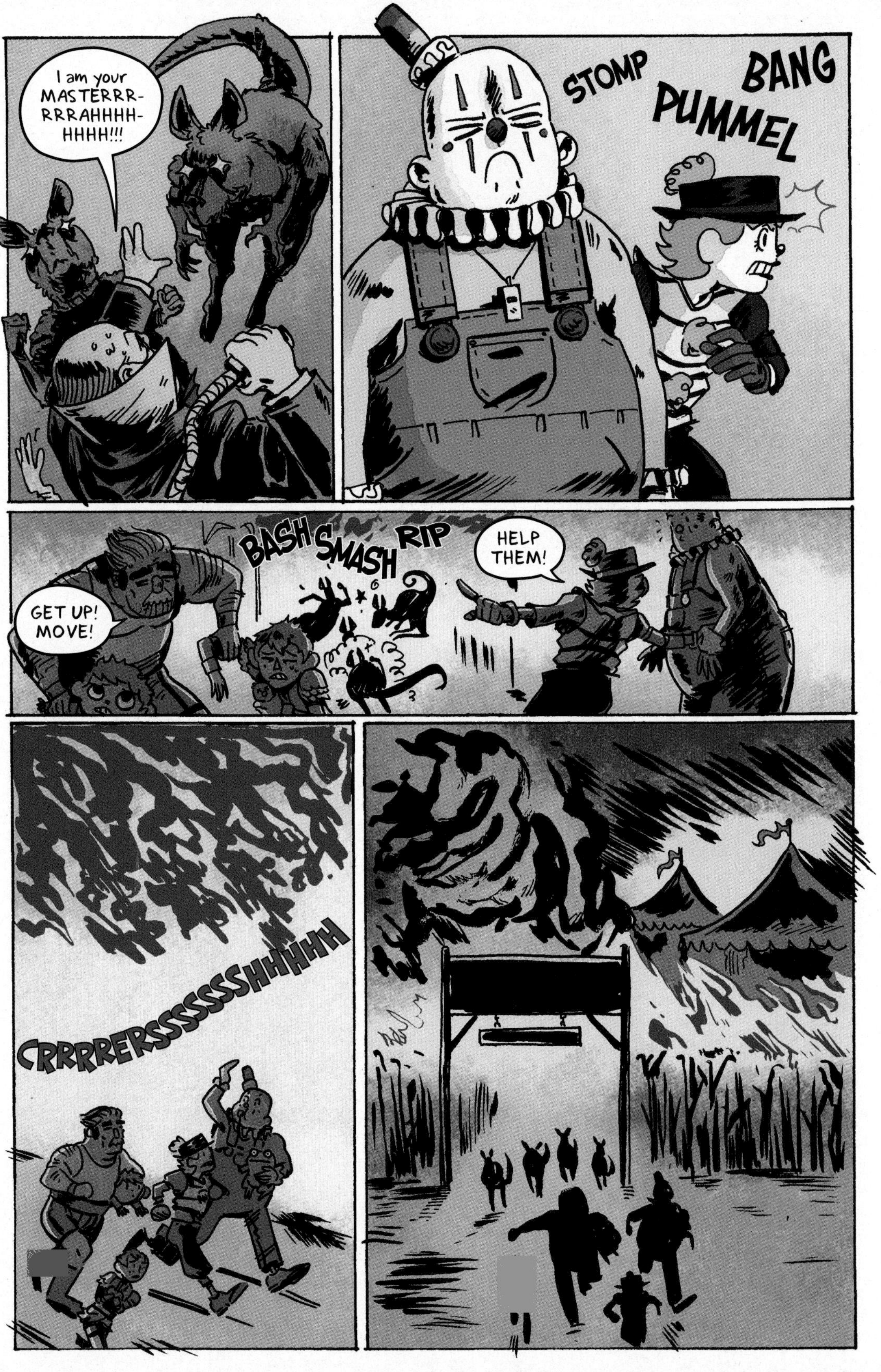
I am your MASTERRRR-RRRAHHHH-HHHH!!!
STOMP
BANG
PUMMEL
GET UP! MOVE!
BASH
SMASH
RIP
HELP THEM!
CRRRRERSSSSSSSHHHHHH

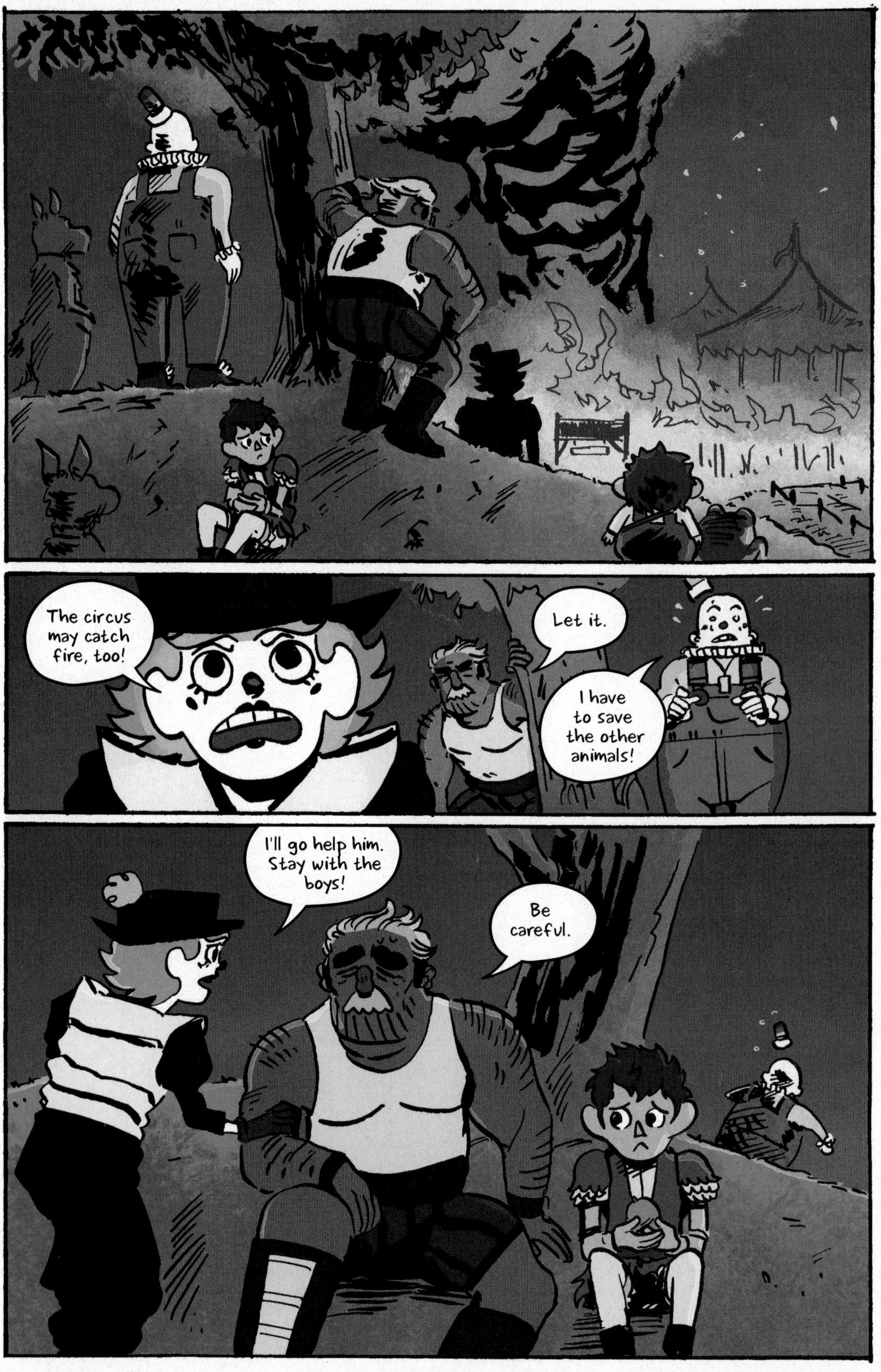
The circus may catch fire, too!
Let it.
I have to save the other animals!
I'll go help him. Stay with the boys!
Be careful.

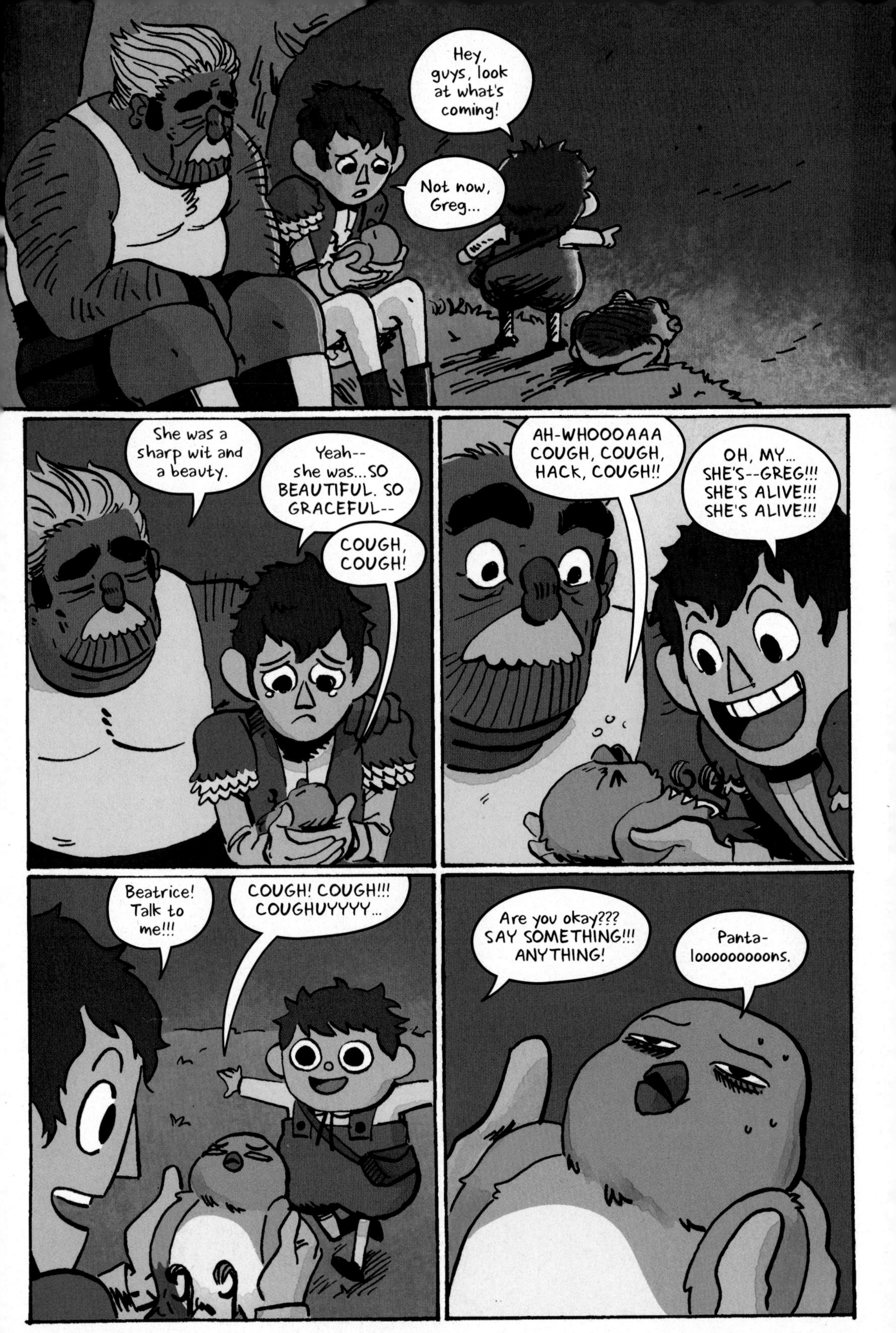
Hey, guys, look at what's coming!
Not now, Greg...
She was a sharp wit and a beauty.
Yeah-- she was...SO BEAUTIFUL. SO GRACEFUL--
COUGH, COUGH!
AH-WHOOOAAA COUGH, COUGH, HACK, COUGH!!
OH, MY... SHE'S--GREG!!! SHE'S ALIVE!!! SHE'S ALIVE!!!
Beatrice! Talk to me!!!
COUGH! COUGH!!! COUGHUYYYY...
Are you okay??? SAY SOMETHING!!! ANYTHING!
Panta-looooooooons.

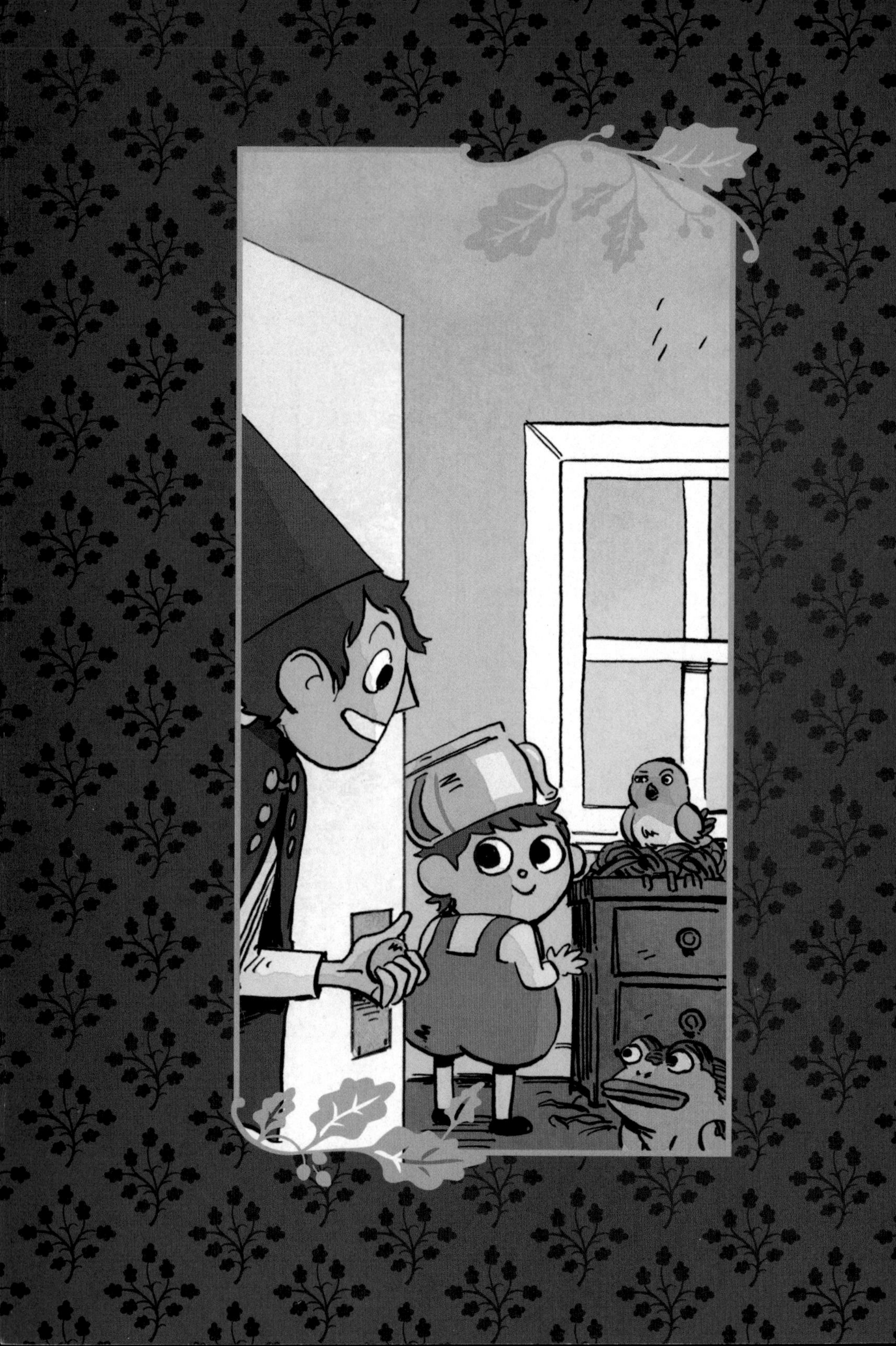

EPILOGUE

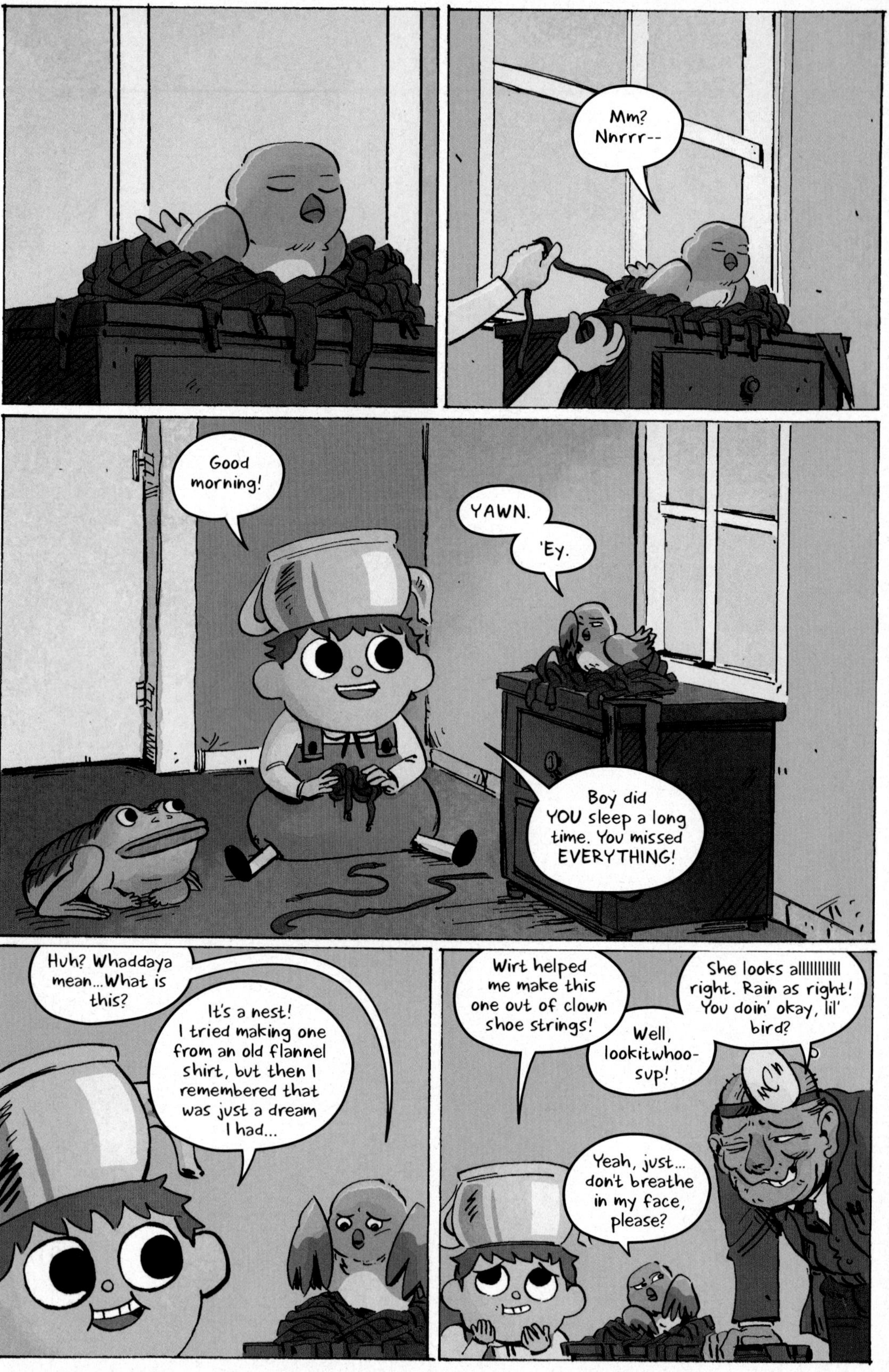
Mm? Nnrrr--
Good morning!
YAWN.
'Ey.
Boy did YOU sleep a long time. You missed EVERYTHING!
Huh? Whaddaya mean...What is this?
It's a nest! I tried making one from an old flannel shirt, but then I remembered that was just a dream I had...
Wirt helped me make this one out of clown shoe strings!
She looks allllllllll right. Rain as right! You doin' okay, lil' bird?
Well, lookitwhoo-sup!
Yeah, just... don't breathe in my face, please?

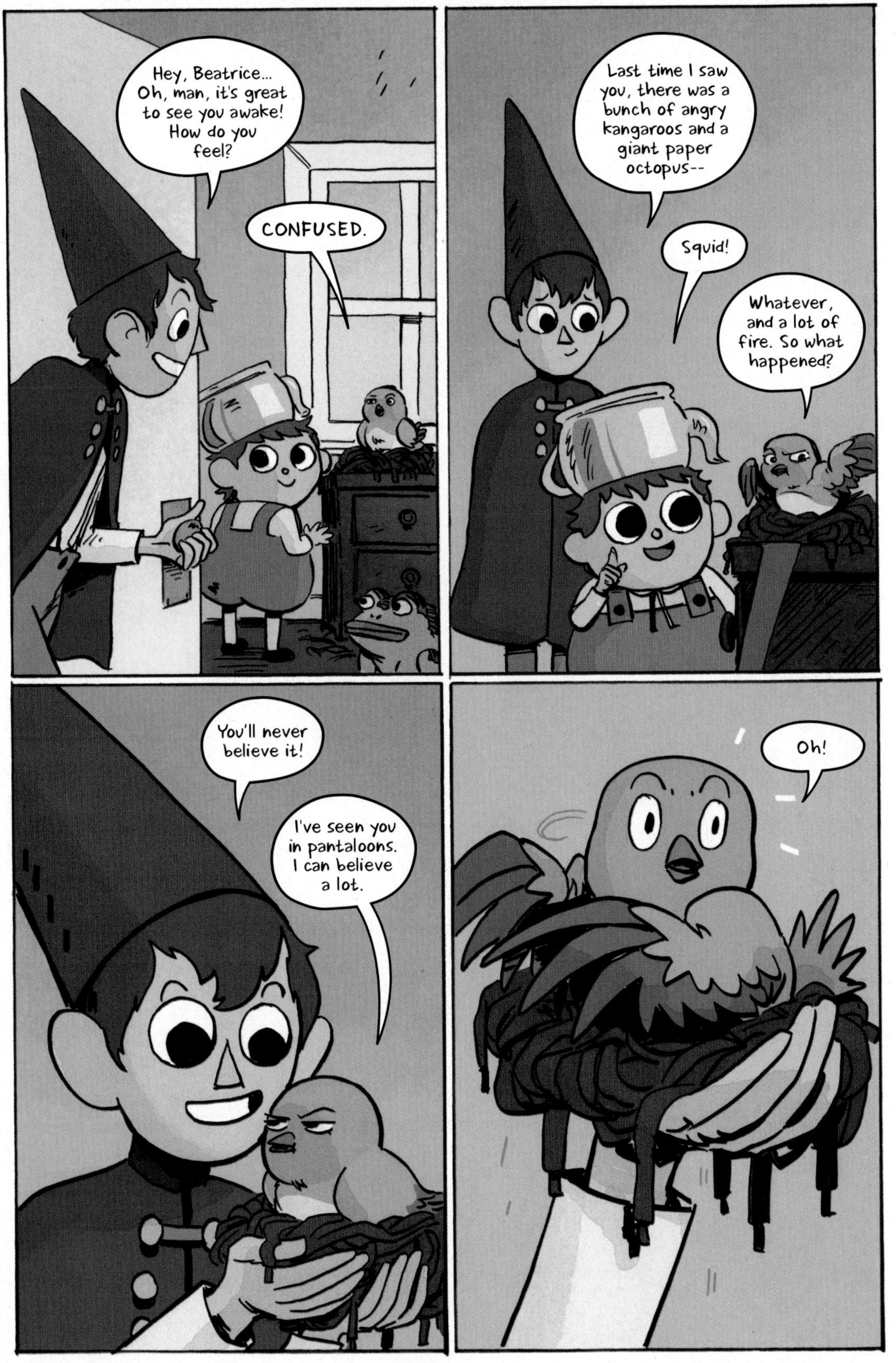
Hey, Beatrice... Oh, man, it's great to see you awake! How do you feel?
CONFUSED.
Last time I saw you, there was a bunch of angry kangaroos and a giant paper octopus--
Squid!
Whatever, and a lot of fire. So what happened?
You'll never believe it!
I've seen you in pantaloons. I can believe a lot.
Oh!

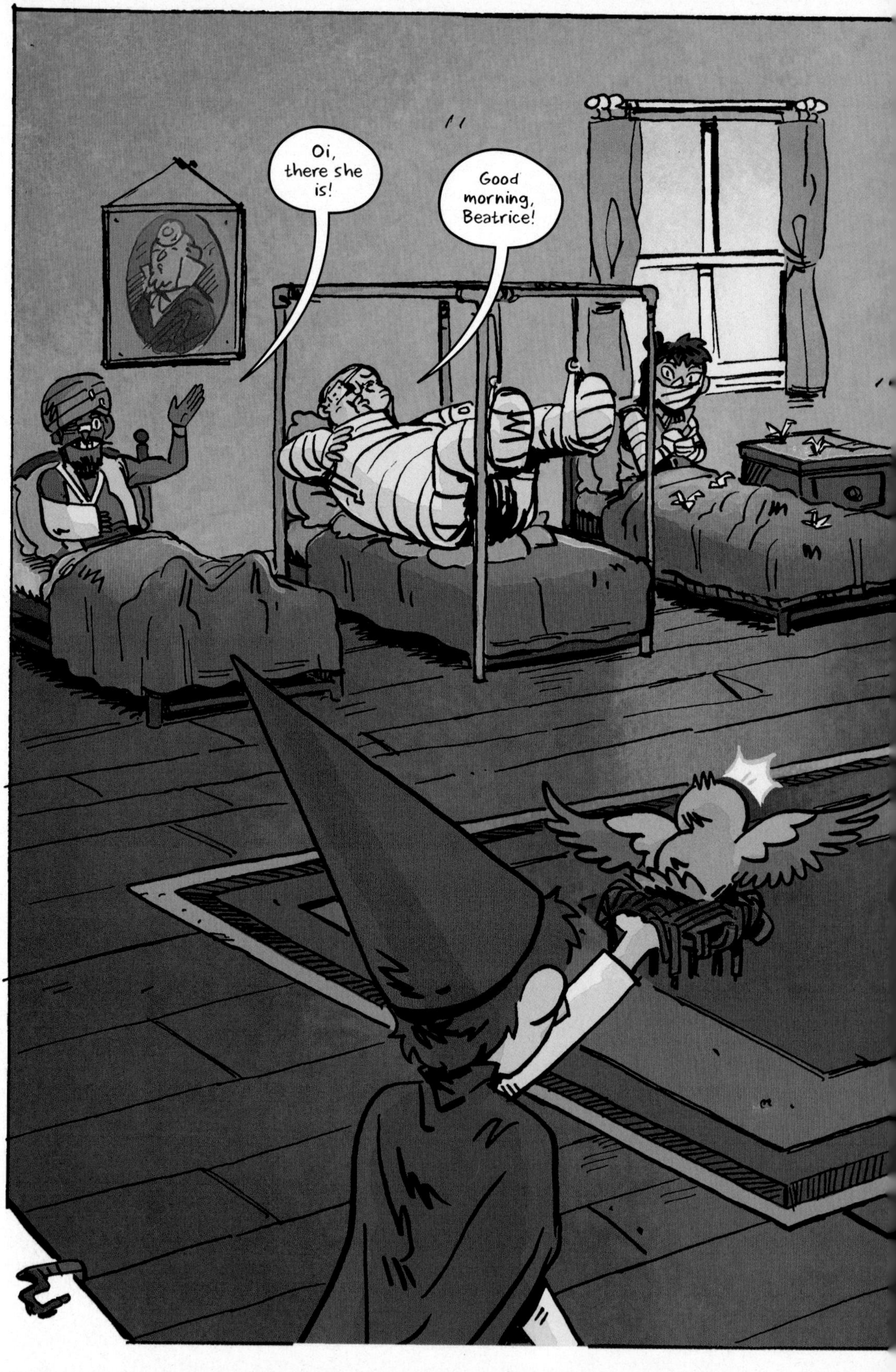
Oi, there she is!
Good morning, Beatrice!

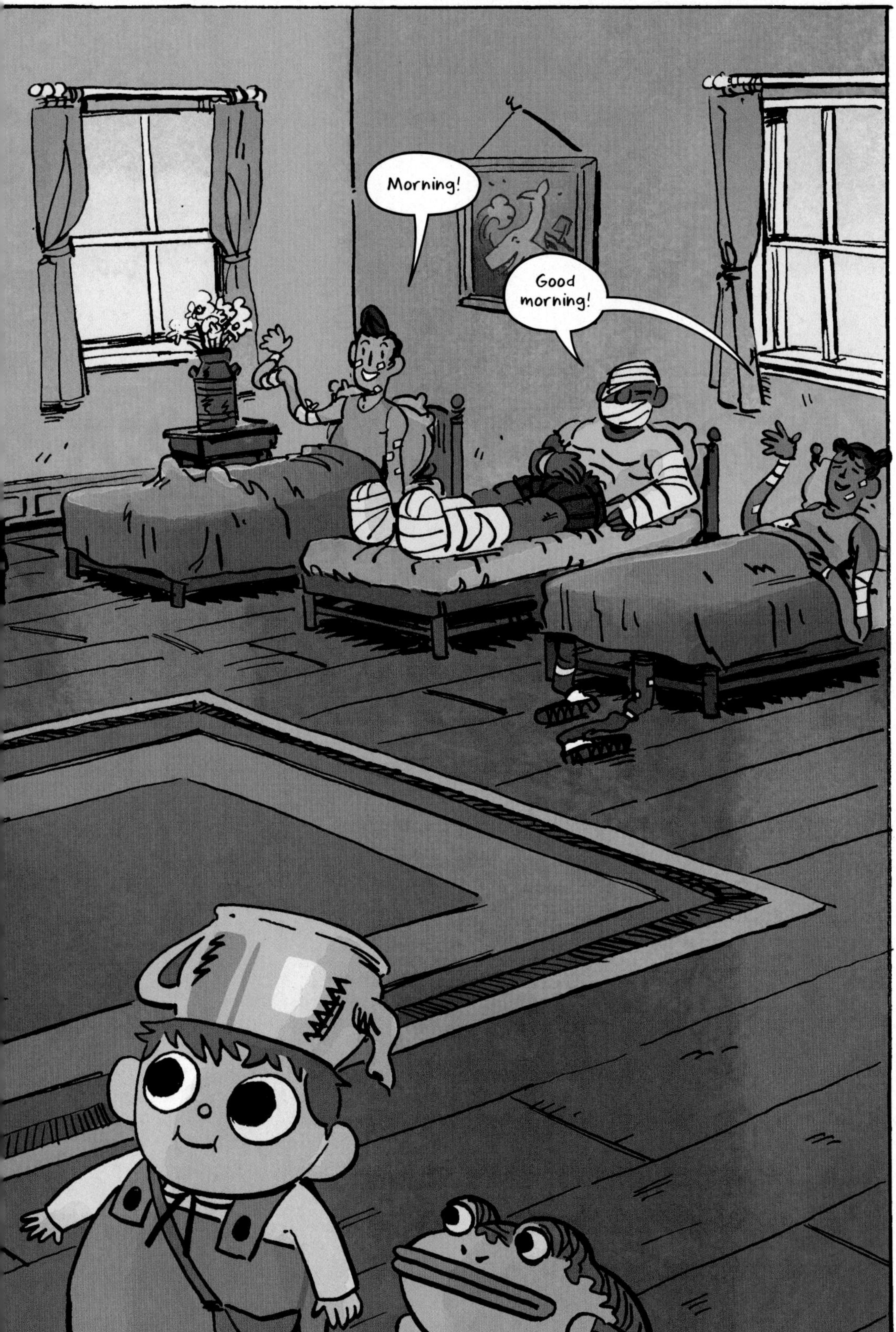
Morning!
Good morning!

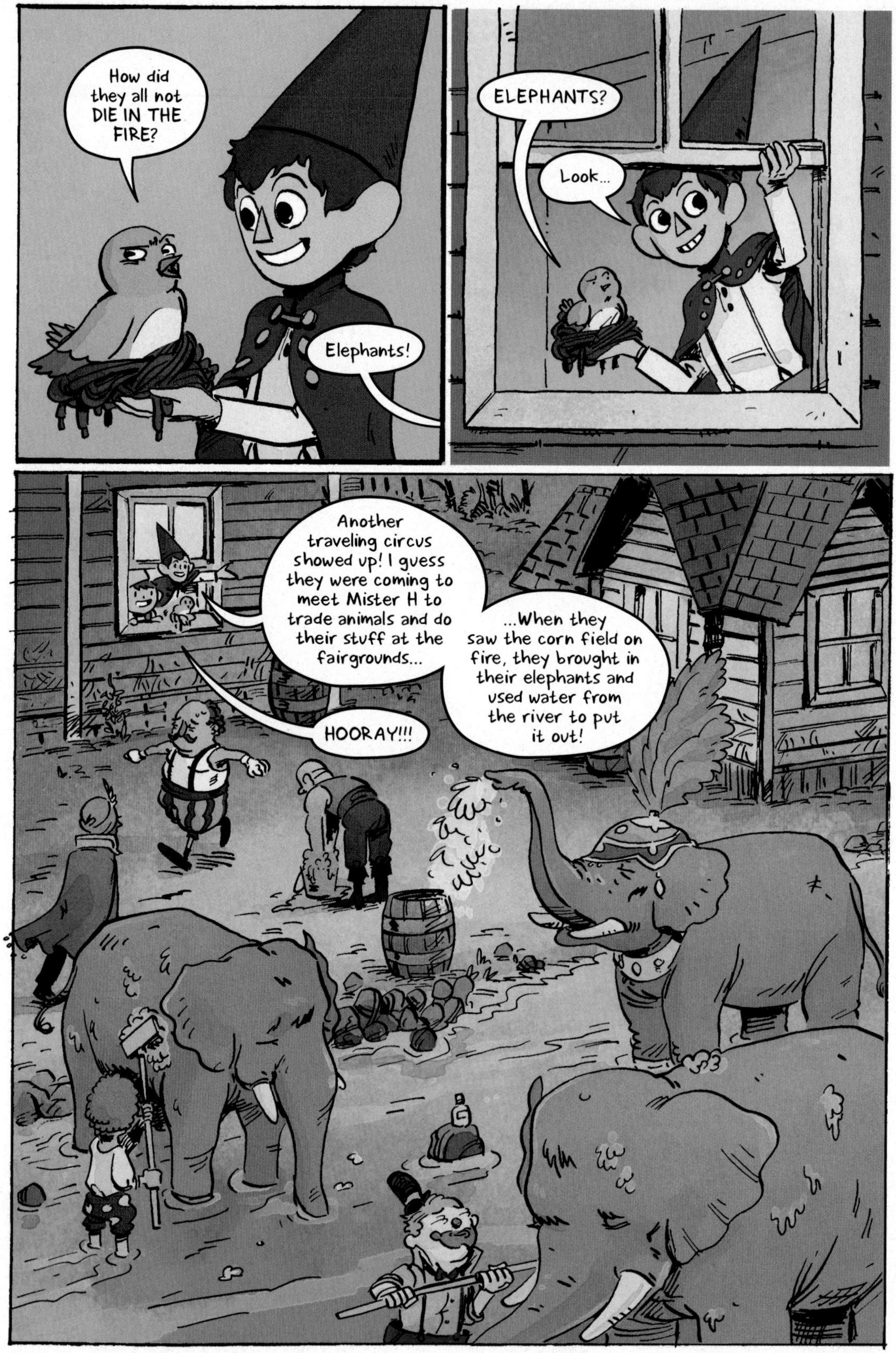
How did they all not DIE IN THE FIRE?
Elephants!
ELEPHANTS?
Look...
Another traveling circus showed up! I guess they were coming to meet Mister H to trade animals and do their stuff at the fairgrounds...
HOORAY!!!
...When they saw the corn field on fire, they brought in their elephants and used water from the river to put it out!

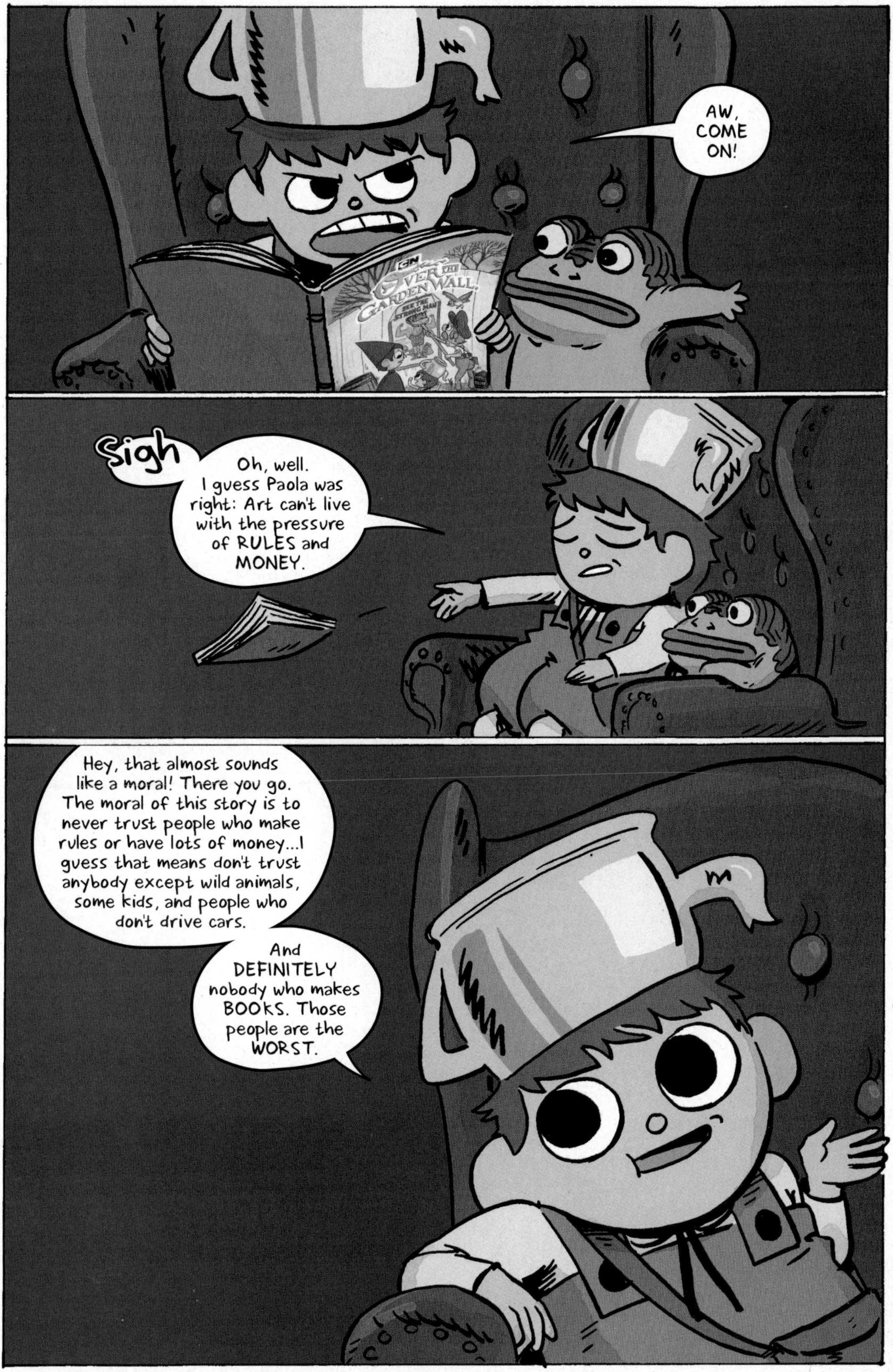
AW, COME ON!
Sigh
Oh, well. I guess Paola was right: Art can't live with the pressure of RULES and MONEY.
Hey, that almost sounds like a moral! There you go. The moral of this story is to never trust people who make rules or have lots of money...I guess that means don't trust anybody except wild animals, some kids, and people who don't drive cars.
And DEFINITELY nobody who makes BOOKS. Those people are the WORST.

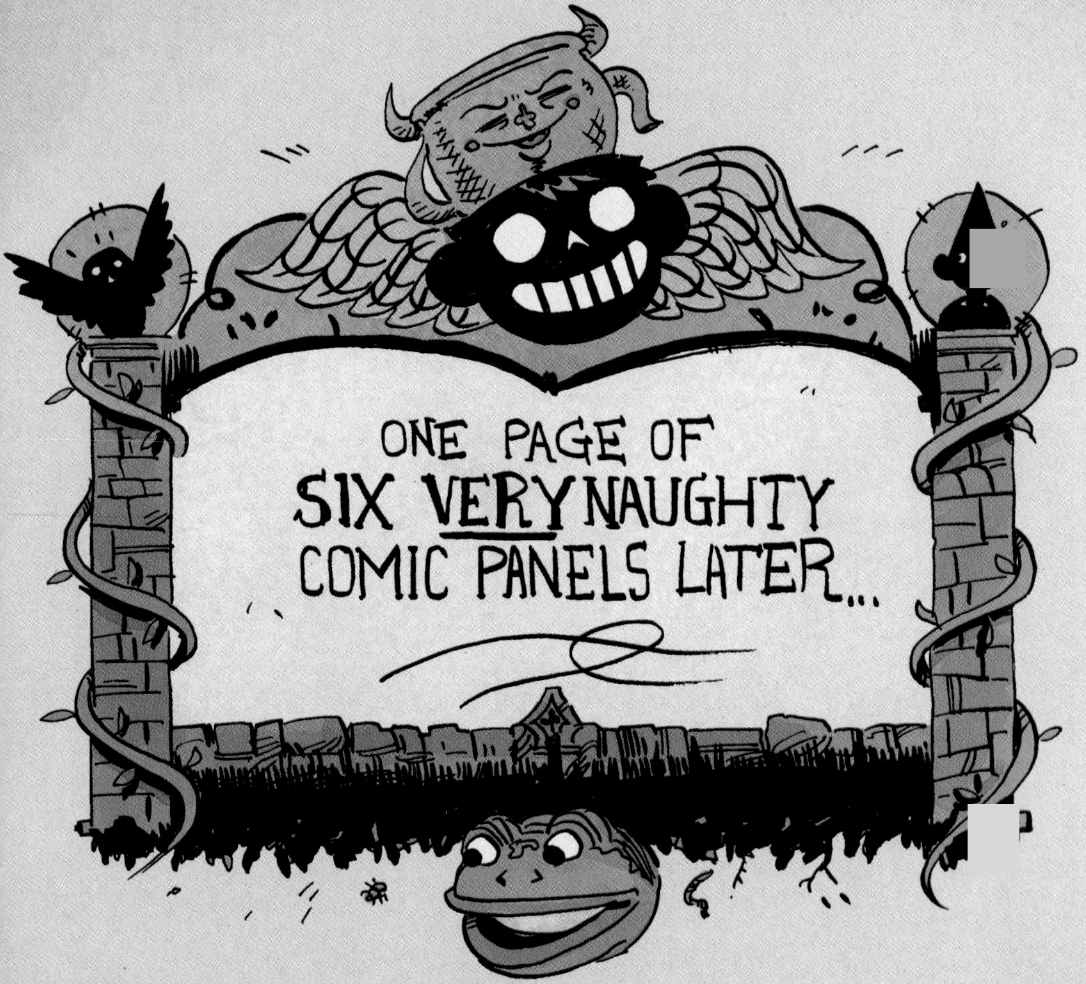
ONE PAGE OF
SIX VERY NAUGHTY
COMIC PANELS LATER...

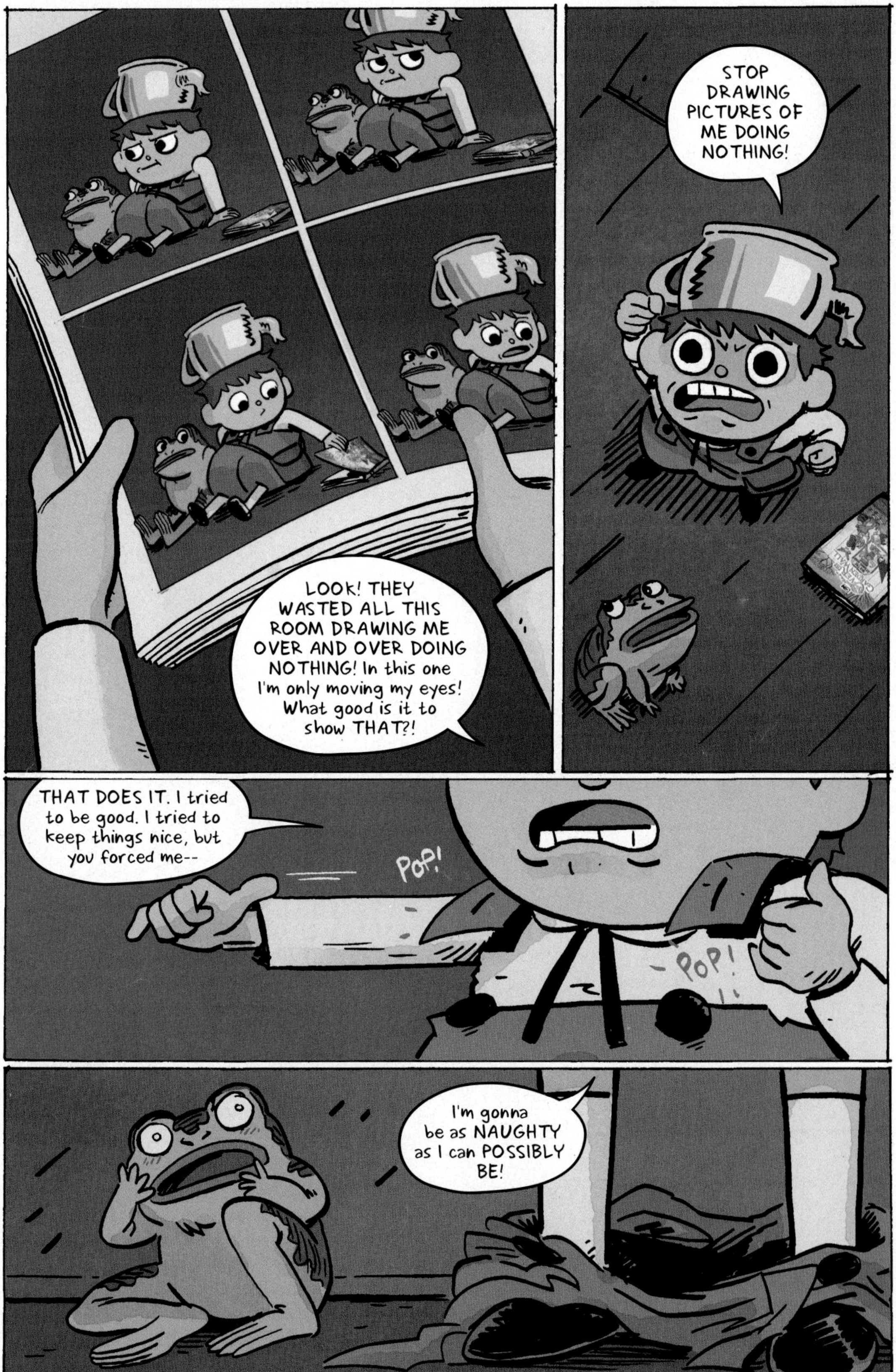
LOOK! THEY WASTED ALL THIS ROOM DRAWING ME OVER AND OVER DOING NOTHING! In this one I'm only moving my eyes! What good is it to show THAT?!
STOP DRAWING PICTURES OF ME DOING NOTHING!
THAT DOES IT. I tried to be good. I tried to keep things nice, but you forced me--
POP!
POP!
I'm gonna be as NAUGHTY as I can POSSIBLY BE!

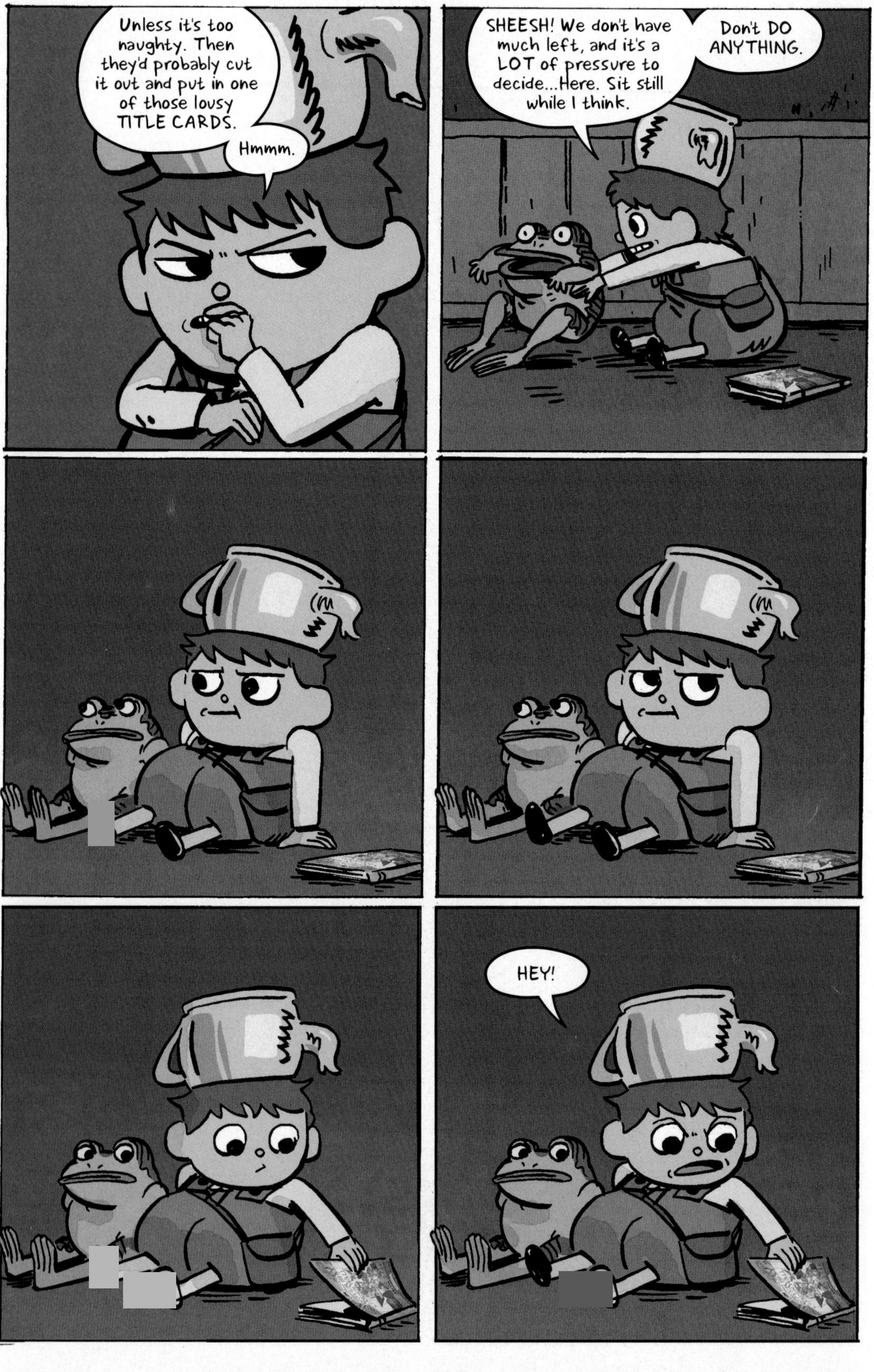
Unless it's too naughty. Then they'd probably cut it out and put in one of those lousy TITLE CARDS.
Hmmm.
SHEESH! We don't have much left, and it's a LOT of pressure to decide...Here. Sit still while I think.
Don't DO ANYTHING.
HEY!

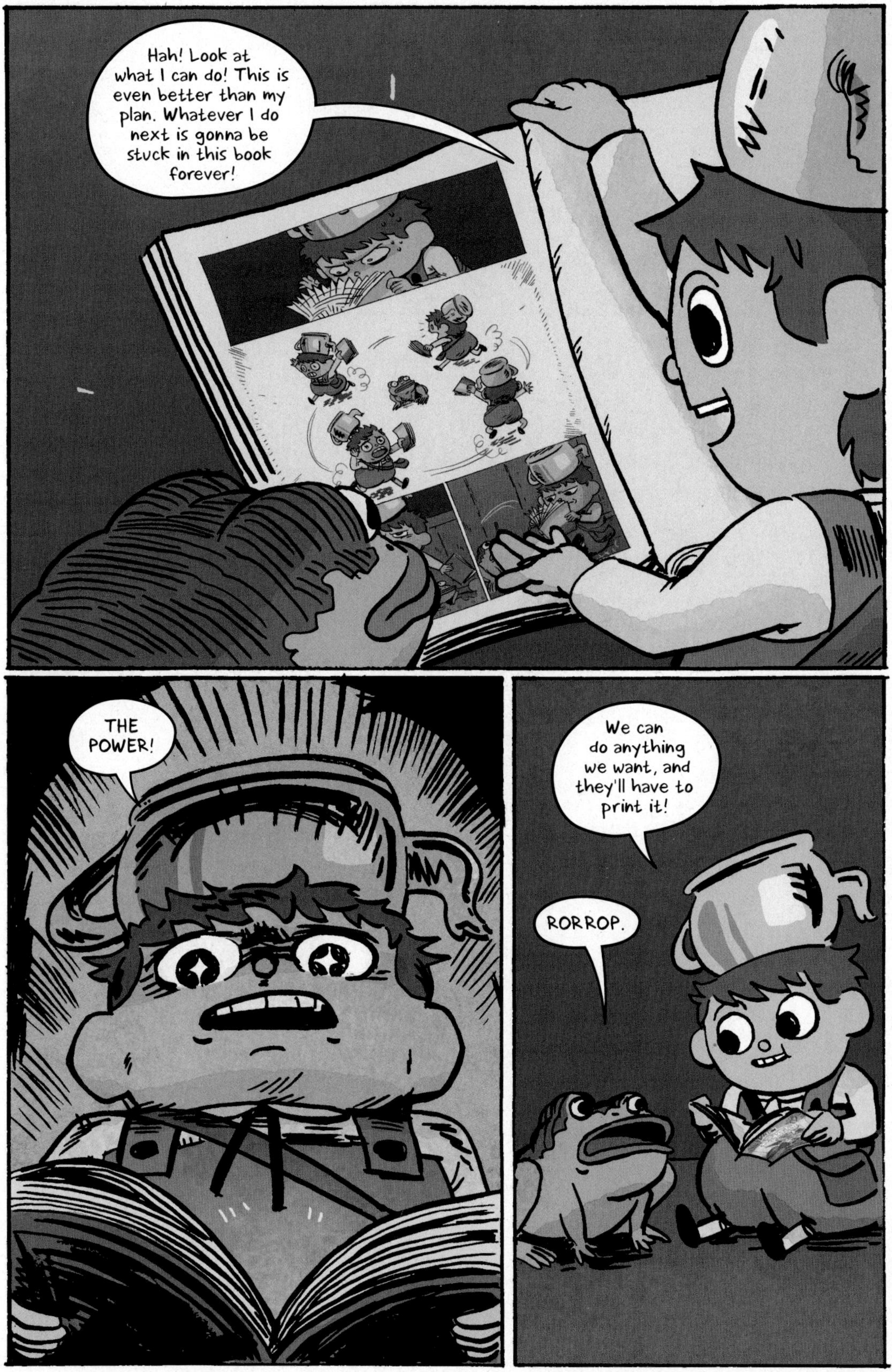

Hah! Look at what I can do! This is even better than my plan. Whatever I do next is gonna be stuck in this book forever!
THE POWER!
We can do anything we want, and they'll have to print it!
RORROP.

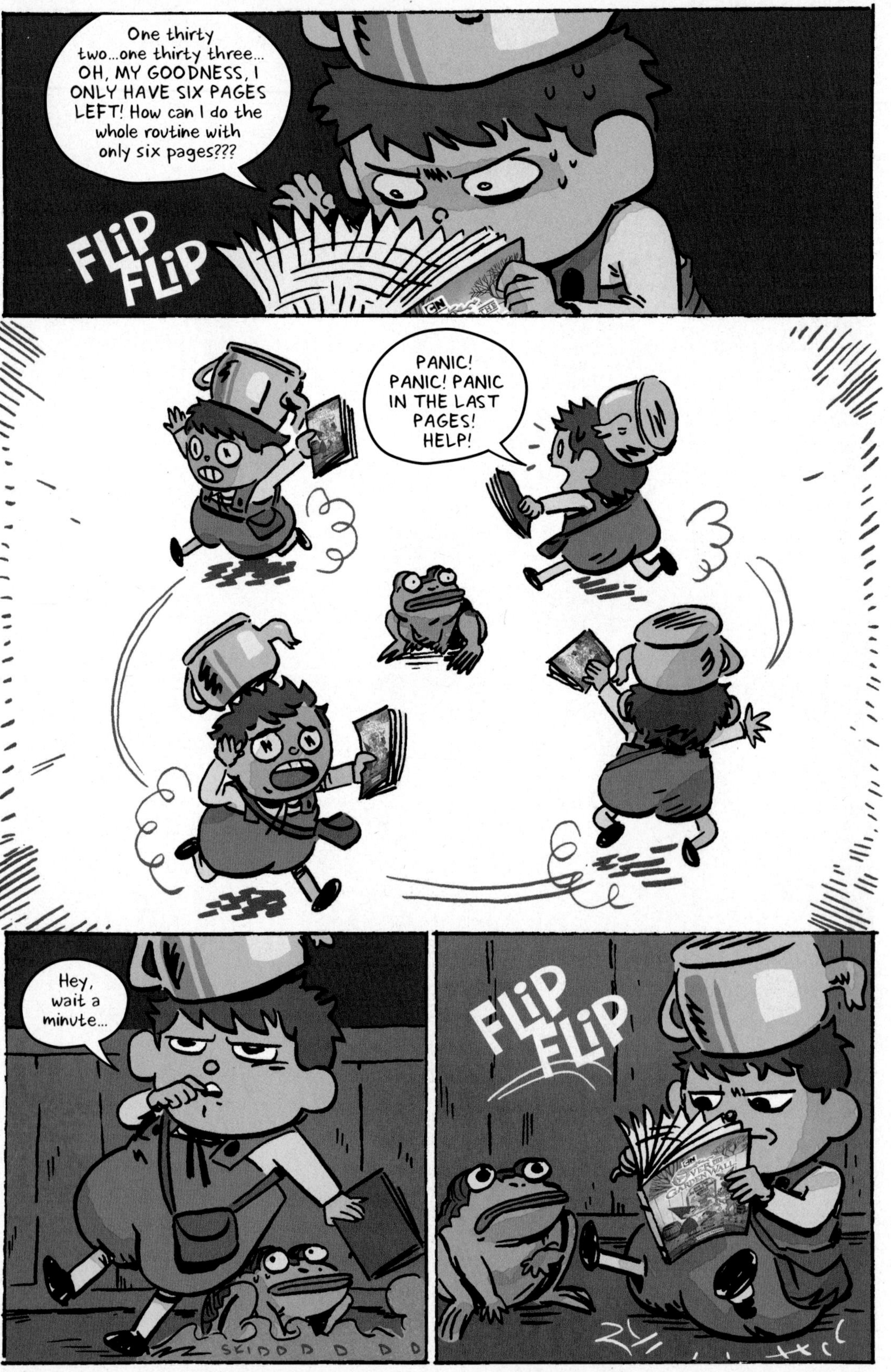
One thirty two...one thirty three... OH, MY GOODNESS, I ONLY HAVE SIX PAGES LEFT! How can I do the whole routine with only six pages???
FLIP FLIP
PANIC! PANIC! PANIC IN THE LAST PAGES! HELP!
Hey, wait a minute...
SKIDD D D D D
FLIP FLIP

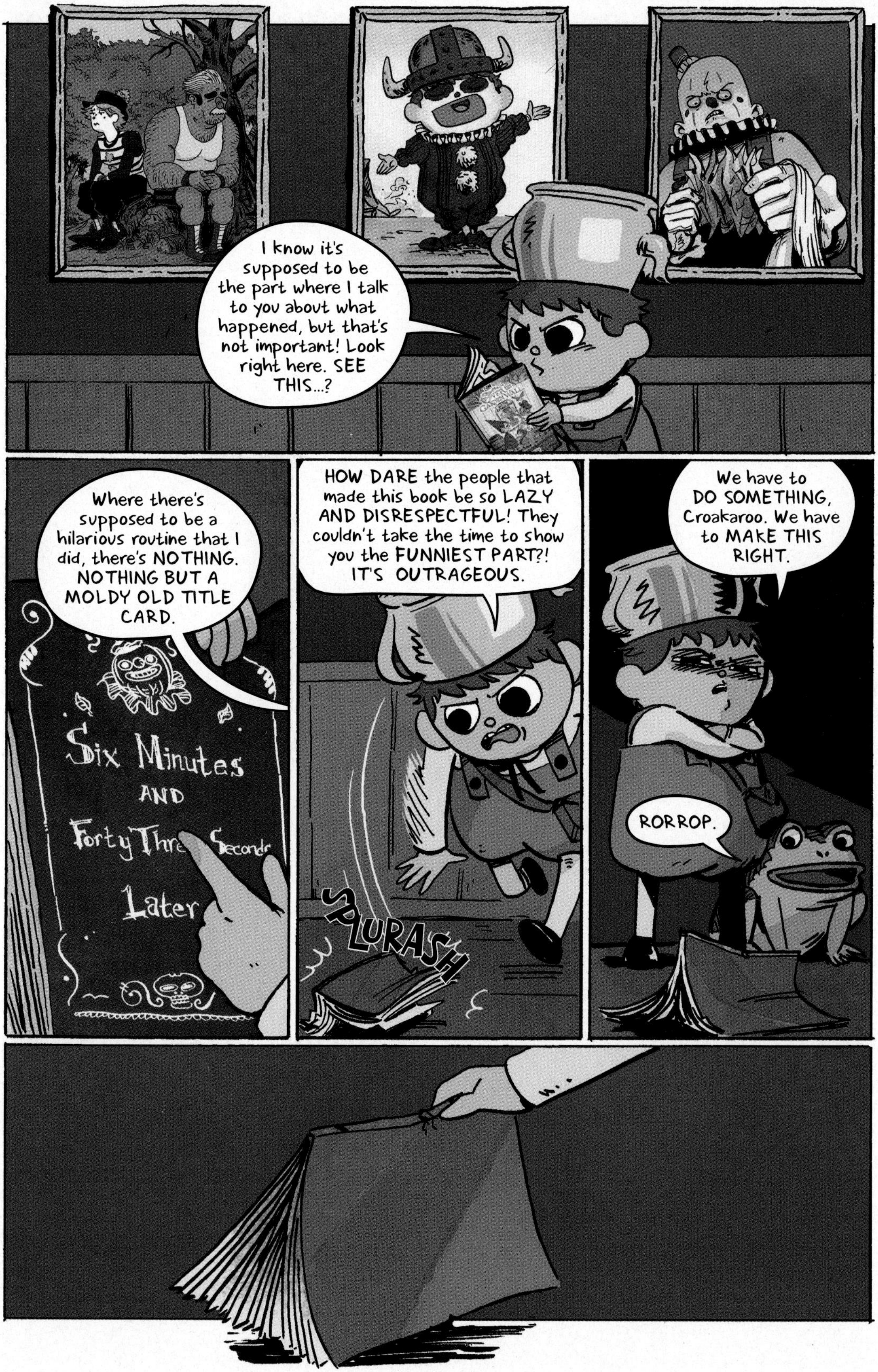
I know it's supposed to be the part where I talk to you about what happened, but that's not important! Look right here. SEE THIS...?
Where there's supposed to be a hilarious routine that I did, there's NOTHING. NOTHING BUT A MOLDY OLD TITLE CARD.
Six Minutes AND Forty Three Seconds Later
HOW DARE the people that made this book be so LAZY AND DISRESPECTFUL! They couldn't take the time to show you the FUNNIEST PART?! IT'S OUTRAGEOUS.
SPLURASH
We have to DO SOMETHING, Croakaroo. We have to MAKE THIS RIGHT.
RORROP.

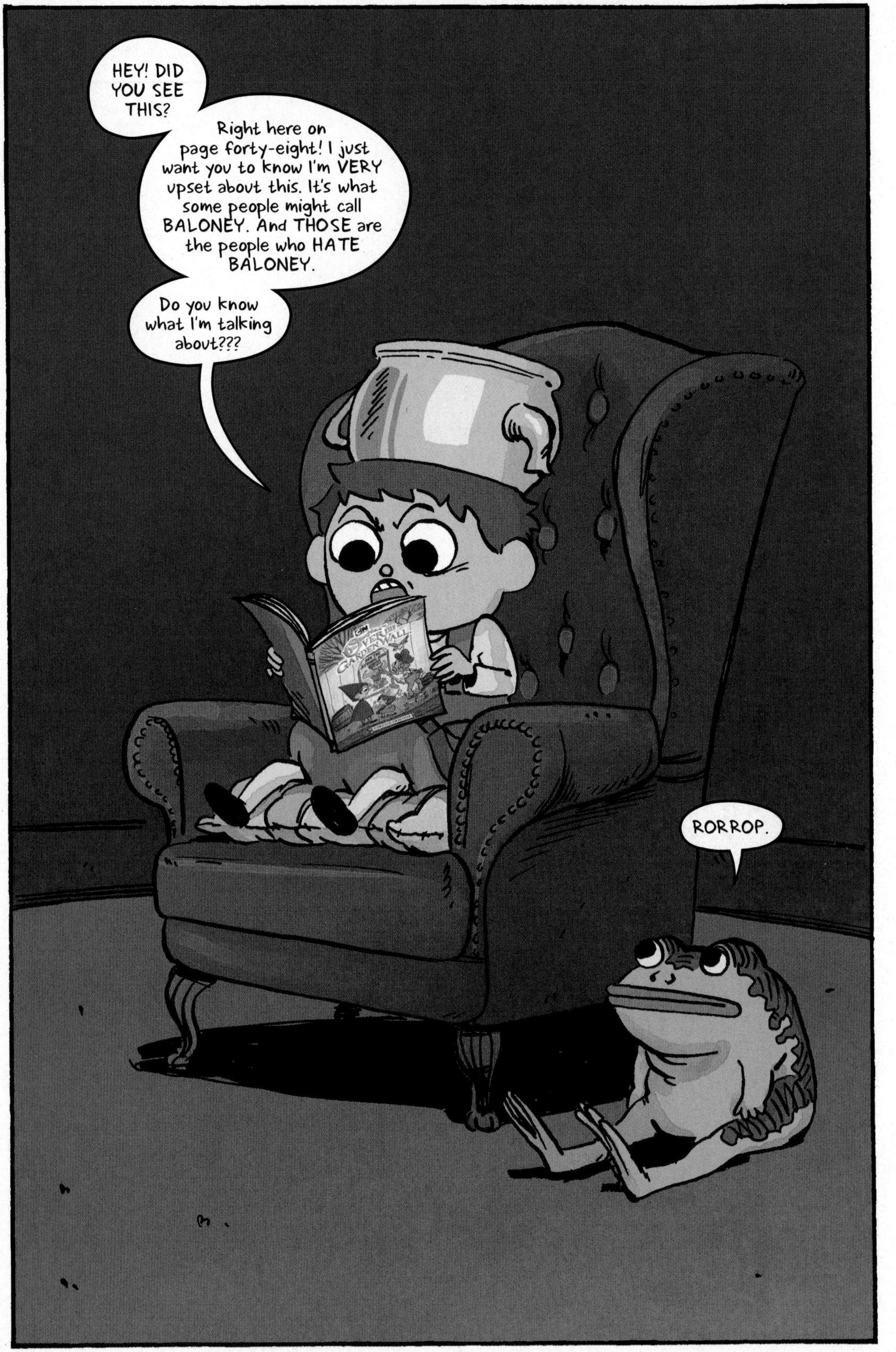
HEY! DID YOU SEE THIS?
Right here on page forty-eight! I just want you to know I'm VERY upset about this. It's what some people might call BALONEY. And THOSE are the people who HATE BALONEY.
Do you know what I'm talking about???
RORROP.

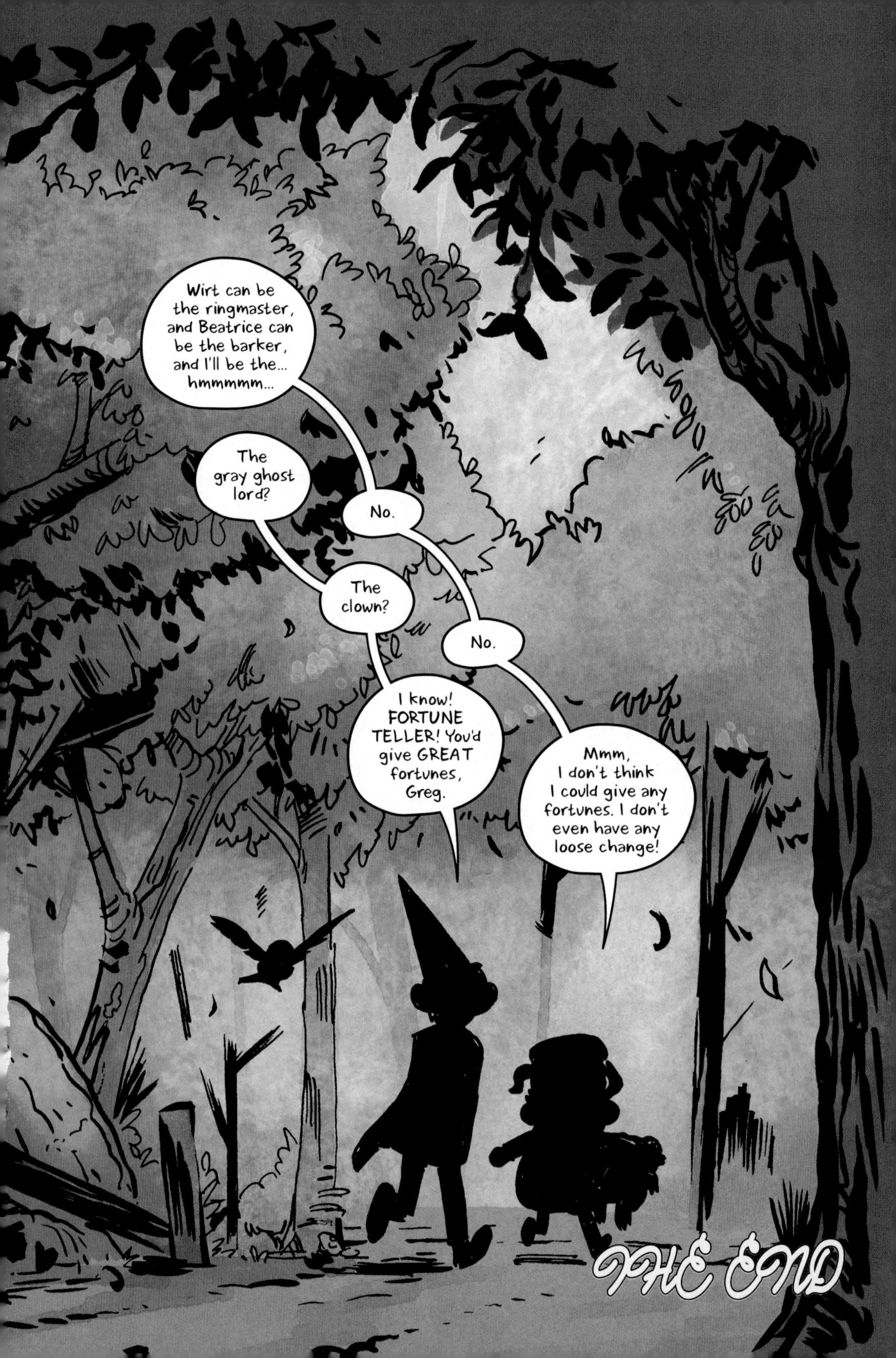
Wirt can be the ringmaster, and Beatrice can be the barker, and I'll be the... hmmmmm...
The gray ghost lord?
No.
The clown?
No.
I know! FORTUNE TELLER! You'd give GREAT fortunes, Greg.
Mmm, I don't think I could give any fortunes. I don't even have any loose change!
THE END

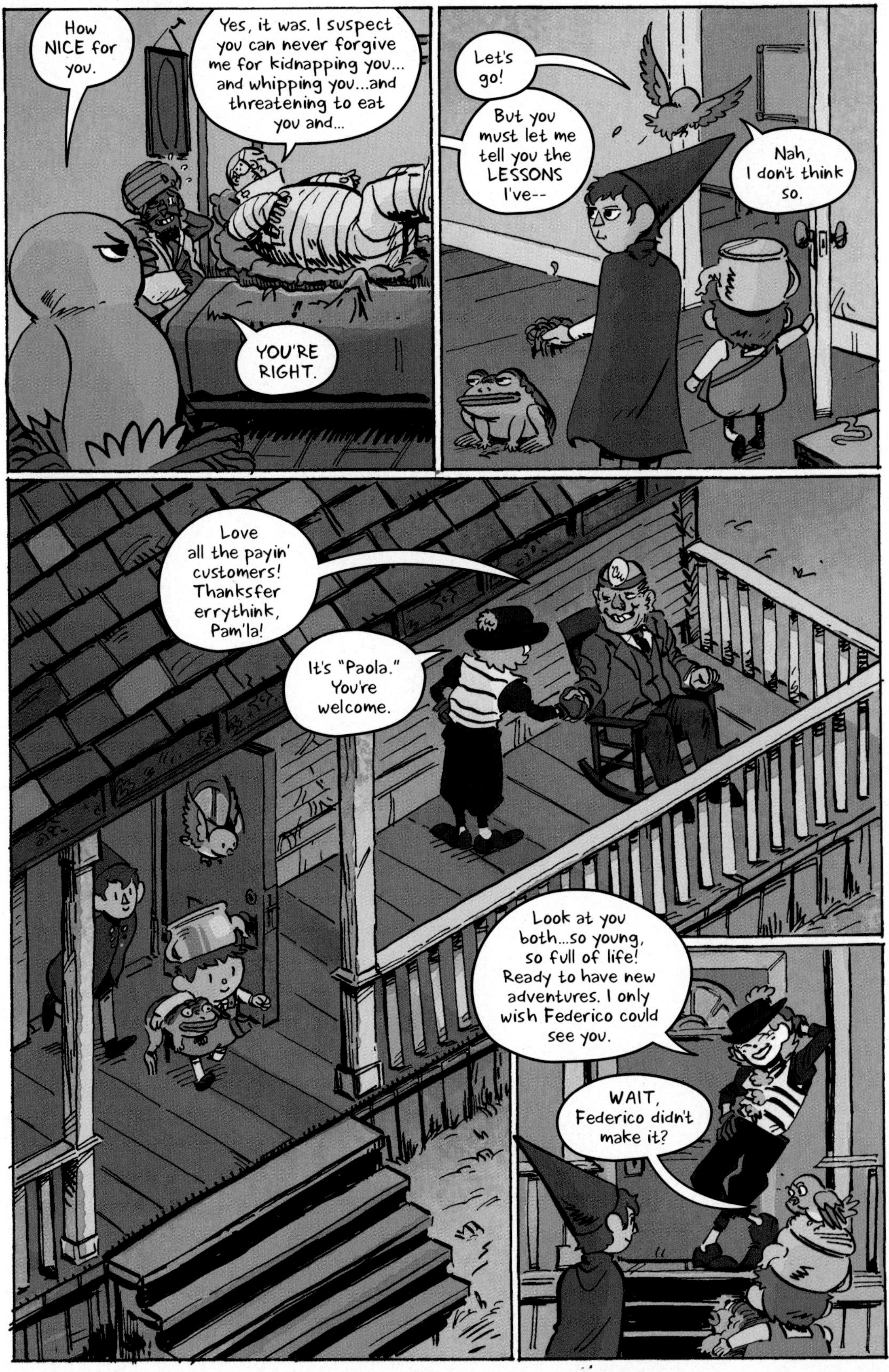
How NICE for you.
Yes, it was. I suspect you can never forgive me for kidnapping you... and whipping you...and threatening to eat you and...
YOU'RE RIGHT.
Let's go!
But you must let me tell you the LESSONS I've--
Nah, I don't think so.
Love all the payin' customers! Thanksfer errythink, Pam'la!
It's "Paola." You're welcome.
Look at you both...so young, so full of life! Ready to have new adventures. I only wish Federico could see you.
WAIT, Federico didn't make it?

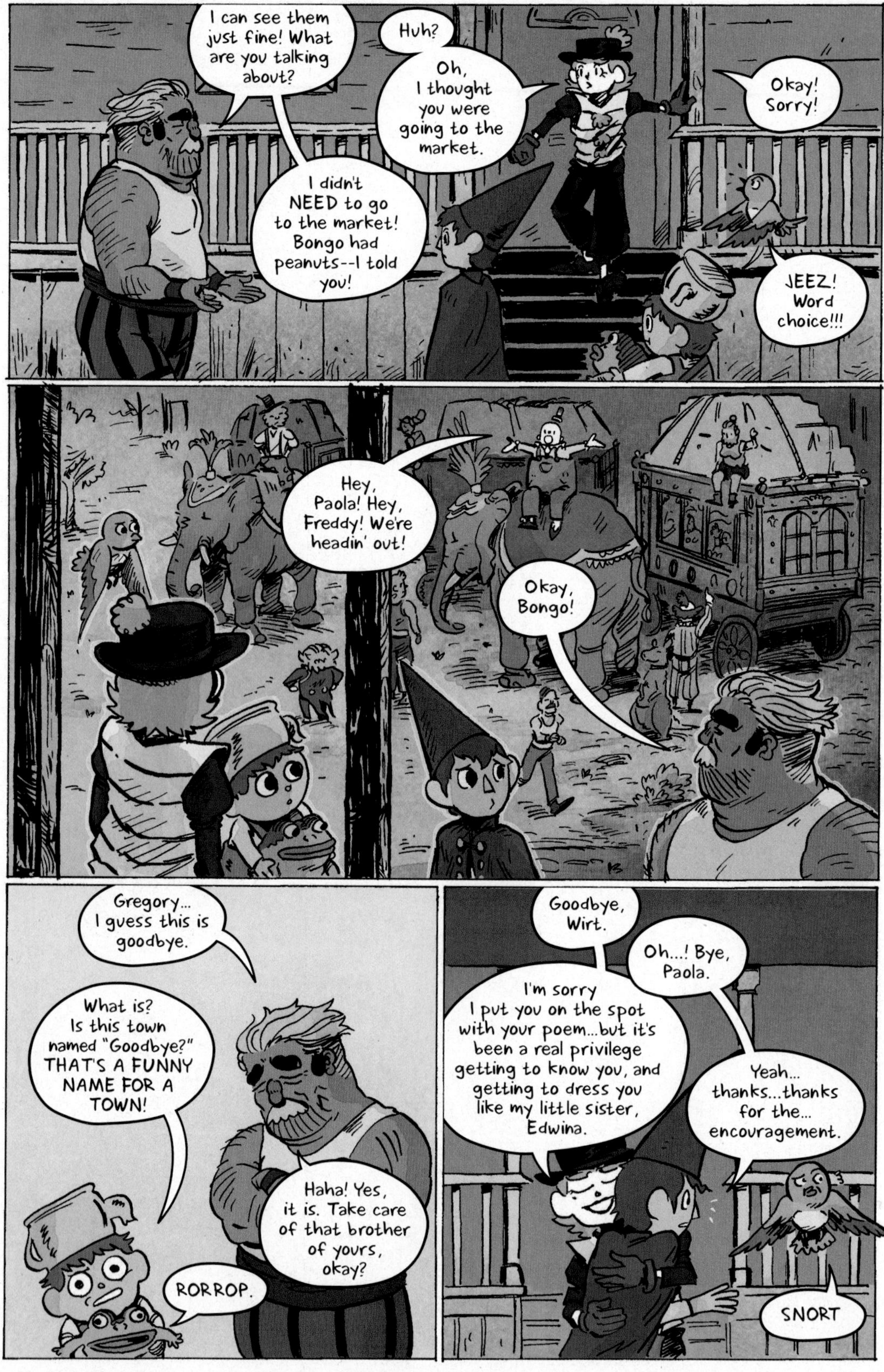
I can see them just fine! What are you talking about?
Huh?
Oh, I thought you were going to the market.
Okay! Sorry!
I didn't NEED to go to the market! Bongo had peanuts--I told you!
JEEZ! Word choice!!!
Hey, Paola! Hey, Freddy! We're headin' out!
Okay, Bongo!
Gregory... I guess this is goodbye.
What is? Is this town named "Goodbye?" THAT'S A FUNNY NAME FOR A TOWN!
Haha! Yes, it is. Take care of that brother of yours, okay?
RORROP.
Goodbye, Wirt.
Oh...! Bye, Paola.
I'm sorry I put you on the spot with your poem...but it's been a real privilege getting to know you, and getting to dress you like my little sister, Edwina.
Yeah... thanks...thanks for the... encouragement.
SNORT

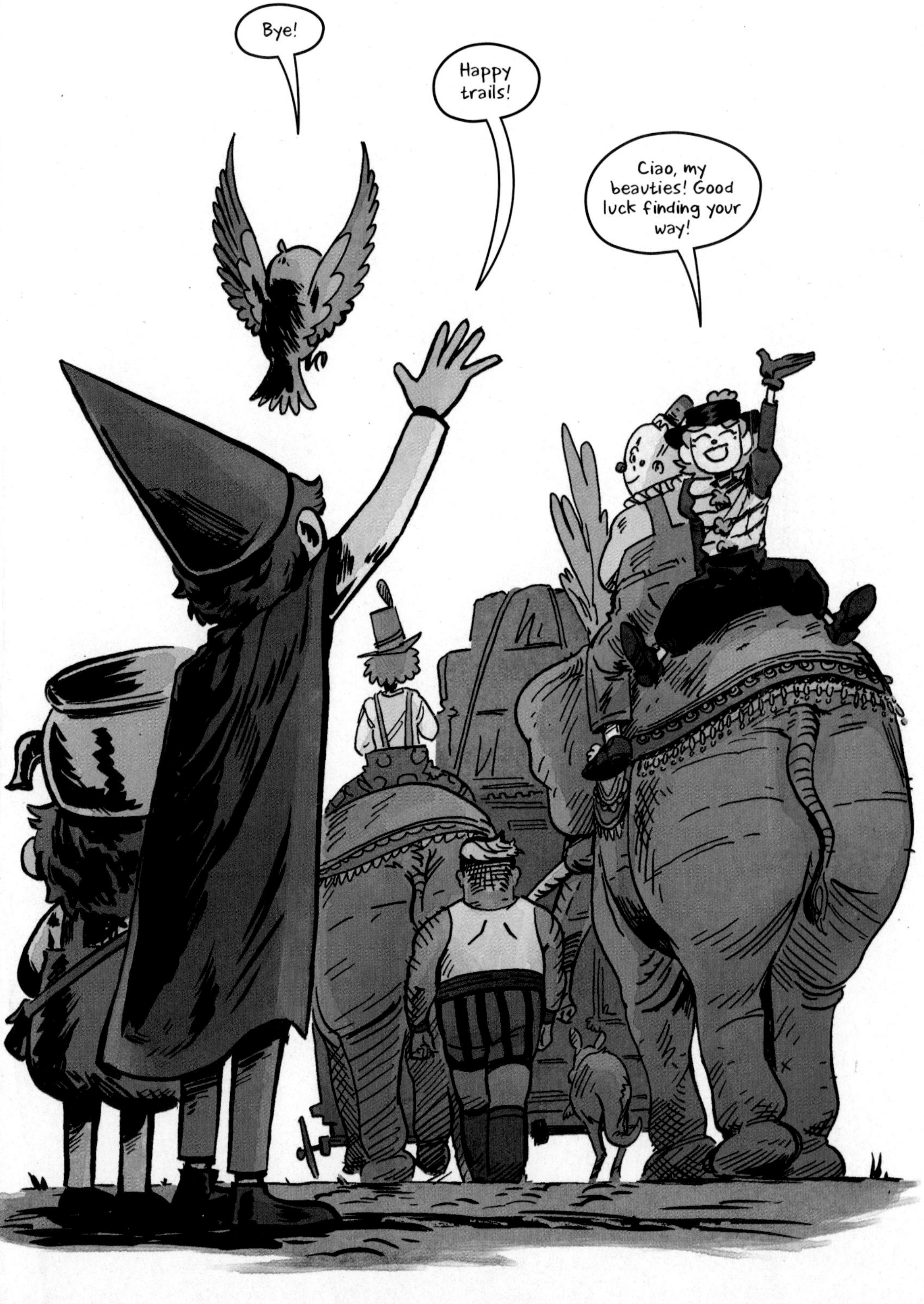
Bye!
Happy trails!
Ciao, my beauties! Good luck finding your way!

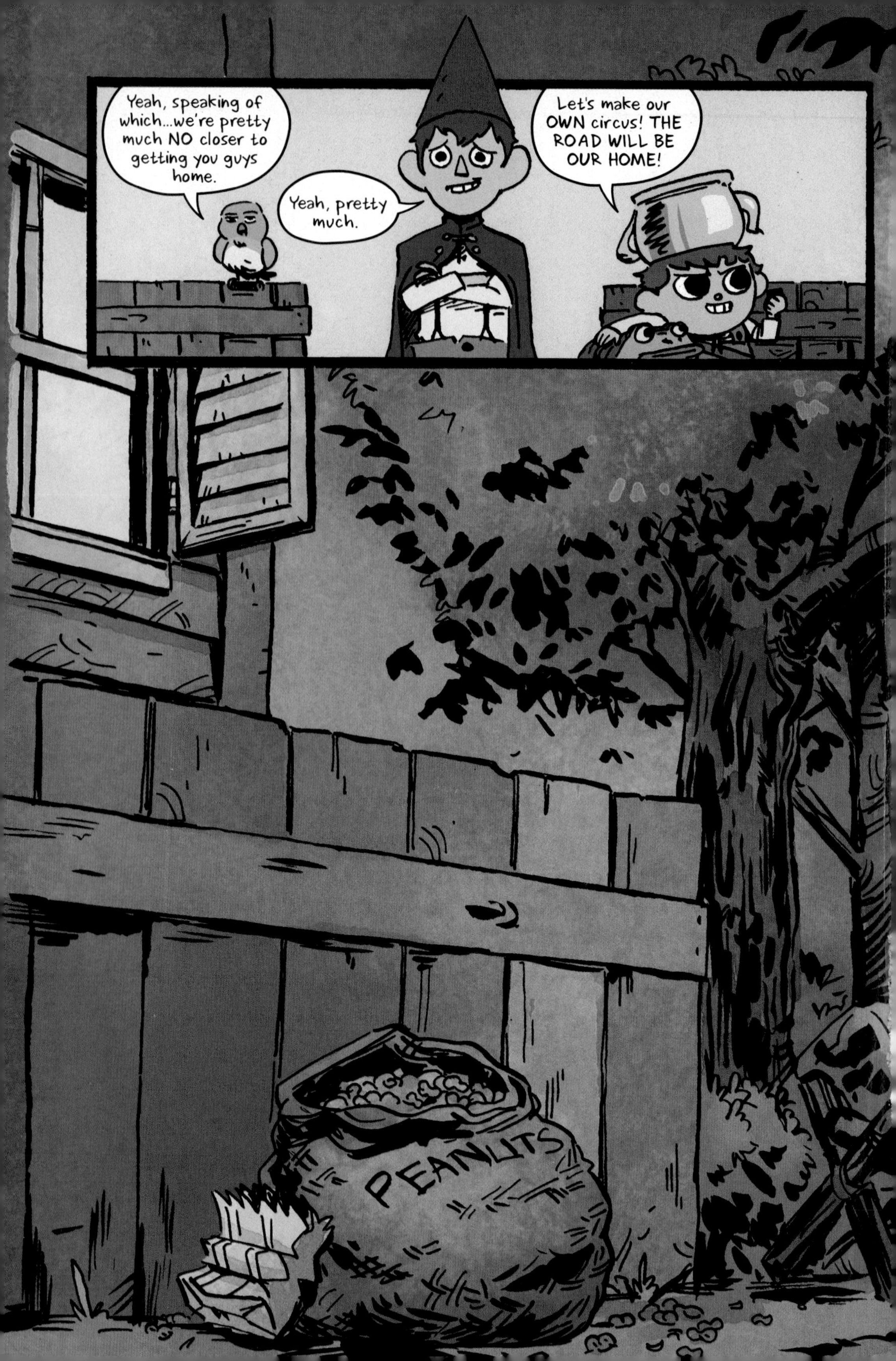
Yeah, speaking of which...we're pretty much NO closer to getting you guys home.
Yeah, pretty much.
Let's make our OWN circus! THE ROAD WILL BE OUR HOME!
PEANUTS

DISCOVER
EXPLOSIVE NEW WORLDS

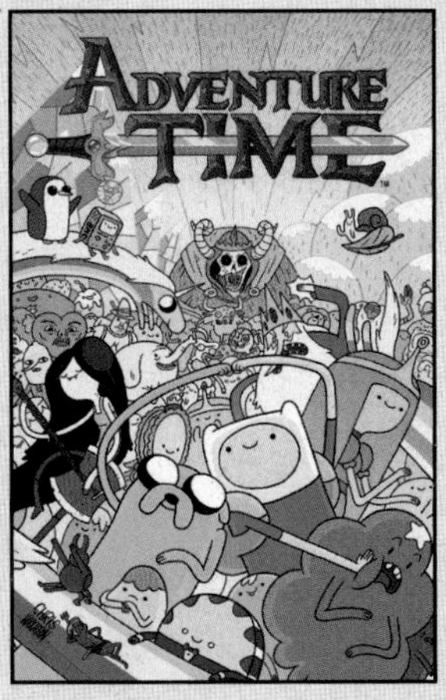
ADVENTURE TIME

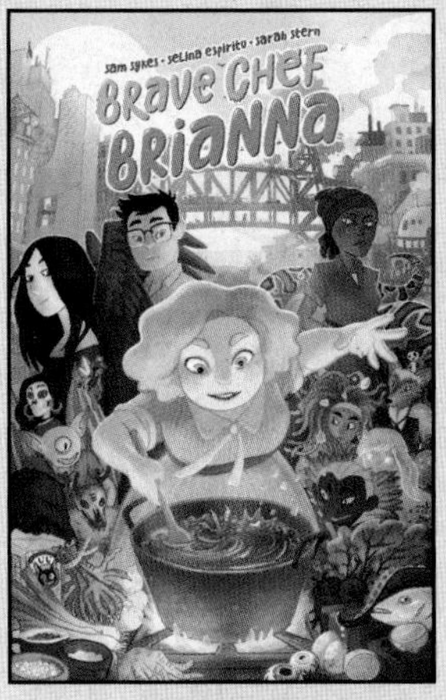
Sam Sykes · Selina Espiritu · Sarah Stern
Brave Chef Brianna

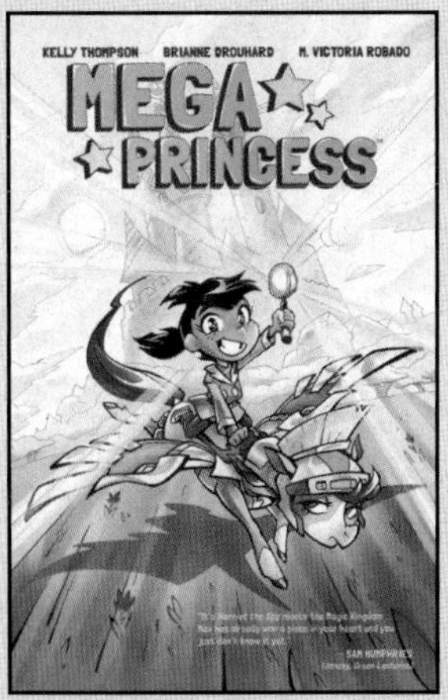
KELLY THOMPSON BRIANNE DROUHARD M. VICTORIA ROBADO
MEGA PRINCESS

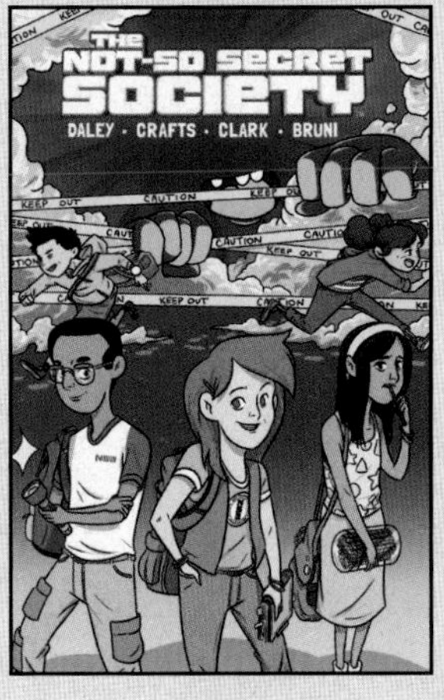
THE NOT-SO SECRET SOCIETY
DALEY · CRAFTS · CLARK · BRUNI

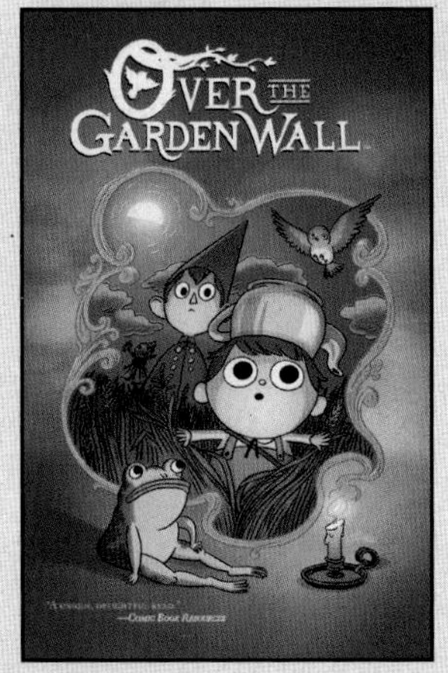
OVER THE GARDEN WALL

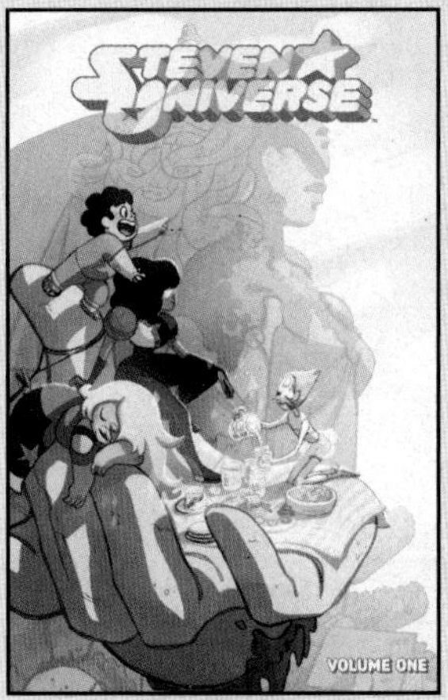
STEVEN UNIVERSE
VOLUME ONE

Adventure Time
Pendleton Ward and Others
Volume 1
ISBN: 978-1-60886-280-1 | $14.99 US
Volume 2
ISBN: 978-1-60886-323-5 | $14.99 US
Adventure Time: Islands
ISBN: 978-1-60886-972-5 | $9.99 US

The Amazing World of Gumball
Ben Bocquelet and Others
Volume 1
ISBN: 978-1-60886-488-1 | $14.99 US
Volume 2
ISBN: 978-1-60886-793-6 | $14.99 US

Brave Chef Brianna
Sam Sykes, Selina Espiritu
ISBN: 978-1-68415-050-2 | $14.99 US

Mega Princess
Kelly Thompson, Brianne Drouhard
ISBN: 978-1-68415-007-6 | $14.99 US

The Not-So Secret Society
Matthew Daley, Arlene Daley, Wook Jin Clark
ISBN: 978-1-60886-997-8 | $9.99 US

Over the Garden Wall
Patrick McHale, Jim Campbell and Others
Volume 1
ISBN: 978-1-60886-940-4 | $14.99 US
Volume 2
ISBN: 978-1-68415-006-9 | $14.99 US

Steven Universe
Rebecca Sugar and Others
Volume 1
ISBN: 978-1-60886-706-6 | $14.99 US
Volume 2
ISBN: 978-1-60886-796-7 | $14.99 US

Steven Universe & The Crystal Gems
ISBN: 978-1-60886-921-3 | $14.99 US

Steven Universe: Too Cool for School
ISBN: 978-1-60886-771-4 | $14.99 US

kaboom!™

AVAILABLE AT YOUR LOCAL COMICS SHOP AND BOOKSTORE
To find a comics shop in your area, visit www.comicshoplocator.com
WWW.**BOOM-STUDIOS**.COM

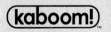

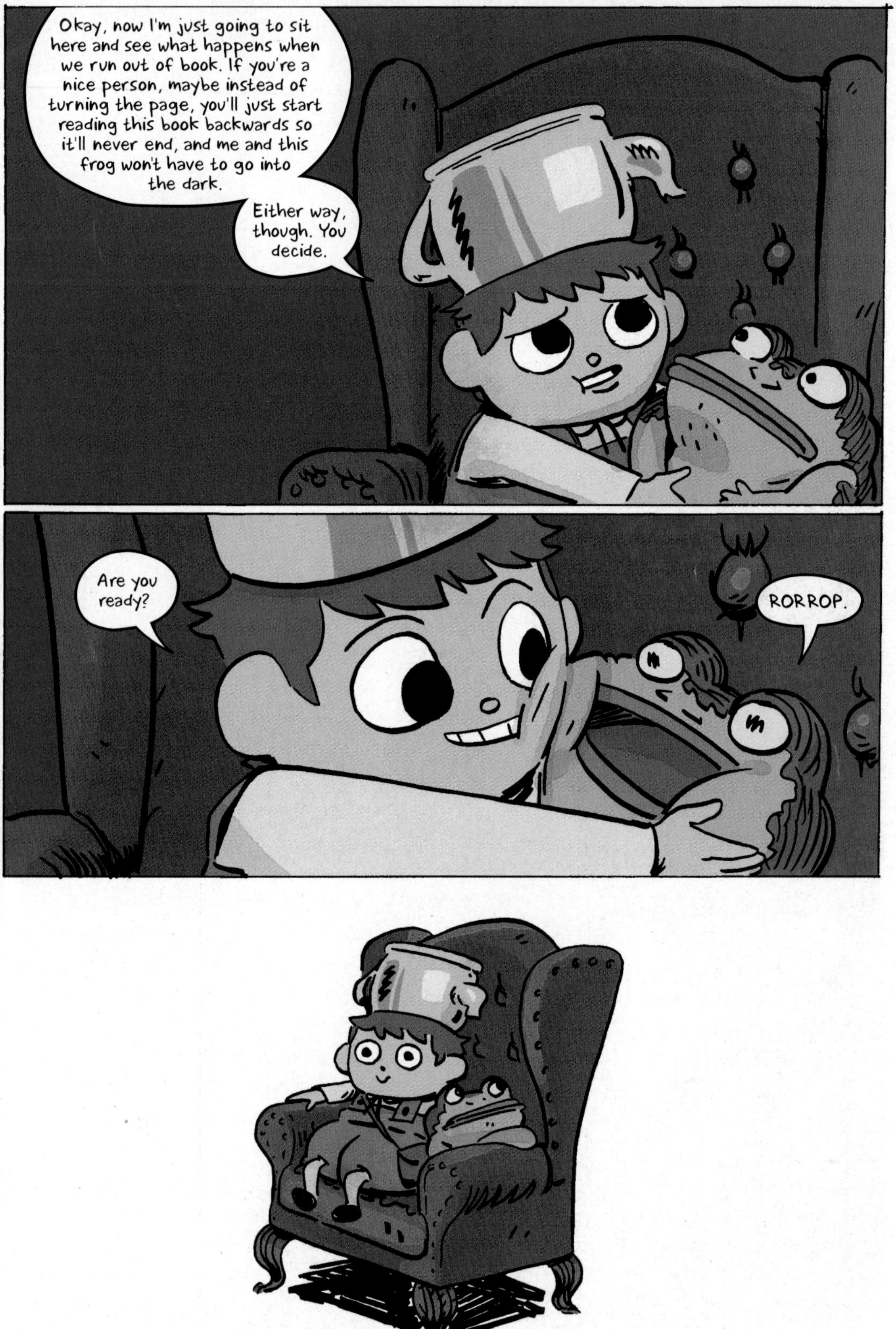
Okay, now I'm just going to sit here and see what happens when we run out of book. If you're a nice person, maybe instead of turning the page, you'll just start reading this book backwards so it'll never end, and me and this frog won't have to go into the dark.
Either way, though. You decide.
Are you ready?
RORROP.